DALLIN THE VIOLET

BOOK 7 OF THE DRAGONWALL SERIES

MELISSA MITCHELL

To you, reader, for taking this journey with me. The release of this book marks the ten year anniversary of starting this series. Thank you for walking this path beside me.

DRAGONWALL
Shadowkeep
Belnesse
Dragonfire Sea
Eagle Lake
Mistport
Redport
Squall's End
Three Horned Man
Scattered Islands
Kastali Dun
Bay of Bandu

Kengr Gate
Northedge
The Gable
Forest
Kaljah
Lincastle
South Sea

PROLOGUE

The Gable Forest

Vigilance eyed the forest with unease. No one had ever flown over its vast expanse. Its magic did not allow it. He was stuck going in on foot. And there was no telling how long he would wander within its depths. But he had to try.

"Are you sure this is a good idea?" One of his generals pawed at the ground, gouging furrows in the earth.

"You know I have no choice."

He'd run out of options. If there was any hope to be found, it would be found here. Some said the magic possessed by the great spriten queen was limitless. He needed to believe she could help him—help all of them.

Sparing a final glance for the dragons who had accompanied him, he stepped into the trees. Their tall forms made him feel small. *Him!* A dragon, heir to the Iron Clan.

As if the forest sensed his need—yes, the idea made him shudder—a path appeared wide enough to accommodate him. He did not question it, instead letting the forest welcome him into its depths.

He began to walk, keeping his wings pulled tightly against his body.

Time felt disjointed here. The trees began to look the same. The backdrop of insect sounds and bird cries never changed. It made him feel as if he were going mad.

He could not have said how long he wandered before he sensed that he had come to the right place. The path opened into a glade large enough to accommodate his bulk. Near its edge stood a female.

She did not face him. Still, he said, *"Please, I seek an audience with Queen Isabella of the sprites. Are you her?"*

It was a silly question, for there was no doubt in his mind as to who she was. She turned to face him. For a moment, he was struck dumb. His first thoughts were of disappointment. Not in her, but in himself. That he was not spriten like her, so that he could claim such a beauty for himself. It was a possessive thought, one born from his true nature.

The female was taller than any mortal, with with hair that spilled down her back like waterfalls of gold. Her eyes, a rich blue, held the depth of forgotten ages. Markings covered her bare skin and vines grew in her wake, blooming at her bare feet with each step. She wore no crown, yet she needed none.

"You speak with reverence. Few dragons do." That she could communicate with him, mind to mind, was a relief.

"I am not like other dragons."

"So I've heard." Isabella's telepathic voice was smooth as water over stone. *"You are called Vigilance. Heir of the Iron Clan. Enemy of Rage. Seeker of peace."*

He inclined his head. *"It would seem that you know me."*

"I know your kind. You seek favors when war turns against you." Her eyes glittered. *"Why are you here, Dragon?"*

He stepped forward, crossing into the glade. The magic around them stirred, like a heartbeat awakened.

"I have flown across half a kingdom to reach you. I have shed blood —mine and others—for the sake of my people. But words...words are beyond us. We frighten the humans. They see us only as beasts. Even the

wise among them misunderstand. But if I could walk among them—if I could speak as they do—they might listen."

"You wish to become human?"

"I wish to become... both." He lowered his head. *"Can you help, Queen of the Forest? Let me take on the form of a man so that I may change the course of this war that is upon us. We need additional aid. We need the help of the humans, of the dwargs, if we are to turn the tide. If I cannot speak to them, they will never join us. And if they do not join us...Rage will win."*

Silence settled between them. Isabella circled him, studying him as if she saw beyond scale and bone, into the fire of his soul.

"You would give up the life you know," she said at last. *"You would embrace humanity, vulnerability, frailty—just for the hope of an alliance?"*

"For the hope of peace."

She paused. Her expression softened, though sorrow lingered behind her eyes. And something else. Something he couldn't quite decipher. A deception that made his scales itch.

"I could grant your wish," she said. *"I could bind your soul to the twin forms of man and beast. But such a blessing comes with a price, Vigilance."*

He wanted to sneer. Of course she would exact a price. He shouldn't have believed a forest sprite would help out of goodwill. Still, he had nowhere else to turn. *"I will bear it."*

"You say that now." Her gaze flicked away in another direction, like she was looking towards something. *"But, no matter. This is as it should be, what is to come."*

"I am not afraid."

"Then step into the center of the glade."

Vigilance hesitated, then moved forward.

Queen Isabella began to sing. They were words of a language he could not hope to decipher. For a few long moments, nothing happened. Then he was struck with power, a force that crawled inside him, burrowing deep. He sucked in a breath. Fire shimmered through his form, his body folding in on itself, talons reshaping into fingers, his mighty tail coiling inward and vanishing. In a heartbeat, where the dragon had stood, now stood a man.

His chest rose and fell in harsh pants, sweat beading his skin. Sweat! He had never known what it would feel like to sweat. And the earth beneath his bare feet? It was so soft, in a way his rough hide had never noticed.

The trees around them seemed to bow towards him. *"This is the blessing you sought,"* Isabella said, her shoulders straightening. Her voice felt as though it echoed through the world. *"But know this: your kind was never meant to walk this earth. The dragons were made from stolen magic. My blessing might flow through you, but that does not make you any more deserving of this world."*

With that, she slipped away into the trees, leaving him naked and alone. A shiver raced down his spine in the aftermath. He opened his new hands and looked down at them. They trembled. Not from fear—but from the weight of what had changed.

He would worry about her words later. Worry about the threat she carried in her gaze. For now, he needed to focus on what this meant for him. For those who were loyal to him. Because far to the north, in his frozen fortress, Rage was ready to rein fire down upon the world.

CHAPTER I
SHADOWKEEP'S HALLS

Claire slammed onto the ground, her body rolling to absorb the impact. She sent a silent prayer of thanks to Talon's shields for all the time spent training her. A snarled curse came from the other side of the room. There was just enough time to erect a wall of air around her before Kane lunged, dagger in hand. He met her barrier and bounced off.

She stood in a dark cave, the only light coming from the sconces on the wall. It threw harsh shadows over the sorcerer's gaunt face. He began to mutter an incant. She felt the power of it battering her protective barrier. She immediately fed it more energy—

"Claire!" Feowen appeared beside her, gripping her arm. He must have followed her through. His sword was drawn, still dripping with blood from the battle they'd left behind.

She didn't allow herself to think about what she'd done. If she did, she'd crumble with terror. A distant press against her mind was the only evidence of Talon's distress. She pressed back, hoping he knew that she was okay...for now.

"We have to go back!" Feowen tugged on her.

"It's too late for that." She glared at the sorcerer, still pushing against her defenses. It was taking more magic than it should have to hold him back. Was it because of this place?

"She's right," Kane scoffed, his eyes flicking towards the waterfall. "It's too late."

"What are you talking about?" Feowen snarled.

"Like everything in Shadowkeep, the water only answers to me. You made a mistake in coming here. I don't plan to let you leave—not alive."

"Let us back through and I won't kill you," Feowen bit out. Kane only laughed.

"Feowen!" She pulled her arm free. "This is my fight. I have to do this."

Kane utilized the distraction, lunging. His blade pierced her barrier. It split open, a combination of the dagger's sharp tip and his incant. Mustering her strength, she shoved both the barrier and sorcerer backwards.

Her pulse raced in her ears, equal parts fear and exertion.

Kane jumped to his feet, his laugh deranged. "Oh, this is going to be so *satisfying*." He disappeared up the stairs.

She took a step—

"Claire, no!" Feowen grabbed her cloak, nearly ripping it free.

She whirled on him. "Do not hinder me! Stay here!"

"What?" Feowen looked at her like she was psychotic. "I'm captain of your guard, if you think—"

Her ire softened. "I know you want to protect me, but it was always supposed to be this way, Feowen. As your queen, I'm ordering you to stand down. Follow if you must, but I command you to stay out of this."

"Claire—"

"This is between me and Kane. You are not to interfere, that is a command, *Prince*."

Feowen's jaw ticked. He looked about to argue. She didn't wait to see what he'd say.

She took off at a dead sprint, urging her legs up the stairs two at a time. Kane's footsteps echoed off the rocky walls above her. A menacing rumble shook the fortress as his magic ricocheted. Behind her, Feowen cursed. She threw up another barrier just as debris rained down around them. Rocks large enough to bash her skull in. She dodged them as they went rolling away. Her foot slipped on one of the damp steps.

"Careful!" Feowen growled, pushing her back onto her feet. "Thanks," she gasped, working to maintain the protective barrier. Only, her magic wasn't doing what it needed to. It felt like wading through mud.

"Something's not right," she cried, feeding yet more energy into her protective wards. Another rumble shook the walls.

"It's this place," Feowen growled behind her. "Tainted with the remnants of dragons and asarlaí. Our magic isn't powerful here."

His confirmation sent ice sliding through her veins. She had enough doubts to begin with. She needed every advantage. Unfortunately, Shadowkeep was working against her.

They continued upward until her thighs were burning. She used her staff like a walking stick to brace her weight. Little good it did. Her breaths came in panting gasps. Behind her, Feowen didn't make a sound. She should have incorporated physical endurance training into her regimen.

Another explosion sounded above. She braced as more debris showered down around them. They passed dark doorways leading to different levels. The footsteps ahead of them had quieted. She paused to listen, slowing her breaths.

What if Kane found a way to escape? No, she couldn't allow it. There was no possible outcome where he was allowed to live, even if she had to die taking him down. The promise would eventually kill her anyway.

A distant sound, like a kicked rock, had her jerking to the left. She glanced at the stairway leading upwards, then decided to take a gamble. "This way."

The massive corridor was dark, save for a few dim torches along the walls. There were gaping doorways along its length. Shadowkeep had once belonged to the dragons. While Kane might have modified the stairs to make them more suitable for human use, he hadn't changed much else. She paused before each room, listening.

"He could be anywhere," she breathed, keeping her voice a low whisper. Feowen was a steady presence at her back, his movements tense. She was suddenly glad he was here despite his earlier attempt to dissuade her.

She called on a mage light, sending it into each room before stepping inside to search. Most were filled with bones of animals long dead, remnants from the dragons who'd once called this place home. A clicking sounded from the corner of a dark room. She sent her mage light high—

She screamed, scampering backwards. A giant spider lunged, its pincers working. Oh, gods! Her mind flashed back to the last time she'd confronted a spider like this. Except, this wasn't in her head.

"Stay back!" Feowen cried, leaping before her. His movements were fluid as he swept his sword around, slicing two of its legs clean off before ducking and rolling. He plunged his blade up into the spider's abdomen. Its screams set the hairs on her arms on end. She took several deep breaths, trying to regain her composure.

If she couldn't face off against a damned spider, she didn't stand a chance against Kane.

The spider curled in on itself as it died. Feowen hummed a little tune, his hand hovering over his blade. The gore disappeared, leaving nothing but starlight silver etched with the markings of magic.

She took a deep, steading breath, her eyes fixed on the markings. She needed courage. She needed to find Kane before it was too late.

A scream made her flinch. It sharply cut off. Tearing her gaze away from the spider, she chased the noise out into the dark corridor to another stairwell. Her mage light followed. The sound of her pounding feet mixed with the roar beating against her eardrums.

She ascended a flight of stairs. Feowen's feet sounded behind her. She emerged into a large atrium and froze. Heat surrounded her, pouring off a wall of flames that blocked her path. She lifted a hand to shield her face. Huddled in the center of the large space was a group of malnourished servants, pressed together inside a ring of fire. Their skin was already perspiring, their worn clothes smoldering.

"Come any closer and they burn," Kane commanded.

Her eyes snapped to him. The chest plate he'd fashioned gleamed in the dancing light. A fresh wave of fury washed over her. That he'd tried to connect the stones. Tried to eliminate all of dragon kind. That he'd committed atrocities. That he *existed*. "You've done enough harm. Let them go."

"Now, why would I do that?"

"Can you control it?" she asked Feowen.

"I'm...trying," he breathed. "This place..." His words were labored. Even for a sprite like Feowen, the taint of evil here was too much.

"It is a place without balance," whispered the king tree, struggling for a foothold here. The staff warmed in her hand, as if that was the only reassurance it could give.

"You must make a choice, Queen." Kane's eyes darted between the staff and her face, as if he didn't quite understand what she held. "These...*innocents*, or me." His grin was cruel. He didn't give her time to decide before he stepped into the shadows and disappeared.

"Go," Feowen cried as the flames licked closer, threatening to devour their prey. "I'll do what I can to save them."

She hesitated. There was no guarantee that Feowen would douse whatever magic Kane had used. Together, they stood a better chance. There were six humans in all. Kane had called them innocent and she believed it, especially given their haggard appearance.

Every second she deliberated was a second Kane gained an advantage. If he made it out of this fortress, she'd be forced to search an entire kingdom for him. There was no telling if she'd get another chance like this.

Deep inside her, the promise flared to life like a puppet master, pulling her in the direction Kane had gone. "Save them," she commanded of Feowen before taking off at a sprint.

"Be...careful," Feowen grunted, his voice calling after her. "Talon would...never...forgive me—"

The rest of his words were cut off as he focused on holding back the hungry tongues of flame desperate to consume. She couldn't think of Talon or his forgiveness. If she thought of her mate, her determination would waiver. She didn't want to leave him behind. Didn't want to risk her life, knowing that she might die. He'd waited centuries for her, and he'd had her mere minutes in comparison. Her death would break him.

"I am the queen of Dragonwall. I am the queen of the sprites. I will not be afraid," she said, repeating it over and over as she raced down Shadowkeep's darkened corridors. There was no telling what direction Kane had gone. Only the pull of her promise guided her now.

Her heart raced with fear at each shadowy doorway, each unknown corner. *Please, gods, let this end.*

She ascended another stairwell and stumbled, shocked to find herself beneath the open sky. She'd found a way out. It was a courtyard, half crumbling. Kane was pacing. That he hadn't simply vanished into the night spoke of his determination to eliminate her. "This ends here, *Queen*. I made the mistake of not ending you before. I won't do that again."

"You're right." She reached behind her, hands searching for the grip of a weapon. Her palm closed around the familiar warmth of Cyrus's sverak. *You can do this,* he whispered. She felt his determination. He'd waited for this moment, to finally put to rights his failure.

Don't leave me, she begged, knowing she'd need his strength.

I'll be with you all the way.

The wind ripped at her hair, beating against the mountainside. She didn't dare look out over the vast expanse. Didn't dare consider how high up they were. The edge of the courtyard had already crumbled into a sheer drop off. She made a note to avoid going near it. Her magic could only do so much, and there was no telling if it would save her from the fall.

Keeping her protective barrier close, she began circling Kane. Her magic was stronger out here, less muted under the oppressive force of the fortress. Kane must not have realized that or he wouldn't have chosen this place. He probably hoped to throw her over the side and be rid of her for good.

He copied her movements, chanting under his breath. Whatever incantation he worked, she needed to be ready. Large chunks of the crumbled fortress lifted from the courtyard, flying straight for her. She pressed harder into her magic, keeping her mental focus as she thought about what strategy she needed.

The debris battered against her magical shield, working to wear her down. Giant chunks large enough to crush her. Sweat beaded on her skin, dripping down her temples. Kane snarled at his failed attempts to break through her wards.

"Enough of this!" he cried.

Changing tactics, new words formulated on his lips, too quiet to hear. Too quiet for her to know exactly what he was planning. The air crackled with energy. She could feel it building, whatever he planned.

She took several steps back.

He swept his hands around in a wide arc then clapped them together. The air all but exploded as a massive force of energy radiated outward from his body coming straight for her. Enough energy to tear her body to shreds. To pulverize her into nothing. Crying out, she crossed her sword and staff. She lowered into a bracing stance just before his magic slammed into her.

CHAPTER 2

SOMETHING FUNDAMENTAL

Shadowkeep

Claire grunted as the force of Kane's power slammed against her protective shield, making it shudder. The immensity of it pushed her back, her feet sliding towards the cliff's edge. She scrambled, trying not to slip. That had been his plan all along, to send her over the edge. Tightening her gip on the staff and sword, she gave a mighty scream as she pressed back, letting his magic flow around her.

Her frantic breaths calmed as the force of it disappeared.

Kane's lips curled in fury.

"Nice try." She straightened, looking him dead in the eye. "Only one of us is leaving here alive. Me."

They began circling again. She focused her mind, partitioning it the way Pelwynn had taught her, then formed a ball of fire the size of her fist. She sent it flying at him. It fizzled out against his barrier. She formed another and another, until they pounded against his shield, wearing it down in bursts of red-orange. Again and again she split her mind. She conjured vines, forcing them to grow out of the stone, bringing life to a place long dead. One of them found a chink in Kane's shield and snaked inside, wrapping around his

12

ankle and pulling. He quickly recovered, using a blade to slice himself free before repairing the damage done to his shield. His face no longer held the smug satisfaction of certain victory. She caught the flash of doubt.

She couldn't lay all her cards on the table just yet. If he suspected she might win, he'd flee to save his skin. This had to end here.

They continued circling as he wove incant after incant, sending spears of energy to tear down her shield. She was forced to block, to fortify, to feed more energy into the protective barrier of air and magic while continuing to fight back. Never was she more grateful for Pelwynn's excessive exercises to sharpen her mind.

Pulling from everything she learned, both mage and spriten magic, she began combining aspects of the elemental pillars to form more and more elaborate ways to break through his shield and deal him a death blow. She remembered the death word the tree had granted her. It had given her permission to use it on Jade just that once. Even if she spoke it here, it would be powerless. She needed to earn this victory.

Each of her conjurings grew more elaborate. Spears of ice that swarmed like bees. A flaming phoenix that spouted jets of water. Vines that twisted into the shape of a cat with thorns for claws. Balls of flame that sparked with lightning. One thing after another, swallowed up by tendrils of Kane's shadows. No matter how hard she tried, Kane's shields never fully crumbled. But they did waiver. There were moments when she snuck through and got a hit in.

He was growing sloppy. He began to pant, the exertion taking its toll on his ancient body. It was taking its toll on her, too. Her muscles trembled with fatigue. She couldn't keep this up forever. Already, she could feel the pull of magic draining her.

"You cannot kill me," Kane hissed. "I am an asarlaí. My magic will keep me going for an eternity."

His words triggered something. Her mind jumped back to the cave beneath the keep. The murals of the first asarlaí inside the mausoleum. "You're wrong," she spat. "Even the most powerful asarlaí can die."

It is time, Cyrus said. She saw his intentions a millisecond before he struck, finding a small crack in Kane's shield—pierced by one of her ice spears. He wormed his way inside. He dove into Kane's mind, taking it captive. In the chaos of their fight, she'd completely forgotten about his mind-bending abilities. How he'd done this once before.

She gasped at the force of Cyrus's ability and the immediate drain on her body. "Cyrus!" she cried out in warning, but it was no use. This *had* to happen. She saw that now. Saw the reason he'd gifted her his soul. For this very moment. So that he could hold Kane captive while the sorcerer was caught in the middle of using his magic. Cyrus took his mind captive, forcing him into inaction. He couldn't stop wielding, couldn't stop feeding power into their surroundings, but neither could he move or do anything to harm her directly.

He was ensnared.

The scene from the mural formed in her mind, of the first asarlaí as his magic was drained. That was the key to it. She would never beat him in a battle of wills. They were too evenly matched. Her only option was to drain him of everything he had.

Cyrus combined his soul with hers, using their joined life force and the magic she possessed to press harder into Kane's mind. He manipulated the sorcerer's magic, sucking more and more of Kane's power free at a faster rate. Kane screamed, his body thrashing.

She gasped, gritting her teeth. She'd never felt power like this. Wasn't sure her body could maintain it much longer.

Thunder rumbled overhead and the sky opened up. Rain began pouring down in heavy sheets. It bounced off her protective barrier, a barrier she no longer needed now that Kane was immobilized. It dissolved.

She refocused her energy, giving more of it to Cyrus. The force nearly ripped the breath from her lungs. She could scarcely breathe.

The crack in Kane's shield grew. Darkness in swirls of blue and black streamed from his mouth and nose, it pooled from his eyes like liquid tears, crawling along the ground as if searching. Images began to assault her mind. She saw how Cyrus had first glimpsed Kane's plans back in the forest, diving into his oily thoughts. More and more images bombarded her mind. Certain scenes stood out. Kane studying in libraries across Dragonwall as he gained power. His trips to Oshea, where he discovered what the asarlaí had become. His efforts to reclaim the stones. His desire to control the kingdom. The secret missions into Kalderland to ally with the ice giants. The goblins.

Pain needled its way into her body. Cyrus tightened his hold, eating through even more of her magic. She screamed, falling to her knees. The pain was immense, even worse than what Kane had once put her through.

Get up! Cyrus ordered. *You must be the one to end him.*

I...can't. She could hardly think as more and more of her energy was syphoned away. Cyrus needed everything to keep Kane's mind captive, as Kane fought back with the last of his power. Still, more and more magic streamed free of the sorcerer's body. A near endless supply.

You must be ready, Cyrus cried. *I will deal the final blow to his mind, pulling what remains of his magic. But you must be ready to deal the death blow. Get up!*

Screaming from the pain and effort, she surged to her feet, using the staff to pull herself up. The sverak in her right hand felt immensely heavy. She could barely hold it. How would she lift it?

Go, now! Cyrus was close. This was it.

She took a single step, and then another, trying not to stagger. Water streamed down her face. Her hair fell in wet sheets around her head. Her cloak and clothes were soaked, adding to the heavy weight of her.

She dragged her feet, one in front of the other. Forward. She had to keep going forward.

Lightning forked across the sky. A boom of thunder followed. It shook her very bones.

Tears filled her eyes, mixing with rain as they fell. Sobs wracked her chest. It hurt. Everything hurt so, *so* much. She tried to breathe, tried to think—

She was in front of him now, staring into the blood-red eyes that had once haunted her dreams. Kane's face was twisted in a snarl. He saw his imminent demise but was powerless to stop it.

"Please." The word was so quiet, she almost didn't hear it. Barely saw the sorcerer's lips move. He begged for mercy, but there would be none.

She was doing this for Cyrus. For Talon. For his shields. For everyone who had lost someone because of this sorcerer.

Power continued to stream free of the sorcerer, draining him. Only now, she could feel an end. Feel that last little bit of resistance that fought with sharp claws to remain inside him. Cyrus would rip it free.

It will take all of me, he said, seeing where her thoughts had gone.

"What?!" she gasped. "Cyrus, no!"

I must do this. We always knew that sacrifices must be made.

Her mind tripped over itself, trying to make sense of what he was saying. The pain consuming her made it nearly impossible. Was he going to sacrifice himself? But how? He was already gone. Wasn't he?

"No," she shouted, backing up a step. If this was the cost, it was...it was too much!

Claire. His voice was only a faint whisper now. In keeping Kane's mind captive, he was wasting away, little by little. *There is no one alive worthier than you to carry the gift of my soul. You gave me more time with my brothers. You showed me what it means to be a part of something greater than myself. A part of history in the making. Watching you blossom into the woman you are today—it was one of my greatest honors. You were always fierce, but now you are so much more. You are brave and honorable. You are just and fair. You are kind. You are wise. You are all the things a good queen should be. You are the best queen this kingdom has ever seen, or will ever see. You shine brighter than all the stars in the sky and you will light this kingdom's way into a better future.*

Cyrus, please. How could he do this to her? How could he leave her when they had been together since the beginning? Surely there was another way!

There isn't. Are you ready?

No! I will never be ready. How can you ask me that?

Because I know you are willing to do what must be done. You promised me, remember? You promised me that you would do this. That you would end him.

Losing you was never part of the promise! she cried.

I am sorry. Give the others my love. Tell them that no amount of time would have been enough. That I love them.

She stifled a sob. *But where will you go? How is this even possible?*

She knew that he'd sacrificed the afterlife to give her his soul. Was this the true end for him? Would he cease to exist? Become nothing?

She had so many questions but he didn't answer a single one. Instead he said, *I love you, Claire.*

She felt the moment he gave the last of himself into holding Kane's mind. Felt as something fundamental inside her broke apart. Felt the world shake as what remained of Kane's power spilled from his body. He screamed in agony. She screamed with him, in heartbreak. The staff in her hand exploded in tandem as the king tree poured its magic into her. The pieces broke apart, pulverized.

There was no time to mourn the loss. Not yet. Because it was now or never. She couldn't squander Cyrus's sacrifice. Couldn't risk Kane regaining even an ounce of magic after what Cyrus had done for them.

Using the last of her energy, she lifted her sword arm. It hurt. Gods, it hurt so damned much. Cyrus's sverak had never felt heavier. Her arm shook. Letting out a fierce battle cry, she swung the blade through the air. Kane's eyes widened and she saw the faintest trace of white around the red before his head was sliced cleanly from his shoulders. It landed on the wet flagstones with a sickening squelch, blood spraying the ground around it. Then it rolled over and over until it reached the courtyard's edge. It disappeared from view, plummeting from the fortress into the depths below. His body crumbled thereafter, into a withered heap.

With the final dregs of her magic, she set Kane's body alight. It burst into flame like dried kindling, lighting up the bleak night. Seconds later, the flames fizzled out until nothing remained but ashes and the charred breastplate with five dragonstones embedded in it.

She staggered back a step.

This should have been her victory. A moment to celebrate. But she could only weep. She'd done what she set out to do, but had lost something fundamental in the process.

"Claire?!" Feowen's voice sounded far away. Everything began to spin. The pain of using too much magic was gone, and yet, everything still hurt. She gulped in air, trying to steady herself. The edges of her vision blackened. The last thing she noticed was familiar arms catching her as she crumbled to the ground.

CHAPTER 3
IMPLOSION

Shadowkeep

Claire's eyes flew open as Feowen shook her awake. He hovered over her, his expression frantic. "Feowen?" Her head ached, like the contents of her brain had been scrambled.

There was a profound ache in her chest. It took a moment for her to understand why. It was the place where Cyrus's soul ought to be, like half of her had been ripped away. He was gone. He'd sacrificed the beautiful gift he'd given her, using it to ensnare Kane's mind. He'd played his role perfectly and part of her hated him for it. Hated that he'd given himself to her, allowed her to get to know him, taken this journey with her, only to leave her in the end.

How could she go on without him?

The same way you always have, he seemed to say, except, he was silent. That was only what she *thought* he might say. A sob built in her chest until it exploded out of her in an anguished scream. Tears followed, blurring her eyes, flowing down her cheeks.

"I'm sorry, Claire, but we have to move." Feowen gripped her shoulder. "The fortress is coming down around us!"

She felt it then, the deep rumbling beneath her. A fresh wave of adrenaline shocked her system. She reached for him, letting him pull her onto her feet. The ground immediately swam up to meet her. "Careful." Feowen's hands clutched her waist. He threw one of her arms over his shoulder to support her.

"Cyrus. He's...gone," she managed.

"Claire, I'm sorry, but there isn't time."

"I don't think I can... I can't do this. I need to..." She tried to squirm away, to sit back down again.

"You can rest as soon as we get you off this mountain." He threw her a worried look.

Feowen was a jokester. Always a hint of a smirk on his mouth, or mirth in his gaze. She'd never seen him quite like this...this *scared*. It made her heart race, crowding out some of her fatigue.

"You there," Feowen cried to the gaggle of servants huddled near the courtyard's entrance. "What is the fastest way off the mountain? Answer me!"

One of the women stepped forward, wringing her hands. "We... we won't make it in time...sir. We're all dead anyway."

"There has to be a way!"

"There's a lift. But..." The woman's eyes darted towards the dark entrance with fear. "It's in a different area of the fortress, far from here. We'd have to go back inside."

Claire forced her muddled brain to work. "Could we climb...?"

Feowen cursed, glancing over to the sheer drop-off. "No. There is no way they'd be strong enough. It would take hours. They can barely stand, Claire. *You* can barely stand. I'd have to carry you and climb." She only vaguely realized he'd said this in *Ednuar*, not wanting the servants to hear.

"I can—"

"No! I'll not risk you. Back into the fortress, all of you. We take our chances."

She gave the doorway a wary look right as Feowen pulled her forward. "Wait! The stones!"

He cursed and released her. The unsavory glare he gave the chestplate said everything. Still, he picked it up. The ground heaved again and she lost her footing. Feowen darted forward to steady her. There was no time to extract the stones. He looked sick as he buckled the piece of armor over his clothes. It didn't quite fit him properly, but she was glad he'd volunteered. She couldn't bear the thought of wearing something Kane had worn, no matter how precious the stones were.

Feowen kept her upright as they moved into the opening to the fortress. He hummed under his breath. She muttered a few words and lights popped into existence around them. Just that small bit of magic seemed to drain what little energy reserves she had left.

Had Cyrus taken her magic with him?

Who would she be without it?

There was no time to question. Feowen was already casting protective barriers around their group as they shuffled cautiously down the corridor. The woman who'd spoken took the lead, her breaths labored as she shuffled along.

A crack appeared, running down the center of the floor. Feowen's humming stopped. "*Varti yifah,*" he swore. "Faster! Run!"

They increased their pace, trying to outrun a crack. The floor began to split and she cried out, reaching for the tendrils of her spriten magic, her affinity for earth, to try and hold the rock together. Her head swam and her vision blackened. Feowen must have sensed her struggle.

"Don't!" he cried. "You are no use to me if you fall unconscious."

"This way!" The female servant darted down a side corridor. "It's longer but—"

"We don't have a choice," Feowen finished for her.

Behind them, the labored breaths of the other servants kept pace.

"Is there anyone else?" she managed.

"No. I already asked. The dungeon was already cleared out for Kane's spiders."

They took another set of passages and found their path blocked by a heap of rubble. Feowen swore again and began to hum, his arm shooting out, the rubble pulverized into dust. They waded through it, continuing down the path—

Then they were through.

"Almost there," the woman cried before stopping short. Her arms flailed. Feowen had just enough time to release Claire and reach for her before she slipped over the edge. A deep chasm stood between them and the other side of the corridor.

"Is there no other way?" Feowen demanded, pulling her to safety.

"None!"

The walls were coming down around them. He glanced around then began humming again. He wasn't as strong as Taylynn—still relied on music to work his magic. But he was far more powerful than any other sprites. A network of vines began to break through the cracks in the rock, attempting to weave a bridge.

A massive crack appeared under their feet and the floor jolted, coming apart an inch, then two, then three.

"Feowen, there's no time!" she cried. "We'll have to jump it."

Feowen's neck bulged, tendons popping out. She could sense his profound fatigue. There was no telling how much of himself he'd spent trying to work against Kane's fire magic earlier.

He released a rough exhale and nodded, too tired for words.

"We have to jump," she said, turning to the others.

"You're coming with me," Feowen said, knowing he needed to get his queen to safety first.

They took off at a run and cleared the distance, barely landing with an inch to spare. She staggered forward to the ground, catching herself with her hands. Her wrists screamed. Feowen was already directing the others to run and jump. A few of the braver servants landed beside her. One slipped and Feowen reached out, pulling them to safety. Two of the older looking servants didn't look like they'd make it. The crack on that side grew to a foot wide.

They backed away. Feowen swore under his breath. Then he was running, clearing the distance between them. He landed on the other side. Either he'd have to make the jump with both servants, or sacrifice one. There wasn't time to go back again.

He made his decision.

Wrapping an arm about each of their waists, he took off at a sprint, pulling them along. He made the jump. She was ready to catch him, a vine already in hand, under her control.

He surged towards them, but there wasn't enough power behind his jump. She saw it as soon as he did. That he wasn't going to clear the chasm. She used the vine, throwing it to slither around his waist just as his eyes widened. Her vision tunneled at the expense of her magic, the effort threatening to blind her. For a moment, the world around her wavered and she lost control. A scream tore from her lips but she forced her magic to comply, using her magic to pull Feowen the rest of the way towards them with the vine.

His body slammed against the wall below, the vine holding firm. "Help me pull!" she cried. The servants beside her jumped into action, taking the vine before it slipped through her hands. They put their weight into it, one step, then another, then another until she saw the top of Feowen's blue hair and the wisps of white hair from his two charges. Both charges were clinging to him. She called on her inhuman strength to make the final heave that brought him up over the lip of the drop.

Feowen helped the two servants over the edge, then pulled himself up. She noticed the tremble in his muscles but didn't comment. She reached out and helped drag him to his feet, her own knees nearly buckling.

"Run!" Their guide cried. They took off at a sprint.

"If we make it out of this alive—" she started to say.

"We are not dying today," Feowen growled.

Gods, she wanted to believe that. She had a mate and a kingdom waiting for her. Oh, gods—how was she going to tell Talon about Cyrus, about his sacrifice.

A tear slipped down her cheek as they fought their way free of the fortress.

When a pinprick of natural light appeared in the distance, the servants began to cry out. Feowen let out a whoop. She urged her feet to move faster.

They broke out into the early morning light. The sun was just peeking up above the mountains. She had to shield her gaze against it. Rumbles continued to shake beneath their feet, growing more violent. The fortress had once belonged to the dragons, but Kane had sunk his teeth into it. Without him, it was imploding.

She cringed as one of the towers split away and dropped to the ravine far below, disappearing into the mountain's mists. It felt like a lifetime of waiting before the resultant crash sounded. They were so, so high up.

"The lift," Feowen breathed, leading them over to it.

"It's got to be operated by someone to lower and raise it," the woman said, biting her lower lip. "Someone will have to stay—"

"No one stays behind," Feowen growled. He began ushering everyone onto the platform.

"What's your plan," she whispered, fighting the tremble in her voice. She was so, *horribly* tired, mentally and physically. She wasn't sure she could even create one of the jasmine flowers Pelwynn loved so much.

A fresh wave of sadness and despair struck her chest. She'd never be able to tell Pelwynn what his training had done for her. That she'd relied upon it to defeat the sorcerer. That his relentless exercises in focus were the key to staying alive.

"I'll use magic to turn the crank." Feowen's voice wavered.

"Are you… Are you sure?" Uncertainty made her stomach clench. They were so close. So close to freedom.

"I think I have…enough."

They situated themselves inside then closed the grate, sealing themselves into the tight box. It reminded her of an elevator. It ran on a metal track down the side of the fortress, with a massive crank that required an operator.

Feowen began to hum and the crank started to turn. She grabbed his hand, squeezing. She offered him what remained of her strength. He looked ready to protest. He must have thought better of it because he didn't. He must have been truly spent.

Her humming melded with his. There was little thought involved. She let her instincts take over. Sprite magic was a part of her and had always been instinctual. She relied upon that now, more than ever.

The box lowered.

She didn't dare look down. The sheer drop was at least fifteen hundred feet, perhaps more. Instead, she turned her face towards the warmth of the rising sun. After being stuck in that dark place all night, lost in its labyrinthine tunnels, where every step was life threatening, the feel of the warmth on her skin was a balm.

The lift jolted and she gasped, her song broken as they began to plummet. Feowen's eyes went wide, his neck muscles straining. He began to hum again, an apology in his gaze. His magic was faltering. She increased the ferocity of her humming, trying to feed him magic. Little black dots popped into her vision. Her body was near collapsing.

She prayed this wasn't the end. That after this, they could rest. She didn't have it in her to do anything else.

"I've got you, Miss." A woman's voice sounded behind her. She felt hands, multiple sets of hands, helping to hold her up, allowing her to take the focus off standing upright. She fed everything she had left into the magic they needed to get down.

"Almost there," one of the older servants cried. "Almost—"

The lift jolted again and several screams rang out. She opened her mouth, her humming turning into words laced with power. She was weaving mage magic with sprite magic, substituting some words for others. Her brain was too muddled to think much about it.

There was another lurch and then a bone jarring thud.

"We made it," several voices cried.

"Oh, bless the gods!"

"They did it!"

"We're free."

She opened her eyes to find the base of the fortress. A massive lake stretched around them. She began to shiver, pulling her cloak tight. Her legs decided to give out. She sank to the floor of the lift, her back against the bars. Feowen sank down beside her. Their heads came to a rest against one another, leaning in for comfort.

There were no words.

How could she ever give voice to the maelstrom of emotions swirling inside her. She'd defeated Kane but lost Cyrus—and Isabella's staff—in the process. They'd nearly died. She's almost lost Feowen—he'd almost lost *her*.

She felt like she could sleep for days, weeks, perhaps even months—

A series of rough grunts sounded, "Well, well, well, what has we found here!"

Several worried voices cried out. The servants shrank away from the lift's bars. She blinked, bringing things into focus. They were surrounded by a band of goblin guards, all armed with weapons pointed right at them. A deranged laugh burst from her chest.

"And here I thought we might get a break," she managed. But they wouldn't be so lucky.

CHAPTER 4
A QUEEN'S NEED

Shadowkeep

Claire didn't feel an ounce of fear at the sight of nearly thirty goblins. She should have. Her magic was spent, she didn't have the strength to stand, her head ached. She was hungry and thirsty. Her eyelids could barely stay open. And yet, after having faced down Kane, it felt as if nothing would ever frighten her again.

"The sorcerer is dead," Feowen said, his voice cold. "Our queen killed him."

The goblins exchanged wary glances, their harsh, guttural words filling the air. She couldn't make sense of them, nor did she care to.

"We can do this the hard way or the easy way," Feowen continued. "The hard way means I kill all of you. Easy way means you go on your way and leave us be."

The goblins hesitated. More muttered exchanges followed. Her eyes fluttered shut. Maybe Feowen would take care of it—

The next thing she knew, he was shaking her awake and the goblins were gone. She attempted to drag herself to her feet. Her body shook from exhaustion. Had she...fallen unconscious?

Feowen moved in, helping her come to her feet. "That's it. Let's get you somewhere you can rest. I don't fancy dozing off in a cage. Not this close to a mountain about to come down."

She didn't have the energy to thank him. They managed to stagger forward. The servants assisted in keeping them upright. There was a dirt path through the foliage. They found a place to settle beside the lake.

"This must be the lake Mikkin and Jamie found the dragons nesting beside," Feowen mused.

"Looks so peaceful," she murmured, her eyelids falling closed.

The last thing she remembered were gentle hands settling her on her back to rest.

When she finally woke, the sun was low on the horizon. Her stomach ached with hunger and thirst. Feowen was awake beside her, gazing blankly out over the water. The servants were huddled together for warmth around a small fire.

It took a few moments, but the events of earlier that day began to fill her mind. A trickle at first. Then a roar.

"We did it," she said, slowly sitting up.

Feowen scooted closer, his eyes sharp with concern. "You're awake. How do you feel?"

She groaned, rubbing her temples. "Like I've been run over by a truck."

Feowen raised an eyebrow. "A truck?"

"Never mind," she muttered. "It's just—I didn't expect this."

"You didn't expect to *not* be dead after vanquishing Kane?" He smirked.

"No." She tried to shove him but it was a feeble push. "I half expected to die getting *out* of there. How ironic would that have been?"

Feowen hummed. "Quite the end to the story. You save the kingdom and get buried in rubble."

She let out a humorless chuckle, her mind drifting back to the chaos of the fortress. She could still feel the weight of her loss—the hollow ache in her chest where Cyrus had been. His absence made her miss Talon's comfort even more. Their pain of separation stretched across the kingdom, across her heart, like a wound that hadn't healed.

Feowen must have sensed her mood shift. He nudged her shoulder. "You've done it before, you know. Traveled across a kingdom to find him."

She offered him a tired smile. "With a dragon at my side. I don't think I can walk it alone this time."

"You aren't alone."

"I'm not, am I." A tiny smile pulled at her lips. A tiny *grateful* smile. Gods, she was so glad to have him with her. Her hand jumped to her neck, nervously fiddling with her pendant. The forest tear was a comfort. So was the pearl she'd strung onto the chain after—

"That's it," she breathed, eyes going wide.

"What?" Feowen frowned at her, his gaze searching.

"Tourmaline."

"What's Tourmaline got to do with—? Oh." He seemed to realize it at the same time as she did.

She closed her eyes, clutching the pearl. Tourmaline had said to carry it with her always, so that he would know if she ever had need of him. Well, she needed him now more than ever!

Uncertain if he could hear her, she silently communicated the depth of her need. Could he feel it, all the way in the forest? Would he come?

When she opened her eyes, Feowen was gazing intently at her. "I don't know if it will work," she said. "But all we can do is hope."

"In the meantime," he said, keeping his voice low, "we ought to see about feeding our companions before they waste away from starvation."

She felt as if she might waste away too. But when her eyes found the small group they'd saved, she winced. Their frail bodies were skeletal.

It didn't look like Kane had fed them at all while they'd toiled away in his fortress. How very like the sorcerer to treat his servants so horrendously, trapping and starving them.

"We'll have to take them with us," she said, switching to *Ednuar*.

"I figured as much," Feowen replied.

"We can find out where they came from, perhaps find a village with villagers willing to help them get home."

Feowen glanced down at the coin pouch he carried. "I think I have enough to ensure they are taken care of."

"Good." Her shoulders relaxed. "Have you regained enough strength to see to their needs? Otherwise I can—"

"No." He placed a hand on her shoulder. "You rest. Let me see to them."

She sighed, relieved. "Something tells me if I try arguing you'll still insist."

"I am many, *many* years older than you. I've had thousands of years to build up a magical tolerance. Nothing you can say will change my mind."

"Fine. But if you're going to grow anything, I could go for a few root veggies and perhaps some pears."

"Consider it done, *Ayas Drollaya*." He moved away to speak with the servants.

Her mind drifted in and out of thought. When she next turned, Feown had fashioned a frying pan out of stone and she caught the scent of vegetables over the fire. Her stomach growled. He handed her a stone cup of water and she drank deeply, thanking him.

There was enough food for everyone to eat their fill. When darkness fell, Feowen ignored the danger fire might pose, arguing that the mountains were too cold for the humans to survive without it, and had even managed to create cotton blankets for them. He also insisted on taking first watch so that she could get more sleep. She was too tired to argue, promising that she'd take over after a few more hours of rest.

When she next opened her eyes, morning sunlight was shining over the mountains. Feowen was alert, his gaze on the forest. "You should have woken me," she chided. "You've not had any rest."

"I'm a sprite. I can go days, even weeks without it if I must."

"Well I'm a sprite too, and I could probably sleep for that long and still feel tired."

He chuckled, some of his old self returning. "You still have human and drengr blood in you, *Ayas Drollaya*."

"I suppose you're right." Her eyes took in all the new growth around them and she smiled. "Nice garden."

"Why, thank you. Rather proud of it."

"We should get moving once they've had something to eat," she mused, gaze darting towards the servants. They already looked better after a good meal.

"Yes, I thought the same. The sooner we get out of these mountains, the safer we'll be."

There was no telling what sort of denizens lurked around Kane's crumbled fortress. The fortress. She glanced up to find much of the mountainous peak gone. It had caved in on itself. Feowen followed her gaze before looking away.

He still wore Kane's breastplate. The only reason he hadn't removed the stones was because he'd already spent so much magic. It only illustrated how weak the ordeal had made him.

She reached for his arm, giving it a squeeze. "Thank you."

He frowned. "For what?"

"For coming after me, for doing this with me. I... I wouldn't have made it without you."

His throat bobbed. "You're welcome, my queen."

Her insides melted. "Don't tell Taylynn, but you're my favorite cousin."

His face brightened. His familiar mischievous grin came out in full force. Seeing it—it felt like everything would be okay.

"I won't say a word." He placed a hand over his heart.

A giggle slipped free and she rolled her lips between her teeth to fight a smile.

"Now," he said, "shall we get away from this accursed place?"

~

Tourmaline appeared two days later. He hadn't come alone. Seven other unicorns trotted behind him, enough for Feowen and each of the servants to ride. Like he'd known.

A sob burst from her chest at the welcome sight, her eyes clouding with tears. "You came!"

He tossed his head. *"I will always come when you need me."* His voice was rich in her mind. She rushed to him, caring little about how undignified she looked, throwing her arms around him and nuzzling his sleek coat. *"Much has happened since we last spoke, Queen."*

"Yes," she breathed, stroking her fingers through his mane. "But, gods, I am glad to see you."

"Nua bualta," Feowen said, greeting the unicorns. They tossed their heads in return.

Their small group had slowly been making their way through the mountains but hadn't gotten far on foot. The servants were too weak to walk more than a few hours at a time. Feowen kept a constant supply of food on hand to nourish them, but it would take more than that to get these poor souls healthy again.

"We need to get them somewhere they can recover," she told Tourmaline. "What is the closest settlement?"

"Much of them were burned by the dragons, but several have begun to rebuild. I know of one near the base of the mountains. It could work."

"Then let's go," she decided. She turned to the servants and froze, taking in their wide eyes. She'd become accustomed to shocking sights, but they hadn't. They gaped at the unicorns.

"Can you ride?" she asked. Most of them shook their heads, mouths hanging open. "Well, we'll start slow, then."

"It's no matter," Tourmaline assured her.

She and Feowen helped the others up until everyone was in position. Since the terrain was rough and the humans would struggle to remain astride, they carefully picked their way over the landscape. It was slow going, but it was better than walking. The unicorns were sure-footed and didn't stumble as they made their way through difficult passes, over rocky and pitted ground.

The day passed slowly. They made camp in the evening and several of the unicorns volunteered to keep watch. Feowen was finally able to get some rest.

They hadn't caught sight of the goblins since their initial encounter. Feowen had long since filled her in. All he'd done was a small little magic trick and they'd shrieked in fright, realizing he was a sprite, knowing they didn't stand a chance against someone so powerful. He'd bluffed of course, since he couldn't have done anything powerful at the time.

But it had worked.

Hopefully they'd tucked tail—metaphorically speaking since they didn't have tails—and run back to Pavv. Not that the little urchins would dare show themselves now that the unicorns were here. Unicorn horns were lethally sharp. No one wanted to be on the receiving end of one of those.

The next three days passed at a painfully slow pace. She rode at the front of the procession, Feowen at the back, to make sure none of the servants fell off their steeds. It gave her far too much time to think. Too much time to dwell on Cyrus.

There were so many times his snide comments had irritated her. Now she regretted ever feeling anything other than undying love for his presence. She'd been appalled to learn he'd planted his soul inside her. Had considered it almost a burden. Now, she missed him more than words could say.

There were so many things she hadn't said to him. Mostly how grateful she was that he'd been with her during her most difficult times. How often had she thanked him for it? Now she'd never get to speak with him again.

A silent tear rolled down her cheek and she wiped it away.

The ground flattened out. Tourmaline interrupted her thoughts to say, *"Now we will make better time,"* and then he was off. He didn't run as fast as he could have. The humans were still frail; they didn't want to risk losing any of them. Still, she was relieved that they would gain more ground, finally.

The sooner she could put these mountains behind her, the

better. She wasn't sure she would ever look at them the same. Wasn't sure she could ever look at them and not see what she'd lost.

The emptiness Cyrus left behind would haunt her forever.

Kastali Dun

Dallin smoothed the front of his brocade tunic. His hands were slippery with sweat. He couldn't linger out here all day. Clearing his throat, he knocked.

"Enter," came Talon's gruff voice.

He fumbled with the door's latch and slipped inside the king's study. Talon sat behind a massive desk piled with missives. He took in the king's appearance, noting how haggard he looked. Talon's hair was a mess, his clothes uncharacteristically wrinkled. When was the last time he'd slept? He almost asked, but refrained. He wasn't as close with King Talon as the others. That kind of closeness would come in time—

"Out with it."

"I'm sorry?" He blinked.

"You're analyzing me just like the rest of them. So?"

"Nothing, Your Majesty."

Talon blew out a breath, pinching the bridge of his nose. "You're my shield, Dallin. Take a seat and say what needs to be said."

He swallowed down the lump in his throat and quickly complied. "I was wondering if you've slept. You look..."

"Awful?"

"What?! No. I didn't mean..." Heat rose to the surface of his skin.

"I know what you meant," Talon huffed, turning his gaze towards the open balcony doors. The sheer curtains fluttered in the sea breeze. Talon's gaze was vacant, like he was trying to focus on something just out of reach. "I haven't slept since she left."

Dallin winced. "Is she...?"

"She's alive. I can feel it." Talon's jaw flexed and he turned back to face Dallin. "Being separated from one's mate is never easy. It pulls on something deep in your chest. It *hurts*. Three days and I'm nearly crawling out of my skin."

Dallin gave a quick nod, like he knew what the king meant. Except in reality, he probably never would. Not just because he was a shield, even though Talon was working to change the charter, allowing shields to take mates. But because he'd never heard of a drengr taking a male mate. Given his preferences...

"How are you recovering from...?"

"Fine. Spending as much time out of doors as possible." It was one of the things he'd struggled with being locked in the dungeons. Having Verath for company—thank the gods—had also helped. Alone, he would have gone mad.

"That's understandable."

"Verath made me spar with him for hours each day. I probably would have wasted away, otherwise. It's made my recovery smoother. I feel back to my normal self, mostly."

"Mostly." Talon nodded, his focus on a small coin he fidgeted with. "That's...good."

"Yeah."

Talon seemed to come back to himself, pocketing the coin. "I called you here because I have a job for you, if you are up for it?"

"What is it?"

"As you know, there has been a rise in crime around the poorer districts in the city, ever since Kane's takeover. I hoped it would die down now that he's been removed from power, but..."

"Things are getting worse."

"Things are getting worse," Talon confirmed. "My informants brought some interesting news this morning. Seems most of the trouble is coming from a gang calling themselves the *Serpent Syndicate*. Or, *Serpents*? Something like that."

"Would you like me to look into it?"

"More than that. I want you to infiltrate them and figure out who's leading them. None of my informants have been able to get close. Calls himself King Cobra."

Dallin snorted. "Not very original."

Talon shrugged. "No surprise."

"Why me? Is this a test?"

"No more tests, Dallin. You're one of us. I think this would be a good fit for you because unlike the rest of us, you haven't quite filled out your form. If I put one of the others inside, people will know he's a drengr just by looking at him."

"I'm still scrawny enough to fly by without suspicion." It wasn't quite true, but close enough. There was nothing scrawny about him, except when compared to other drengr.

"Not a slight against you. Just convenient, is all. I could have had one of my guards find someone for the job but I'd rather it be somebody I implicitly trust."

Warmth exploded in Dallin's chest. "I'll do it."

He didn't even need to think about it. Since removing Kane from power, there'd been an unending list of messes to clean up. Talon had borne the brunt of it, which wasn't a surprise. The king threw himself into the work as a distraction. Still, if he could pick up some slack, he would. Doing things like this, helping the king and his kingdom, was one of the reasons he became a shield.

"Good." Talon nodded towards a pile of tattered clothing on the nearby sofa. "I had my servants collect that earlier. Find a room to rent in the Pauper's District. You'll need to come up with a false identity, fully integrate yourself into society. Maybe get a job. Not sure how long it will take you to work your way into King Cobra's inner circle."

"And once I do?"

Talon blew out a breath, running a hand through his tangled hair. "I'll leave that up to you. I'm certain the man in question is Oshean. Someone who came over when Kane stole the throne. Cells are full enough as it is. Not sure I want scum like that in my dungeons."

"Do shields regularly engage in...less savory things?"

"More than you might guess. We keep it hushed up."

"Understandable."

"Keep your appearances here at the castle to a minimum—less chance of being spotted and blowing your cover. You can come and go, as long as it doesn't risk anything. Report to me whenever necessary—telepathically. If you get yourself in trouble, I expect you to get yourself out of it. But, if it gets really bad, don't hesitate to send for one of us."

"Of course. Is that everything?"

"That's everything." Talon stood and he followed. Talon rounded the desk and extended his forearm. They embraced and his king clapped him on the back. "Be careful, Dallin."

"I will. Thank you for trusting me with this."

"I know you can handle it." Those words meant everything.

He grabbed the clothes and retreated to his chambers to prepare.

RIGHTEOUS ROSE SMELLED like rancid vomit, sweat, and stale ale. He wrinkled his nose as he stepped inside, trying to acclimate to the stench. He'd picked this tavern on a whim. It was half full—a good sign. It appeared to be a mix of day-drunks and suspicious clientele, perhaps using the location as a meeting place.

The back of his neck prickled. He felt eyes on him as he crossed the room, his boots sticking to the floor as he went to the bar and pulled up a stool. There wasn't much in the travel sack he carried, so he plopped it on the surface beside him.

A frazzled maid stepped over. She wore a kerchief on her head but it didn't do much to tame the frizz of hair escaping. She might have been pretty if the hardships of life hadn't sucked the joy out of her. That's how everyone in this part of the city looked. Made worse by what they'd suffered at Kane's hands.

"You're a handsome one," she teased. "What can I get you?"

"Whatever you got on special." He ignored her flirting.

She noticed his disinterest and said, "Ain't got no specials."

"Fine. Pint of ale then." He kept his voice a little louder than necessary.

The maid nodded, setting about her task. When she set a drink in front of him, he handed over two steelies. Enough to pay for the drink but no tip. She took it, but the enthusiasm in her expression fell. He wished he could tip her. Gods, she looked like she could use it, but he had a reputation to uphold and it wasn't one that advertised him rolling in coin. "Looking for a place to rent. I'm new in town. Looking for work, too, if you know of anything."

"Don't think I can help you," she said, her voice firm. He didn't miss the way her eyes darted to the corner of the room as she said it. Then she scurried off and busied herself cleaning.

Right. Well, then. He took a sip and fought the urge not to cough. The stuff tasted like piss—not that he knew what piss tasted like. More just what he expected it to. Is this really what they served in the Pauper's District? Gods, it was horrible. He sighed, letting his shoulders fall. Using the next several minutes, he considered his plans for the day.

It wasn't that he wasn't thrilled by the prospect of doing something useful for the king. He was. It was more that he hated the idea of being cut off from everyone back at the keep. Or rather, one person in particular.

If he was going to do a good job here, he needed to go all in.

He'd looked for Jamie before leaving the keep, but hadn't found him. The best he'd done was leave a letter in Jamie's quarters telling him he'd be gone for the foreseeable future. He hadn't said more than that, for fear of anyone else coming across the note. Still, he'd try to find Jamie to explain when he could. Until then, he hoped he wouldn't take his disappearance as disinterest.

Not that he knew if Jamie was interested in him. Not like *that*. They were friends, and he was glad. It wasn't a good idea to get tangled up with a human. And yet, there was something about Jamie that drew him in.

Silly, since he wasn't even sure if Jamie would ever consider him as more than a friend. Wasn't sure if he'd even *want* to be friends after he found out Dallin's...preferences. It's why he hadn't said anything. Perhaps it was better to simply keep things as they were.

He took another sip, fighting the urge to puke it back up. No wonder the place smelled like vomit. Probably from the crap they served.

A stool beside him scraped. He'd heard the approach of footsteps but feigned surprise, whipping his head around as one of the patrons took a seat beside him. He looked to be in his early thirties.

Forcing himself to appear nervous, he took another sip.

"So, you new in town, eh?"

"Yup."

The first thing that struck him was the stranger's eyes. They were unique. One was gray the other hazel as they roved over him, taking in the threadbare clothes the king had provided. The pants weren't quite long enough for his tall frame. Didn't fit him the way tailored pants did, which illustrated how spoiled he must be if such a thing irritated him. The tunic pulled uncomfortably in all the wrong places. Too tight in the shoulders and arms. He worried he might bust the seams open if he had to lift anything heavy. Given how cheaply it was made, that wouldn't come as a surprise.

Funny enough, the stranger beside him was dressed better than he was—a good deal better. Almost too good to be seen in this part of the city. He hoped that was a good sign. Especially when the man said, "You look like a strong fellow. Where you from?"

He pretended to contemplate his answer. "Lincastle. Worked the docks before..."

The man's eyebrows raised. "Before?"

He cleared his throat and rubbed the back of his neck. "Got caught up in some...stuff. Decided to try my luck elsewhere. Everyone says Kastali Dun is a mess after all that happened. Thought I might settle here for a bit."

Something akin to interest lit the man's eyes. "I see. So, couldn't help but hear you're looking for room and board? Work?"

"Yup." He took another sip of the gods-awful liquid in his tankard.

"Might be able to help ya."

"Truly? Would be forever grateful."

"Friends and I got a job coming up." The stranger pointed towards the group in the back. "Need strong hands like yours. Lots of lifting. Need someone who understands discretion. Fifty-five steelies for a night of work. You in?"

Dallin sat up straighter. There was no telling if this man and his crew had anything to do with the *Serpent Syndicate*, but if they didn't, perhaps they could refer him to someone who did. That meant doing good work and finding an in. "I know all about discretion. I'm up for it."

"Good." The man rubbed his jaw, looking over Dallin's clothes again. "You'll need to wear something dark. Need to blend in tonight. We're meeting here at midnight."

"Not a problem." A thrill shot through him. He didn't have much information to go on but given the lack thereof, it was probably something illicit.

"As for a room to rent, got a place upstairs. Few of us shack up here."

Dallin looked over at the bar maid. She pretended to ignore them but he was certain she was listening intently to their conversation. Interesting.

"Oh, don't mind her. She's just following orders. I decide who gets to settle in this neighborhood."

"Understood. I don't have much—"

"How about I take it out of your pay for tonight? Twenty steelies a week for the room—which is cutting you a fine deal. That leaves you thirty-five. If all goes well, I'm sure I can find you more work in the future."

"That...that would be great. I would forever appreciate it."

"Good. Then I'm Martel, but my friends call me Crazy Eyes. And you are?"

"Derek. Derek Lanover." He opted for something close enough to his real name. Easier to remember. "Don't got a fancy nickname, though."

"Good to meet you, Derek." Martel chuckled, holding out his hand. He fought a grimace, hating the way humans shook hands. It had always grated him. He didn't want to feel a stranger's palm against his. Better to grip their forearm and feel the kind of strength they carried beneath their tunic sleeves. "Maybe you'll earn one if you find a place with us."

He let bright hope light his expression and eagerly said, "I wouldn't mind that!"

"Good. Then follow me."

Dallin stood. Hesitating, he grabbed his tankard and forced himself to chug the remaining liquid. It wouldn't do him any favors to appear wasteful. Wouldn't match his persona. It settled uncomfortably in his stomach, reminding him of the charmed life he lived. Then he turned and followed Martel to a small space off the main room of the tavern. There was a desk piled with papers, two chairs, and an armchair in the corner. Martel went across the room and opened a cabinet.

His lips parted with genuine surprise. "You own this establishment."

"Indeed. Welcome to the *Righteous Rose*. But don't be deceived. Nothing righteous or rosy about it."

Martel laughed at his own joke so Dallin snorted and said, "Got it."

Martel handed him a tarnished key. "Room six, just upstairs. Got a shared pit toilet at the end of the hall. Bathing costs extra. Nora will bring you a pitcher of warm water for five steelies, or cold for three—ain't included in the weekly rent. Otherwise there's a well at the end of the street if you want to pump your own water."

"Understood. Thank you."

"We'll see you in the main room at midnight. Don't be late," Martel warned. Something in his expression said that there'd be dire consequences if he was.

"I won't be," Dallin assured him. With that, he grabbed his travel sack and headed upstairs to settle in.

CHAPTER 6
A CUTPURSE

Kastali Dun

Dallin crouched low, holding his cover beside Greedy Remy and Steve. Gods, half of them had nicknames, which told him they'd been doing this a while. It was well past midnight. He'd donned his only pair of dark clothing, an ill fitting pair of pants and tunic, then strapped on a poorly made dagger he'd found in the folds of his cloak.

"That's the signal," Steve said, keeping his voice low. "Let's go!"

They took off at a sprint, crossing the warehouse yard. They'd been paired up in groups of twos and threes. There were fifteen of them in total. They'd received the majority of their instructions before leaving the *Righteous Rose*. The basics, at least. Martel was smart to keep details to a minimum. Seemed he worried about their trustworthiness.

He filed that bit of info away.

As they approached the warehouse's southern door, a pair of guards stepped out of the shadows, weapons lifted. Greedy Remy and Steve were on them. Dallin hesitated for obvious reasons. Low gurgles were the only sign that their throats were quickly cut before the bodies crumpled to the ground. Their eyes glassed over, unseeing.

Dallin's stomach roiled. *"I don't think I can do this."* He sent the silent thought to Talon paired with an image of the guards' lifeless bodies. The thought of disappointing his king made him squirm, but not nearly as much as what he was doing here.

Infiltrating a crime ring, sure. Killing innocents? It went against everything that made him who he was as a drengr and a shield.

"I know I am asking a lot of you." Talon's words were measured.

"I could have protected them," he argued.

"Yes, and then your charade would be at an end. Your new crew would have killed them regardless of your presence."

"It's not right."

"I know. They will keep at this behavior until someone puts a stop to them. You could act tonight, but that would only stop this job. In a few days, another gang will be at it again. Only then, you won't have any idea what their plans are and how to stop them."

"What if I play along but tip you off before it happens?"

"That might work for a few instances, but you're a new addition to this group and they will surely grow suspicious if their efforts are thwarted." There was a hesitation and then, *"Do what needs to be done, and quickly. Find out who King Cobra is and eliminate him."*

"Derek!"

"What?" Dallin blinked.

"What's the matter? Never seen a dead body before?" Steve was studying him with suspicion.

Damn it. "No, I... Sorry—just needed a moment."

"Well, come on then. Ain't got all night. Boss is expectin' us." Steve nudged him along. He tried to ignore the bodies on the ground as he passed them.

Talon was right. This would have happened with or without him. He just hated being a part of it, even knowing that his involvement would hopefully bring an end to the *Serpent Syndicate*.

"There you are." Martel appeared in front of them. The other smaller groups gathered around them. "No trouble?" Martel asked, his gaze assessing.

"Just a little case o' first-time jitters from this one here," Greedy Remy joked, elbowing him. He elbowed the man back, trying not to inhale the rancid scent of Remy's breath.

Martel gripped his shoulder. "You good."

"All good, Boss." He swallowed down the bile churning in his gut.

"Good. Then let's get started." Stepping away, Martel addressed everyone. "You all know what to do. Get going."

They moved through the warehouse keeping to smaller groups. Fast Fingers joined up beside them. "What happened to Dagger?" Steve hissed.

"Took a sword to the gut," Fast Fingers gritted out. "Told him not to toy with the guards on the north end, but he wouldn't listen. Wanted to have a little fun. Serves him right."

Dallin blew out a breath. At least one of their group had gone down. Not that it made up for all the guards they'd killed, all so they could steal the precious merchandise housed within *Warehouse Twenty-Three*. This one was owned by a *filthy rich* merchant, according to Martel. He had orders from the Syndicate himself to rob the place.

As they moved around, he caught sight of precious artworks, beautiful pieces of furniture, rare vases, and more. Greedy Remy cackled with glee when they found a jewelry box filled to the brim with pearls and jewels. They began quickly stuffing it into sacks as Martel guided them on what to pilfer. They had a wagon just off the premises for everything. All of it would go to King Cobra, to line his pockets. He didn't need to be great at math to know fifty-five steelies per person for a fifteen man job left a lot remaining once these items sold.

It wasn't the thievery that bothered him. Talon would reimburse the merchant, no doubt. It was the loss of life. He couldn't let himself think of the guards, if they had families, friends, loved ones. Gods above, he was going to be sick. He couldn't afford to be. The last thing he wanted was to hurl his guts all over the precious artwork he was toting through the warehouse.

As soon as he was out in the night air, he breathed easier. He dumped the artwork and went back for more. The job took about two hours. When they were finished, they set off through the city. Two horses were used to pull the contents they'd taken.

Warehouses lined the docks along the bay. Nearly fifty of them. The noise from the taverns one street over helped drown out any sound made by the horses hooves and creaking wagon wheels. It wasn't abnormal for workers to work late into the night on this side of the city. Ship cargo didn't wait when sailors had time tables to keep. Still, they couldn't be seen in a group so large.

Martel sidled up to him before dismissing the majority of their group. "You did good tonight."

He withheld a snort. "Thanks, Boss. I'll do better next time. Just not used to killin' is all."

Martel nodded. "Figured. There's a lot of unsavory work we got, but usually, there's some killin' involved. I'll keep that in mind for future jobs. Try an' put you on the ones that don't—"

"No, no. It's fine. I'm no pansy. I just needed to get my head around it. Don't want no special treatment or nothing."

Martel eyed him. "You sure?"

"Absolutely." The last thing he wanted were small, inconsequential jobs. Those wouldn't get him to the top. He needed to make his way up to King Cobra, and soon. Seeing those guards on the ground in a pool of their own blood only reinforced the need.

"Good. That's good." Martel looked pleased. "I take it you're all in then?"

He swallowed, steeling his nerves. "I'm all in."

"Excellent. Well, then. I'll have your pay for ya in the morning. Run along now.

Martel made good on his word the following morning. Dallin was sitting with the others, cringing his way through burned porridge. It wasn't the porridge but the company that stoked his unease. Or, well, who was he trying to fool? It was both.

Still, he forced himself to appear at ease. Martel dolled out their earnings. As mentioned, he kept a portion back to cover this week's rent. "I 'spect you boys will be off to the market to spend all that?"

"Not me." Steve pocketed his coin. "Got a girl down the way—owe her a visit."

"What do you say, Derek?" Greedy Remy clapped him on the back. "Fancy a bit of fresh air?"

"Absolutely." Inside, he was shriveling in on himself. He'd much prefer to go off on his own, but that wouldn't earn him any favor with this crew. He was stuck with them, at least until Martel saw him as an asset. Then, perhaps, he might move on to something better.

It was easier once they reached the bustling market. The fresh air and crowd loosened his muscles. He kept close to the others, keeping an eye out for a new tunic that fell into his desired price range. He was back in the one from yesterday, but gods, it was uncomfortable.

"So, how'd you get the nickname for Fast Fingers," he asked the man beside him as they browsed goods.

"Oh, that? Funny story—that." It was Greedy Remy who answered. "He's always been a good pickpocket. But one day we was meeting with a few nobles. We was under cover on a job. This was before Kane, mind you. Anyway, Fast Fingers here went to shake hands with one of 'em. Stole the man's signet ring right off his hand, didn't he? None the wiser."

"You're joking," Dallin said, looking at Fast Fingers with a new appreciation. No—not appreciation. Sure, it was impressive. But it only made him more wary of the crew he'd infiltrated.

"Good at what I do," Fast Fingers merely said, lifting his chin.

"And what about you? Why Greedy Remy?" he asked, looking at the short, dark haired man at his side.

"Oh, that's been dubbed the Meat Pie Heist." Jester, one of the others said.

"Meat Pie Heist?" He withheld his snort.

Greedy Remy groaned. "They'll never let me live it down, they won't. But I tell you, the goose was worth it. Love me some roast goose."

Jester and Fast Fingers both snorted. "Enough that you got your face bashed in by Crazy Eyes when it was all done with."

"Still worth it," Greedy Remy said.

"What happened with the Meat Pie Heist?" Dallin couldn't help his curiosity now.

"We was working a nobleman's house that evening—fellow and his family got called out of town to his sisters in the countryside. Was supposed to look like an emergency. Took them straight away, just before they was ready to sit down to dinner. Weren't no emergency, mind you. That was all Crazy Eye's doing. He had it set up real clean. No one was to get hurt. Anyway, Remy was newer—eh, Rem? He was our lookout for the night. Was supposed to stand near the servant's entrance just inside the cookery to keep watch. I was charged with rounding up the servants into the hall to keep an eye on 'em while the rest of us cleaned out the house. 'Sept there was some nice looking dinner sitting out on the cookery table, since it weren't served up to the family after all."

"You didn't!" Dallin looked at Greedy Remy, taking in the man's large belly. He already knew how much Remy loved food.

"Never let a good meal go to waste!" Remy looked as if the thought was a worse crime than murdering an innocent.

"We found him in the alley. He'd absconded with a whole roast goose, platter of meat pies, and the nobleman's best bottle of wine. Guards managed to get in the back entrance, turning it into a bigger fight than it were supposed to be. We all got away in the end. But ever since then, it's been dubbed the Meat Pie Heist."

"Some 'o the best meat pies I ever had," Greedy Remy said, a wistful look on his face.

The rest of the crew just laughed and they continued on their shopping. He wanted to hate these people, and he did. But he couldn't help but recognize that there were parts of them that weren't all bad. Nothing was ever entirely black and white.

They spent hours strolling up and down the aisles, browsing booths and wares. He was sifting through a pile of second-hand clothes when a familiar voice drifted towards his ears. He froze. Jamie.

His head snapped up and he spotted Jamie across the way, chatting amicably with Mikkin and a couple of guards. The dwarg and goblin weren't present. "See someone you know?" Greedy Remy appeared, putting a hand on his shoulder.

"What? No."

The desire to get close to Jamie was fierce.

"He's a pretty one, I'll give you that." Greedy Remy bobbed his head in Jamie's direction.

"Think I should go say hi?" he teased.

"Only if you make it worthwhile." Remy winked. He tensed, then relaxed, realizing what Remy had meant.

"Let's try my luck," he decided. "You lot keep back while I work, yes?"

A couple of them hooted with excitement.

He set off to stalk Jamie through the stalls. As he closed the distance between them, his heart set off at a gallop. He stepped up beside him and tossed an arm around Jamie's shoulders, making himself look like an amicable fellow eager for a friendly conversation.

The guards drew weapons but he waved them off saying, "Now, now, I don't mean him any harm."

He caught a glimpse of his gang, hanging back several paces to watch.

"It's all right—" Jamie began. He tugged Jamie along to cut him off and keep him walking.

"Don't turn around, but we're being followed."

"Dallin?! What in the name of the gods is going on?" Mikkin grumbled from beside them. "Jamie said—"

"You don't know me," he hissed before either of them could blow his cover. "Now," he lifted his voice higher. "What's a handsome fellow like you doing in the market today?"

Jamie's cheeks flushed. "Why are we being followed?" he whispered.

"Just play along," he said out of the corner of his mouth.

His crew was far enough back. As long as they kept their voices hushed, they wouldn't be overheard. He quickly explained what he was doing, keeping the details to a minimum. Talon didn't want him giving away too much info. Truthfully, he didn't want Jamie to know exactly what he was tangled up in. Would Jamie look at him differently if he knew what had gone down last night? If he knew he'd stood by while innocents lost their lives?

His stomach instantly soured. All the excitement of seeing Jamie fled. No, better not to say anything.

They kept their heads bent together for a while. He played friendly, acting as though he was meeting Jamie for the first time. A few minutes later, he said, "I'm going to take your coin purse. Talon will give you a new one. Wait a few moments until I get far enough away, then raise the alarm, understood?"

Jamie sighed. "Very well."

With that, he slipped his hand out and cut Jamie's purse. Then he clapped him on the shoulder and bid a loud farewell. His crew gazed at him, mouths agape. He flashed them the purse before pocketing it, walking towards them.

A cry went up into the crowd. He noticeably flinched, eyes locking with Greedy Remy's. Then—

"That man stole my coin purse!" Jamie shouted into the crowd. "Guards!"

His feet were already moving. He raced past Greedy Remy and the others, disappearing into the sea of bodies. His crew's calls of excitement and encouragement made his feet go faster. They knew better than to follow. That would only draw attention to his retreat.

All the better for him. He could disappear for a time and free himself of their company for a bit. He snatched a hat from a nearby vendor's stand, slipping around the stall to pull it firmly over his head. Then he disappeared back into the crowd. It only took him a few minutes to lose the guards. Chuckling, he made himself scarce, making his way from the market into the city's maze of streets. He kept to the lower districts, hoping to memorize the lay of the land. He hadn't spent much time down here in the past, so he decided to explore.

The remainder of the day was spent memorizing his new stomping grounds.

"I hear the king's got you on a special mission." Verath's voice interrupted him at one point. *"Be careful."*

No doubt Mikkin and Jamie had returned to the keep, informing some of the king's inner circle of what had happened.

"I will."

When he returned to the *Righteous Rose* for dinner, it was to hoots and cheers. He found his crew at their usual place in the back corner. They clapped him on the back, offering their congratulations. His bold act of thievery had cemented his place among them. "That was some good sleight of hand!" Fast Fingers cried. "That pretty boy didn't even see it coming. That will teach him next time, making friends with the wrong sort. Served him right."

Dallin could only grin. He'd managed to tell Jamie they wouldn't be seeing each other much over the next few weeks. He'd also gained clout with his new crew. Two birds, one stone.

"Where'd you get off to, anyway?" Greedy Remy demanded. "We coulda enjoyed some of that coin you grabbed."

"Too bad," he said, grinning. He held up the now-empty purse. He'd given it all away to the needy, slipping coins into outstretched hands during his exploration. "There wasn't much in the purse to begin with, but I found myself a nice brothel to lay low in for the afternoon—spent the whole lot."

A chorus of hollers sounded.

A firm hand clapped him on the back as Martel appeared beside him, his face relaxed. "Heard about your little show today. Be more careful next time, eh? I have it on good authority that the person you stole from is staying up in the king's castle. Those were the king's own guards you ran from. Pick a better target next time, eh? Don't need to lose you to the dungeons."

"Oh, come now, Crazy Eyes!" Steve shouted. "The man's celebrating his success! Let 'em alone for the night to bask in it."

Martel snorted and shook his head.

"Apologies, boss." Dallin feigned chagrin. "Didn't think too much about it. I'll be more careful next time."

Martel studied him with that penetrating gaze of his. "See that you do. And next time, rather than shacking up at the brothel, use your earnings to buy a new tunic. That one won't last you much longer."

"Sure thing, boss."

Martel stared at him a beat too long. Did the man suspect him? No, surely not. Martel nodded then disappeared back into the tavern's office and he blew out a breath, relaxing into the booth. His cover wasn't blown. At least, not yet.

CHAPTER 7
PEACE FOR LANDOW

Landow

Claire shielded her gaze against the sun, taking in the small village. There wasn't a cloud in the sky, creating a brilliant scene where the wilderness met the horizon. It was generous to call this a village. There were only a few newly constructed buildings. The rest were tents.

"Welcome to Landow, Queen." Tourmaline came to a stop.

Landow...

Her eyes widened. She recognized the name immediately. Not just because Reyr had come here, but because Mikkin's travel companion, Jamie, was from here.

Cries went up as townspeople noticed their arrival. The group laying thatch on a nearby building stopped to gawk.

"Gods above!" A young dark-haired female strode over. "You..."

"Well met," Claire said, swinging her leg over Tourmaline and dismounting. "I'm—"

"The queen!" the woman finished. "It's the queen," she called to the others who gathered behind her. Everyone fell to one knee.

"Please, rise!"

They were slow to follow orders. The woman's gaze fell on Tourmaline and the others. She gasped. "Are those—"

"Unicorns, yes." Claire allowed the villagers a few moments to recover from their surprise. Feowen appeared beside her. "We're hoping to rely on your hospitality for a day or two," she announced. "These people have been rescued from Shadowkeep. The sorcerer is dead."

"Dead?!" several voices cried. The word was echoed around the mass of villagers.

"Bless the gods." The woman's face brightened.

Another female pushed to the front of the group. She was older. An older male appeared beside her, hovering. "Please, can you tell us if our son, Jamie—"

"You're Jamie's parents!" A grin broke out on her face. "Oh, I am so glad to meet you." She rushed forward and pulled the woman into a hug. "Mary, right? And you must be Tynen."

"How'd you know?" Tynen eyed her suspiciously.

She burst into laughter. "Your son talks about you! All good things, I promise." Both their faces flushed. "I met him back at the war camp before we reclaimed Squall's End. Saw him again right before we reclaimed the capital."

"He's alive and well?" Mary seemed to hold her breath.

"Alive and well," she confirmed. "He's taken to spending time with our new shield, a young drengr named Dallin." She thought of how she'd caught Dallin sneaking looks at Jamie during some of their dinners together, before Kane had bound her memories.

"Oh, that's wonderful." Mary and Tynen shared a meaningful look. It had to be hard, living so far from their only son. Not knowing whether he was okay. "Thank you for such happy news."

"How are things here?" Feowen asked.

"Rebuilding is on schedule." Tynen glanced around. "It's slow work, to be sure. Most of us are good with our hands."

"We hate to impose—"

"It's no imposition, Majesty. You're welcome here as long as you need. Ain't much to look at now, but it'll get there. We can fix you up in the lodge there. It's where we gather and take our meals. You'll be right comfortable—your companions too."

"They haven't a home anymore," Feowen said. During their journey out of the mountains, they'd learned the servants were all that remained of a small village west of here, one that had been destroyed by dragons. "We would like to see them settled."

"We'd be happy to welcome them, that is, if they'd like to stay."

"They haven't much to their name," Feowen added. "I have given them what I had in coin to help them make a start. I do not wish for them to be a burden."

"It's no burden at all," Mary assured them, her expression sincere.

"Thank you." Claire felt immediate relief.

They exchanged a few more pleasantries before the villagers got back to work. Mary and Tynen saw them comfortably settled in the main lodge. The unicorns chose to roam freely and enjoy the wilderness surrounding the settlement. They promised to return when she had need of them.

Talon's mind pressed against hers—a faint, inquiring thought. His dim presence was a constant thing, always there. With an entire kingdom between them, their bond was muted. Still, she managed to send him a few reassuring thoughts, that she was alive, safe. Perhaps when the distance between them shortened, she'd be able to tell him what had happened.

In part, it was a relief. She didn't yet have the words to tell him what had happened with Cyrus. It would be difficult to witness Talon's grief.

After a simple meal of fresh bread and meaty stew—during which she told Mary and Tynen everything she could think of about Jamie—she and Feowen retreated to a quiet place outdoors to talk. "How are you holding up?" he asked as they made themselves comfortable in the shade of a large oak.

"I'm managing." She sighed, plucking a piece of grass and twirling it between her fingers. "I miss Cyrus. I miss my mate even more. I miss Kastali Dun, our friends, my cat."

Feowen chuckled at the mention of Batty.

"With Kane's servants settled, we could return to the capital. The unicorns could have us there in a week, perhaps less."

She blew out a breath. The idea was enticing. Talon was out of his mind with worry, despite her reassurances. He wanted her back in his arms—she could feel that much from the bond. She wanted the same. But...

She eyed Kane's breastplate, nose scrunching with distaste. "We must destroy the dragonstones."

"I was hoping you would say that."

"It's the responsible thing to do. We can never let something like this happen again."

"No, indeed we cannot. Any ideas?"

"The king tree will know."

"I was hoping you'd say that, too." He grinned, bumping his shoulder against hers.

"Already eager to return to your trees," she teased.

"I miss the forest, yes. But I miss Jeanine, too."

"What's going on between you two? Things have gotten pretty serious."

He barked a laugh. "I cannot believe it has taken you this long to pry into my business, *Ayas Drollaya*."

"Well, you know, I've had other things on my plate."

"Indeed."

"So?"

"Are you *ordering* me to tell you?"

It was her turn to laugh. "I could, you know. But I'd rather you confided in me as a friend."

"I like the sound of that." His expression turned contemplative.

As far as males went, he was ungodly handsome. She hadn't ever seen him that way. Technically they were cousins, albeit distantly. She'd only ever had eyes for Talon, scars and all. But she could see what Jeanine saw in Feowen. It wasn't just his good looks, but his personality. How could anyone not love his teasing nature? He was a joy to be around.

She had meant what she'd said days ago. She was truly glad he'd jumped through the portal to come after her. Not only because she would have died without him, but because she truly enjoyed his company. The only other male she would have liked to have on a journey across Kastali Dun, besides her mate, was Reyr.

"I have never loved another the way I love Jeanine," Feowen admitted.

"Does she know?"

"Yes. I've told her." His voice turned wistful. "I have also never felt my immortality more keenly than I do now."

"Because she will age and you will not." It wasn't a question, unfortunately.

He blew out a breath, appearing more young than she'd ever seen him. "It's not fair, is it? The drengr get mates. They can take another life and tie it to theirs, connecting their lifespans together. We sprites? We cannot do that with humans."

She frowned. "You're right. It's not fair at all. It forces sprites to be with sprites. What sprite would want to fall for a human only to know that their time together will pass in the blink of an eye?"

"Thanks," he muttered.

"Sorry." Her heart sank painfully. "Just...speaking hypothetically."

"Yeah..." His gaze settled on some faraway point in the distance. "I would still rather have her for the brief time we get together than not at all. Better to make the most of every moment we have."

"I love that." She blinked back tears. The truth was, she would be forced to watch Feowen's heart break as Jeanine aged. He was right. It wasn't fair. Why did the drengr get mates but sprites didn't? The tree was always talking about balance, but this wasn't it.

She couldn't help but wonder if there was something she could do to fix this.

"So...the forest," Feowen said.

"The forest," she confirmed. "We should get some rest today and leave at dawn. If we make good time, I reckon we will be there in a couple of days. I can seek out the king tree and ask for its advice. There has got to be a way to destroy the stones without harming anyone."

"Agreed. And after that?"

"Well, assuming it doesn't send me on some ridiculous quest to accomplish the task, I hope we might return to the capital. I cannot stay away from Talon too long. My poor king will lose his ever-loving mind." Feowen huffed in agreement. "I hate to think of how he's behaving right now. Hopefully he's not breaking things or yelling at people who don't deserve it."

"I wouldn't be so sure." Feowen's lips twitched.

"Oh, stop." She swatted his chest. "He's not *that* bad."

"Says his *mate*! Did you forget how the two of you met?"

She gave an exaggerated sigh. "You had to bring that up, didn't you?"

"Well, I wasn't there. I only heard about it from Koldis."

"Koldis told you?"

"Big mouth, that one."

She snorted. "He's going to be your brother-in-law, you know."

"Technically, no. Sprites and drengr don't do weddings. We aren't human. So, no."

"Oh, come on. That's a dumb technicality." She frowned. "Wait, sprites don't do weddings?"

"No. We do life ceremonies."

"How did I not know that?"

"Probably because you never witnessed one while you were there. Plus, like you said, you've had other things on your plate."

"Will you tell me about it?"

Feowen grinned. "I would be happy to, *Ayas Drollaya*. Seeing as it is the queen who presides over them when they occur. But you cannot tell anyone else. It is a very sacred ceremony."

"You're being serious," she realized.

He placed a hand over his heart. "Upon my honor, I am."

He spent the remaining afternoon telling her all about the life ceremony. He spoke of the saplings grafted together by happy couples, symbolizing two life forces coming together as one. Baskets presented full of their most prized possessions, things they would take with them as they embarked upon their new life together. Sacred words spoken, promises made between them in sight of their queen and other witnesses. Feasting and dancing, allowing happy couples to celebrate with their friends and loved ones late into the night.

"It sounds beautiful," she said, not mentioning that it sounded just like a wedding ceremony, even if Feowen said it wasn't. "Do you think you will want that with Jeanine?"

He hesitated, something unreadable passing over his expression. "She doesn't have the magic to grow a sapling alongside me."

Her stomach twisted uncomfortably. "What if we found a way to modify the ceremony? She's human, after all. Maybe it can be some of her culture mixed with yours?"

He blinked. A slow smile spread across his lips. "I like that suggestion. Thank you. I will think about it."

She would, too, because she hated the idea that Feowen and Jeanine had only a short span together. Perhaps she shouldn't interfere. Let Feowen enjoy the time he had with her. But still, she was never one to let something sit—not something like this. If she could find a way to give them a happy, long life together, she absolutely would.

That evening, the villagers of Landow surprised them with a feasting ceremony. It was modest, but that didn't matter. What mattered was the honor they paid her. Having a queen and prince in their midst was something unheard of.

The women fretted over her, insisting upon dressing her in a lovely lavender gown someone had graciously donated for the occasion. The generosity brought her to tears. These people had lost so much, and yet they were still so giving. Her hair was washed and braided into a crown upon her head as they fussed over her.

She and Feowen presided over the feast, sitting at a high table they'd set aside for the occasion. Afterward, they surprised the villagers by pooling their magic together to grow a series of beautiful fruit and nut trees in the area that would become Landow's new town square.

The villagers had decided to shift the location of Landow

slightly west, so that they didn't rebuild on top of the ashes of their old settlement. The memories were too painful. Those who hadn't left to seek refuge in Squall's End had remained at the expense of their lives. She encouraged them to speak the names of the ones they'd lost, standing in front of each tree. She then sent several villagers to gather some of the ashes, which they then sprinkled at the base of each tree to offer life and a promising future.

Sleep came easier that night. A sense of peace settled over her. The finality of the ritual had reminded her that Kane was truly gone, and that these people could move forward with their lives.

The next morning, they called for the unicorns. Mary was in tears as she bid them goodbye. She and Tynen had given her letters to deliver, not just for Jamie, but for Mikkin, too. Then she and Feowen set out with the unicorns for the forest, leaving a newly transformed village with new villagers in their wake.

CHAPTER 8
COMFORTING THOUGHTS

Falmont

Jovari landed on Falmont's battlements and roared. The stone beneath his grip trembled. Koldis landed beside him. *"A bit dramatic, don't you think?"*

"Why not? Let's make sure they know we're here."

"Oh, I'm sure they know. Hard to miss the twenty drengr we've brought."

"True." If he could have smirked, he would have. Still, his draconic lips peeled back in semblance of one. *"Now, shall we? I, for one, would like to put an end to this nonsense sooner than later. I've got a mate to return to."*

Koldis snorted. *"You aren't the only one..."*

Things between Jovari and Leah had taken a turn for the better. It might have taken him time to get his head out of the sand, but in the end, he'd managed to patch things up between them. Hopefully. She'd kissed him, hadn't she? Since departing, he'd replayed it countless times, lingering over the way her body felt in his arms, the way her mouth made him hard in all the right places. Gods, he finally understood why his brothers struggled when separated from their mates. He was half crawling out of his skin.

62

How did Koldis manage? He had to be the strongest of them. Taylynn went wherever she pleased and Koldis bore the separation without complaint. He half wanted to congratulate the male for it. Same with Talon. He'd been separated from Claire multiple times. It had driven the king half mad, but he'd managed to keep himself together.

The sooner they wrapped this up, the sooner he could return to the capital.

He had plans for when that happened. He would charm her. Woo her. Win her heart.

Flapping wings behind him signaled the arrival of their drengr forces. They landed just outside the walls. Falmont was the largest city in Celenore. It was unsurprising that Oshea's sorcerers had chosen this place for their new academy. It was on the coast, with easy access to trade. While its ports weren't as impressive as Kastali Dun's, they were comparable.

Transforming, he descended the stairs to the gatehouse. Koldis was hot on his heels. A group of trembling guards hovered in the corner of the room. He breathed a sigh at seeing them in Dragonwall's livery. "Is there a reason the gate is closed?"

"Forgive us, milord." One of the guards bravely stepped forward. "We... We were instructed to keep it closed—punishable by death."

"Understood. No need to fret now. I'm overriding your orders. Get it open."

The guards jumped into action, relief etched in their expressions.

He and Koldis ascended the stairs, back up to the top of the walls, surveying the city below. It was a third the size of Kastali Dun. Still, a significant population. His jaw clenched with distaste at the sight of foreign banners flying above the keep. The symbol of a black tower flapped in the wind.

"What do you think?" Koldis asked, casually slipping his hands into his pockets. "Think they'll cooperate without a fight?"

"Almost hope they don't."

Koldis sighed. "Me too, but there's been enough bloodshed. I'm sick of it."

"Agreed."

A bell tolled in the distance. He caught sight of the belfry towering above Falmont's keep. Someone was sending a warning.

Their forces poured in through the gates, twenty drengr in human form accompanied by their riders, bows nocked. The king had wanted to send more, but the battle against Oshea's forces last year had taken a massive toll on Fort Kastali, reducing its numbers by half. Now more than ever, the future of the drengr felt uncertain. Would their end come sooner than anticipated?

That was a worry for later. For now—

"Shall we head them off?" Koldis lifted his brows.

"Let's!"

Koldis quickly relayed instructions to their comrades below, informing the drengr to sweep through the city on foot. All Oshean forces were to be rounded up. Anyone who put up a fight would be killed, but any who surrendered would be spared and put on trial. Not that they deserved that small mercy.

A small group was sent directly to the port, to oversee any fleeing forces.

Jumping from the battlements, he shifted back into his dragon form, Koldis beside him. They flew over the city in less than a minute, landing in the largest courtyard of the keep. It was smaller, more similar to the keep in Squall's End.

Falmont was the ruling seat of Celenore's dragondom. He had no idea what had become of its lord—Lord Blake Caffrey. Hopefully not dead.

Cries rang out at their arrival. He caught sight of servants cowering in the shadows. A glint of armor drew his attention to the nearby portcullis. A handful of guards stood motionless, their mouths gaping. Their uniforms were the telltale black of Oshea's *Black Tower*. He knew enough now to know that the sorcerers from Oshea had their own academies. That was part of why they were here, to start new ones on Dragonwall's soil.

Jovari offered a feral grin and said, "What's the matter? Weren't expecting a band of drengr on your doorstep so soon?"

"Who is in charge here?" Koldis demanded striding forward, not bothering to demand they lay down their weapons. What was the point? A handful of blades was nothing to them.

One of the Oshean guards stepped forward. "Wielder…. Wielder Kaamal," he managed, looking about ready to soil himself. "He's—in the great hall."

"Excellent." Koldis hesitated before adding, "The rest of our forces are on their way—sweeping through the city as we speak. They've been commanded to kill all who resist. You will lay down your weapons and surrender or die. The choice is yours." Koldis didn't wait to see if they complied, turning his back to march into the keep. Jovari followed.

Wielder Kaamal was not, in fact, in the great hall. After a bit of searching, they found him in his chambers frantically packing as he prepared to flee. Koldis kicked down the door, making the walls shudder. The wielder spun on his heel and cried out, throwing his hands up in surrender while muttering an incant that made fire leap from the braziers, directly towards them. Koldis muttered a counter-incant, mostly to protect their clothes.

"I wouldn't bother with fire," Jovari taunted, drawing his sword and pressing the tip against Kaamal's chest. "We're dragons, remember?"

"Forgive me, my lords, I was just leaving."

"Hmm. Not so fast, I think." Jovari looked him over. "We'd like to ask you a few questions before letting you go."

"You'll let me go, then?" A glint of hope lit his eyes.

"Possibly." Not likely. "After all, I'm sure you were only here on orders from your superiors."

"Exactly that!" Kaamal latched on to that.

"Where is Lord Caffrey?" Koldis demanded.

"Lord—Lord Caffrey?"

"Don't feign ignorance," Jovari scoffed. "It's unbecoming. The lord you supplanted. Where is he?"

Kaamal's face paled. "The...dungeons?"

Jovari rocked his jaw from side to side. "And the other wielders?"

Kaamal hesitated. "There are no others."

Jovari huffed. "I don't buy it."

They made quick work of gagging him so he couldn't speak anymore magic. Then they bound his hands and dragged him into the great hall. Two of their drengr kept an eye on him while they set out in search of his comrades. They found several more wielders attempting to flee. They'd abandoned their things entirely. These they quickly gagged and bound, dragging them to the hall with Wielder Kaamal.

It was clear that while they had red eyes and looked like asaralí, like Kane, they weren't quite that. Their magic was younger. It hadn't taken much to overpower them. If anything, they reminded him more of scholars than sorcerers. Still, it would not be wise to underestimate them.

The other Osheans who'd surrendered were also brought to the great hall. They were all confined on the side of the room. Punishments would be awarded befitting the crime.

"Oh, thank the gods!" A woman rushed into the room. She wore a fine gown but looked as if she'd seen better days. "My husband. He—"

"You must be Lady Caffrey."

"Yes," she cried, her eyes wide with relief. "They took him. I don't know if he's still alive."

He directed a group of drengr to head down to the cells below the keep. Nearly half an hour later, they dragged an unconscious but alive lord into the great hall. Lady Caffrey wept with relief while Koldis set about healing the man's injuries. It was a benefit, having someone like Koldis with them. He was the best healer in their inner circle.

After the lord was safely settled in his bed to recover, Koldis and Jovari set up court, listening to the grievances of all those affected by the wielders. It took nearly all day to hear everything. Many of the keep's guards had been imprisoned or killed in

Oshea's quest to maintain order. Innocent citizens had lost their lives, fighting back.

It was a mess.

In the end, those who were merely acting on orders were put on a ship and sent straight back to Oshea with orders not to return, punishable by death. The wielders and guards with positions of authority didn't receive that mercy. The following day, when Lord Caffrey was well enough, they allowed him to sentence the culprits responsible for wreaking havoc on his keep and his city. They were all beheaded.

It was done at mid-day, when the sun was highest in the sky. Nearly the entire city turned out to watch. These people deserved justice.

Lord Caffrey begged them to stay a second night, but there were still two other cities to liberate. Two cities under the thumb of Oshea's Black Tower. It would take another week, perhaps two, to sweep up the coast, freeing Dragonwall's citizens before returning to the capital.

Just the mere thought made the ache in Jovari's chest intensify.

"How do you do it?" he asked Koldis as they set off for Vlonset, farther north along the coast. *"How do you hold yourself together when you're separated from Taylynn?"*

"It isn't easy," Koldis said after a long pause. *"It hurts something fierce."*

"And yet, you manage."

"Do I?"

"It seems so."

"It might—on the surface. But inside? My heart is screaming." There was another long silence and then, *"Leashing my mate to keep her close would diminish her. One does not leash the wind or the waves. Taylynn is wild like the forest. It grows where it will, and flourishes when left to its own devices. It is what I find most precious about her, most beautiful. The wildness. It speaks to my heart. So, despite missing her with a fierceness that steals my very breath, I know it is this pain that allows her to be who she is truly meant to be. I take comfort in it. And..."*

"And?"

"I make sure that every moment together is treated preciously. I collect those moments in my mind, to reminisce upon when we are apart."

Just like what he'd been doing with the memory of Leah's kiss.

"Will you seal your bond when we return?" Koldis asked. *"The king should have the charter amended by then."*

His shield brother hadn't been overly nosy since departing the capital. Koldis knew that they'd kissed, but that was it. He'd smartly let the topic drop after that.

Now that Jovari had a few days to come to terms with things, he found himself a little more eager to discuss his mate. Especially after Koldis had opened up about his feelings for Taylynn. *"She wants to wait,"* he admitted.

"Oh?" There was no judgment in Koldis's tone.

He hesitated. *"She's been through a lot. It's not my story to tell. But I know she wants to use Kastali Dun as a fresh start, a way to find herself."*

"Like taking up a job in the library?"

"Exactly."

"Hmm." Koldis sounded thoughtful. *"As I said, there is no controlling the ones we love. We can only provide them with whatever support they need to allow them to flourish. I am confident that once Leah finds peace with her new life, she will be eager to have you completely."*

Jovari's chest warmed. *"I will do whatever I can to make her happy. She's my mate."*

"I know. At the end of the day, that's exactly as it should be."

Beneath them, the coast disappeared, replaced by the dark blue depths of Stormy Bay. It would take the remainder of the afternoon to cross, but if they made good time, they'd reach Vlonset by morning. Koldis's words comforted him. It hadn't changed how he felt, or the pain of separation. But talking about it had helped.

Not for the first time, he wondered what Leah was doing at this very moment. Was she carrying around a stack of books to shelve, wearing those cute spectacles he'd caught her wearing? Or perhaps she'd finished for the day. He could picture her curled up in the library, a book in hand, engrossed in a story. Picturing her like that brought him comfort. Knowing she was safe and hopefully happy, waiting for his return. He savored it. He'd need as many comforting thoughts as possible to get him through the coming days, until he could finally reunite with her.

CHAPTER 9
LOSING ARCHERY

Kastali Dun

Saffra swore under her breath as her bowstring twanged. The arrow went wide, missing the target entirely. She notched another and fired. It missed. *Again.* Frustrated, she repeated the motions, growing angrier and more agitated. She couldn't hit the target. A tear rolled down her cheek. She quickly wiped it away before another took its place.

Her arms began to shake. Each iteration grew more impossible. A sob escaped her chest. Her entire hand sized up and she dropped the bow, trying to fix the cramp.

There wasn't enough air in the world to keep her breathing.

"Saffra!" Her name was more a growl than anything. Her vision swam, but she managed to stay upright. Damn it. It's like he could sense her distress. They weren't yet mated, and he still knew. When had he gotten here? How long had he watched her struggle?

Bedelth appeared, taking her shoulders. "I'm fine," she cried, trying to fend him off. He only held on tighter. She hated the worry and guilt clouding his gaze.

"You're not fine," he bit out. "Come on. You've had enough for today."

"I just need to practice more—"

"You've been out here for two hours," he nearly roared. He took a breath and calmed himself. Crouching, he gathered her things and ushered her from the practice grounds. She numbly allowed him to lead her away.

Her skin prickled uncomfortably. She could feel curious eyes on them. The practice grounds weren't crowded today. Most of the king's soldiers were tied up, putting things to rights after Kane's disappearance. Those who did have time off certainly didn't want to spend it practicing. But there were enough eyes that there'd be talk tomorrow.

What would they say? That the king's prophetess could no longer wield a bow? That she couldn't even strike the target?

She tried not to let bitterness fill her.

A click sounded and she realized Bedelth had ushered her into his chambers. She hadn't processed the walk through the keep. He pulled her over to a nearby sofa and dragged her onto his lap. "You're being too hard on yourself," he admonished. Another sob burst free, and then another. He made shushing sounds, wrapping his arms around her. That only made it worse.

She was too strong for this. Too strong to let go. Why now?

She'd managed to keep it together until today. She hadn't cried when the sprites healed her. Hadn't cried when she discovered that half her arm was a ruined, shriveled mess, the muscles completely destroyed. She hadn't cried at all. Until now. There was really no reason to.

She was lucky to be alive. Bedelth had nearly died. So had she. They'd barely made it out of that crumbling fortress with their lives. The vodar had almost bested them.

She'd had weeks to come to terms with it. It wasn't until today—

"It's all right. Let it out."

"I can't...even...hit the...target," she managed between gasps. She knew it was silly. She was *alive*. They were *alive*. Losing her ability with archery was a small price to pay. Sure, she couldn't muster the strength needed to fire a bow, but she could still use her arm...mostly. She could still brew concoctions. She could still hold a book. She could still hug her mate. Kiss him. Be with him.

"I know it's silly."

"It's not silly. Archery has been a part of your life. It's the thing that grounded you after so much was lost." He was so right. "You gave up your family, everything you knew, to come and work for the king. Archery allowed you to process and settle in. Gave you something that was uniquely yours."

"I know."

"You'll get it back again."

"Will I, though? I..."

"You said it yourself. You just need more practice."

"I think I'm just kidding myself." He was silent at her admission. "I don't think I will ever pull a bowstring with this arm."

It was covered, but she knew if she looked at her bicep, she'd find a ghastly sight. The wound from a vodar blade was lethal. The poison had eaten away at the tissue of her arm, burrowing its way through her muscle. Bedelth had gotten her to the sprites just in time. They'd contemplated amputating her arm entirely but had found a way to heal it instead. As a result, the skin looked blackened and had a texture that reminded her of tree bark. It was solid to the touch, from nearly her shoulder to her elbow. She could straighten it, move her elbow and her hand and wrist worked fine, but her strength was completely gone.

"What if you switched arms?" Bedelth pulled her out of her misery.

"Switched arms?"

"Yes, what if you held your bow with your injured arm and used the other for nocking and firing."

"That's preposterous."

"It's not. Plenty of swordsmen who injure their dominant arms are forced to switch. It's one of the reasons we encourage soldiers to practice with both arms."

"I..." She blinked. Could she? Did she even want to? "I don't know."

"Think about it." He turned her on his lap until she straddled his hips. A look of pure determination replaced his usual guilt. He'd done nothing but apologize since the near death experience. She'd seen in his mind that he blamed himself. She was his to protect—despite how preposterous it was for him to take the blame. If he could do this one thing for her, help her gain some of her life back, he would.

She knew that there'd be no fighting him on this. She didn't want him to feel guilty, and admonished him every time he apologized. But maybe this was something that would help both of them.

He brushed his fingers over her cheek before cupping the back of her neck and pulling her mouth in for a kiss. She collapsed against his chest, letting the warmth of his lips push everything else from her mind. The kiss was soft and reassuring.

She didn't want that. She wanted heat and hunger. Feeling brave, she roughly nipped at his lower lip, drawing blood. He huffed, tightening his hold on her until their mouths battled for dominance.

She felt the strain of him beneath her and gave in to the will of her hips.

Soon they were breathing hard, chests heaving. He knew her body, even if they hadn't yet sealed the bond. Knew her better than anyone, except perhaps Dax. But soon, he would know her better than even him.

That thought no longer sent a pang of sadness roaring through her.

"Talon amended the charter," he gasped, pulling away as they both tried to catch their breath.

"What?" It took a moment for her addled brain.

"Just yesterday. He drafted up the document that will allow shields to take mates. He has only to sign it, which he will do at the next council meeting. It's all but done."

"But... Why would he do that when he's got so much else going on?"

"Because sometimes a little good is especially important in the wake of something horrible. We've all been through hell, Saffra. He wanted to give us something good. Me and you, Koldis and Taylynn, Jovari and Leah—"

"Leah?!" She snorted. "We'll see if those two ever get together."

"He apologized to her and made things right—just before he left."

"He did?" Her brows knitted together. Koldis and Jovari had left days ago. Leah hadn't said anything. In fact, she'd been bringing the woman to dinner in the dining hall each night, all but dragging her from her work in the library. Leah hadn't said a damn thing. She wouldn't judge her, though. She knew better than anything how complicated mate bonds could be.

"Anyway, my point," Bedelth emphasized, "is that if we want to, we can." Quick as an adder, he nipped her bottom lip. She gasped.

"Are you suggesting—?"

"Possibly."

Heat exploded in her core. The thought of Bedelth carrying her to his bed. He'd touched her, tasted her, but he'd never claimed her the way a drengr claimed a mate. Her breaths quickened.

"I..."

He leaned in, running his nose along the column of her neck, sending shivers of desire over her skin.

"We should wait." The words were out quicker than she expected.

Bedelth pulled back and blinked. "You wish to wait. Is this about Dax—"

"No! Gods, no." She ran her fingers over his face to reassure him. "You said he hasn't signed it yet. And... I want a ceremony. I want Claire to be here." His muscles relaxed beneath her as understanding settled in. "I want you, Bedelth. I want you more than I've ever wanted anything."

"No, you're right. It would be better, for us and our friends. So that they could join in our happiness."

"Exactly." She pulled her lower lip between her teeth. She would probably hate herself for it later, when he took her to bed for the night. When his fingers slipped between her thighs leaving her hot and desperate. But for now, while she was thinking more clearly, she knew it was the right thing to do.

"Especially because I highly doubt Koldis and Taylynn will grant our friends any kind of ceremony."

Bedelth snorted. "Those two? They'll run off to the forest together and seal their bond beneath the trees, I'm certain of it."

"Exactly." She chuckled. "So we should be the ones that make our friends happy. The ones who set the precedent. Especially because of—"

"My parents."

She laughed, pinching him. He swore under his breath. "We're not even mated yet and you're already finishing my thoughts." He nuzzled her neck. She could feel the smile pressed against her skin. "It just seems right. Like the final stand against them, you know? A way to show that you are your own person, you make your own decisions, and you don't need their approval."

Bedelth had always struggled with his relationship with his parents. They had been a heavy influence on him taking the oath to become a shield. He'd spent his entire life trying to please them, to earn their love, when it should have been given freely.

She loved that her own parents had accepted him as if he were their own. Just the thought of them had her mood brightening. She was doing the right thing, waiting to seal the bond. Sharing their joy with her friends and family felt *right*.

"Do you think they'll come—my parents?"

"If they don't, I'm never speaking to them again," she decided.

He huffed. "They wouldn't dare suffer the wrath of the king's prophetess."

"They're too ambitious to make an enemy of me."

"Anyone would be a fool to do such a thing," he growled, nipping at her earlobe. "So, shall we set a date?"

"We don't know when Claire will return—"

"True, but something tells me nothing could keep her away for long. So let's assume it will happen approximately a month from now. Then, once we're certain of her return, we'll finalize the date."

"I'm in. All in."

"Good. Now, what do you say we go flying before dinner. I love the sky at sunset, and I long to be in your mind."

Her heart fluttered. She'd long since gotten past the nerves of sharing her mind with him. Being close to death had forced her past it. There were moments during their race to the forest when she'd felt him so deep inside her, taking away her pain, that she still felt the phantom touch of him within her.

"I would love that," she decided.

He took her hand and led her to the king's tower. It was mostly empty save for Talon's servants. A door closed and Jeanine emerged from one of the lower levels. "Oh, hello you two."

"Jeanine." Saffra rushed forward and hugged her. "How are you holding up?"

"Me, oh. I'm fine. Why wouldn't I be?"

"Come now."

Jeanine scoffed. "I wish you all would stop doing that. He's not my mate or anything. Not like what Talon's going through. Everyone keeps acting like I'm going to crumble or something. I'm sure he's fine. He's Feowen."

"He's Feowen," Saffra repeated, knowing that was explanation enough. They had to believe that the sprite prince was fine, because if he wasn't, that could mean Claire was in even more danger.

They still had no idea where she was, only that she was alive.

"You two going flying?" Jeanine asked, clearly eager to change the subject.

"Yes, and—" She cut herself off, glancing at Bedelth. He gave a small nod. "We've decided to set a tentative date for our bonding ceremony."

Jeanine gasped, hands covering her cheeks with excitement. "Truly?!"

"Yes, but...don't say anything to the others yet. We will tell them tonight, during our meeting."

"Oh! Everyone is going to be so excited."

"That's the hope." Saffra pulled her bottom lip between her teeth.

"Well." Jeanine looked between them. "Have a good flight. See you at dinner." She slipped away before they could say anything else.

Saffra watched her go, brow furrowed. "I really hope she's okay. I know he's not her mate, but that doesn't mean they love each other any less."

Bedelth ran a comforting hand down her back. "Trust that they will be fine."

"You're right." She offered him a bright smile. Together they ascended the tower stairs to the very top. The queen's garden was the tallest vantage point in the keep. It had become their designated place to take off into the sky. While the drengr could leap from whatever courtyard or balcony they wished, it wasn't so easy when they took riders with them. This offered privacy so others wouldn't talk and gossip.

He shifted into his beautiful sunset orange scales and she vaulted onto his back, the movements effortless even despite her weakened arm. His mind was immediately joined to hers as her skin made contact. She quickly buckled herself into the straps of the harness. *"Ready, mate?"*

"Always!"

Springing from the ground, he took off into the sky.

CHAPTER 10
FORT SQUALL WITH REYR

Merrian shielded her gaze against the setting sun. The sight of Squall's End and its adjacent fort was beautiful. Though nothing compared to her first sight of Kastali Dun when Reyr had leapt into the sky. It was unlike anything she had ever experienced.

The excitement had long worn off.

King Talon had given Reyr an important task. When he'd begged her to accompany him, her refusal had been impossible. Here she was, nearly six days later. Their pace was grueling. She wasn't used to sitting astride a dragon all day. The promise of a soft, feathered bed and a hot bath was all that kept her mood from spiraling.

It would have been easier if they could communicate. She wasn't his mate, so they were forced into silence. Well, she could talk *at* him, but she'd have to yell over the rush of the wind.

They saved their conversation for evenings when they made camp. That had become her favorite part of the day, sitting beside Reyr, listening to his stories and sharing hers. They'd spent so much time locked in that dungeon cell saying very little. Mostly because her anger towards him—rightfully deserved—and his overwhelming guilt, hadn't been conducive for conversation. Now they had catching up to do.

At the sight of the fort, Reyr roared in anticipation. His cry was answered by several more roars. A wing of drengr flew in a pattern out over Stormy Bay. They changed direction, coming straight for them. Nerves sent butterflies fluttering in her stomach.

Flying with a drengr was frowned upon—something only mates did together. Reyr hadn't let that stop him from bringing her along. He'd promised that they would travel the kingdom together, and while this wasn't technically part of their kingdom tour— which wouldn't happen until things calmed down—he still wanted her with him. The group of drengr formed around them, their riders grinning. She felt their curious stares but didn't let it intimidate her. By now, everyone in the kingdom had probably heard rumors of her involvement, standing in as queen in Claire's absence.

A twinge of unease shot through her. There hadn't been any time to get to know Claire. She'd disappeared through a water portal and they'd left a mere day after. She knew next to nothing, except that Claire had followed Kane to his fortress and was meant to battle him.

Had she survived?

Reyr descended towards a large courtyard near the front of the fort. She braced for impact. As soon as he landed, she unbuckled the harness straps and swung her leg over, dismounting. It had taken days of practice to get to this point. She liked to think she was more skilled now, but that didn't stop heat from flushing her cheeks as people watched their arrival.

"Uncle!" A tall drengr male strode forward. He looked like he could be Reyr's own son. She had to blink several times.

Reyr was quick to transform beside her. He gave her arm a gentle squeeze before turning to Byron. "Nephew, good to see you." They pulled each other into an embrace.

"I've just informed Tam that you've arrived. She's got her

hands full, but should be along in a moment." Byron stopped and turned to her. "You must be Merrian."

"You already know my name?" She threw Reyr a look.

Byron chuckled. "My uncle might have given me a heads-up yesterday that you were coming. We're glad to have you. Come, let's talk in my chambers. I'm sure you're weary from the journey."

"Thank you," Reyr said, clapping Byron on the shoulder.

She glanced around as they left the courtyard. There were several sets of scaffolding constructed in areas that required repairs. The fort had been busy with rebuilding after the wild drag-ons. Seeing it now, she was reassured by their progress. They'd have it completed in next to no time.

Byron led them into a large apartment. It was richly furnished with dark wood and cream colored upholstery. "I hope I'm not too late," a feminine voice sounded behind them.

Merrian spun around, taking in the dark-haired woman. Gods, she was just barely on the tail end of adolescence. "You must be Tamara," she blurted. "I'm Merrian."

Tamara grinned. "Yes, I know! I'm so pleased to meet you!" Without waiting for an invitation, Byron's mate rushed forward and pulled her into a tight hug. "It's just awful what that monster did to you. Just awful!"

"Oh." Her stomach squirmed uncomfortably. She didn't like to be reminded, but it was thoughtful of Tamara to show concern. "I'm just grateful that it's over."

"Yes, thank the gods." Tamara turned her attention to Reyr and grinned shyly.

"Lady Tamara, good to see you looking hale."

"Thank you, Uncle."

Reyr huffed, pleased. "The progress you've made on the fort is incredible. You were barely getting started when I left. Now look at the place."

"Well, I should hope so, it's been nearly a year," Byron said. "Come, let's get comfortable." He led them to a sitting area before pouring them something to drink. She opted for water to quench her thirst. "I've got food on the way," Byron added. "So, let's talk about your task, yes?"

"You already told him?" Merrian scowled at Reyr.

"Well, I gave him a brief summary yesterday when I made contact."

"So he knows we're looking for the freed captives?"

"Indeed," Byron said. "I'll do you one better and save you the search. The majority of them are here in the city. We started a program as soon as Captain Bennett began his efforts. Families all over the city have volunteered to temporarily take them in. Those we don't have space for reside in some of the overflow housing that was constructed after part of the city burned. It's why progress on the fort was slower than we'd hoped. We allotted the majority of our resources to the city."

"That was kind of you," she observed, impressed.

"It is our duty as drengr to care for the kingdom's people in whatever way possible. Given that it was our cousins who destroyed their homes, our failure to protect them from it, they are our first priority."

She nodded in agreement. "And what of those who lost their homes? What of the homeless and sick?"

"We've got funds in place. I am not sure it is enough, but we're doing all we can."

Something told her that just like in the city of Kastali Dun, it probably wasn't enough. "You won't mind if we get involved. I'd rather be the judge of that," she found herself saying.

She half expected Byron to grow defensive but instead, a relieved smile tugged at his lips. "Not at all. I welcome it. If you find any areas we can improve, I'll get a meeting set up between you and Lord Rhal."

She blew out a breath. "Good. That's... Thank you."

"Now," Byron looked at Reyr. "You promised me one hell of a story. So? Get talking."

Reyr barked a laugh. The food arrived shortly thereafter. A collection of warm savory pies that they could eat with their hands. Reyr unloaded everything, telling Byron and Tamara exactly what had happened after Talon's disappearance through the gate. She let him talk, filling in the parts about her appearance and how she stood in as Claire's body-double.

"Oh, that must have been so stressful," Tamara said, offering her a concerned look. "I can't imagine the weight on your shoulders. Especially being new to all of this."

"It wasn't easy." She threw Reyr a glance. Not necessarily to guilt him.

He winced and said, "I didn't make it any easier for her, I'll admit."

Without thinking, she reached for his hand and squeezed. Byron and Tamara noticed. She quickly moved to pull away, but Reyr wouldn't let her. He tangled their fingers together. The gesture was so bold and unexpected, her cheeks flushed.

Reyr cleared his throat before continuing the story. When he got to the part about Claire disappearing, Tamara paled. "We've got drengr wings in the vicinity, up north. Surely we can send a search and rescue team."

"I don't think that will be necessary. The queen is resourceful, and Feowen is with her. If I had to guess, she's long gone from Shadowkeep."

"Then, you're sure she's been successful?" Tamara's face lit with hope.

Reyr's face softened. Merrian couldn't help but feel a *little* jealous. It was irrational, she knew that. She had no claim on Reyr. Besides, he wasn't interested in the queen *like that* anymore. "I don't doubt Claire's abilities. I'm sure."

"Gods above." Tamara folded her hands in her lap. "I hope you're right."

"We must still remain vigilant," Byron said. "I've received word that Oshean ships are still arriving up and down Dragonwall's coast, hoping to claim their fair share."

"The king is working on that," Reyr assured them. "He sent Jovari and Koldis to remove several opportunists from power. A few of the sorcerers from Oshea who thought to plant themselves in big cities."

"Good," Byron said. "They will see it done."

They spent a few more minutes in discussion before Reyr said, "We've had a long day. We should retire for the evening."

"Oh, of course," Tamara said. "Your old room is still available."

"I told you to give it to someone who might need it."

"Everyone I offered it to refused," Byron groused. "Something about not wanting to step on Lord Reyr's toes."

Reyr sighed. "Fine. What of Merrian?"

Tamara bit her lower lip. "Accommodations are scarce. We've got all unmated females bunking in groups of six or more. Even with much of the fort rebuilt, we've had an unusual surge in volunteers hoping to make a life here. People who didn't want to move back to their villages."

"I should imagine no one wants to go back to a village that's been destroyed," Merrian said. "But it's no matter. I can bunk with Reyr. I mean—if it's all right?"

"Oh." Tamara's eyes darted between them with a knowing glint. "Of course."

They were all adults here, weren't they? Sure, it was something the nobility would balk at, but she wasn't nobility. And she certainly wasn't a virgin or a prude. Who cared what others thought about her?

"Fine by me," Reyr said, an eager sparkle in his gaze. "I've got a sofa in the sitting room I can sleep on."

She opened her mouth to argue, then shut it. Surely they could manage to share a bed without making it awkward. Except, the moment she thought that, her cheeks flushed. What would it be like sharing a bed with Reyr? Why did she love the idea so much?

She imagined Reyr's hands on her body. Oh, gods—

She needed to stop. Now.

Reyr was a shield. There was no way he would throw himself at someone like her. Then again...

She glanced down. Reyr was still holding her hand.

"Well, that's settled." Byron stood, a mischievous smile tugging at his lips. "I'll come to collect you at dawn, take you around to the city to meet some of the rescued captives. Safe to say they will be overjoyed to know they can return home. Then we can work on getting them safe passage south."

"Excellent." Reyr stood, pulling her with him.

They said their goodbyes.

When he led her to his chambers, she found herself exploring with open curiosity. "It's the room I grew up in," he admitted. She spun to face him, surprised. "My parents were fort leaders here, remember? Davi and I shared these chambers. He didn't move into the fort leader chambers until my parents passed. I upgraded our separate beds for a single. It became just mine after that, but...his presence still lingers here. Memories of growing up together. All that."

"Oh." Her breath whooshed from her lungs. "I... It must be hard, seeing the reminders of him. Are you... Are you going to be okay?"

His expression crumbled. He pressed his lips between his teeth. That he showed her such vulnerability broke something in her, too. She was hurting because he was hurting. "Truthfully, if you were anyone else I'd tell you I was fine. Even Talon believes I am more healed than I actually feel."

"But I'm...not anyone else?" Her heart began to race.

"I think you and I have been through too much to lie to each other. Don't you think?"

Pleasure coursed through her. "You're right. Thank you. You can talk to me, if you need."

His eyes fixed on the opposite wall, going unfocused. "Losing him was hard. I took it hard. Disappearing for a while...it helped. Healing is a slow process. It's different for everyone—as I'm certain you can understand. Some days I think I'm getting there, and others feel like it just happened."

Her throat thickened. "You're right. I understand."

"I know—I know you do." She'd lost people she loved, too. Her entire family.

He scrubbed a hand over his face then fixed his gaze on the couch. "I'll find some spare blankets. Make yourself comfortable. You can take the sleeping chamber."

"Reyr." She reached for him, squeezing his hand. "I don't want to force you out of your own bed."

He snorted. "I'll be fine. Go ahead."

She was tempted to argue. The only reason she didn't was because her nerves had taken over. Maybe he didn't *want* to share a bed, and she'd only embarrass herself by insisting. So, she nodded and accepted his request.

As she tucked herself in for the night, she couldn't help but let her thoughts run away. She was sleeping where Reyr had slept for many years. All she could do was picture him here, until an ache built between her legs and she was left entirely frustrated. At last, sleep finally found her, but it was mostly dreams filled with his face, his hands, and the heat of them searing her body.

CHAPTER 11
SARAPHINA'S HOME

Reyr watched Merrian carefully. Gods, she was amazing. How had he ever believed her inferior? The way she handled each rescued captive, every word from her mouth thoughtful and sincere. It had something flaring to life inside him. An ache he hadn't thought he'd feel again, one even stronger than the feelings he'd felt for Claire.

Thank the gods he'd opted to sleep on the sofa while they were here. He wasn't sure he could keep his hands off her during this journey otherwise. Especially not now.

True to his word, Byron had met them at dawn, sharing a rushed breakfast before escorting them to Squall's End. He'd introduced them to Tessa, a woman in charge of helping Lord Rhal oversee the rescued captives while they stayed in Squall's End. Though she appeared at least a decade older, Tessa reminded him a lot of Merrian. It was no surprise that the two immediately connected.

Tessa spent the entire morning acting as their guide. She'd taken them to homes and encampments housing hundreds of displaced captives. When they weren't meeting with people, Tessa and Merrian had their heads together, whispering and smiling. He was happy to keep his distance, walking behind them as more of a chaperone.

Merrian had met with as many as possible, offering kind words of reassurance, letting them know that the king had reclaimed the throne. That they would be returning home. Their joy over the news never got old.

"I'd like to visit a few of the shelters before we return to the fort," Merrian told Tessa as they finished up at one of the encampments. "I wanted to get a feel for how things are for the homeless citizens of Fort Squall."

Unlike the makeshift encampments for the rescued captives, the shelters were places for those who had called Fort Squall home most of their lives.

"Oh." Tessa hesitated, a look of pleased surprise settling into her expression. "Of course. I'd be glad to show you a few. The city has ten in total."

"That's probably too many to squeeze in this afternoon."

"Indeed." Tessa wore a soft smile. "But if you have time tomorrow, I can always take you to the rest."

Merrian threw Reyr a questioning look. This trip wasn't technically intended for this, yet, he couldn't possibly say no. They were here on the king's business, but what harm would it be to take a few hours?

"Whatever you wish," he said, finding it impossible to deny her anything.

Merrian smiled. "I'd like that," she told Tessa. "If you have time, that is. I'm sure you are busy—"

"Oh, I'll make the time." Tessa led them up the road, stopping before a rundown building. Reyr frowned. The wooden walls had started to slant, the boards warped from too much exposure to the sea air. One of the gutters hung askew. The sign out front read *Gillman House*.

"This is one of the worst of them," Tessa said by way of explanation. He couldn't help but wonder if she'd brought them here on purpose. She lifted her hand to knock. "I think you'll see why momentarily."

"Looks as though it might collapse around us," Reyr muttered, half tempted to refuse Merrian entry. What would happen if the thing came down while she was inside? He would stay close to her, just in case. He could shield her, if nothing else.

An older male opened the door a sliver, glaring out at them. "What'da you want?" he growled, glaring at Tessa. It was clear he recognized the woman and considered her a nuisance.

"Brought you some visitors, Abel."

"Don't want no visitors. Certainly not the likes of them." He started to shut the door but Tessa planted a foot in front of the doorjamb. "This is a place for people without homes."

Tessa sighed. "Even so. We'd like to come inside."

"Don't need no inspectors nosing around my business."

"Abel." Tessa's voice was whip-sharp. "This is Lord Reyr and Lady Merrian. He's one of the king's shields—a drengr. I can promise you he's strong enough to muscle his way through the door if he chooses to. Best not refuse."

Reyr pressed his lips into a line to keep from smiling. Truth be told, he was less and less enthusiastic about going inside. He had no plans of shouldering his way inside if Abel refused them entry. But Tessa was clearly determined.

Merrian stepped forward. "Hi! I'm Mer," she said brightly. "I just wanted to drop by and see if you needed any help with things, or perhaps some coin to help with..." She glanced up at the state of the building's exterior. "Upkeep and things?"

"Coin, eh?" Abel's face brightened with greed. "Why didn't you say so before?" He stepped back into the darkened entry, opening the door wide.

"Shouldn't have said that," Tessa warned Merrian under her breath.

Merian merely shrugged.

They entered a dimly lit foyer with rooms on either side. "How about a tour?" Merrian suggested, keeping her voice light.

Abel grumbled then said, "Fine. Come along."

The thought of coin had clearly motivated him. He led them around the first, second, and third floors of the building. There were close to forty people staying in Gillman House. They shared rooms along the top two floors. He counted upwards of eight beds in some rooms. Abel Gillman was the sole proprietor of the building. He didn't charge people to stay here, but he did require a small fee if they obtained work while living under his roof—a piece of information that had Merrian's jaw tightening when she learned of it. The rest of the money Abel received was through payouts from the city's lord. That information wasn't surprising. It was how shelters like this functioned. The ruling body always allotted funds for those in need. In the case of shelters, the funds were paid to the person who ran the establishment to be spent on food, clothing, and incidentals for those living there.

When Merrian asked to look over Abel's financial ledgers, he flat out refused. "But I could help you spot any inefficiencies in how the funds are spent. Perhaps there's a way we could make the money stretch—"

"I ain't showing you no ledgers!" Abel barked, his expression turning from greedy to downright defensive. Merrian's mouth opened and closed. They stood outside Abel's office, the dim light of the hallway casting shadows over everything.

Reyr backed up several paces. Keeping his voice low, he said to Tessa, "He's not spending it properly, is he?"

The woman pressed her lips together, giving her head an angry shake.

"You got a problem with how I manage my affairs, you can take it up with Lord Rhal," Abel sneered.

"Very well," Merrian said, attempting to keep the peace.

Reyr half wanted to lunge at the man for speaking to her like that. Merrian wouldn't take kindly to him fighting her battles, though. So he held himself in check.

"Do you mind if I spend some time with the patrons upstairs, at least? Once I'm done there I can come back down and give you the coin I brought." It seemed she had caught on. Perhaps she was worried Abel would demand she leave. Reminding him of the coin she'd promised changed his mood.

"Fine." He backed into his study. "I'll be in here when you're finished."

With that, he slammed the door in her face.

"Well," Tessa said brightly. "Now you see what I mean."

Merrian only scoffed, giving Abel's door a dark look.

Once she had spent some time with the residents and offered to heal those who suffered from common maladies, she gave Abel a small bag of coin, one Reyr was certain she'd drastically lightened after discovering his deceit. Abel seemed to sense it too, because when he weighed it in his hand, he threw her a mocking look before shutting himself back in his office.

It wasn't until they were out on the street that she said, "Why is he allowed to do that? It's obvious that he's using the stipend he receives on himself!"

Tessa walked them out of earshot of Gillman House before saying, "Abel Gillman is one of several who owns a building he's turned into a shelter. Like the others, he gets away with quite a lot since the building is his own. The lord governor is far too busy to look into matters such as these. Most people find it easier to turn a blind eye, especially when the less fortunate are involved."

"It's absolutely despicable!"

"I couldn't agree more!"

"And there are others? Like this?"

"A few." Tessa sighed. "Not all the shelters are this way. The ones who actually do good work are overcrowded. As you can imagine, they're the most popular so their beds fill the quickest."

Merrian threw Reyr a look. He knew exactly what she wanted without having to speak a word. "Let's arrange a meeting with Lord Rhal," he found himself saying. "We can discuss the matter with him before we leave."

Merrian blinked. Perhaps she hadn't expected him to be so eager to help. "Are you sure there will be time?"

"We'll make time."

"Thank you." Her voice was low and breathy. He loved the sound of it. He gave a quick nod.

"Would you like to see a few others before you head back to the fort?"

"Please, lead the way."

Tessa spent what remained of the afternoon light showing them around. It was much the same. The other three shelters she took them to looked slightly better than Gillman House, but only slightly. Fortunately, she ended their tour on a positive note, taking them to Wisteria House. This one was kept up and had a lovely garden out front with wisteria growing along trellises.

"Oh!" Merrian looked delighted at the sight of it. "I wasn't expecting that."

"Saraphina is a good...*friend* of mine," Tessa said. Reyr didn't miss the way she hesitated over the word friend, wondering if there was something more she wasn't saying. "This is the best shelter in the city and it shows."

Tessa unlatched the gate, leading them through the small garden and up the front steps to a massive town home. It was in one of the nicer neighborhoods."

"Some of the folk around here were none too pleased when she turned her home into a shelter. Worried they'd get the wrong sort. Crime and all that. But there's never been a problem. Part of that is because Sara only takes in a certain kind of person."

"What do you mean?"

"You'll see soon enough." Tessa rang the bell out front. "Sara, it's me! Got some visitors for you."

A young girl answered the door, immediately squealing with delight. "Tessa! Tessa!" She lunged, wrapping her arms around Tessa's legs.

"Hello there Layla."

Layla backed up, turning suddenly shy. "Hi," she breathed.

Reyr watched Merrian's expression soften at the exchange. He would have given all his worldly possessions to know what she was thinking at this very moment.

"These are my friends, Merrian and Reyr."

"Oh." Layla looked over at them, her face flushing.

"Can you tell Sara we're here?"

"Yes!" Layla rushed off. A few moments later, a middle aged woman appeared. Saraphina had dark hair with strands of gray running through. She was short and curvy, with a gown that accentuated those curves.

Tessa and Saraphina shared a long, fond look. There was definitely something between them, though they held back in the presence of company. "You've brought me guests!"

"Indeed." Tessa stepped back and gestured. "This is Merrian—"

"Mer," she corrected.

"*Mer*. And this is her traveling companion, Reyr."

"Lord Reyr!" Saraphina put a hand over her heart. "I am so sorry for your loss."

Reyr stiffened, then relaxed. There was nothing but sincerity in Saraphina's words. Normally, saying sorry was an off-the-cuff response. But it was obvious that she meant it.

"Thank you," he managed.

"They're in the city for a few days on the king's business, and wanted to have a look at the shelters here. I already took them to a few—Gillman's included." Saraphina's face darkened at the mention of Abel's establishment. "But I thought we'd end the day on a positive note."

"Well!" Saraphina brightened. "You came to the right place." She glanced out past them at the darkening sky. Evening was fast approaching. "We're preparing the evening meal. I know it's probably not a fare you're used to but if you'd like to join—"

"We would love to!" Merrian said, breathless. She threw him a questioning glance, realizing that she'd spoken for him.

"It's no problem." Silently, he sent a quick thought to Byron, letting him know they would stay out later than planned. His nephew was quick to answer.

"Good! Then come!" Saraphina ushered them inside. "And please, call me Sara. Saraphina is too formal for my tastes."

"Sara. Wonderful. Thanks so much for opening your home to us."

"I'm honored. Let's start with a tour, shall we? Then we can join the others in the cookery."

The tour was quick. Sara's home was exactly that. It wasn't a massive building in one of the poorer districts. It was a large, three floor house. Sara had used the space economically. She'd had the larger rooms remodeled into smaller ones. Even though some of the bedrooms were more closets than anything, she had a good reason for doing so.

"Most of the women and children who come here are running from abusive relationships," Sara explained. "Be it from their husbands, brothers, or fathers. A lot of times, they're wary of getting close to others and want their own space—to heal and all that. I found it better to have smaller rooms that they could keep to themselves, rather than bunking them all together. Gave them a piece of their lives back, you know."

"And you only take in women and children?"

"Yes." Sara nodded, leading them back down to the main floor. "While this house specializes in women and children who've been traumatized, I make the occasional exception based on the person's character. No adult males, though." She gave Reyr a look.

"Is it going to be a problem? Me being here?" The last thing he wanted was to trigger someone suffering from trauma. He knew how large and imposing his form was. He didn't want to make any of this house's inhabitants uncomfortable.

They stopped outside the cookery. He could hear voices within, women chatting while they prepared the meal. Children, too.

Sara sighed. "You are very kind and thoughtful for asking. I cannot say for certain, but I have my suspicions. Why don't I pop in and ask. You are a drengr, after all. Everyone knows that the drengr are honorable."

"Please, ask. If it's too much trouble, I can wait outside while you lot take your meal. I'd be happy to eat later."

"Oh, nonsense. You won't be going hungry on my watch." Sara

slipped into the cookery. The voices dropped low. His drengr hearing picked up every word as the mistress of the house asked around. There were several excited exclamations but mostly silence.

Sara stepped out a moment later, twisting her fingers together. "There are a few who—"

"Say no more," he lifted a hand to stop her. "The last thing I want is to put these women through more than they've already been through."

Sara's shoulders relaxed.

"Sara," Tessa said. "Why don't we just take dinner out on the front porch?"

"Oh! Yes!" Mer perked up. "I saw a charming table and chairs overlooking your little garden."

"Are you sure?" Sara looked between them.

"Yes, that way we don't disturb any of your occupants."

"Well," Sara chewed on her bottom lip. "There were a few who were eager. The children especially."

"Let them come out to meet us, then." Merrian was already grabbing his arm and leading him back down the hallway as she spoke. "That way no one feels as if we're invading your home."

In the end, they made themselves comfortable at the porch's table. The garden was small, and the street beyond gave the occasional entertainment as passersby rushed home for their meals. The table sat six, so they were comfortable. A few of the more eager house occupants saw to serving them their meal, and several children rushed out to greet them. They were mostly interested in him.

He wasn't surprised that they treated him like a character from their favorite bedtime story. There were plenty of rumors circulating about him, about the role he played against the wild dragons. He gave each child plenty of attention.

He couldn't help but notice the fond looks Merrian gave each of them. Something pulled in his gut. He'd never considered that she might want children. The discussion hadn't even come up. Not that he should be thinking of such things. But, he'd be blind if he hadn't noticed her beautiful eyes and generous curves. And he'd be lying if he hadn't imagined kissing her a few times over the past week.

But if she wanted children—she'd never get that with him. It would be unfair of him to have any kind of romantic relationship when he couldn't give her what she longed for. A sense of disappointment washed over him and he pushed it down.

No, better that they remain good friends so he didn't risk ruining this thing between them.

The meal passed in a rush, and they spent a happy evening sipping a dessert wine that Saraphina brought out to entice them with. One she kept for special occasions.

When they finally left Saraphina's, it was with a good sense of the differences between how a shelter ought to be run and how most of the shelters in the city were. Merrian kept up a constant chatter of all the things she wanted to address with Lord Rhal as they made their way back to the fort. He made a mental note to make the arrangements first thing in the morning.

Once back in the fort, he begged off to go and speak with Byron.

"Oh, but aren't you tired?" Merrian fussed with the stitching on the hem of her tunic, looking uncertain. They stood outside the door to his chambers.

"Quite, but I get few opportunities like this to return to Fort Squall and I need to make the most of it."

"And you are sure you don't need me there?" She almost looked hopeful, like she wanted him to bring her along.

"No. You need to rest. Especially if we're to meet with the lord governor tomorrow."

"Right." She saw the dismissal for what it was but didn't let her disappointment show. "That is important."

"Exactly."

If he spent one more moment in her company, he was certain he would take her by the arms and capture her mouth in a claiming kiss. There would be no coming back from something like that.

"You head on to bed and I'll be along in a bit," he promised.

Only once she was behind the closed door did he let out a deep breath.

He *did* go and find Byron, but only to give him a brief overview of their day. Then he took to the skies, heading out over the bay. What he needed was a nice, cold swim to cool the fire in his blood. He dove from the sky and plunged in, careful to keep a good distance between him and the other boats floating in the bay. He swam for a time before emerging back into the sky.

When he returned to his chambers, he listened for the sound of Merrian's breathing. It was steady, but he was almost certain she wasn't sleeping—pretending, more than likely. He quickly made himself comfortable on the sofa. Not that there was any comfortable way to sleep for someone like him. It wasn't until the quiet stretched out around him that he finally heard her breathing shift into sleep. Eventually, he drifted off to the sound of a woman he wanted but wasn't sure he should ever have.

CHAPTER 12
THE TREE'S ADVICE

The Gable Forest

Claire relaxed as the forest came into view, a blur of green that quickly grew. They'd been traveling for two days. It would have taken twice that for a drengr. She was desperate to finish her task and reunite with Talon. Desperate to heal the gaping hole Cyrus had left behind, a hole only Talon could help mend.

Tourmaline slowed his pace. *"Riltar Outpost, Queen."*

She took in the familiar sight sitting just outside the line of trees. It looked different without the heavy snows of winter. Spriten banners flew from the building's gabled roof. The last time she'd been here was with Taylynn, when they'd borrowed unicorns to wake Fright.

A cry of surprise went up. One of the sprites in the horse paddock had spotted them. He jumped over the fence, rushing to the main building. A few minutes later, the doors were thrown wide as several sprites streamed out to greet them.

She and Feowen dismounted.

"Nua bualta, Ayas Drollaya, Sariho Feowen." One of the outpost

97

attendants rushed over, his face glowing with delight. "I am Bellas, the one tasked with overseeing this outpost."

"*Nua bualta*," she and Feowen echoed the common greeting.

"Surely my eyes deceive me?" Bellas went on to say in the spriten language, gawking at the black unicorn. "You ride with Tourmaline?"

"Indeed." She stroked a fond hand down the unicorn's flank. "But we will have no more need of him or his companions."

Tourmaline nudged her, his tongue flicking out near her ear, making her squeal. *"Fare thee well, Queen. I will always come if you have need of me."*

"Thank you," she told him, truly grateful that he'd come to their rescue.

A few moments later, Tourmaline and the remainder of his unicorn companions trotted off, disappearing into the forest. She breathed a sigh, turning back to Bellas. "I need to send a message to the king—as quickly as possible."

She wasn't sure how long her task would take, but Talon needed to know that she was safe, that Kane was dead.

"My queen also requires refreshments and rest," Feowen added, reminding her that she hadn't eaten all day.

"Of course." Bellas bowed. "If you will follow me, we can see to your needs."

The other sprites gave murmurs of greeting and respect for their prince and queen as they passed.

Once indoors, she didn't waste a moment. Bellas provided writing supplies. She scratched out a quick note to inform Talon of all that had transpired. There was no concern of private information being intercepted. Bellas promised to send one of his own with a unicorn to take the note directly to the capital. "I have others, too, if you wouldn't mind?"

"It is no problem, *Ayas Drollaya*."

She had hoped to deliver Mary and Tynen's letters herself, but there was no telling how long she'd be away.

After a quick meal she managed a few hours of sleep. The urge to reunite with Talon didn't allow for more than that. She'd never be at ease until she was in his arms again.

His presence was stronger in her mind now. She even sent him a few words, telling him that she was safe and that Kane was dead. She sensed his relief. *"I love you, mih cralla."* The words were a faint whisper, almost too quiet to hear, thanks to the distance and the forest between them. Mates communicated better over long distances, but there was still more than half a kingdom between them.

Bidding the outpost attendants farewell, she and Feowen set off into the forest. She breathed deeply, brushing her hands over the bark of trees. She felt the ever-present awareness that permeated every living thing. It almost felt like home, but not quite. Home was where Talon was, but it was a close substitute. A smile pulled at her lips. She'd missed this *so much*.

Cyrus would have missed it too, she realized. Her budding smile faded. He'd grown just as fond of the forest as she. Now he would never experience it through her again. But he *would* be happy for her. Happy knowing she was here.

"Hil zanih," Feowen said, his voice careful in light of her sudden melancholy. *Welcome back.*

"It is good to be back," she murmured, trying to ignore the heaviness in her chest.

"I missed it too." Feowen went to the nearest tree and pressed his forehead to it, humming with delight.

The breeze rustled her hair. With it, faint words called to her. *"Seek me... Seek me..."*

"Do you hear that?"

"Indeed." Feowen straightened, glancing around. "The tree wants us to find it."

"Us, or me?"

"Us, I think. Or else I would not hear it."

"Interesting." She held out her hand to him. "Shall we?"

"Let's." Feowen's smile was soft. He laced his fingers through hers and they set out.

~

FEOWEN'S GASP was the first sign that they'd reached their destination. His steps faltered as he gaped up at the beautiful giant. "I forget that you have not been called into its presence as Taylynn and I," she murmured, taking in the same sight. A thrill shot through her, the same excitement each and every time she witnessed it.

"Welcome, Queen, Prince, to my dominion. I see that congratulations are in order. You have done well, Claire." The disembodied voice had her skin erupting in goosebumps. A quick glance at Feowen's neck showed the same reaction. His pulse drummed heavily, out of nerves, most likely. Few were permitted to look upon the tree unless they were here to partake in its fruit, embarking upon the final passage of their life.

"It's magnificent," Feowen whispered.

"Thank you, Prince," said the tree. Who would have guessed a giant tree could be so smug? *"You have brought me a treasure, I see."*

Oh. Right. That.

Feowen quickly removed the breastplate Kane had constructed. His magic made quick work of the metal, until all five stones were removed. She took Fright's stone, slipping it into her pocket. She withdrew the black stone Taylynn had slipped to her before everything had gone to pieces. Feowen handed her the other stones, but she kept them in her other hand. Separate.

A familiar sense of power and greed swept through her. It wasn't the same as when she'd first experienced it, all that time ago in her farmhouse while Cyrus recovered outside. She was stronger now, with magic of her own. She was no longer as susceptible to the whims of power.

"Can you help us?" she asked. "We must destroy the stones."

"The stones cannot be destroyed." The tree's voice rang through her mind, abrupt and final. Her breath caught, a knot tightening in her stomach. *"To destroy them would be to destroy all that comes from them."*

A fresh wave of panic took root as she thought about everything they had been through. "The stones pose a risk to all dragon kind. We cannot risk another opportunist like Kane coming along."

"*No you cannot,*" agreed the tree. "*Which is why they must remain safe.*"

Safe?! The thought terrified her. Look how well that had gone before.

There was no immediate danger, sure. But what about thousands of years from now? When the world forgot how horrible this war had been. Would another sorcerer come along and decide they wanted the same thing Kane had?

"*You assume there will be drengr left by then, Queen.*" The tree had read her thoughts. Its words made her insides turn to ice. Dragonwall without dragons. Without drengr. It was impossible to imagine. Horrible to consider.

This wasn't her first time hearing about it, but Kane had always been the bigger threat.

"*Isabella created the drengr, but so too did she curse them. Only one child born of each pair, except in the rare cases of twins or even triplets.*"

"There were triplets?!"

"*Once, long ago.*" The tree sounded amused by her surprise. "*A very lucky pair, to be sure.*"

She blew out a breath. "She doomed them. Doomed us all."

"*She tried. But all is not lost.*"

"It can be fixed?"

"*You are of Isabella's blood. If such a thing is to be undone, it can only be undone by you.*" Hope exploded in her chest, pushing her panic aside. She'd woken Fright, hadn't she? Reversing Isabella's magic once before.

"But how would I even begin to fix it? She traveled around Dragonwall and cast her magic upon each dragon that was willing to receive the blessing, didn't she?"

"*She did.*"

"Then I would need to go around to every drengr and cast some kind of counter-magic?"

The tree was silent for several moments. *"Or you might find a more efficient way of doing things."*

Her thoughts turned over. There was something in the tree's voice. It had a solution and was waiting for her to come to the same realization. "The stones," she breathed, glancing down at what she held in both hands. "If I destroy them, I destroy the dragons and drengr. But if I bring them together, I could turn them to stone, as was intended."

"Indeed. If you so desire."

She took a step back, sputtering. "You mean, if I didn't wish to, it wouldn't happen?"

"You possess all five stones, that makes you the master of all dragon kind." Her breaths came faster. *"As a master over their kind, you have the power to do whatever you wish. Something even Isabella wasn't capable of, given that she never possessed all five."*

"Oh, gods." The implication set in. No one should have this much power. "So I could bring the stones together, but instead of sending the dragons back to stone, I could work magic that would alter the way they procreate."

"I should think so, yes. Intention is everything. Kane wanted the stones to harm dragon-kind."

She thought it over and gasped. "Could I also make it so that females can become drengr too?"

"I don't see why not," said the tree. *"The world is desperate for balance, after all."*

Balance. Of course. She tried to take a deep breath but was suddenly lightheaded. "I think... I think I need to sit down."

Feowen jumped forward. He'd been silently observing this entire interaction. He took her arm and guided her to a wooden bench that had not been there moments before. She sank onto it, keeping a firm hold of the dragonstones in her hands. She was still careful not to bring the black one into contact with the others, just in case the tree had been wrong.

Feowen crouched in front of her. Their eyes locked. She whispered, "This could change everything."

"I know," he whispered back, his voice laced with hope. Giving her shoulder a squeeze he stood, moving about the clearing to examine everything.

The sound of the babbling brook was soothing.

When she'd had a moment to digest everything, she said, "So I use the stones and just...cast my magic over them?"

"I believe that is the gist of it."

"You don't know for certain?"

"Like with many things, Sprite Queen, there must always be a healthy dose of faith. Trust in yourself and your abilities. Trust that this is the balance needed. Trust that it will work."

She blew out a breath. If the tree's theory was correct, then when she brought the stones together, they wouldn't automatically render all of dragon-kind into stone.

She glanced over at Feowen who was watching her intently. "Might as well test the theory."

Holding her breath, she brought the black stone into contact with the others...

Nothing happened.

Then again, how would she know? The others could be turning into stone at this very moment. Oh, gods!

"Trust yourself," the king tree said again.

She closed her eyes, focusing on the power in her hands. She felt it then, the steady hum of magic. The life that flowed through each stone was the same life that had lived in each of the first dragons. The same life that lived in all the drengr now, as well as the mothers and hatchlings in the Forest Clan's cave. They were safe.

"So...now I just need to figure out the magic to undo the curse," she mused.

"It will come to you."

"And after that?"

"When you are ready, bring the stones to me. They cannot be destroyed, but I believe I know a way to keep them safe forever. Out of the hands of anyone in this world."

"You would hide them in another?"

"Something like that, a plane no living being has access to."

"That... That could work." She blinked and glanced around.

Night had fallen. "I need a way to carry these until I can devise my counter-curse." She thought of the breastplate Kane had fashioned. How he'd magically placed each stone in its holder.

An idea came to her and she crouched on the mossy forest floor. Feowen moved in to watch her over her shoulder. Summoning a series of vines, she twisted them into various knots to secure the stones into a kind of necklace. "How is starlight silver made?"

"It is summoned from the stars," Feowen said, then realized why she was asking. He crouched beside her, taking her hand in his. "Let me show you."

He began to hum. She soon joined her voice with his. Bright flashes appeared, like the very stars above were finding their way through the trees. Shimmery liquid began to coat the delicate vines, spreading over them. It hardened, turning a bright silver.

When they were finished, she slipped the necklace over her head. It was a thing of beauty, each stone delicately encased in tiny threads that held it in place within the thin, twisting vines. Until she was ready to cast her magic. She didn't know exactly what would be needed, but she already had an idea.

"Do you know where Isabella was when Vigilance first found her? Where it was that she blessed him?"

"No" Feowen frowned, thoughtful. "But I do know it was somewhere in the forest."

She turned to the king tree. "Do you know?"

"Shall I show you the way?"

"Please."

A path appeared. Steadying herself for what came next, she reached for Feowen's hand, pulling him forward.

"Good luck, Sprite Queen." The tree's voice faded in her mind. When she next turned around, it was as if it had never been there to begin with.

CHAPTER 13
EXPLORING THE CITY

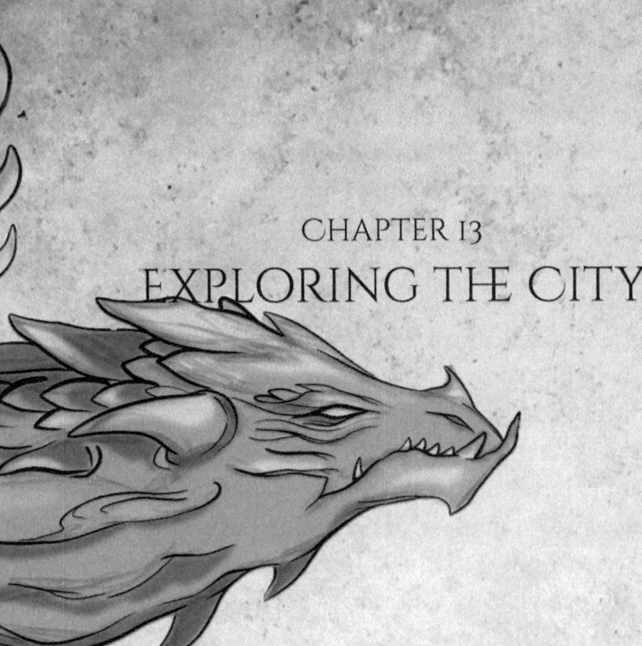

Kastali Dun

Leah followed Saffra's instructions and tipped her head back into the bowl of hair dye. "There. Now move your head back and forth," Saffra instructed, looming over her. She gently turned her head from side to side, ensuring that she coated every strand of hair. The liquid was cool on her scalp. She was lying on her back looking up at the ceiling, braced on her elbows while Saffra dunked her tresses into the brew she'd concocted. This was Saffra's second attempt. The first one hadn't worked—it washed right out.

"How long should I stay like this?"

"Just a few more minutes, I think. To be sure."

"You know, normally when you dye your hair you've got to leave the paste stuff in for thirty minutes."

"Well, *normally*, you're not using magic." Saffra stood and moved away, bustling about to put away her ingredients. "I promise, it will work this time."

"Is it working?" Jocelyn appeared in the doorway, striding into Saffra's chambers. She had a basket hooked around her on her elbow. "Desaree and I just got back from the market."

"And where is Desaree?" Saffra asked.

"Where do you think?" Jocelyn teased, pulling things out of the basket, setting them on the table. "With Verath."

"Are those berry coils?!" Saffra demanded. Jocelyn froze, then continued setting the pastries out. "I haven't had one in ages! Not since...before."

"What's a berry coil?" Leah asked, trying to twist her head to see what Jocelyn held.

"Only the most delicious sweet treat the market has to offer," Saffra said, walking over and snatching one. She immediately groaned as she took a bite.

Jocelyn snorted. "I wouldn't call them the *most* delicious. But they are divine. Here." She walked into Leah's field of view and held up the pastry. It had swirls of dark purple jelly threaded through it. She caught a whiff of sweet bread, cinnamon, and something tart. Jocelyn took a bite and closed her eyes. "So good."

"Okay, you're both being unfair!" Leah's stomach growled. "Can I get up yet?"

"Yes, just a moment." Saffra spoke through a mouthful then licked her fingers clean. "Let me grab a towel."

She guided Leah into a sitting position, careful to wrap her hair and pat it dry. When she removed the towel, Jocelyn gasped. "It worked!"

"Like I said." Saffra sounded smug.

"Mirror! I need a mirror," she demanded. Jocelyn rushed off then returned seconds later with a hand mirror.

She held it up and squealed with delight, turning her head this way and that. "Oh! It's perfect." It was the exact shade she'd hoped for. Just a little darker than lavender. "Do you think it will fade?"

"I'm not sure." Saffra chewed on the inside of her cheek, glancing down at the bowl. "If it does, I'll modify the concoction next time for better longevity."

"You're incredible. Has anyone ever told you that?"

Saffra's lips pressed together like she was trying to withhold a smile. "Thank you."

"I'll take care of that." Jocelyn scooped up the bowl and left to dispose of it.

She patted her wet hair, wishing now more than ever for a blowdryer. She hated having wet hair, but like many things, she had to get used to it. This was her life now. She wouldn't change it for anything.

If only Claire was here. An ache formed in her chest as she recalled their last hug. She'd grown closer to Claire's friends, but they would never replace her bestie. More than a week had passed since her disappearance.

Jocelyn returned and they sat around the table devouring the berry coils. The pastry was exactly as delicious as she expected. It reminded her of a cinnamon roll, except with some kind of berry jam added, and a slightly different shape. Not too sweet, and just tart enough to make her tastebuds come alive.

"So, how is your work in the library?" Saffra asked, leaning back contentedly.

"Oh!" She immediately brightened. "It's wonderful. We've nearly finished most of it. There are books that still need some restoration, and some that can never be repaired. But I think the damage could have been far worse, all things considered. I've already lost count of how many volumes I shelved and restored. I finally memorized the locations of all the sections, too. I thought the organization a little strange at first, but it wasn't too hard once I got the hang of it. Take the history sections, for example. They were the hardest to figure out because there's two floors. And..." Her words faded as she took in their expressions, beginning to glaze over. "I'm rambling, aren't I?"

"No, no!" Saffra pressed her lips together, trying to fight a soft smile. "Okay, just a little. But I'm glad you love working there. Claire will be so excited to learn that you're settling in."

"Yeah. I can't wait to tell her." Silence fell. They all worried about Claire in her absence. She was desperate to recapture the moment, if only to lift their spirits. "We should be ready to re-open the library for scholars in the next week."

"That's great news." Saffra immediately perked up. "I've missed escaping to the library."

"Yeah..." Leah chewed on her lower lip.

"What's the matter?" Saffra leaned forward.

"Master Roland said outsiders aren't permitted in the library. Is that really true?"

"Oh. Well, traveling scholars and various courtiers from—"

"No, I meant, like *normal* people. Like, if someone from the city wanted to come and borrow a book?"

Saffra sat a little lower in her chair. "Well, it's the royal library. There have always been rules like that."

"But what about everyone else? Are there no other libraries in the city?"

"Libraries in the city?" Saffra frowned. "I'm sure some of the the wealthier people have libraries—"

"Yes but the average person can't just go and borrow a book."

"I see what you mean." Saffra gnawed on her lower lip, contemplating.

The door burst open, halting their conversation. Desaree chose that moment to waltz in. Her eyes immediately zeroed in on Leah. "There you are! A little birdie told me—okay, it was Verath—that someone's mate just returned."

Leah blinked, then immediately shot to her feet. "Jovari?"

"Unless you're mated to someone *else* we don't know about." Desaree waggled her eyebrows.

She ignored Desaree's teasing and glanced between the others. "He's back? But, what if he comes looking for me?"

She was hardly presentable in her current state, in the simple homespun gown Jocelyn had lent her, now covered in dust and splatters of hair dye from Saffra's first attempt. Never mind that the hem was a little too short and showed off her ankles, which was *apparently* not the fashion here.

"Then we'd better get you ready." Saffra rushed off, then returned with a dark green gown. "This should look beautiful with your hair and skin tone."

Leah's lips parted. "That's..." It looked like something a fairytale princess would wear. She hadn't missed the fact that Dragonwall's nobility dressed like something out of a Disney movie. But she'd been too wrapped up helping with the library's restoration to worry much about her own appearance.

She shouldn't care now, either, except this was Jovari. After the way he'd kissed her...

She'd spent every day in his absence replaying it. Now she was a ball of nerves. Suddenly, she wanted to look beautiful enough to take his breath away.

"Come on." Jocelyn grabbed one hand and Desaree grabbed the other. Saffra simply stood, grinning. "Fortunately you have us. We've plenty of experience with this sort of thing."

"You're in good hands," Saffra clarified.

An hour later, she was transformed. Her hair, which had mostly dried by the time they got ahold of it, was artfully done up with small braids and twists and knots. She had no idea what magic Desaree had worked. Jocelyn had applied some light makeup to her face. Saffra had helped with the gown. While it was a little shorter than it should be, they'd adjusted it to fit rather well.

"I feel like a princess leaving for a ball," she admitted. Saffra snickered. "I still can't believe people put this much effort into their appearance every day."

"Welcome to court," Saffra said, "where everything you do, say, and wear will be used to take your measure."

Just then, there was an impatient knock on the door. "Yes?" Saffra called.

"Saffra?" Her heart jumped at the sound of Jovari's voice. "Is Leah in there with you? I can't find her."

She opened her mouth and managed a croak. How embarrassing. She cleared her throat.

Jocelyn was already at the door, opening it. "She's here. Come in."

Jovari swept into the room, wearing a freshly pressed tunic and pants, his auburn hair swept back. The moment his eyes fell on her—sweeping over her from head to toe, his gaze lingering on her lavender hair—he froze. "Oh." The word was a soft exhale. The tips of his ears flushed slightly. It wasn't much. One would have to stare to notice it.

Her stomach fluttered and she managed to say, "Were you looking for me?"

"I... Yes." He blinked, coming back to himself. He rubbed the back of his neck. "I wanted to see if you were free? I promised to show you around the city when I returned." There came a quiet snicker from one of the girls. "I've got some spare time if you—"

"Let's go." She strode forward and grabbed his arm, all but dragging him from the room. She managed to throw a glare at the others on her way out, just in time to catch Saffra doubling over, holding in a fit of giggles. Jocelyn quickly closed the door behind them. It didn't hide the outburst of laughter that followed.

"They're acting like a bunch of children," Jovari muttered.

"You noticed, then?" she teased.

He repositioned her hold so that her arm was draped through his. "Did I notice," he scoffed.

"So, the city?" She had to bite her lip to hold back her excitement. She had refrained from leaving the keep because he'd promised to show her around. It hadn't been difficult, considering she had plenty of work to keep her busy in the library.

"You're going to love it," he announced.

"I can't wait. Lead the way!"

Their walk through the keep didn't take long. Courtiers bowed as they passed. She didn't miss the lingering gazes of several beautiful women. She forcefully buried the jealousy that threatened to rise each time.

He was *her* mate. They had no claim on him, even if they had probably shared his bed at one point or another.

The noise increased ten-fold once they were through the portcullis. She couldn't stop her wandering gaze. There was so much to look at. The quaint buildings, the cobbled streets, the horse drawn carriages and wagons. Small groups of people strolled, some of the women carrying parasols to block out the sunlight. It reminded her of something out of a movie.

None of it felt real. She had to pinch herself several times as they walked. This was her life now.

"This is the shopping district," Jovari explained, taking her along a lane packed with storefronts. "It's one of the places least affected by Kane's takeover."

That didn't surprise her. No doubt the poorest were the ones to suffer. She didn't want to think about Kane, didn't want him to sour her first escape from the castle, her first escape from all the hard work she'd done to reverse his damage.

"Let's go in here," Jovari said, his eyes lighting up as he pulled her toward a narrow shopfront with a carved wooden sign reading "*Wonders of the Realm.*"

"Oh!" She couldn't help her surprise as they stepped inside. The shop was dimly lit, shelves and display cases packed with curiosities from floor to ceiling. Glass jars filled with dried herbs and powders lined one wall, while shelves of intricate carvings, polished stones, and foreign trinkets filled another. Delicate chimes made of seashells and copper wire tinkled softly near the entrance. The scent of dried herbs, spice, and something faintly earthy filled her nostrils.

"Mistress Tyra's had this shop for decades," Jovari said, his eyes scanning the shelves with interest. "She stocks treasures from all twenty dragondoms."

An elderly woman emerged from behind a beaded curtain, her silver hair arranged in an elaborate knot atop her head. A pair of spectacles perched on her nose. "Lord Jovari," she said with a quick curtsy. "What an honor."

"Mistress Tyra." He nodded respectfully. "Just showing my— Leah—around the city."

Leah's heart tripped at the way *my Leah* sounded on his lips.

The woman's eyes flicked to Leah, lingering on her lavender hair with open curiosity but no judgment. "Welcome to my humble establishment," she said warmly. "Please, explore to your heart's content."

"Pick whatever catches your eye," Jovari said, already moving toward a display of polished river stones from the Northern Barrier Range.

She bit her lip. She'd received her first payment two days ago. It was far more generous than what she'd expected. The king had something to do with that. She'd wanted to ask him why—to inform him that she didn't need special treatment or extra handouts. She had every intention of working hard for everything she earned and being paid fairly.

She'd already been given her own accommodations and had been shocked to discover that she wouldn't be paying rent. Her small apartment in the *Hall of Kings* was already furnished beautifully with a sitting room, bedroom, and bathing chamber. Apparently it had been Claire's old apartment before she'd moved into Talon's tower. She wasn't required to pay for food, either. That came out of the king's coffers.

At first, it hadn't made sense. There were at least fifty nobles living within the keep. How did the king manage to pay for everything? But then she'd discovered that everyone living there was required to pay both room and board—everyone except for Talon's special guests.

She'd wanted to protest. Coming here was a chance to make her own way. But she also knew that if she did, Claire would refuse. So, she would accept the help just until she could get on her own two feet. Then, she'd figure something out. Maybe she'd save up for a house—one of the adorable townhouses she'd seen just outside the castle. That meant she needed to be frugal with her money.

"Leah?"

"What? Oh." She blinked. Jovari had already gathered a few items: a polished blue stone, what appeared to be a navigational compass, and a small bone carving of a dragon.

He stared at her. "Something wrong?"

"No! I just—sorry, I got lost in my own head." Embarrassed, she wandered to a glass case displaying delicate jewelry. There was a necklace with a pendant that reminded her of a snowflake, crafted from silver so fine it looked like it might melt if she touched it. Next to it lay a bracelet woven from copper wire and tiny pearls. She moved to another display, drawn to a collection of small glass bottles filled with colored sand arranged in intricate patterns.

When she finally selected a small brass trinket box with a design of stars etched on its lid, she turned to find Jovari watching her with an expression she couldn't quite read.

When she set the small trinket box down beside Jovari's items, he frowned. "That's all you want?"

"Yep." She made a popping sound with her lips. He eyed her a moment longer before pushing everything across the counter toward Mistress Tyra. "No, wait! I was going to—"

"Surely you did not think I expected you to pay for any of this."

"I am perfectly capable of paying my own way." Her cheeks flushed with heat. Money had always been tight, making her extra aware of when others took pity on her and tried to pay. She knew that Jovari didn't pity her, but it still brought too much of her past roaring to the surface.

Jovari must have seen something in her expression. His jaw rocked back and forth before he said, "I admire that you want to take care of yourself, but I am the one who invited you out today, and doing this for you would make me tremendously happy. Please, let me."

She worried at her lower lip. "All right."

"Thank you."

Their items were carefully wrapped in soft cloth and placed in small drawstring pouches. She couldn't help her delight when Mistress Tyra handed her the bag containing her trinket box. Coins were exchanged before they headed back out into the sunshine.

Jovari immediately pulled out the polished blue stone, turning it over in his palm. "This is from the lakes near Fort Squall. When you hold it to the light, you can see patterns that resemble dragon scales." He held it up, letting the sun shine through it. "See?"

Her breath caught as she spotted the subtle scale-like patterns in the translucent blue stone. "It's beautiful."

"It's for you." He placed it in her palm, his fingers warm against her skin.

Her eyes widened. "What? But you just bought—"

"The compass and carving are for Durlan—my father. His naming day approaches." He closed her fingers around the stone. "This reminded me of you—of our bond."

She stared at the stone nestled in her palm, its color shifting in the light—sapphire to cerulean to a pale, gentle blue, like sky reflected in still water. Like his scales. "Thank you," she managed, her voice unexpectedly thick with emotion.

Their eyes locked as she clutched the stone. Sparks crackled between them. He seemed to lean in, their faces less than an inch apart. Her heart sped up in anticipation. Her eyelids fluttered closed—

The clatter of a horse-drawn carriage had them jolting apart.

Jovari cleared his throat. "Come, let's keep walking."

They spent the remainder of the afternoon walking through the city. The market by the docks was one of her favorites. She told him about the berry coils she'd tried earlier. Eventually they ended up at a small plot of land called the public gardens, smack in the middle of the city. It didn't compare to the royal gardens, he explained, but it was open to everyone.

That immediately got her mind working.

"What would you think about public libraries?" she asked as they walked past beds of flowers. "Similar to these gardens. Somewhere people who can't afford to buy books can go to enjoy them. In my world, there are library cards and memberships, which are often free. Patrons can go in and show their library card and it allows them to borrow a set amount of books. They must return them by the due date if they want more. I never imagined that you wouldn't have something like that, but Saffra said there aren't any."

"You're right. There aren't—none open to the public, that is."

"So maybe there should be."

Jovari steered her to a bench, half hidden by overgrown bushes. They sat down together. "You have a kind heart, Leah."

"Okay. Is that your way of saying you don't agree?" She kept her irritation in check, wanting to hear him out.

He sighed. "I guess I'm not sure how something like that would work."

She frowned. "It works just fine in my world."

"Very well... What's to stop people from simply coming in and taking the books?"

"Jovari!" She failed to hide her surprise. "You shouldn't assume the worst in everyone."

He reached for her hand, lacing their fingers together and resting it on his lap. "You're right. As a shield, I've seen my fair share of unsavory people. It's in my nature to automatically be suspicious."

"Everyone deserves a chance. I think people will be so glad to have an establishment that lets them borrow and read books, that they'll cherish it and treat it well. Sure, there are always bad apples, but that doesn't mean we should punish everyone for it."

"What would the running of this establishment look like?" he asked, with genuine interest in his expression.

Her heart leapt. It was like he'd opened the floodgates. She spent the next hour telling him all about how libraries in her world worked. He interrupted a few times to ask questions and seek clarification. When she finished, he was silent for several moments.

"We should draft up a business plan for it," he decided. Her lips parted and she failed to form a response. Jovari seemed oblivious to her surprise as he continued. "The king has funds set aside for various public works. If we could come up with a convincing argument, get the council to vote in its favor, then we'd have a real chance at implementing it."

"You would help me with something like that?"

"I'd help you with far more than that—with anything you wanted."

"Wait." She pulled back, reclaiming her hand. Her sudden withdrawal made him frown. "Are you just saying that because we're mates?"

She didn't want him to feel obligated simply because fate had forced them together.

He barked a laugh. "In part, yes, but not entirely. It's a good idea, Leah. I think Kastali Dun has been through a lot. Something like your public library could improve everyone's quality of life, especially those less fortunate. It could help. The city is huge. We could start one as a test, and if it works, open several more across the city."

Her heart turned to mush; she had to fight back tears. "You mean that?"

"I do." He tucked a strand of her lavender hair behind her ear. His eyes traced the action. He licked his lips and said, "I didn't get a chance to tell you how much I like your new hair, by the way. Your favorite color."

"You remembered."

"I remember everything you've ever told me." He inched closer, giving her the opportunity to pull away. When she didn't, his lips brushed hers. Her breath whooshed out. She kissed him back, softening against him as he pulled her closer. His hand cradled her jaw, the other wrapping around her shoulders.

The kiss didn't last long. They were in a public place and she could feel eyes on them. The garden's patrons had stopped to watch.

"I'm guessing public displays of affection aren't that common in Dragonwall."

Jovari didn't release her as he chuckled, their breaths mingling. "No. Not all that much. But I've never been one to care for my reputation."

"I'm sure you haven't," she teased, biting her lower lip.

His eyes dipped to her mouth. He shook himself, pulling away to say, "It's getting late. I should get you back in time for dinner."

"Lead the way." She stood and reached for his hand. He happily took it. Their audience quickly scattered. She wouldn't be surprised if rumors of her library plan spread through the city in the coming days, given all the eavesdroppers. That idea left her smiling.

Jovari led her from the gardens and back through the city. For the first time in weeks, she felt like she could truly build a life here and be happy doing it. There was so much to hope for, so much to look forward to, and knowing Jovari was there to walk the journey made her heart burst with warmth.

CHAPTER 14
THE FIGHTING PIT

Kastali Dun

Dallin stood in the shadows watching a pair of fighters lay into each other. The ground was already stained with blood. Basher was on a winning streak after killing the night's earlier victor.

He was a mountain of a man, all muscle and hard lines. Not quite as tall or powerfully built as a drengr male, though. His eyes were cold and his expression was cruel. He enjoyed this sort of thing, taking lives.

Basher feinted left before landing an uppercut to Rogue's chin. Rogue's head jerked to the side, his entire body dropping to the ground. The crowd erupted. Hundreds of voices sounded in a maelstrom of noise that echoed off the warehouse rafters.

The haphazard stands had been hastily constructed and towered above the small fighting pit. Hundreds filled the benches, hungry for entertainment. This sort wasn't legal. Not when it involved fighting to the death. That seemed to make people more eager for it.

Basher dropped to the ground, straddling Rogue, landing punch after punch to the man's head. His fist was already a bloodied mess, made bloodier with each blow. He tossed his head back and howled with delight. There was nothing left of Rogue's face by the time Basher finished with him, just a bashed in mess.

Basher got to his feet and roared, spreading his arms wide. As if he were a warrior worthy of praise. The crowd ate it up.

Dallin swallowed down the bile coating his throat. It was a disgusting practice—one without honor.

"Sure you want to do this," Steve whispered, squeezing his shoulder. Steve was the most sensible of the crew. "That man's got a mean streak."

Mean was an understatement.

"Oh, come on." Fast Fingers scoffed, clapping Dallin on the back. "This kinda thing builds character."

"Only one of you's coming out alive," Steve said, ignoring Fast Fingers. The rest of the crew was already in the stands. They'd whooped with delight when he'd informed them of his intent to fight. He'd decided after one round that Basher needed to die. The world would be a better place without him in it. Basher was from a different street crew. Most of them answered to King Cobra though. Those who earned Cobra's trust joined his inner circle and became Serpents.

It's what Dallin was working towards.

He'd been with his gang for nearly a week. In that time, he'd joined them on two more jobs. Both had left him feeling disgusted. As if he didn't already have enough to grapple with mentally. But that's why he was here tonight—why he was doing this. Even if half his gang thought he was crazy.

There were rumors that King Cobra was hidden somewhere in the stands, watching. Word on the street was, he'd killed his last personal guard. Something about a betrayal. Now he was looking for a new one to take his place. What better way to find a skilled fighter than in the pit? Only the best came out alive, and Dallin intended to walk away with his life.

Two attendants rushed into the pit, dragging the dead body away. Blood trailed in its wake. He wondered if the dead man had family. If he'd stepped into the pit in hopes of winning the massive purse of coin up for grabs. Desperate people had little to lose.

"Any more takers?" The pit master stepped into view, his voice booming. "We got time for one more fight before we close out for the night. What do you say? We give Basher the winnings? Or does one more brave soul think they're strong enough to challenge him?"

Silence fell, everyone eager to see if anyone was stupid enough to step forward. Dallin waited one beat, two, three before striding out of the shadows. "I'll have a go."

The crowd roared, hungry for a bit more entertainment. Hundreds of assessing eyes raked over him, probably noting that even though he was tall, he didn't have Basher's bulk, acquired over his decades of life. Not that it mattered, even if he hadn't fully developed into his mature drengr form yet.

"You sure about that young man?" The pit master eyed him, clearly skeptical.

Dallin locked eyes with Basher and said, "Never been more sure of anything in my life."

Basher's expression was eager. No doubt imagining him as an easy kill. Good. He hoped the man underestimated him.

"All right, then. You know the rules?"

"You mean that there are none?" The crowd liked his answer, some of them erupting into delighted laughter.

"Exactly. No rules. No weapons. You fight to the death. Only one of you walks outta here alive tonight."

"Understood." He hadn't taken his eyes off Basher.

"Good. Then what's your name? Your fight name, not your real name. Don't need to be giving any extra information here tonight."

He wanted to choose something meaningful like Vengeance or Retribution, but he needed to look young and hungry, even a little stupid. His gang hadn't picked a name for him yet, so whatever he picked would stick. "Wasp."

"Wasp it is." The pit master turned towards the crowd. "Last fight of the night. Hurry up and place your bets. Basher versus

Wasp." The din of conversation rose as people began discussing the match's outcome. Coins were exchanged.

"You had better be careful." Verath's voice sounded in his mind. He didn't show any surprise. He should have guessed his mentor would be here tonight.

"I know what I'm doing."

"I know you do."

His gaze flicked around the stands. He immediately spotted Verath and Imeir, but only because he was purposefully looking for them. They wore shabby cloaks, their hoods drawn. They had squeezed themselves in with the audience. How the people around them hadn't realized that two drengr were here was beyond him. It was enough to shut down an operation like this.

Verath wasn't warning him because he was worried for Dallin's safety. He was worried he'd blow his cover. After all the effort he'd put into this mission, he had no intention of it.

The pit master backed up to the edge of the pit then shouted, "Begin!"

Basher wasted no time. He charged, his face morphed with feral intent. Dallin stepped aside, keeping his breaths steady and his mind clear. Basher looked to be in his forties. Sure, the man had some years on him, but that didn't mean much. Not when he'd been training religiously since before he'd fledged, hours upon hours every day, from some of the best teachers in Dragonwall. Learning to fight with his body was a requirement before he'd picked up a single weapon.

Basher growled and lunged again. He'd already memorized the brute's fighting style. Basher hoped to use his bulk to his advantage. He'd battered nearly all of his opponents with sheer strength. The crowd screamed and stamped their feet. The noise was thunderous.

This time, he let the man land a hit, wincing. He was no stranger to pain. It was nothing compared to the punch of a mature drengr. They began trading blows. He was careful to tone down his fighting skill. More importantly, he couldn't afford a single hit to his face. If he did, his body would heal too quickly, alerting everyone as to what he was. He allowed Basher to succeed in other places, like his torso and legs.

When Basher planted his fist into his abdomen, he doubled over, then took the opportunity to maneuver around him and bring the man to the ground. Basher recovered quickly, scampering backward to put space between them. It was surprising that a man of his size could move so fast. It was no wonder he'd killed six men tonight. He was skilled.

The crowd cheered with approval. They loved that he'd taken Basher down a peg. People loved a good underdog story, and he looked every bit the part.

His drengr ears picked out a single voice cheering from the audience. He didn't dare look, knowing what he'd see. In a moment of weakness, he'd told Jamie that he planned to be here tonight. They'd only seen each other once after that day in the market, when he'd returned to the keep to meet with his shield brothers.

Stopping by Jamie's room had been inevitable. He'd tried to keep away, but couldn't help it when his feet took him there. After the stunt he'd pulled in the market, he wanted to give Jamie a better explanation.

Eventually, he'd let slip his plans for trying his luck in the fighting pit, hoping to catch King Cobra's attention. He hadn't expected Jamie to show up, especially not with Mikkin. They were dressed like everyone else here, disguised to look like commoners and not people from the keep. He'd felt equal parts anger and excitement at the sight of him. Anger because Jamie was at risk in a cutthroat crowd like this. The drengr part of him wanted to protect him. But there was also excitement. He was desperate to show off. Perhaps it was a little embarrassing that he was pining over someone he wasn't sure he could have, but that was the way of things, wasn't it? He couldn't help his feelings any more than a clock counting time, the waves lapping at the shore, the stars shining in the sky—

"Think you can best me, *boy*?" Basher taunted, wiping sweat from his brow as they began circling again. "I eat lads like you for breakfast."

He screwed his face up in disgust. "Didn't take you for a cannibal, Basher. Sounds terrible."

Basher spit on the ground. "That mouth ain't going to be so smart once I knock your teeth out."

"Oh yeah?" He grinned wide. "You mean *these* pretty teeth? I rather like them." He turned towards the crowd. "Don't you?" Hoots and hollers followed his question, his audience soaking up the spectacle. "See? I think they like me better than you."

Basher's face darkened and he lunged. They fell into another round of blows. He let the man land a few before imparting a series of punishing punches and jabs, making Basher curl over and scurry away.

They danced back and forth like this for another five minutes. He needed to make the fight look genuine knowing King Cobra was watching. Basher was already tired from his previous fights, so it was easy to wear him down until the male grew sloppy. He waited for the perfect moment before spinning around behind him. In movements nearly too quick for a human—just believable enough —he grasped Basher by the head and twisted. The snap echoed louder than it should have, like a twig breaking in the winter silence. Basher crumpled, all that muscle and rage undone in an instant. Dead.

He should have felt something—taking a life was no small matter—but he felt absolutely nothing but relief, knowing a male like this was off the streets.

For a second, the crowd gaped. He'd caught them off guard and they hadn't expected the fight to end so abruptly. Perhaps they wanted more of a show. Wanted to see him beat Basher into a pulp, just like the male's namesake implied. That wasn't him. He'd claimed the name Wasp for a reason. His bite was quick and painful.

The roar that came was deafening. Everyone shot to their feet. He finally locked eyes with Jamie.

He expected to find disgust on his friend's face—disgust for so easily killing a man. Even knowing Basher deserved it. He found nothing but approval in Jamie's expression. His shoulders relaxed with relief. Forcing a grin on his face, he lifted his hands to the raucous audience.

"Just goes to show, muscle isn't everything," he cried, leaning into his underdog persona.

His audience cheered even louder. *Wasp. Wasp. Wasp.* The chant began, growing more frantic. Jamie took up the chant with everyone else. He couldn't help but wish it was his real name on Jamie's lips.

As his gaze circled the hundreds in attendance, his eye caught on one man who *wasn't* cheering. He knew instantly who it was. King Cobra didn't look all that different from most men. Physically fit, dark hair, shadowed eyes, a heavy brow, and a beard just thick enough to disguise part of his face. His gaze was shrewd, taking him in. Perhaps he should have looked away, but he couldn't help himself. Couldn't help the challenging stare he threw back at the leader of the Serpents. A dare, more than anything.

He'd proven himself here tonight. Would King Cobra seek him out? Would he invite him into his inner circle?

The attendants rushed forward, breaking the spell. He glanced down, watching as they dragged Basher away. When he next looked up, King Cobra was gone.

A bag of coin was thrust into his palm—his winnings. He looked down at it, blinking. A sense of unease crept into the pit of his stomach. He'd been paid to kill tonight. Didn't matter who, the idea of taking coin for a life sickened him.

His gang rushed down from the risers and out into the pit. Before he realized what was happening, they'd swept him up on their shoulders, parading him around like royalty, shouting about all the drink they planned to ply him with once they returned to the *Righteous Rose*. He was desperate for one more glimpse of Jamie.

When he turned to find him in the departing crowd, their eyes met. He felt his throat bob as he swallowed, wishing more than anything he could return to the keep tonight, even if it meant spending a few minutes in Jamie's company. It would be too risky. Mikkin placed his hand on Jamie's shoulder and ushered him away. Moments later, his own gang carried him out of the warehouse and set him on his feet.

They'd only just stepped out into the night when a cloaked man stepped in front of him. "Got a message for you from the boss," he said. The rest of his gang fell silent, crowded in around him. "Come by the *Tacky Stag* at noon tomorrow."

"And who might your boss be?" he challenged.

"Think you already know." The man pulled his hood more firmly into place and disappeared into the shadows.

Greedy Remy whooped. "Well I'll be damned! Bet that was one of King Cobra's lap dogs!"

Steve clapped him on the back. "Looks like you got yourself noticed with that fight of yours."

Exactly as he planned.

They began pulling him along, down the darkened streets until they reached the Pauper's District. "Just remember where you came from, *Wasp*," Fast Fingers nudged him with an elbow. "Don't forget us when you start runnin' in that circle."

"Wouldn't dream of it," Dallin lied.

"Eh, maybe you can put in a good word for us, yeah?" Jester said, hopeful.

"Definitely," he lied again. These weren't good men. Yes, desperate people did desperate things, but there were far more honest means to make a living. They'd chosen this life instead. It was why he'd done his best to remain separate. He didn't want to know about their mothers or their brothers and sisters, their lovers. The people they'd leave behind if they died. Most didn't have families anyway, which made it a little easier.

When they entered the *Righteous Rose,* Martel was waiting. "Heard you won yourself a fight."

Word traveled fast. Martel had his own network of spies. Young lads, mostly, desperate for a steely.

"You shoulda seen 'em!" Jester said, beginning to act out a fight scene with an invisible foe. The tavern was nearly empty at this hour, but there were a few patrons swaying in their seats near the bar. He caught the barmaid eyeing him hopefully. She'd done that a lot lately, even offered herself to him, telling him she wouldn't charge. He'd gently refused, though he didn't have it in him to admit the real reason why.

"How about a round of drinks, on me?" Martel announced, eyeing him shrewdly. He still didn't like the way Martel's gaze was always assessing him, as if he could see right through him. It was why he was so careful not to slip up.

Drinks were passed around. They lifted their cups. "To Wasp," they toasted, clanking them together before drinking deep. Martel participated. Their small group gravitated towards the back booth to settle in for a few hours of fun. Fast Fingers pulled out a deck of cards.

A hand wrapped around his arm, halting him. He flinched, knowing it would be Martel. "Hope you understand what you're getting into," the man growled, keeping his voice low. "The others might not see it, but I do. You're hiding something. You have been since the day you showed up here. I didn't see it then, but I see it now. Don't give me a reason to regret this."

"Wouldn't dream of it," he lied.

Martel gave him one more penetrating look before walking off. He brushed off the encounter. Surely Martel had his suspicions, but he doubted the man had any idea who he *really* was.

He lifted his winnings and said, "Deal me in! I've got money to spend!"

His new friends hooted with excitement, making room for him in the booth.

CHAPTER 15
A GAME OF RUE

Kastali Dun

Dallin winced against the bright sunlight streaming in through his window. He groaned and flopped over. His bed in the *Righteous Rose* was pitiful, at best. Not only was it sized for a more average person, but he felt every lump prodding his back. He wanted to keep sleeping, but not like this. He missed his bed at the keep, which made him feel beyond spoiled, knowing most people slept on beds just like this one.

A bell in the distance began to toll. He counted before shooting out of bed. Eleven in the morning. He'd slept late! Not that it was any surprise.

He glanced around his small closet of a room, gathering his bearings.

Last night was a blur of gambling and spirits after they'd returned from the fights. He'd had a splitting headache by the time he'd turned in—close to dawn. It hadn't lasted long, thanks to his drengr blood. Getting drunk wasn't nearly as easy for him as it was for humans, but since he wasn't a fully mature drengr yet, he was still more susceptible.

He eyed his clothes draped over the room's only chair, letting out a groan. Another day of wearing ill-fitting attire. Another day of playing the part of a street rat. But after last night's fight, his luck was about to change.

Jumping into action, he quickly dressed, locked up his room, then thundered downstairs. His stomach growled, but he ignored it. Perhaps he'd go flying later. He'd much rather hunt a nice, fat grazer than resort to half-burnt porridge. Just the thought made him shudder.

"Wasp!" It took him a moment to realize Jester was calling him over from their booth in the back. He already had trouble remembering he was supposed to be Derrick. Now Wasp. Sighing, he headed over. "You look better than I feel," Jester groaned. "Must be a pretty boy thing."

They'd all given him a hard time about his *supreme good looks*.

"A good night's sleep will do that to a person," he lied. Jester didn't look like he'd slept at all. He was already buried in a cup, which he quickly drained. "Why aren't you still abed like the others?"

"Wanted to see if you wanted accompaniment to your...meeting. You know, someone to have your back?"

He suppressed a groan. Jester was the last person he wanted to have his back. But he couldn't very well say that. "Sure, come along then."

He'd planned to ask for directions, but it turned out that Jester knew the way. The Tacky Stag was a fifteen minute walk. They loitered around out front for a bit so that when he entered, he was right on time.

The tavern was packed. He felt eyes on him as soon as he walked in. Clearing his throat, he marched over to the bar. "Hi there, handsome," a young bar maid sidled up to him. "What can I get ya?"

"I'm supposed to be meeting—"

"Wasp." He turned at the sound of his name, coming face to face with a large man wearing a scowl. "Boss says to bring you over to his table."

"Right." He looked up at the blushing maid. "Until next time."

"Your friend isn't welcome," the burly man added, eyeing Jester.

"Oh, yes. I'll just be right here." Jester climbed onto a stool and grinned salaciously at the maid.

"Going to have to search you first."

Dallin sighed, then indicated that his escort should get on with it. It wasn't as if he carried much. A single knife that looked as though it had seen better days was removed from the belt at his waist. His escort stowed it in his own bandolier, then led the way across the room. He was taken to a booth shielded by a curtain. It was gauzy and semi transparent. He saw a couple of shadows moving behind it, their voices low as they conversed.

His escort parted the curtain and said, "Cobra, he's here," giving him enough space to see the occupants within.

"Good. Good." Cobra waved a hand, offering Dallin a disarming smile before turning back to the booth's other occupant. "Mek—we're through here. See that you get yourself on that dock tonight. Take the spider with you."

"You want me to bring Tuck—?"

Cobra's motions were fast. Before Mek could move, Cobra was leaning over the table, a blade at the man's throat. He stared at Mek, his expression serene, as if holding a man's life in his hands was a simple transaction. Like he was merely paying for a new waistcoat. "Some prey don't realize they've been swallowed until it's far too late. Mind that you do as you're told. I pay you to act, not to think. Not to ask questions."

Mek paled. "Of... Of course, boss. S-sorry." Sweat beaded Mek's forehead. "I'll see it done."

"Good." Cobra sat back, as if nothing had happened. "Slither off with you, now."

That was all the invitation Mek needed. He scrambled from the booth. Dallin stood just out of the way to let him by.

Cobra turned his attention to him and graciously said, "You must forgive me. I never strike without cause." He couldn't help his audible swallow. The man was downright sinister as his penetrating gaze flicked over him, taking in his rumpled clothing. "Long night?"

Dallin cleared his throat. "Might have had one too many drinks with the boys. Nothing I couldn't handle. To celebrate an' all that."

Cobra hummed. "Venom is only deadly when mishandled. Come. Have a seat."

Dallin casually sank into the booth across from Kastali Dun's most dangerous gang leader. His heartbeat spiked. He was here—in Cobra's presence. This was something he'd worked towards for over a week. His desire to jump over the table and break the man's neck made his fingers twitch. He could do it. In just a few moments, this would all be over.

In his excitement, he sent a few projections to Talon. The king immediately followed up with questions, taking in the scene the way Dallin had. Making note of the bodies filling the tavern. *"It is too risky and you know that,"* Talon warned. *"Do not be rash. I put you on this mission because I know you understand discretion."*

"Aye, Your Majesty. It was merely wishful thinking."

"Understood. Stay the course. You are nearly there."

With almost twenty bodies filling the tavern, he'd have a right time killing the gang leader and escaping with his life. While he was a drengr, his odds, twenty-to-one were slim when all of them were armed. Sure, he could transform and blow the tavern to smithereens, but it would create the kind of publicity Talon wasn't interested in.

There would be too many questions. Namely, why hadn't Talon used the law to apprehend Cobra? The judicial system existed for a reason. The king couldn't merely go around killing whomever he pleased without putting them on trial before the court. If he did, his people would lose trust in him.

"Well then. I summoned you here because I'm looking for a new personal guard," Cobra said, getting right to the point.

Dallin blinked, focusing on the man before him. "Pardon my frankness but, from what I just saw with Mek, it looks like you can take care of yourself."

Cobra hummed, not interested in his flattery. "I want someone watching my back."

"And you're hoping I'm fit for the job."

"Something like that."

"You want me to prove my loyalty, then?"

"Even snakes know how to be loyal to those who feed them. Isn't that right, my sweet?" Cobra looked down. A hiss came from the inside of his sleeve just as a black head appeared. Snake eyes pinned him from across the booth.

He didn't have to feign his flinch as a snake slithered out of Cobra's pocket and began to wind itself around the man's forearm. Cobra cooed, stroking the little reptile's head. Snakes might have been considered distant relatives to dragons, but they'd always given him the creeps. They had no arms or legs. No wings. It was downright unnerving.

After a long beat of silence, Cobra turned back to him. "I want more than loyalty. I want trust. But the thing with trust is, it's like warmth on a cold stone. Slow to build and easy to lose."

"I've no intention of losing it, and I'm happy to prove myself however you like." At this point, he was willing to say whatever necessary to free himself of this man's presence and the snake now slithering over the table.

"Wonderful. One must shed old skin to grow." Cobra watched his little pet before turning back to him. "Got a couple of jobs for you—to give you a chance to earn my trust. If you're willing to work with my personal crew and prove your worth, I'll promote you to my own personal guard. The pay will be vastly better than whatever you were getting under Martel's employ. Are you in?"

"Do I have a choice?" He already knew the answer. Knew a man like Cobra wouldn't show his face to a nobody and let them walk away without ensnaring them in some way. That wasn't how people like Cobra stayed in power, stayed hidden.

"Smart young man." Cobra eyed him. He hesitated. "Spend the rest of your day getting your affairs in order. Let Martel know he'll be compensated for you, since I'm sure it will wound him, losing you." Cobra spoke like he was livestock to be bartered for. "You start tomorrow. You'll have a room upstairs so you're close to the crew."

"Understood."

They talked logistics a few more minutes before he departed. When he looked around, there was no sign of Jester. His mug was still there, half finished. He got a prickling sensation down the back of his spine that kept him from asking the bar maid where his *friend* had gotten off to, because he had a feeling he wouldn't like that answer.

THE KEEP WAS BUSTLING as he exited one of the secret passages that placed him two floors below the *Hall of Kings*. He contemplated for several moments before slipping upstairs to change. It was stupid, but he wanted to look his best. Sure, Jamie had come from a simple farmer's life and was no stranger to homespun clothes. Yet, he couldn't help himself.

Slipping into his chambers, he leaned his back against the door and sighed. Now *this* was comfort. He had half a mind to shed his clothes, bathe, and then cocoon himself in his plush bed for the rest of the afternoon, napping. But if he was gone too long, Martel and his crew might start asking questions.

This was his last night with the gang. They'd expect him to spend it celebrating his promotion into the city's most notorious ranks. The Serpents had developed quite the reputation in Kastali Dun's underbelly.

Groaning, he went to his wardrobe and quickly selected a forest green brocade tunic and beige pants. The color would bring out his eyes and look good against his pale skin and freckles. Then he quickly shed his clothing in a heap and ventured in the bathing chamber.

He groaned as he sank into the steaming pool.

He might have taken longer than necessary to bathe, mostly

because he missed the luxury of it, but he was soon dressed and slipping out of his chambers. He moved quickly through the keep seeking out Jamie's accommodations. Servants and other passersby on business bowed respectfully when they saw him.

He still wasn't used to it, the kind of attention he received. Back home, he'd done everything he could to hide in the shadows. It wasn't easy, being the son of a fort leader. His father had a massive reputation, given that he had once served Talon's father as a shield before retiring to Fort Edge. Not just that, but his father was the oldest drengr to find a mate. No one had expected him to have an heir. Generally, fort leaders passed their titles down to the next of kin, even if a vote was required. Occasionally, the vote swung in a different direction, and a new line of drengr took over. But more often than not, it was expected that the son would follow in the father's footsteps.

He wondered if his father was disappointed in him for running away so disgracefully.

His cheeks burned as he thought of the incident that had cemented his decision into place. He didn't like to recall it. Hated remembering the look of shock he'd seen on people's faces when he had been discovered.

He stopped at Jamie's door, taking a deep breath. Maybe he was getting worked up for nothing. Jamie could be away, and then he would have wasted his efforts for nothing.

Bracing himself, he knocked—perhaps louder than necessary.

"Just a moment." Jamie's voice was muffled.

Dallin's heart kicked up. Was it stupid that he'd come here? Would Jamie wonder why he'd chosen to visit him when he could have spent what little time he had visiting Verath or one of the other shields? Or reporting to King Talon?

Before he had time to question it further, the door swung open. Jamie's eyes landed on his face and widened. "Dallin." A flash of something unreadable crossed Jamie's features, there and gone before he could read it. He hoped it was happiness at seeing him, but he couldn't quite tell. Was Jamie upset with him?

"Had some time on my hands, thought I'd come by."

"Oh. Right. Of course." Jamie cleared his throat and stepped aside. "Come in I guess. That is, if you'd like to, I mean."

"I would." He strode inside and eyed Jamie's apartment. It was smaller by half compared to his own, and there was only a small sitting area and bed. The rooms on this level shared a communal toilet and bathing chamber at the end of the hall. It made the plumbing easier in a keep of this size.

"So..." Jamie glanced around, his eyes landing on a pile of clothes. He rushed over and began straightening, a slight flush creeping up his neck. His movements were tense, stilted. Yes, something was definitely wrong.

"Jamie, that's not necessary. Really. You should see my room." It was an outright lie. His chambers were free of clutter, not a single piece of clothing out of place. He wasn't sure why he said it, except that he wanted Jamie to feel at home in his presence. Whatever was going on with Jamie's mood was throwing him off.

Jamie didn't stop his fussing, quickly trying to fold the mess of clothes. He wouldn't meet Dallin's gaze.

Taking a deep breath, Dallin strode forward and wrapped a hand around Jamie's wrist. The feel of his skin beneath his fingers made his heart jump. Their eyes finally met, Jamie's going wide at the contact, and he quickly dropped his hold, stepping back a pace. "Really, I don't mind the clutter. Leave it. This is your space. You should be able to have it however you like."

Jamie dropped the tunic back onto the messy heap and nodded. "Right. So..." He rubbed the back of his neck, looking away again. Why wouldn't he meet Dallin's eyes? "You're back from your mission?"

"Just for a few hours. Things are about to get more serious, though. I'm not sure I'll be back for a while." He'd be under intense scrutiny once he was working for Cobra. He couldn't risk unnecessary trips into the keep. He gave Jamie an abridged version of what had happened that day. He was careful to keep things vague. Just enough so that Jamie understood the severity of the undertaking.

All through his retelling, Jamie still refused to look at him.

Something was definitely wrong. He took hold of Jamie's wrist again and said, "Come here." Leading him over to the sitting area, he indicated that they should sit. He released Jamie and took a seat across from him. "Tell me what's going on."

"What are you talking about?" This time, Jamie snapped the words sharply. Gone was his timidity. The change was abrupt. Jarring.

"Jamie," he warned.

Ever since they'd met, Jamie's mood towards him had been hot and cold. Sometimes he blushed and grew quiet, shy. Other times he avoided him or even ignored him. But he'd never snapped at him.

Blowing out a breath, he leaned his head back against the sofa and closed his eyes, trying to think. When he opened them, he said, "Your mood swings will be the death of me. Tell me what I have done to warrant your ire. Is it my coming here? You want me to leave?"

"No." The word was out quickly. "I mean..."

"Then what, Jamie. I cannot read your mind. If you do not tell me, then I'll be forced to draw my own conclusions. So far, those conclusions haven't been great. Sometimes I wonder if you dislike my friendship and wish you'd rather not know me. Other times, it's the opposite. Just tell me what has you irritated so that we can move past it."

He watched Jamie's throat bob. As far as age went, they were fairly evenly matched. He was twenty-four and Jamie was just past twenty. While Jamie was considered a man by human standards, he was still considered just shy of adolescence and still not fully mature by drengr standards. But sometimes, it seemed as if Jamie was the adolescent and not him. He needed patience if he was to navigate this. He reminded himself that Jamie had come from a rural village and hadn't been exposed to the world the way he had.

"You put yourself in danger last night."

Dallin opened his mouth to deny it, then froze. He'd never been in any danger. There had been zero doubt in his mind when he confronted Basher. But that wasn't what this was really about. At the heart of it, he saw what was eating at Jamie.

"You're worried about me?"

"Of course I'm worried about you, you...you...you idiot!" Jamie jumped from the sofa then began to pace.

Dallin's heart took off, beating so forcefully his chest all but vibrated. Jamie cared about him. As...a friend? Or something more? He wanted to ask. Gods, he did. But then he remembered the look of disgust he'd confronted the last time he'd let his feelings run away with him.

"I'm sorry if I worried you, Jamie. The king gave me a mission. I did what I had to."

"Right," Jamie muttered, not looking at him.

"Jamie," he snapped. He'd never taken a snappish tone with him before. Jamie's head whipped towards him, their eyes meeting and holding. "I'm sorry. All right? I'm sorry for worrying you. I'm sorry for that, I really am. I had to do it."

Jamie's throat bobbed. Their gazes continued to hold, until Jamie blew out a breath and his shoulders dropped. At last, he nodded. "I know. It's... I know you can take care of yourself. I shouldn't have worried."

"No, that's not... I like that you worried over me."

"I... You do?"

It was on the tip of his tongue to say *yes*. Instead, he said, "Can you forgive me?"

Jamie pressed his lips between his teeth, then nodded. "Forgiven."

Dallin felt a smile break free. "Thank you."

"When do you have to be back?"

"Not for another hour or so, why?"

"Fancy a game of rue?" Jamie's eyes darted towards the table where there was already a deck of cards and several dice waiting.

"I'd love that. Especially if it means I get to school you, yet again."

Jamie snorted, walking over to the table and dragging out a chair. "Doubt it. Not this time."

He couldn't help his eager grin as he took a seat across from Jamie and waited. He watched Jamie's hands as he shuffled, mesmerized by the motions. As he lifted his cards, he barely saw what he held. Yes, perhaps Jamie would get the better of him this time around. He'd already done that with his emotions. What was one more thing?

CHAPTER 16
REVERSING A CURSE

The Gable Forest

Claire and Feowen followed the path the king tree set for them. Two days passed, spent enjoying the forest and all it had to offer. They did not hunger or thirst, utilizing their ability to seek out food and water, or simply magic it into existence. They rested on beds of moss when sleep was needed.

It made her think of how much she'd grown. There was pride in that. Knowing that things hadn't been easy, but that she'd fought through it and come out better for it. Cyrus had been with her every step of the way—until he hadn't. Maybe if she'd been stronger, more prepared, he wouldn't have needed to sacrifice himself.

And yet, his sacrifice had been inevitable. She was coming to realize that. To stay with her all her life would have been selfish. She needed to be happy that he had finally moved on. That he might have his chance at an afterlife.

"I wonder if the tree is testing our patience," Feowen muttered as night began to fall. Neither of them had any idea where they were.

"It reminds me of all those quests when I first started learning spriten magic."

"Perhaps you will come away with new marks."

"I don't have much bare skin left for that."

"There's always your face," he teased.

She burst out laughing—the first since she'd lost Cyrus. "No, I hope not. I'd like to keep me looking like me—"

The path opened up around them, dead-ending in a large clearing. She gasped, grabbing Feowen's arm to stop him. "I think this is it."

The space was plenty large enough for a dragon, even if the trees surrounding it didn't look as though a dragon could have passed between them. He hadn't flown in. The forest's magic didn't allow that. It must have created space for him when he'd needed it, knowing that he sought Isabella.

She stepped into the center of the clearing and closed her eyes. A hum of invisible magic permeated the air. It was hard to describe, only that she could feel something monumental had happened here, long ago. The stones around her neck seemed to vibrate in recognition.

"It's hard to believe," she mused. "An entire race and it started right here, with the first drengr."

Feowen hummed behind her.

She brushed her fingers over the necklace of stones about her neck. There had been plenty of time to think about the magic she would use. The words. This was not her first time undoing Isabella's magic. She'd woken Fright with Taylynn by her side. Now, she had Taylynn's brother. The parallel wasn't lost on her.

Unlike waking Fright, this would be monumental. "Feowen, come." She held her hand out for him.

"My queen?" His voice was tentative.

"I need you for this. You will do this with me."

"But—"

"No buts. Come." She opened her eyes and turned to him as he stepped forward, slipping his hand into hers. The stones around her neck all but vibrated with energy against her skin. She was in contact with each of them. Felt the magic within them as surely as she felt the importance of this place. They would be with her every step of the way.

"You need not speak the words with me," she told Feowen. "Simply be here with me. Share your magic, whatever you are willing to give. Hum along if you wish. " She would pick a familiar spriten tune so that he might. It was the words and the intent that mattered most. Even more important was her decision to use a little of her drengr magic with what Pelwynn had taught her. She was born of two bloodlines. Even though Isabella's magic had been wholly spriten, doing it this way felt...*right*.

Her hand trembled slightly as she squeezed Feowen's, the weight of the moment pressing down on her. The air seemed to thicken, each breath slower, heavier. She closed her eyes, blocking out the flickering shadows of the forest. A sharp wind rustled the leaves, whispering secrets, but she was still, determined.

She focused—mind, body, and magic—blurring the edges between herself and the forest. The stones around her neck nearly pulsed against her skin, responding to her. The magic was there, waiting, eager. She could feel it, like a heartbeat beneath the earth itself. She took a slow, measured breath. *The world had waited long enough. She had waited long enough.*

Her voice cracked the silence of the clearing, soft at first, as if testing the air. Each word she uttered lingered, vibrating with intent. Her throat tightened but she pressed on, feeling the weight of her purpose in every syllable.

At first, there was nothing—only the echoes of her own voice and the distant hum of the forest. Then, a shift. A subtle pull. Her heart thudded louder than her voice. The air seemed to change, to grow thicker, more alive. Her magic, her connection to the world itself, surged beneath her skin, desperate to answer the call.

But this wasn't just any magic. This was the magic of creation and destruction. She could already feel it, the strain tightening across her chest. The world was watching. It had waited fifty thousand years for the balance she offered. Ages ago, the asarlaí had created the dragons. Their very existence upset the balance, but the life they brought into the world further shifted it. Isabella should have made that right when she created the drengr. The king tree had offered her the chance to right an age-old wrong. She hadn't. She'd been selfish and conniving. She had only made things worse.

Now, it was finally time to fix that. The words she sang were in *Ednuar* but roughly translated to:

BEAUTIFUL IS *the gift of life.*
   She stole that with her heart of strife.
   The words she used,
   A curse she wrought.
   Sewing promises he surely bought.
   He took her blessing,
   Accepted with an eager heart.
   He did not see the darkness,
   Saw only a fresh start.
   He did not know the price to pay,
   It would come for all someday.
   There would be a reckoning,
   It is here and now.
   I am that reckoning.
   Upon this sacred ground beneath my feet,
   A blessing made laced with deceit.
   Restore the balance between male and female,
   With no limitations on fertility.
   Rein in a new age.
   A new beginning, a blank page.
   To right a wrong that shaped a race,
   I offer here my blood in her place.

SHE DROPPED Feowen's hand and pulled her spriten blade from its sheath. Continuing to hum, she dragged the sharp edge along her palm, making a deep cut. She didn't flinch, didn't hiss with pain, even if it surged up her arm. It was a small thing compared to what

Isabella had done, compared to all those she'd hurt with her self-ishness.

Squeezing her palm, she let the blood pool and fall to the forest floor. A price. One that would undo Isabella's curse. The queen had eventually paid for her deceit—but not enough. She'd lost her only daughter to a different world. But Claire was the result of that, and she'd come to make amends.

The blood spread, dark and pulsing against the earth beneath her feet. It sank into the ground, but not quickly. No, it lingered, as if the earth itself was considering the offering. Her heart stilled for a moment, a flash of doubt creeping in. Was it enough? Was it the right price? Surely she had paid enough by now.

Then the ground began to stir. At first, it was slow. Just a ripple, like a sigh in the earth's bones. But then the tremors quickened, and the air crackled with rising energy. Her breath caught in her throat. Vines shot upward, snapping into place like living things, racing to form shape. The clearing was alive with magic—vines twisting, flowers blooming, branches stretching toward the sky.

A large form was quickly taking shape. It felt like time itself was warping. She didn't move. She had no choice but to watch as the massive figure rose—powerful legs, a muscular body, wings unfolding in a burst of verdant life. It was too much, too fast, and yet... It was breathtaking. A dragon made of foliage and flowers. Vigilance reborn. She could barely breathe, hardly daring to believe it was real.

And yet it was. Because she had done it.

A laugh that sounded more like a sob burst from her lips. It was beautiful. *He* was beautiful.

A breeze kicked up around them. On it, a gentle whisper that sounded much like the king tree. *"It is done. Return to me."*

She turned to Feowen, her eyes were blurred with tears. His were too. The immensity of the moment came crashing down around her. First one sob exploded from her chest, then another. Until she fell into his arms crying, her shoulders shaking with emotion.

She'd done it. For an entire race, she'd erased Isabella's awful desire to render them extinct. She'd given new mothers a chance to hold not one child in their lifetime, but many. She'd given future females born of the drengr the ability to shift, when those of the past had never had it.

"Shhh...." Feowen combed his fingers through her hair, comforting her. "Shh..."

"I can't... I can't believe that worked."

"The world was hungry for it—ready for it."

"I know. It's just...after how hard everything has been lately, it's nice that something wasn't."

"Oh, I don't know about *that*. Had you tried this a year ago, I think you would be singing a different tune—pun intended, of course."

Her tears morphed into a bark of laughter. She stood and wiped her eyes. "I suppose you're right. Gods, he's beautiful." She walked over to the giant effigy. It was nearly the size of Talon. She brushed her fingertips over the leaves, caressing a jasmine blossom. The sight of it reminded her of Pelwynn. What would he think, seeing this?

"He would be so proud of you," Feowen said, as if reading her thoughts.

"You think?" she hiccuped.

"I am sure of it. Claire, what you have done, not just with this but with Kane, as a monarch both for the drengr and sprites." He shook his head, the levity in his voice making her straighten her spine. "You are an incredible woman. I am honored to call you family. To have witnessed all you have done. I cannot wait to see what else you will do for our kingdom."

"Feowen..." Her tears, which had almost stopped, started all over again.

"I know," he murmured, leaning in to kiss her forehead. "Why don't I give you some time alone with him?" He motioned to the effigy. "I'm sure the king tree can afford us a few extra moments."

"Thank you. I'd like that."

He crept away, not going far, just enough to disappear a few feet down the path. She walked around the effigy and found a place to sit, somewhere she could gaze upon it in full, where she could come to terms with everything she'd done. When she closed her eyes and focused her senses, she could tell this place had changed. The magic here was more meaningful.

Her tears stopped and her lips pulled into a smile.

Gods, she was a ball of emotions. She needed Talon to balance her. The sooner she could wrap her arms around him, bask in his comfort, the better. She couldn't wait to share the good news with him. Not just what she'd done here for the entire drengr race—the fact that they would never be limited to just one child—but for the little magical presence she was all but certain she now sensed growing inside her.

WHEN THEY FOUND the king tree a second time, it was to discover Taylynn sitting beneath it. A fierce joy burst in her chest. "Taylynn," she cried at the same moment as Feowen said, "Sister! I should have known you'd be here waiting."

They rushed forward, pulling Taylynn into a group hug.

"Talon! Is he—?"

"Fine. Grumpy as ever, but fine," Taylynn said. "Your disappearance sent him into a rage, but he reined himself in."

Fondness for her mate had warmth coursing through her. "I'm sure you had something to do with that."

Taylynn huffed. "I might have had a few...*choice* words to offer."

"What news?" Feowen asked, eagerly.

"Jeanine is fine. No need to fret, Brother." Feowen's shoulders relaxed. "I left a few days after things settled. The king has his hands full, as I'm sure you can imagine. My mate was sent away with Jovari, and I knew I would be needed here." Taylynn shot Claire a meaningful look.

"You knew I would come?"

"The king tree works in mysterious ways." Taylynn's eyes darted to the tree before she added, "Well?"

"Well, what?" Claire blinked.

Taylynn laughed, the sound so pure that every living creature in proximity quieted to listen. "*Well*, the tree has told me of your adventures. But I would like to hear it from you."

"Oh. Right. I did it," Claire breathed. "I killed him." Taylynn nodded as if this was absolutely no surprise whatsoever. "And, I used the stones to help me reverse Isabella's curse. The drengr will be able to have more than one child now. And I worked something in that will allow future females born of the drengr line to shift. I think. I guess I won't know for certain until there's proof. But…"

A soft smile pulled at Taylynn's lips. "That's good. I should like that, I think. For my future daughters to possess the ability to shift. To be able to have more than one child." Taylynn's eyes darted to her brother. "I want my children to share what we do."

"Aww, sis. I love you too." Feowen grinned, then hooked an arm around Taylynn's neck, sloppily dragging her against him the way an annoying brother would.

"Feowen," Taylynn screeched, breaking free to glare at him.

"I never had siblings," Claire admitted. "But I should love for my child—*children*—to share that. What you both have."

Taylynn's eyes darted down to Claire's belly and then away. Gods above. Did she suspect the same thing Claire did?

She cleared her throat and said, "The tree has offered a way to protect the stones. Now that we have all five, it has offered to keep them safe."

"That would have been nice before," Taylynn grumbled, to which the roots around the tree protested. They backed up several paces.

"It's because it needs all five together. Oh! That reminds me." She reached into her pocket and handed Taylynn Fright's white stone. "You should have this."

"No." Taylynn backed up a step. "You keep it. Or—do with it whatever you wish."

"Perhaps I should give it back."

Taylynn's expression softened. It was clear the princess had grown fond of Fright in the time they'd spent together. "I think that would be a kind gesture. One of trust."

"Are you ready?" The tree's voice sounded in their minds.

"Yes." Claire turned to the others. "I'd like to do this alone, if you don't mind?"

"Very well. My brother and I will be just here, outside the clearing." Taylynn dragged Feowen away.

She turned to the tree, pulling the necklace of stones over her head.

"Set it upon my roots," the tree advised. She followed its instructions. The roots began to wiggle and writhe. Moments later, the necklace with all five stones was swallowed up. *"They will be with me in a different world, one where no one will ever look."*

"Then, it's done?"

"It is done." There was a hesitation and then— *"Ask what is on your mind, Queen."*

It always seemed to know what she was thinking. She bit her lower lip, then told it what had been bothering her for days, ever since she and Feowen had talked of Jeanine.

The tree listened patiently, then said, *"For your service to this kingdom. For their service, as well. I will grant you this one request. But know that I do not defy fate's laws lightly."* Her eyes widened, both because the tree was willing to help, and because a thick branch grew out of its trunk near her eye-level. Six purple fruits materialized and ripened. They reminded her of plums, albeit magical ones. These were different from the golden fruit the sprites ingested when they were ready to leave this world behind. *"Take them. They are yours."*

Her heart skipped a beat. Was it truly offering this to her? It almost didn't feel real. Afraid it might rethink its offering, she quickly pulled her cloak free. She carefully plucked each fruit and wrapped them safely into a bundle. The tree explained what would be needed before it sent her on its way. She couldn't help her grin, the way her chest burst to share the news. But she would hold this one a little closer to her chest—for now. Until the time was right.

She found Taylynn and Feowen bickering. They both perked up at the sight of her. It was on the tip of her tongue to tell them what she'd done. Instead, she kept her lips pressed into a line.

"It is done?" Taylynn asked, eyes glittering with desperate hope.

"It is done," she confirmed. In time, they would discover what else it was that she had managed.

"Excellent. Then let us depart for Esterpine." Taylynn hooked an arm through hers and her brother's and they set off for the heart of the forest.

CHAPTER 17
SPRITEN MESSENGERS

Kastali Dun

Talon removed the next sheet of parchment from the stack and slid it in front of him, immediately taking note of the heading. His shoulders straightened with interest. He quickly read through the contents, making sure the chronicler had gotten the wording correct. Pleased, he sat back to survey what remained of his lower council.

Nearly half had either died at Kane's hands, or been removed after Kane's rule. He had hoped his council members, out of everyone, would not succumb to dishonorable behavior during those dark days. Unfortunately, some had used Kane's rule as an excuse for it; he'd promptly removed them from power. Those currently sitting in the room had been pardoned. A few had gone into hiding. The others had been forced to swear allegiance to Kane, but had refused to act dishonorably, even if it meant putting their own lives at risk. Those were the kinds of people who deserved leadership roles under his rule.

Clearing his throat, he said, "I have decided to amend the oath sworn by my shields. Mathis, is this the final document?"

"Aye, your majesty." Mathis stepped up beside him. "All it requires is your signature."

"What amendment?" Lord Luwai Zaki inquired, sitting straighter in his chair.

"Read it for yourself." He passed the parchment over, letting Lord Zaki read it. The council members shifted uneasily. They never liked change.

"You wish to allow shields to take mates? But...that's unheard of."

"It is unheard of because Dragonwall's first king wrote it into law."

"Yes, but that law exists so that your shields are never forced to choose between loyalty and love."

"Yes, well, now they may. If it comes down to a decision for them to choose a mate over my own life, I should hope they chose that of their mate's."

"You would risk death—?"

"If it meant making my shields happy? Yes. Besides...that's all it is. A potential risk."

"Forgive me, Your Majesty. You might be capable of taking care of yourself. You are one of this kingdom's most powerful kings, yes. But what of future kings to come?"

"If a future king cannot protect themselves with the help of a handful of shields, then that king is probably not fit to rule."

"A handful of shields? What's to stop all your shields—all future shields—from taking mates."

"Nothing." He understood both sides of the argument. But he had no intention of backing down. "I have added a clause that allows a shield to step down if they feel they are unfit, after taking a mate."

"But—the oath is for life."

"It doesn't have to be," he growled. Forcing himself to relax, he took a deep breath. It didn't matter that he knew Claire was safe. Didn't matter that they'd managed to exchange a few whispered endearments days ago. It didn't matter that she had confirmed Kane was well and truly dead.

Being separated from her had his temper on a short leash.

The room fell silent. At last, he said, "There's nothing stopping future kings from amending the oath to better suit their needs."

"Laws are not written to be changed so easily."

"This one is!" He slammed his fist on the table, making everyone in the room flinch. "This law—this *custom*—is between a king and his shields. It is a matter pertaining to the race of drengr. Are you a drengr, Lord Zaki. What about you, Lord Bertalan? I didn't think so. For matters such as this, I have the final say. That I am even informing you is a courtesy."

"With all due respect," Lord Glover said, "I believe most of us are merely worried about your legacy. Should anything happen to you, when you have not secured the throne for future generations."

Talon let his head fall back against the chair, closing his eyes. "I do not yet have an heir. I am well aware of this. But I do have a queen, and it is only a matter of time."

He would never dare admit how much he yearned for it. The thought of his mate carrying their child. He hadn't allowed himself much space to consider it. She'd brought it up that day in the forest, before she had regained her memories—that they hadn't used protection. He couldn't help the selfish desire, the selfish hope, that he'd gotten her with child in the many times they'd come together since.

"None of us is criticizing you," Lord Glover amended. "I am merely stating the source of our concern."

"Your concern is noted." Talon reached for the document, which had now circulated the table. "Mathis, a quill, if you please."

Mathis rushed forward, setting out what he needed. He dipped the tip of the quill into an ink pot and hesitated. Then he signed the document, making sure to send a projection of the monumental moment to his shields so they could witness it. Several more duplicates were produced, and he signed those as well. The records of their laws were housed in multiple places, including copies kept in the keep's innermost vault for safe-keeping.

He lifted each parchment and handed it to his steward. "Very good," Mathis said as he took the final one. "I will get these placed with our records."

"If that is all—" He surged to his feet. He knew there were other matters but right now, his clothes felt too tight for his skin.

"Actually—" Mathis looked ready to protest.

"Save it for another time." He turned and fled the room. It took mere minutes to reach the nearest courtyard. He was just about to shed his skin in exchange for scales when Koldis's voice stopped him.

"A delegation of sprites and unicorns have been spotted en route to the capital."

His heart leapt. *"Claire?"* He knew even though he asked, that she would not be with them. After hearing her faint whispers, she'd gone silent. She'd gone into the forest and hadn't yet come out.

There was a hesitation and then, *"I'm flying out to meet them now."*

"I'll join you." He jumped into the air, taking to the sky. He spotted Koldis. His shield banked, coming around to meet him. Together they took off north.

It was less than fifteen minutes before they found the group of sprites and unicorns. They'd already slowed to a steady trot, likely on purpose, to give the capital enough warning.

His chest deflated when he didn't see Claire among them, even though he'd already known. That hadn't stopped him from hoping. Gods, he missed her.

They descended. The group spotted them and came to a stop. Closer, he counted three spriten males along with a shockingly large number of unicorns. He transformed, landing on two feet. Koldis did the same.

He didn't waste time in striding forward to greet them. "Nua bualta," he said. *Well met.* Despite the absence of his mate, he was damned glad to see them. "Aahm tir?" *What news?*

All three sprites dismounted. If they were surprised to hear him speaking their language, they gave no sign. *"Ayas Drollaya,"* they said in unison, returning his greeting with respectful bows. He'd never thought to see the day when sprites offered their respects to the likes of him. But, being mated to their queen did lift his esteem in their eyes.

One of them stepped forward, continuing in Ednuar, "I am Luthias. This is Garrik and Virion. Our princess sends word. The queen has returned to the forest. We are here to collect her guards. Princess Taylynn recommends we return with haste. Here is her missive."

Luthias produced a small bit of parchment. Talon quickly broke the seal and read over its contents. His heart leapt at the words. He looked up at Koldis, who wore an eager, almost desperate expression.

"Taylynn invites us to Esterpine, to witness her coronation. Claire is ready to abdicate the spriten throne."

Koldis immediately brightened. "When?"

"As soon as we can be ready. I have a few matters to take care of. That should give everyone time to prepare." He looked over the unicorns. There were certainly plenty.

Noting his gaze, Luthias said, "Forgive me, but as you know, the unicorns refuse to carry your kind. I hope you will not be offended—"

"It is no matter. We can fly."

"Good. The princess wished for all those close to Claire to attend, should they wish it. We did not know how many, so we brought as many as were willing to come."

"You cannot leave Kastali Dun unprotected," Koldis warned, already anticipating what would happen when he announced the news to his inner circle.

"The threat of Kane has been neutralized. Surely—"

"It would be unwise," Koldis warned.

He sighed. "I know. Let us discuss it with the others. In the meantime—" He turned to Luthias. "Do you wish to see the capital? Or do you and the unicorns prefer to remain here."

Luthias and his companions threw dark looks to the city's towering walls in the distance, blanching somewhat. "I cannot speak for my companions but I wish to remain outside. We will assemble just outside the city gates and wait for you there."

His companions gave their own murmurs of agreement.

"Very well. We will gather the others. Please allow us several hours to set our affairs in order."

"Of course, Ayas Drollaya." Luthias bowed his head, then returned to the others, mounting up.

Talon gave Koldis one final glance before jumping from the ground and morphing. He took flight, racing back to the capital. He'd already sent projections to Bedelth, Dallin, Jovari, and Verath by the time they returned. Once they assembled in the tower, it was to find the majority of their inner circle present.

He repeated the news and wasn't surprised by the arguments that followed. Everyone was eager to see their queen, even if it meant traveling to the forest. But Koldis was right, he couldn't leave the capital unprotected.

Dallin was in the middle of a mission and would be no help ruling until he completed his task. Desaree was practically in tears when Verath assured her that he had no intention of leaving Dallin alone, and that she would have to travel to Esterpine without him if she intended to go. In the end, she chose to stay so as not to be parted from him. Bedelth agreed to stay with Verath, to help out with court and ensure nothing went amiss. Since Reyr was in the north, he wouldn't be going either. That left Jovari and Koldis.

"You should go," Jovari said to Koldis. "Your mate is there, and you rarely get to see her as it is. You need to be there for this."

Koldis looked uneasy, his eyes darting to Leah. They all knew how much Claire valued her best friend. But they also knew that Jovari would hate remaining behind if Leah chose to go. In the end, Leah made the decision for them.

"I have my work here," she said. "Jovari and I are in the middle of our library project. It's better if we stay behind."

Two days ago, Jovari had barged into his study, a drafted proposal in hand. They'd argued over it for several minutes, until he'd agreed and put the matter before his lower council. The vote had been favorable. Even if it hadn't been, he was sure Jovari would have found a way to make it happen. Each of his shields had a small fortune to their names. He paid them well enough for it. But in the end, the proposal had earned funding directly from the royal coffers, fueled, in part, by taxes.

"Very well then. Jovari, you and your mate will remain here."

"Not a problem."

With that sorted, only he and Koldis would fly. Claire's queen's guard and her handmaidens would travel by unicorn. The girls insisted on writing letters, which he promised to deliver to Claire upon their arrival. He also promised to return her to the capital as quickly as possible.

Hours later, they said their goodbyes. From his vantage point in the sky, he watched the unicorns depart, knowing they would reach the forest far sooner. He informed them not to delay. He and Koldis would make their way in their own time.

The two of them did not bring any others. The fort had lost too many drengr already. None could be spared without putting the capital at risk.

Paying Kastali Dun a final glance, he and Koldis set off in search of his queen.

CHAPTER 18
A LETTER

Somewhere Along Celenore's Coast

Merrian grinned, tilting her head back. The sun was a welcome contrast to the crisp air while flying. She and Reyr had departed Squall's End the day before yesterday, flying south. Lord Byron didn't know Captain Bennett's exact whereabouts, only that he was somewhere between Squall's End and the capital, keeping a safe distance from the coast to avoid detection.

Now that people were no longer being captured and sold to slavers, Byron's drengr could come home. The only problem was, they were too far from their fort leader's reach. Reyr had offered to locate Bennett and inform everyone that Dragonwall was free, that the drengr helping him could return home.

That turned out easier said than done.

She knew enough about drengr telepathy that distance played a big role in how far their voices could reach. Reyr had told her his plan, that he would fly out over open water away from the coast, and call out for the fort's drengr traveling with Bennett in hopes of locating them. It felt like searching for a needle in a haystack.

They returned to the coast each night to make camp on the

beach. She liked having Reyr all to herself again. He was popular everywhere he went, but especially at Fort Squall.

She thought back over their time there. True to his word, she'd gotten a meeting with Lord Rhal to discuss the circumstances the city's homeless and less fortunate faced. She'd expected the lord to flat out refuse additional aid. Instead, he'd been thoughtful and receptive, promising to reevaluate the budget and ensure that those who needed it received more funding. She'd warned him about some of the shelters, of their greed. Lord Rhal had promised to ensure that the increased funds wouldn't be misspent.

She'd left the city riding on a high. It felt good to make a difference. It felt good to know that she'd helped those who needed it.

Reyr's roar split the air. He turned, changing direction over the water to head further out. It could only mean one thing. He'd located Bennett's ship.

She blew out a breath, relieved.

It took three hours before she spotted the small cluster of ships. There were three. Reyr descended directly for them. She realized just before he back-winged what he intended. He was too large to land on the deck of any ship. Not to mention, his weight in dragon form would probably sink them.

All three had let down their anchors, furling the sales to keep them stationary.

Reyr landed in the ocean, his massive body bobbing in the rolling water. He paddled to the closest ship, coming up alongside it. "You there," someone called down to her, a male drengr by the looks of him. "Grab the ladder and climb up."

She threw a dubious glance at the ladder. Her legs were belted into the harness, keeping her safely on Reyr. Once she freed herself...

Well, here went nothing. Following the drengr's orders, she managed to jump from her perch to the ladder, grabbing ahold of it. Her heart raced. She could feel Reyr's eyes on her, his head craned to watch.

No harm would come to her, of that she was certain. The worst that might happen was she slipped and fell into the water. But Reyr would be there to grab her. She just didn't fancy a swim, that was all.

She reached the top. Strong arms pulled her the rest of the way over. She was breathing hard by the time she got her footing.

Her stomach immediately heaved. "Brace your legs. It takes some getting used to," the male said. "I'm Samuel, by the way. One of Fort Squall's drengr."

"Merrian," she offered, grasping his forearm in greeting. The deck was a flurry of activity as people rushed about. The other two ships looked much the same.

"Welcome to the *Lady Faith*. Captain Bennett will be along in just a moment."

There came a spray of water as Reyr launched back into the sky. He didn't go far, circling around before dropping towards the deck. Transforming. He landed beside her with a thud.

"Sam, good to see you," he said, reaching for Samuel's arm.

"You as well, Lord Reyr."

"Your mate?"

"She's belowdeck, having a nap."

"Ah."

"Come this way." Samuel led them across the deck as they intercepted who she presumed was Captain Bennett.

"Lord Reyr!" Captain Bennett nearly roared with delight. His eyes darted in another direction, fixing on one of the deck hands who had frozen in place, a rope in hand. A look of worry washed over Bennett's features before disappearing. "Wasn't expecting you! Heard you got locked up."

"I did." Reyr looked in the same direction Bennett had, then frowned. His body went rigid and she immediately knew something was wrong. Perhaps she'd spent enough time around him to simply glean these things.

"Is that who I think it is?" Reyr all but growled.

"Not sure what you're talking about."

The person—a woman, she realized—seemed to shake free of the surprise and turned to rush off. Reyr jumped forward and caught up, grabbing the woman around the arm. "Caterina?!" He appeared more shocked than anything.

"Take your hand off of her, my lord," Bennett ordered, coming up beside them. "You might be a king's shield, but this is my ship and you have no authority here."

Reyr huffed, dropping her arm. The woman—Caterina—looked between them with an unreadable expression. The only sign she was nervous was the pulse jumping rapidly in her throat.

"Do you have any idea who this is?"

"I know exactly who she is."

"Then you know that she is—"

"What I know is that if it weren't for her, you wouldn't have had any warning before that Oshean fleet reached your shores. If it weren't for her, some of my crew wouldn't be alive today. If it weren't for her—"

Bennett stopped himself, his chest heaving.

Reyr took a step back, lifting his arms in a placating gesture. He turned his focus on Caterina. "So, this is where you ended up, then? We all wondered when you fled."

Caterina squared her shoulders. "I made a new life for myself. I wasn't going to let the king behead me, or sit around in a dark dungeon for the rest of my life."

Merrian suppressed a shudder. She knew all too well what it was like being confined in the castle's dungeons. Reyr seemed to feel the same, because his throat bobbed and he gave a quick nod.

"You cannot arrest her," Bennett warned, as if worried Reyr would make off with her any moment.

Reyr blew out a breath, running a hand through his hair. "I have no intention of taking her back with me. I already have one passenger, and I wouldn't subject her to the likes of you," he said to Caterina.

Caterina merely shrugged, taking his insult in stride.

"Lord Reyr," Bennett warned. "May I ask why you have graced us with your presence?"

Whatever joviality the ship captain had initially possessed at seeing Reyr had vanished.

Reyr held Caterina's gaze a beat longer before dismissing her and turning to the ship captain. "I apologize for my less than savory arrival. I come bearing news. Kane has been dethroned."

There were enough people within earshot that a cry of celebration went up, echoed by others further away as word spread through the crew and over to the neighboring ships traveling with them.

"Now that's the kind of thing I can get behind." Bennett nodded with approval. "I take it Byron sent you?"

"He did indeed."

"Excellent. Come, let's meet in my cabin. I'm sure you'd like some refreshments after your journey."

"Thank you. We can't stay long."

Bennett motioned for them to follow. Cat was left standing on the deck, watching.

Merrian couldn't help but wonder what it was she'd done to anger Reyr. She wanted to ask, but knew better. Especially not in Bennett's presence. It was obvious that the captain cared about her. She'd wait until later.

～

When they emerged back out on deck, she had to blink away the brightness despite the overcast sky. There wasn't a lot of light belowdeck. Reyr had spent the time catching up with Bennett, letting him know everything that happened while the captain had been at sea, rescuing captives. He'd also informed him that the king wished to grant Bennett and the other ship captains a medal for services rendered to the kingdom, along with a large sum of money as a reward.

Bennett had been modest, first trying to wave it away. "I was only doing what was right for my kingdom. Plenty of others rallied against Kane, too."

"But few of them had the impact you did," Reyr argued. "You rescued thousands."

Bennett only huffed. She hadn't missed the shyness that came over him. In the end, they'd gotten a promise from him. He would venture to the capital at his earliest convenience to accept the reward.

Just before they'd left his cabin, Bennett had pushed the idea of granting Caterina a pardon for what she'd done to help Dragonwall. "That isn't in my authority to grant," Reyr had said. But he agreed to take the matter before the king.

The activity on deck was more subdued. Several deckhands lounged, a couple with caps pulled low over their eyes to nap.

"How do you feel?" Reyr leaned in to ask.

She shivered as his lips brushed her ear. "Still not great." Her hand went to her tummy, trying to quell the seasickness. The sooner they got off this boat, the better.

Reyr straightened. His jaw ticked as his eyes swept over her, taking in the absentminded way she'd reacted. He turned his attention back to the captain. "Bennett, I think you have all you need from us. We're eager to be off again."

A slight flush crept over her cheeks. She hadn't expected him to care so much, but she found that she liked it. Liked knowing that he wanted to ease her suffering as quickly as possible.

Bennett's gaze scanned the eastern horizon. "You sure you won't stay? Looks like there's a storm along the coast. You'll have to pass right through it."

Reyr hesitated. She saw the indecision pass over his features. "We have time yet," he decided.

She blew out a breath, relieved. She wouldn't be stuck here.

"Very well. Just be careful."

They bid Bennett a quick farewell.

Reyr jumped from the deck and transformed, taking to the sky. He circled once before landing in the water beside the ship. It rocked as the water settled. Her stomach heaved into her throat.

Oh, gods. She'd have to climb down the ladder again, all while trying to hold down the contents of her stomach.

"This way, miss." One of the deckhands guided her over to the side of the ship.

"Wait!" Caterina appeared on deck, rushing over to her. It took a moment to realize she had a sealed letter, which she thrust into her hand. She gaped in surprise, failing to react. "I know I'm asking a lot, but when you return to the capital, could you give this to its recipient?"

"Uhm…"

Caterina didn't wait for an answer, rushing away. She glanced down at the folded parchment. A name was scrawled onto its surface. One she recognized.

Reyr's impatient warble spurred her into action. She tucked the letter into her pack and rushed over the edge of the ship. "There you go. Just hold tight to the rungs. We've got you," her assistant said, keeping hold of her shoulders as she swung her leg over, searching for the ladder. When she managed to get both legs on the other side, she began to climb down and the supportive hands disappeared.

She held each rung in a white-knuckled grip. The faces above grew smaller as she scaled the massive side of the Lady Faith's outer hull. Reyr was just there. She glanced between herself and his hulking form. He extended a wing to make it easier, so she wouldn't have to jump.

What if it didn't hold?

His impatient snort reminded her to move. Muttering to herself, she managed to set her feet onto the leathery membrane and stagger across. She blew out a relieved exhale as she buckled herself into her harness. Reyr put some distance between them and the ship, then heaved his body out of the water. Water droplets rained down around him, glittering as they fell back into the sea.

His powerful wings beat, taking them higher. He circled the trio of ships once, roaring a goodbye, then took off east. She saw the storm clouds better now. They straddled land and coast.

Reyr flew swiftly, taking them straight into the heart of the storm. The wind kicked up. It was a testament to his abilities as a dragon that he managed to battle it and stay the course. She hunkered down, curling her cloak around her and her pack, drawing it over her face. It didn't matter. She was soaked in minutes.

She wasn't human, and thus, wasn't too concerned about catching a chill. That didn't stop her limbs from trembling with cold. She pressed herself close to Reyr's scales, soaking in every bit of heat he had to offer.

The wind worsened. Her chattering teeth could soon be heard above the noise of Reyr's wing beats. But land appeared, a long stretch of beach with rocky cliffs. She nearly groaned with relief as Reyr began to descend, taking them to the ground.

"The storm is too intense to fly through," he yelled after he'd landed and she'd dismounted. The storm raged around them, lightning forking through the sky. The resulting boom made her jump. "Come! I spotted a set of sea caves over here."

He took her hand and pulled her in the direction of a rocky outcropping near the beach. Her feet slipped over the rocks, but Reyr kept a tight hold of her as he guided her up the steep incline. It wasn't easy to reach the open mouth he'd found.

She was clinging to him by the time they made it under cover. The wind picked up even more. Lightning forked the sky in rapid succession, followed by each sonorous boom, all but shaking the small cave's walls. It was quieter here.

When she looked up, it was to find Reyr's eyes fixed on her. She took in his soaked golden hair, the flush of his skin, the rapid rise and fall of his chest. He had never looked more beautiful to her. She had never felt such an ache as she did now.

She licked her lips, trying to think of something to say. The action drew his eyes directly to her mouth. He let out a groan that had her insides tightening.

"Gods damn it," he muttered. Then his lips were on hers, his mouth crushing hers, his arms caging her against his solid body.

A tiny mewl of surprise broke free, swallowed up by his kiss.

She couldn't breathe—couldn't think.

His tongue swept in and she parted her lips on instinct. The way his tongue tangled with hers. This was a male who knew how to kiss, who knew how to take what he wanted and give in equal measure. Her nipples tightened beneath her top. The feel of fabric against them as they rubbed against his chest...

Oh, gods.

She was lost.

A draconic rumble vibrated between them. Reyr wrenched his mouth away, his lips already dark red and swollen. Hers would look much the same, though it would take them a little longer to heal back to their original state.

Reyr stared at her, his eyes bright with surprise. "You... That... I shouldn't have—"

"Don't you dare!" She was shocked by the demanding growl of her voice.

"Don't you dare say that was a mistake."

"Oh, it wasn't a mistake." Reyr stepped back, putting distance between them. He ran a hand through his wet hair, making it slick back.

"Then what is the problem?" she demanded. If anyone had a right to shut down their kiss, it was her, after how he'd treated her all those months. Even if his apology had been genuine.

"I had a million reasons why we shouldn't do this, but suddenly I can't remember a single one."

She snorted, stalking towards him. She discarded her pack along the way, letting it drop to the cave's floor with a wet thump. There was very little light to see by, just what the gray gloom at the entrance let in. "Then I don't see what the problem is."

With that, she pushed up on her tiptoes and kissed him again. If they were stuck in this cave for gods only knew how long, she may as well make the best of it. That started with his mouth. Who could say where it would end.

CHAPTER 19

BEING BROKEN

Kastali Dun

Saffra winced as the arrow clattered to the flagstones, the sound jarring in the otherwise morning quiet. "Try again." Bedelth's voice was calm, a direct opposite to how she felt. She made another attempt to nock an arrow, this time clumsily managing to get it in place. It was like trying to write with her opposite hand. Awkward and messy.

Praying the arrow would stay, she drew her arm back. The motion was jerky, not smooth like it should've been. The string went taut. She released. To no one's surprise whatsoever, the arrow went wide, sailing so far past the target it was comical. It flew out over the keep and out of sight.

Her shoulders dropped.

Bedelth muttered an incant, reaching out. Seconds later, the arrow returned, its momentum slowed enough that he caught it. "Again." He handed it to her.

She rocked her jaw, staring at him but refusing to take it. "This is pointless. We've been at it for over a week."

"And how long did it take you the first time?"

"Years." She sniffed. "But that's different. I didn't know

165

anything about the mechanics of bowmanship. Now I do. That gives me an advantage."

"You still cannot expect to master something like this in mere weeks."

"Or maybe, I've got a bad teacher," she snapped.

Instead of looking irritated by her insult, which had been her intention, Bedelth calmly set the arrow back in her quiver and bridged the distance between them. Pressing his front flush to her back, he took hold of her waist and bent down until his mouth brushed the shell of her ear. "Is that what I am? A bad teacher?"

"Clearly."

He made a humming sound, nipping at the lobe of her ear. It made her shiver. "Perhaps you are right. If I were a good one, I would not be doing this." He pressed a trail of open mouth kisses down the column of her neck that made her immediately forget her irritation. "I wouldn't distract you from the matter at hand. I wouldn't think about what you look like bare, without all this fabric in the way." His fists clenched in her gown. "I wouldn't be so distracted by the sight of you while I'm trying to teach you. Wouldn't be explaining the mechanics of nocking an arrow while thinking about what you taste like between your legs."

Her knees chose that moment to wobble, heat licking up her spine like fire catching dry tinder. "Oh, gods."

He tightened his hold on her before she could crumble, his mouth continuing to sweep up and down the column of her throat. "You're right. I'm a very, very bad teacher. But I'm too selfish to let you cast me aside. So I'm afraid you're stuck with me."

"Bedelth," she gasped as his hand made its way over the fabric of her skirts to cup between her legs. Oh, gods. She needed him.

As quickly as he'd begun, he stepped away, taking every ounce of his heat with him.

"Again. And this time, don't pull the bowstring so tight. It's a lighter draw weight for a reason. You're straining your arm too much."

"You... You expect me to—"

"I expect you to confront this the way you have confronted

everything in life. You are not a quitter, Saffra. Do not think you can cow me into giving up."

"You can't just...just *touch* me like that and then expect me to focus."

"Hmm." He turned to the chair beside him and flipped it around, straddling it and resting his arms along its back. "Think of it as part of the exercise."

"You're unbelievable," she muttered, her mood darkening. She half thought he would rescue her from this and offer her a way to forget all her troubles.

It didn't matter that they were in the queen's tower garden, which had become a popular place for everyone in their inner circle. Didn't matter that someone could have discovered them. Not in the heat of the moment, when all she wanted was a measure of relief. A distraction from the idea that she might never shoot properly again.

Sighing, she positioned her bow and went through the motions of knocking an arrow. Her bow arm shook—

"Stop." Bedelth was out of the chair in an instant, standing beside her. He moved to correct her position. "You cannot lock your bow arm. You know this."

"I know!" she growled, her irritation exploding. "You don't think I know that?"

"I know you do."

"It's... It's the only way I can hold it properly now that I've lost all my strength in that arm."

"Not all. But yes, I see your point." He moved her arm slightly, forcing her elbow to bend a bit more. "Try it like this, with me bracing you."

"I'm not sure what good that—"

"Humor me, Saffra."

"Fine," she groused. Gods. She was being insufferable. It didn't help that her tutor was her mate and that they were both stubborn.

Nocking her arrow again, she went through the motions, drawing the bowstring taught. With Bedelth's steady hands on her bad arm, holding it in place, it didn't shake and the slight bend in her elbow gave her more control.

"Good," he murmured. "Now release."

She did. The arrow flew true, landing just on the edge of the target.

A surprised laugh fell from her lips. "It worked. Well! All I need is you by my side, holding my arm so I can shoot. Wonderful."

"Your sarcasm isn't helping." He released her arm and blew out a breath. "We're done for the day."

"What?"

"You heard me. Collect your things. I have court shortly anyway."

"But... No. You go to court and I'll keep practicing."

"No."

"No? You think to control me?"

"I think to strongly advise you not to push this any further. Not today. There's something I would like to try with you, if you will trust me. Do you, Saffra? Do you trust me?"

All the fight went out of her, her shoulders dropping. She moved forward, pressing her forehead into his chest. "You know I do."

"Thank you." His arms came up around her, holding them together. "Leave this here, we'll try again tomorrow. Besides, you have plenty of other things to occupy your time this morning with all our bonding ceremony preparations. Didn't Des have a florist scheduled this morning?"

She jerked. "Oh, gods! I forgot. How could I forget?"

"Hmm... Let's see. Perhaps because this archery thing is eating you up inside? Come. You aren't late yet."

They gathered their things. Bedelth led her down into the king's tower and through the keep, dropping her off at the parlor where Desaree was waiting. He gave her a gentle kiss on her forehead before striding off. She watched his back retreat down the corridor, every step echoing in her bones. Strong. Steady. Unshakeable. She'd once thought of herself that way. She still wanted to.

With Talon and Koldis out of the city, and Dallin off on some secret mission most of them knew nothing about, Bedelth's duties had increased. She made it a point to update him on all the preparations each evening, and left any important decisions for that time, so that he could be included.

"How did it go?" Desaree asked.

"Horribly, if I'm being honest." They all knew she was trying to relearn archery with her opposite arm.

"At least your tutor is easy on the eyes."

That startled a burst of laughter out of her. "Yes. True. Though that isn't always a good thing." She thought of the way he'd distracted her. She'd purposefully tried to rile him and instead, he'd remained calm and returned the favor. Gods. Talon's shields were expert tacticians. It shouldn't have surprised her that he would handle their interaction so effortlessly.

Now she was left aching. That had probably been his plan all along. With him occupied most of the day...

"Let's just get this over with," she decided.

"Oh no you don't." Desaree took her shoulders, forcing their eyes to lock. "This is your bonding ceremony. You only get one. Some people dream of this kind of thing and don't ever get one, so you're not rushing through it or treating it like some unsavory task to be completed."

Her chest squeezed. "I... That was thoughtless, Des. I'm sorry. You're right."

Desaree would never get a ceremony with Verath. How could she behave like this, knowing that? Verath and Des loved each other. No one doubted it. But she wasn't his mate.

She often wondered if Des might have some kind of wedding instead, like what humans did, even if Verath was a drengr. Perhaps they could have some kind of hybrid of the two. It was on the tip of her tongue to suggest it when Jocelyn popped her head out of the parlor.

"Are you two coming? She's got everything all set up."

"Let's go," Des said.

What followed was an hour of discussions about which orange and white flowers would make the best bouquets and all the locations within the keep they would place them. There would be flowers in giant pots in the entry when guests passed through the portcullis. There would be flower garlands strung from some of the parapets. There would be flowers in the dining hall and throne room.

"And you can get everything sourced in time for our ceremony?"

"Of course, my lady." Evgenia made a few notes on the parchment she carried. "We have a number of flower farms. I have already informed them that a hold should be placed on the majority of their orange and white selections, to ensure we will have enough."

She eyed the collections on the nearby table. Evgenia had made a number of sample arrangements for her to assess. They were all beautiful combinations. She'd never considered flower arranging to be the art that it was, but it was clear that Evgenia had an expert hand at it, giving her a whole new appreciation.

Claire's bonding ceremony hadn't stuck to a set of colors. She could have done black but there weren't a lot of options, and so they'd gone with every color. It had been absolutely beautiful. Her decision to highlight Bedelth's scales was a conscious one.

"There now, I think that is everything I need." Evgenia made a final flourish of notes on her parchment and looked up. "Do you have any more questions for me?"

"None, I think." Desaree threw Saffra a glance to confirm. She shook her head. "Excellent. Thank you, Evgenia. I am confident you will handle these matters perfectly. Once the final date is set, we will be sure to notify you so that you have plenty of time to source everything."

"Excellent, my dears." She hesitated. "I'd rather not carry all of these out of here."

"Oh, good!" Jocelyn clapped her hands together in delight, then pressed her lips between her teeth to calm herself.

"We would be more than happy to enjoy these arrangements."

"Wonderful, they're yours," the florist said, beaming. "I've got all I need, then."

"I can escort you out," Jocelyn offered. The keep could be properly confusing to those who weren't used to its many corridors and courtyards.

"Thank you." Evgenia bowed and swept from the room, leaving Saffra with the faint scent of marigolds and a strange tightness in her chest. This was really happening.

She cleared her throat and said, "Do you think Leah will want a few?"

"Oh I think she'd love that. Let's surprise her and place them in her room."

"Great. I'd like to save that one for Bedelth. It will look perfect on his table."

They summoned a few servants to help them carry everything. The servants oohed and awed over the gorgeous arrangements. And since they had a few extra, they sent them off with arrangements of their own to enjoy.

By the end of it, her mood had remarkably improved.

When she found herself alone in her room, she took a seat out on the balcony to look out over the sea. The same sea that just last year, had been dotted with enemy ships, intent on capturing the city. They had lost many lives. Drengr, rider, and human alike.

For all the grief she carried over the loss of archery, she had so much to be grateful for. She had her life. Her mate. And soon, they would celebrate their bond with all of her closest friends. Her archery wasn't her identity. She needed to remember that. Just as being a seer wasn't her identity.

If she had to find new pursuits, she would. But Bedelth was right. She wasn't a quitter. She owed it to herself to keep trying, and she would.

A flock of seagulls caught her attention, swooping down towards the waves. She leaned forward to watch them, catching sight of a gull that moved a little funny. It took a moment to realize part of its wing was missing, causing it to fly slightly lopsided.

Her chest squeezed with a pang.

The seagull stuck with its comrades, flittering about in the waves below. It dove under the surface then reappeared, a small fish in its mouth. The sight of its success brought a smile to her lips. Even with a dysfunctional wing, the bird still managed to fly and eat. Being broken wasn't an end, it was simply the beginning of a different kind of strength. She promised herself that she would remember that from now on.

CHAPTER 20
THE SNAKE'S SHADOW

Kastali Dun

Dallin followed the female servant upstairs, stopping before a door halfway down the hallway. "Just a moment," she said, giving the door a quick rap before slipping inside. He nodded to each of the guards bracketing the door. The servant popped her head back out. "He'll see you now."

"Thank you." She nodded and slipped back out, hurrying down the hall.

He went inside, his shrewd gaze making note of everything in quick succession. The apartment was less elaborate than he'd expected. Spacious, yes, with a sitting area, work space with a desk, and a sleeping chamber through another doorway. There were rugs, but they were shabby, and vases with faded paint. The paintings looked like they'd been picked more for coverage than beauty. Wall sconces cast everything in a mix of light and shadow.

He'd expected gilded statues for all the coin King Cobra pulled in with the jobs he ran.

"Ah, you're here." Cobra sat forward, stroking his pet snake as it coiled around his arm. He'd since learned that the snake's name was Sable and it was female. "Blaise, Nighthawk, we're done here. Please ensure you do not disappoint me."

"Never, boss." Blaise and Nighthawk stood. They nodded in greeting before passing by. He'd worked a couple jobs with them since moving in with Cobra's crew.

"Come. Sit, please." He quickly complied. "Can I get you something to drink?"

"No, thank you."

One thing he'd quickly learned was the value Cobra placed on manners. He wore words like 'please' and 'thank you' as a snakeskin to disguise the venom beneath. While the crew didn't display manners towards each other, they did for their boss.

"Very well. I thought we were due for a chat."

"Of course." The back of his neck prickled. He'd been with the Serpent Syndicate for nearly a week, had done several jobs with them, integrating himself into their ranks in much the same way he'd done with Martel's team at the Righteous Rose. So he'd been waiting for a moment like this. Waiting for Cobra to seek him out.

"You're settling in to my den?"

"Well enough."

"Yes, very good." Cobra stroked Sable again.

"I've kept an eye on you—just one, mind. You've got spine. I admire that in a meal, or a man. I'd hoped to give you longer to integrate. To prove yourself. I prefer to let matters uncoil naturally, see. But there's a big meeting coming, and I want you at my back for it."

Dallin sat up straighter. "You're promoting me?"

Cobra hummed. "Think of it as a probationary trial. You do good at this meeting, and I'll pull you in full time."

A shiver of satisfaction raced down his spine. He was more than eager to get a move on with this mission. It had been far too long since he'd been up to the castle. Far too long since he'd seen Jamie, not that he didn't think about him too often for his own good.

"When is the meeting?" he found himself asking.

"Tonight." Cobra's gaze was intense, assessing.

He knew better than to ask what the meeting was for. He

recalled Cobra's words to Mek. The people in Cobra's crew were paid to follow orders. They didn't ask questions unless it was to seek clarification on a job.

"I'll be ready."

"Good. See yourself out." Cobra turned back to his snake, effectively dismissing him.

He returned to his room to plan. He frowned at the open door. He was certain he'd shut it earlier. Cautious, he pushed it the rest of the way open and stepped inside. His eyes darted over the space. It wasn't much bigger than his room at the Righteous Rose. The amenities were the same: a bed, set of drawers, a bedside table, and a chair in the corner. A worn rug underfoot and a few drab paintings on the wall was the only warmth it offered. His eyes landed on his pillow. Quietly, he shut the door behind him and strode across the room. There was a small slip of parchment waiting.

When he read it, his blood chilled.

I KNOW *who you are and what game you're playing.*

HIS FIRST INSTINCT was to reach out to King Talon. If someone had discovered his identity, the whole mission could be in peril. And yet, whoever this was hadn't gone straight to Cobra. If they thought he was playing a game, they clearly wanted in.

He could reach out to Verath, seek his mentor's advice. Yet, something held him back. A need to prove himself. To do this on his own.

The game wasn't up yet.

He crumbled the note in his hand. Whoever it was, they'd show themselves eventually. He already had his own suspicions as to who it might be, but he'd have to wait.

Perhaps he'd picked up a thing or two over the last week. Snakes were patient. They struck only when they were sure of their prey.

Did that mean he was becoming more ingrained in the Serpent Syndicate than was wise?

No.

He whispered a word of magic, incinerating the note. The heat was a warm welcome to his skin. Seconds later, ash flaked to the floor.

He needed to become like the enemy he intended to eliminate, and that meant becoming a serpent. As much as he hated the idea, it was necessary. He just hoped he could end this—end Cobra—before the syndicate's venomous teeth sank too deeply into his skin.

THE MEETING, as it turned out, was held in an underground croft below one of the warehouses near the docks. It had a damp, musky feel to it. Only a few torches cast pools of yellow light.

He followed Cobra in to the meeting, staying close on his heels. The epitome of a perfect guard. They were the last to arrive at the long, rectangular table. A table that barely fit in the room. They'd brought a few of their crew, bigger men good for fighting, should they need back-up. They were left to wait just outside the door, squeezing together in the corridor.

Dallin recognized some of the faces at the table, waiting for Cobra to take his seat. Cobra was methodical about it, moving like a snake. He took up a protective stance at Cobra's back. Other personal guards had already done the same.

"Ah. I see you've gotten yourself a new guard," one of the men at the table said to Cobra. "Heard he was one of yours, Martel."

"Indeed, he was." Martel's assessing gaze landed on him. He gave a nod of respect to his old crew leader, hoping to diffuse some of the sudden tension. Martel didn't return it. "It looks like he's settling in nicely with the Serpents. Only a week and he's already in a position of power."

"He's shown teeth," said Cobra. "I respect that."

"Indeed." Martel ran a hand down his face with feigned thoughtfulness. "You know who's *not* settling in well?"

"No," one of the other men groused, "but I'm sure you'll enlighten us anyway."

"But certainly." Martel smiled. "That king's new guard. What's his name? Dallin or some such? Heard he hasn't been seen at the keep in weeks. Some folks say he's gone...missing. Doesn't sound like *he's* settling in that well."

Martel's eyes locked with his, sparking with challenge, as if waiting for him to react. What did he think he'd do? Transform here and now? He wasn't some juvenile incapable of controlling his urges.

"Never cared much for the king's business, myself," one of the men said, clearly uninterested in this latest gossip. "Too much drama."

"That's rather unwise of you, Bullseye." Cobra stroked his sleeve. Sable was hiding within. "After all, the tighter the coil, the sweeter the surrender." The occupants immediately settled down. Cobra's words, more often than not, had a sinister effect on those around him. "Now, let's move on to business, shall we?"

Martel's gaze continued to dwell on him. He dismissed the crew leader, letting his stare go blank on the opposite wall. It wasn't as if he feared the man. He could crush him in an instant. But he did worry about what it meant for his mission. He wouldn't put it past Martel to pull Cobra aside at the conclusion of this meeting.

Cobra reached into his coat and drew out a narrow ledger bound in black snake hide. The spine crackled as he opened it, pages covered in precise, curling script. He set it on the table and, with a fountain pen of tarnished gold, began making neat little notations as each leader spoke.

From his position just behind Cobra's chair, he caught a glimpse of the entries. Some of them made little sense, others too much.

"Anyone have anything pressing they'd like to report?" Cobra's gaze settled on the table's occupants.

A woman with dark hair and a fang strung about her neck, spoke up. "The magistrate in Goldrow's gettin' skittish. Wants double for lookin' the other way. Says we're bringing too much heat."

Cobra's fountain pen scratched. The line entry read, *Goldrow: M—50d/"favor" doubled. replace?* He didn't look up as he said, "Does he want double, or does he want out?"

A pause.

Another man grunted. "Could be both."

Cobra sighed, the sound almost affectionate. "Then we give him a vacation. A permanent one, if need be. See to it Finley, but quietly."

"Yes, sir." Finley gave a cooperative nod.

Cobra made a strikethrough of his previous note, the action a deliberate flourish. The room was silent but for the soft scratch of pen on parchment as more notes flowed. Cobra spoke again, his tone light but eyes sharp. "And the shipment from Oshea?"

As he asked, he penned another line, *Oshean heathroot—new batch in via pier 6. Too hot for Hollow distros?*

Dallin's stomach tightened at the reference to Oshea. Imports from the east were still flowing through, even after the dust had begun to settle in the wake of Kane's rule.

"Three crates landed at Pier Six two nights past. Sealed and marked. Old symbols—Oshea's, still being used."

Dallin's jaw clenched. He didn't know what Heathroot was, but he'd heard rumors of a new drug circulating that gave people added energy. Plenty of laborers would be desperate for longer hours to earn extra pay, even if it turned to addiction and even death.

Cobra flipped a page, writing something in shorthand he couldn't decipher. "Let's distribute through Hollow District first, see if the taste still sells. If the healers start sniffing, burn the rest."

"It will be done," one of the occupants answered.

Sparks danced in Dallin's eyes as he watched the blind devotion to which everyone behaved. They dared not object to any of Cobra's orders. His rule here was absolute.

The meeting continued on in much the same way, Cobra going down the list of his ledger, making notes and asking questions. This was the first time he'd gotten a real understanding of just how much influence and reach Cobra had. It was frightening. His fingers itched to snatch the ledger and take it straight to the keep. How much evidence could they find to condemn these gangs? It was no wonder Talon wanted him eliminated. He just needed to figure out how to do it. Quietly.

Now that he was in a better position within the syndicate, he would pay careful attention to Cobra's day to day schedule. There was sure to be a time when the syndicate's leader isolated himself.

A few people chuckled, making Dallin blink and come back to himself. Cobra smiled faintly and reached up to stroke Sable's pale head as she slithered lazily around his neck. "That is our cue, I'm afraid. Sable gets testy when she's hungry. Let us take our leave."

With those words, Cobra brought about a quick end to the meeting.

Chairs scraped as the others began to stand. Cobra was quick to rise. He dismissed himself before everyone else, striding out. Dallin fell into step behind him, eager to put as much distance between himself and Martel as possible.

The other crew members who'd accompanied them followed, keeping close but not too close. Not enough to be suffocating. "Ah. A nice night, is it not?" Cobra strolled casually along the docks as they made their way towards home base. "What do you say, my sweet?" He lifted his sleeve. Sable stuck her head out, tongue flicking the air.

Dallin bit down on his teeth, tearing his gaze away. If he hadn't looked away just when he did, he might have missed the glint of metal, the sparkle of it as it sailed through the air, end over end. His hand shot out and he snatched the dagger by the hilt, his body rotating with the momentum. There was a beat of silence. Then their crew began shouting orders. Several of them rushed off to investigate the darkened alley.

"Sir, are you all right?" Dallin immediately turned to Cobra.

"Fine. Thanks to you."

"Ah. Looks as though someone was trying to assassinate you." The sound of Martel's voice materialized beside them. There were a few other meeting attendees who had also been walking in the same direction. They hung back to observe. "Lucky you should have such a...*quick* guard at your disposal."

"I don't believe in luck," Cobra said, unruffled as ever. "You've been paying Wasp a lot of attention this evening, Martel. Do not think I have missed it. One would think you are suspicious of him. Or do you dislike that he chose to work for me."

"I would never try to withhold an asset you wished to acquire, sir."

"Smart man. Then you are suspicious of him?" Cobra's gaze on Martel was one of cool assessment. When Martel did not give an answer, Cobra said, "A viper does not hiss without cause, but neither does it strike its own tail. If there was any reason to suspect Wasp's loyalty, it has been shattered this night. Let me see that knife."

Dallin handed it over, ignoring Martel's penetrating gaze. His heart beat a little harder in his chest. They were out in the open, with more than a few onlookers. If Martel chose this moment to voice his suspicions, there would be few options available to him.

The last thing he wanted was to disappoint Talon.

Cobra hummed in consideration, turning the dagger over in his hand. Sable had long since retreated back up his sleeve.

A few of their crew returned. "No sign of anyone, sir. We checked the alley and neighboring streets."

"I did not expect it," Cobra murmured. "Here, Blaise, take this and see if you can discover where it came from."

"Of course, sir."

"Martel, good night to you. Wasp, let's go." It was a command to follow.

He turned to leave, but not before Martel pressed something into his palm. The action was too quick to notice, but as he made his way back to The Tacky Stag, he fisted the bit of parchment Martel had passed him. He wasn't sure what it would say, but if it was anything like the note he'd received earlier today, it wouldn't be good.

"That was quick work on your part," Cobra said. "Once again, you prove your mettle."

"Just doing my job, sir."

"And a good job at that."

"How are you not more unsettled? A second later, that dagger would have embedded in your skull."

"You think an open blade unsettles me? I've slithered through worse dens than this, and I still came out with venom to spare."

The response shouldn't have bothered him and yet, it did. He repeated those words as they entered The Tacky Stag, as he said goodnight to the others and made his way to his room. Cobra's calm collection bothered him. It made him feel like the man was always three steps ahead. If there was anything good to come of tonight, at least he'd have less reason to doubt Dallin now that he'd proven his worth. Especially after the way Martel had behaved. That man had grown all the more suspicious.

Locking the door behind him, he leaned against it, breathing. When he was ready, he lifted his fist and opened the note.

～

YOU'RE NOT *the only one with secrets. Midnight. Righteous Rose. Come alone—or I start talking.*

～

IT WAS the same handwriting as before. This time, he knew he had no choice but to act.

CHAPTER 21
SOULS LOCKED AND BOUND

Claire fidgeted on the spriten throne. Her latest gift, a massive bouquet of glowing purple flowers was placed out of the way, on a side table with the other gifts she'd received. She'd been at this all day, holding court. It was different from how court was held in Kastali Dun. In the capital, it was mostly grievances and matters of law to be settled. In the forest, sprites often managed to settle things among themselves. Sitting here was more a matter of formality. Mostly, it was accepting the respect each patron offered, which included gifts.

It had been four days since she'd said goodbye to the king tree with Feowen and Taylynn. They'd only just arrived last night, enjoying their time together as they traveled through the forest. Before bidding her goodnight, Taylynn had insisted she sit on the throne first thing the next morning. "Your people haven't seen you for months. They wish to pay their respects," she'd chided. So, here she was, wondering what in the name of all the gods she would do with so many gifts.

This had happened the last time too, when she'd returned with Talon. The difference was, Kane had been alive and she'd needed the support from her spriten people on her quest to defeat him. Now he was gone.

She'd never meant to hold the throne for so long.

It was time to return home, to Kastali Dun, but before she could do that, the crown had to pass to Taylynn. Only, she hadn't seen the princess since last night. Had Taylynn scampered off somewhere to avoid the inevitable? What was the requirement to abdicate, anyway? Did she simply throw up her hands and say, "I quit?" Or was there some kind of formal ceremony? She almost snorted. Knowing the sprites, there'd be a ceremony.

The murmur of voices picked up. An aisle formed, allowing a group of sprites to pass. It took only a second for her to realize who they were.

"You're here?!" she gasped, shooting to her feet.

Feowen froze beside the dais, his eyes locked on the woman he loved. "Jeanine," he breathed.

Claire was down the dais in a blink, racing across the crystal floor, her ethereal gown swishing around her legs. She came to an abrupt halt as the group fanned out. Feowen quickly formed rank beside them until all eight of her guards stood in a rigid row. As one, they saluted her formally before bowing.

Her mouth opened and closed, a wash of emotions flooding her. They were here—alive and unharmed after all that had transpired in the capital when she'd vanished. She couldn't help but glance past them, wishing, *hoping* that Talon was there with them. But she didn't feel him in her mind the way she ought to. She would have felt their bond flare to life—felt his presence if he was in the forest. Instead, the forest's magic continued to work, maintaining the barrier between them.

She wouldn't let her disappointment over his absence darken this moment. "Rise, please!"

They moved as one. It was at that moment that she caught sight of Miera and Selphie lurking in the background. They came forward when she motioned to them.

"Well met, all of you!" she said in Ednuar, grinning widely. Then, before she could stop herself, she launched herself at them, hugging each of her guards and handmaidens in turn. It was very undignified. Especially when a small sob of joy passed her lips at the sight of Jeanine. "Talon's only a couple of days behind us," her friend whispered.

"What?!" she gasped.

"He and Koldis departed with us, but we had the unicorns so we reached the forest sooner. They should reach the forest any time now."

"How?! How is it you're here? The unicorns?"

"Taylynn sent for us. We received her missive days ago."

"She did?" Claire straightened, glancing around as if she expected Taylynn to step out of the shadows. That meddling female! Of course she'd already set her plans in motion. It shouldn't have surprised her.

She glanced at Feowen, who hadn't taken his eyes off Jeanine. She all but snorted at the hungry expression he wore. "You have my permission to greet her, you know. Don't hold back on my account."

Feowen's expression flickered, a war between propriety and desire. Desire gave in as he broke rank and reached for Jeanine, catching her up in his arms. Jeanine squealed. Their mouths were locked by the time he set her back on her feet.

Claire took a step back, addressing the rest of the hall in Ednuar. "Court is dismissed. Thank you for all the wonderful gifts. Please, have a lovely day."

With that, she strode from the giant hall, leaving the crystal palace behind. "Where are you going?" Feowen cried, jogging to catch up to her. Behind her, her guards formed ranks.

"I'm going to get my mate."

"There are emissaries waiting to escort him to Esterpine when he reaches the forest," Jeanine informed her.

"That's all good and well, but I'm going regardless."

There was a snort. She thought she heard someone mutter *mates* under their breath. She didn't turn to see which guard it was. Let them tease all they wanted.

If they had a problem with turning around and retracing their steps, they didn't voice a single complaint.

SHE FELT it the moment Talon breached the barrier and stepped into the forest. The swell of their minds melding together again. A gasp slipped from her lips and she staggered sideways. Feowen was there to catch her, gripping her shoulders as he straightened her.

As if the forest had sensed her eagerness, it had turned a two day journey into half that. They'd been waiting mere hours near the mouth of the forest just beyond Ellia outpost.

She raced down the path, rounding a particularly large tree—and there he was. She barely registered the presence of others. Koldis beside him, an envoy of guides ready to lead him to Esterpine.

Their eyes locked, minds locked, souls locked—bound together by fate and love.

She couldn't move as thoughts and images flowed between them faster than light. He saw everything in a brief instant—Kane's defeat, Cyrus's final death, the magic she'd worked to break Isabella's curse. All of it.

She saw all of him, too. The pain he'd grappled with in her absence, not knowing if she was truly okay. The heavy burdens he'd faced as he set out to heal their kingdom. The late night meetings. The number of missives that kept him tied to his desk.

"Claire." Her name was a desperate plea.

She broke free of the emotions freezing her in place and sprinted to him. She launched herself at him. He huffed as he caught her up in his arms, staggering back a step. Her legs wrapped around his waist. Then she was kissing him everywhere. His forehead, his eyes and nose, his cheeks, his chin, the corner of his mouth. Every scar that had become dear to her.

When their mouths crashed together, a burst of fireworks exploded in her chest. She gasped, kissing him harder. His tongue was desperate as it parted her lips and slid between them. Their kiss was messy and beautiful in equal measure.

Her stomach hollowed out as desire built a nest in her core. Talon inhaled—his draconic senses picking up on the scent of her need—then growled a low warning.

A throat cleared. Koldis. "Shall we just leave you to your passion, then? I, for one, would like to find my mate."

She pulled back slightly, smiling against Talon's lips, keeping her eyes locked with his. The silver had changed, swallowing up the whites of his eyes, while his pupils had morphed into draconic slits. She knew his control was tenuous. Were it not for their audience, he would have taken her against the nearest tree. "Careful," he warned as the image invaded both their minds. "Do not tempt me, *mate.*"

She trapped her bottom lip between her teeth, holding back a breathy moan as she freed her legs and slid down his body, feeling the hard ridge of him against her as she did. Gods, she needed him. *Right now.*

But she was a queen, and queens had more control than that.

Turning to Koldis, she took him in. They shared a silent smile before she opened her arms in invitation. "Come here, you menace."

He chuckled, then offered himself to her. She wrapped him in a tight hug as he lifted her off the ground. "You are well?" she asked.

"As well as can be expected. Better, once I set eyes on my mate."

"I know the feeling," she mused. "Well then, let us not delay, yes?"

"I would appreciate it." He kissed the top of her head as he set her on her feet.

She didn't tell him that before they'd left, Taylynn had been nowhere to be found. Something told her that the princess knew very well that Koldis was here. She would show herself when she chose.

To the envoys, she said, "*Shalaya. Mi bei darmah sasam. Skailah eah ayas stoloah.*" Letting them know she had no need of them and that they may return to their post. They bowed and thanked her, retreating.

Their journey back to the city took two days. She reined in her frustration, wondering if the king tree had done it on purpose. Talon never left her side. It was as if he couldn't bear to be without her touch for more than a moment, keeping her hand firmly in his. She half expected him to join her whenever she slipped away to see to her needs, but fortunately he didn't. Not that he was ever truly apart from her, not with the bond they shared.

They spoke very little aloud. It wasn't necessary when their minds could cover topics much faster. *"It kills me that you had to bear the loss of Cyrus all over again—and alone for so many days,"* he admitted.

It had nearly killed her, losing Cyrus for a second time. Talon hated that she hadn't had his support to help her through it. Hated not being there for her when it had happened. But he was here now, and he would grieve beside her. They would heal together.

She hadn't told Koldis yet. The king wanted to tell all his shields together. It would be easier that way.

The only thing Talon hadn't yet seen was the news she was keeping to herself. For now. She'd buried it deep in the one place she swore she wouldn't hide from him again. But it was only until they could be alone. She wanted all of his joy all to herself. Besides, she wasn't one-hundred-percent certain. There were no pregnancy tests in Dragonwall. She wasn't sure what methods were needed to determine something like this. Did she simply wait until she missed too many periods? Surely there was another way.

Taylynn, unsurprisingly, materialized before the gateway into the city. Koldis let out a whoosh of breath before striding over to her. He didn't give her time to pull away as he captured her mouth in a crushing kiss. Claire pressed her lips between her teeth, fighting a smile. Call her a hopeless romantic, but it made her heart so happy to see other people getting to experience the same kind of love she and Talon shared. Especially when it was someone she cared about.

"Well, I think we ought to give them privacy," Feowen said,

attempting to continue into the city as he walked past the two love birds.

"Not so fast." Taylynn pulled back, making Koldis grumble with irritation.

Claire half snorted. The drengr were such a broody, possessive bunch.

"We must discuss what comes next—for all of us."

"Surely it can wait," Koldis said. "We've barely just arrived."

Taylynn shot him an exasperated look. "There is the matter of Claire's abdication—my ascension to the throne."

"So...you aren't trying to avoid it?" Claire hedged.

Taylynn sighed. Sometimes she looked so very ancient. The expression on her face left Koldis frowning. "It can no longer be avoided. You are Dragonwall's queen. Much as I wish to pin this on you, our people will not be content with an absent queen. Moreover, the forest needs its queen here to be truly strong and healthy."

Koldis's hand tightened in Taylynn's. Claire knew that he hated this part. Hated knowing that he and Taylynn would never have a traditional relationship. But she also knew it was a sacrifice he was willing to make for the sake of their bond.

"I'm ready to abdicate," she said, feeling Talon relax beside her.

"Good. Ceremony preparations are already underway. Spend today recovering from your journey," she said to the others. "Because tomorrow will be a long day."

"A long day, how?" Talon asked.

Taylynn pressed her lips together, hesitant. "Our people are insisting on a day of celebration, followed by a ball to end the night. Much has happened, Your Majesty. Kane has been defeated, balance restored, and a new queen for the spriten throne. That warrants proper recognition, don't you think?"

"I suppose," Talon grumbled, glancing at his mate. Claire only squeezed his hand in reassurance. If the king could have things his way, he'd take her away somewhere private and keep her all to himself for the next week, preferably the beautiful cottage in Ashvale.

"Not a half bad idea," he told her.

But the reality was, there wasn't time to lounge around in each other's arms. There was still too much to be done to heal the king-dom. Too many duties back in the capital awaiting them.

"You knew I would need to get back soon, that's why you orchestrated all this," she said to the princess.

"Yes, I had a feeling that once you went back to the capital, I would be hard pressed to get you back here anytime soon. The forest needs its queen, and much as I am unenthused about taking the crown, my duty will always be to the health and happiness of this place."

"Is there anything I must do to prepare?"

"Nothing at all, beyond showing up tomorrow."

"Then I will be there. Now, come." She tugged on Talon's hand, leading him through the archway into Esterpine.

TALON CARESSED HER BARE SKIN, tracing circles over her marks as he held her close. His touch was tender, yet laden with the emotion they shared. They were tangled in the sheets of her bed within the crystal palace. The room was quiet save for their heavy breathing in the aftermath of what they'd shared. After returning, they'd promptly retreated to the privacy of her suite where he'd quickly divested her of her clothes before sinking into her. They'd spent the past three hours reaffirming their love for each other over and over.

She felt heavy and sated and had no plans to get up anytime soon. "There's no need," Talon murmured against her before kissing the top of her head.

"We'll have to eat eventually."

"I'm perfectly content to enjoy you as a snack until then."

He began nibbling along her neck, making a laugh burst from her chest. "Talon," she groaned. "Mercy. Please! I cannot go another round. Not yet."

"Just relax, I'll do all the work."

"Talon!" she cried again, gripping his face to keep him from going lower. There were things they needed to discuss first, now that the joy of their reunion had calmed.

"What is it?" He came alert, already sensing the turmoil within her mind.

"I… I didn't show you everything when you arrived," she admitted. His throat bobbed, eyes darting down to her belly. She tensed. "Wait, you know?"

"That you are carrying our child? I suspected," he breathed.

"How?" She tried to search his mind but he began to speak again.

"I cannot explain it. I sensed it the moment you were in my arms two days ago. You smell different, like your scent has changed. At first, I thought it might be the loss of Cyrus. But I can feel something just here." He placed a hand over her belly.

"Then… I really am pregnant?"

"Yes." He pulled back to look at her. "And… You are okay with this? After everything we have been through?"

She studied him for a long moment, feeling the weight of their shared history, the pain of their losses, the joy of their reunion. Her heart ached, but it was a warm ache. One that whispered of new beginnings. "I cannot tell you what the future will hold, but we'll face it together. After what we've been through, we can handle anything. So, yes. I'm okay with this."

His lips curved into a slow, joyful smile. She realized in that moment, searching inside his mind, that he had been withholding his emotions, fearful of clouding and overpowering her own. He wanted to make sure she was ready for this. He hadn't wanted to influence her decision. "I don't doubt any of what you've said. We will face this together."

"Together," she echoed. She shifted, coming up to her knees so that she could be at eye level with him. "I… I just wish Cyrus was here to share this with us. I know he is finally at peace. A peace he deserves. But I'll miss him."

"He would be so happy for us," Talon murmured, sadness

coloring his voice. "But think of it this way, the fates took his loss and in return, gave you something beautiful."

Tears sprang to her eyes, one of them falling free. "I was thinking the same thing."

"*Mih cralla.*" His expression crumbled to one of devastated joy. He finally let the full force of his emotions free. "I am beyond happy in this moment. I want to beat my chest and roar to the heavens. I've gotten my mate with child. There is nothing more fulfilling for a male like me, than to fill your belly with my young."

She let out a sob mixed with a laugh at his possessive words. A drengr through and through. He chuckled and pulled her onto his lap so that she was straddling him. "Did you expect anything less of me?"

"Never."

Their mouths crashed together and she found that he was already hard and ready beneath her. Perhaps she had just enough energy to go another round. His fingers tangled in her hair until her head was pulled back and she was held captive to his mouth as it traced a hot path down her throat. His teeth paused over her pulse point, beating rapidly. "I'm going to take you over and over until you are drowning in pleasure. Just need to make sure the baby takes, you know?"

A breathy laugh escaped her lips. "I'm not sure that's how it works, darling," she said.

"Let me have my fun." With that, he positioned her over him, sliding in deep. Then he made good on every word.

Kastali Dun

Dallin slipped into the Righteous Rose three minutes to midnight. He pulled the hood of his cloak back and was immediately met by several whoops. "Wasp!" Greedy Remy was out of his chair in a flash, the portly man moving over to whack him affectionately on the back. He stank of ale. "Thought you were too good for the likes of us, eh? Haven't come ta visit 'til now."

"Never too good for the likes of you, Remy." He looked at the others offering nods of greeting. They were gathered around their usual booth in the back, the evidence of a card game in full swing. Steve was there, and Fast Fingers, too. He didn't see Jester, confirming his previous suspicions that someone had quietly gotten rid of him after his initial meeting with Cobra.

"Come have a drink with us," Spindle called.

"We're about to deal a new hand," Ratcatcher added.

Martel appeared in the corridor, his face shadowed, and signaled for him to follow.

"No time for cards or drinks this night," he said, offering them a salute. "Sorry friends. Got business with Crazy Eyes."

A few groans followed in his wake.

He entered Martel's office to find the man already sitting behind the desk, his chair leaned back, hands folded over his trim stomach. He hesitated, then strode forward and sat in the empty chair across from him. They stared at one another.

It was Martel who broke the silence. "You know what I like about you, *Wasp*? You're clever and adaptable. You listen more than you talk. That's rare around here."

Dallin remained silent.

Martel's lips curled. "I've been watching you. Noticed pretty early on that you're not here for coin or power. You're too clean. Too precise. Like a soldier in disguise. That got me thinking. Digging. It's not hard to guess who you're working for." Martel leaned forward, placing his elbows on the desk. "Anyway, I think we might have something in common, you and me."

Dallin lifted his brows. "And what's that?"

There was a long pause, and then, "I don't like the way Cobra runs things. He's got more power than any one man should have. He's too cruel. Too...dark. Plays with knives like they're toys and people like they're rats, his own prey to be consumed."

"What is this then, a proposal?"

"Something like that." Martel smiled again, all teeth and careful calculation. Dallin waited. "When Cobra's body grows cold on a brothel bed and the dust settles, I want to know who will take his throne."

Dallin suppressed a shiver at Martel having so easily guessed what he was about.

King Talon wanted a quiet death for Cobra, something that couldn't be traced back to his rulership. He'd hoped that by eliminating Cobra, the rest of the syndicate would fall. But Dallin was already doubting that. He'd seen the way Cobra structured things. The way he'd delegated power. The moment he fell, someone would step into his place. Perhaps they wouldn't be as cruel or calculative, but they'd still have enough skill to lead, or else they wouldn't seize the opportunity.

Cutting the head off the snake didn't always mean the body

followed. They'd hoped it would. But in this case, he wasn't so sure.

As if reading his mind, Martel said, "Whoever takes over, it ought to be someone who understands quiet power, someone who won't turn this city into a slaughterhouse."

It shouldn't have surprised him that Martel wanted to throw his hat into the ring. "You assume too much."

"What can I say, I'm a man of assumptions. And leverage." Martel slid something across the desk. A folded bit of parchment. He was getting sick of Martel's missives. "Think of this as...insurance. A name. One that would interest you in your...pursuit."

Dallin reached for it. Martel leaned back, watching him.

He didn't open it, instead slipping it into his pocket.

Martel gave him a tight smile. "We need not agree to anything tonight. Just know that I am not your enemy. Not unless you make me one."

"I'll think over what you have said." He stood, giving the man a curt nod.

Martel had taken a gamble tonight, inviting him here. Knowing what he was—a king's shield. Knowing Dallin could have slit his throat and slipped out the back.

Instead, he left the crew leader alive and slipped out the back with the knowledge that his secret was not as secret as he'd hoped. In the darkness of the alley, he removed the slip of parchment. It was a single name. *Collier*.

It sparked a memory, one that set a new plan in motion.

With the use of the secret passages, he slipped into the castle. His cloak shielded his face. He could have removed it now that he was here. After what Martel had hinted at the other day, the fact that he hadn't been seen around the palace in some time, that people had noticed his absence, didn't bode well. Especially not since it allowed Martel to draw his own conclusions. But it was late, well past midnight, and most of the keep's occupants were asleep anyway.

Before he realized it, he found his feet taking a familiar path. A pair of guards passed, throwing him suspicious looks. He waited until they rounded the corner, then doubled back, stopping outside Jamie's door. A pale glow seeped from beneath it. Why wasn't he abed at this hour?

Pulling his lower lip between his teeth, he hesitated and then knocked. There was a long pause, and then the sound of bare feet on the floor before the latch clicked. The door swung open to reveal Jamie's narrowed eyes.

"Dallin? What...?"

He pushed through without an invitation, eager to get out of the corridor at this hour. Truthfully, he wasn't sure when the guards on patrol would return to this corridor. The last thing he needed was suspicious talk. The sight of a cloaked stranger on Jamie's doorstep at an unsavory hour.

He pulled the hood of his cloak back, revealing his face.

"It's the middle of the night," Jamie said.

"Astute observation. I wouldn't have knocked had I not seen your light."

"Well, I'm glad you did." Jamie snapped his mouth shut as soon as the words were out. A flush crept across his cheeks and he cleared his throat, massaging the back of his neck.

Dallin's gaze zeroed in on his hand. His fingers were stained. "What are you...?" His words died as his gaze darted over to the desk, cluttered with pages upon pages filled with neat, precise writing. His feet were moving before he thought better of it.

"No!" Jamie rushed forward and quickly began collecting up the pages.

"What's the matter? What is it?" He tried to peer around Jamie's shoulder.

"Nothing." Jamie shoved the pages in a drawer and slammed it shut.

"Got some letters to write?" Except they hadn't quite looked like letters.

"Something like that."

"Oh, come on. You can tell me."

Jamie pulled his lower lip between his teeth. Dallin had to look away rather than bear the sight of it.

"What if you laugh?"

"Why would I laugh?"

"I don't know." Jamie sounded hesitant. He marched over to the nearest sofa and threw himself down upon it. Vexed.

"Come on, Jamie. Please. You don't have to hide anything from me." In fact, he rather loved the idea of Jamie sharing literally everything with him.

"Fine. If you must know. I've been doing a lot of reading since I got here, and anyway, lately I've felt rather inspired."

"From reading?"

"Yes, from reading!" When Dallin arched a brow in question, Jamie sighed. "I have all these...stories in my head. You know? I thought...well, it's pretty stupid actually. But after all that happened with me and Mikkin. And the dwargs. The Stone Road. All that. Thought I might try my hand at storytelling. I've always loved stories."

"Storytelling..." There had been pages upon pages of words he'd shoved into that desk drawer. His eyes widened. "You're writing a book!" It was completely unexpected. And yet, the moment the idea struck, he could see it perfectly.

"I don't... I'm not sure... It's just a few stories, that's all."

"Stories you plan to turn into a book...?" His eyes immediately darted to the bookshelf packed with tomes.

Jamie lifted a shoulder, averting his gaze. "Maybe."

"Can I read it—what you've written so far?"

"No!"

Suddenly, he wanted nothing more than to race over to the desk and abscond with every page. But he knew that would be a betrayal. If Jamie didn't trust him to read his words, he couldn't force him. Besides, gaining Jamie's trust, his permission, was a much sweeter victory.

"If you ever change your mind, I would love to see what you've written. With your experiences in the wild and your love of stories, I'm sure it will be a tale worth knowing."

Jamie's throat bobbed but he seemed to relax. Dallin fought the urge to take the seat next to him. He was here for a reason, and seeking Jamie out had only been a momentary distraction. "I wish I could stay longer."

"You can't?" Jamie sat up straighter, a small frown pulling at his lips.

"I need to head down to the dungeon. There's someone I must meet with."

"I... I could go with you." The suggestion was more hopeful than hesitant. He had it on his tongue to refuse when Jamie added, "It could make good fodder for my future stories."

"Damn you." It's like Jamie knew exactly what to say to tempt him. Jamie's entire face transformed. He was handsome to begin with, with sharp cheekbones and bow-shaped lips. But when he smiled, he was positively heartbreaking. "Get a cloak. Let's go."

As if he could refuse him.

The walk to the dungeon took ten minutes. He was always hyper aware of time when he was in Jamie's presence. They spoke in hushed whispers as he answered questions, catching up on everything that had happened to each of them over the past week.

The warmth of Jamie's room was quickly replaced by cold darkness as they descended into the bowels of the keep. He felt it like a phantom touch, shredding what remained of his earlier happiness. His lips pressed into a thin line as he fought the childish urge to flee. Memories of his confinement during Kane's rule battered against his mind. Months spent in the darkness, forced to swallow down dragon's bane potions that zapped his power and befuddled his mind. Were it not for Fewoen's appearance every so often, he would have been lost for all those months. Verath too. It was a small mercy that the two of them had been forced into a cell together, even if it had made the situation more cramped. He'd have gone mad all alone.

He pushed the thoughts aside, focusing on the task at hand. He was stronger than this. He needed to act like it.

Collier was in his cell. Either Kane hadn't known he was rotting down here or hadn't cared to free him knowing that he was. All the better. While he'd never met the man Verath imprisoned, he knew enough about what Collier had been involved in. Most prominently, that he had provided the poison that had killed Desaree's mother.

"Well, well, well...to what do I owe the pleasure, *Drengr*." Collier broke into a fit of coughing. He was all skin and bones. Looked closer to death than life.

"I need some advice on poisons." Perhaps he could have asked Saffra, but the king had wanted to keep this business quiet, and Saffra had done enough in their fight against Kane and the wild dragons. He didn't need to drag her into this.

"What makes you think I'd be inclined to give you what you seek."

"Name your price."

Collier's eyes lit with surprise. "A bed. Better living accommodations."

"You didn't ask for your freedom."

"You think I'd be stupid enough to reach that far? Would you grant it?"

"No. Not for anything in the world." He didn't want a man like this on the streets. "But I can improve your living conditions. In exchange for a poison brewed."

That had the poisoner sitting up straighter. "You'd let me brew again?"

"You would be under careful watch, and just this once. I need something that will stop a heart. One specific heart. Something that won't look suspicious. Needs to look like natural causes. I'm certain you can make it happen."

It took several moments, but Collier managed to climb to his hands and knees, then push himself up to his feet. He wobbled. Dallin was ready to rush forward and catch the frail man should he fall. Gods, he might not even live to see the poison brewed if he keeled over here and now.

"Sure he's up for the task?" Jamie murmured out of the side of his mouth.

"I'm up for it, boy. You give me my living conditions, and the ingredients and tools I'll need, and I'll give you your poison."

"You have yourself a deal. Make a list. I'll get you what you need."

"A list." Collier's voice was flat.

"I can help with that," Jamie piped up. It turned out that he had a spare bit of parchment in his pocket already, along with a charcoal pencil. When Dallin shot him a questioning glance he shrugged and said, "What? You never know when inspiration might strike. The other day I was in the dining hall and I had this idea about a cave bear and a young maiden—" He cut himself off, swallowing.

"I'd like to hear more about this cave bear," Dallin said, lowering his voice to a purr. "Just not here."

"Right." Jamie flushed. He quickly looked away, over to Collier. "Well, I'm ready when you are."

Once they had everything composed, they departed. Jamie offered to see to the procurement of everything on the list, promising that it wouldn't be too difficult. "That will allow you to focus on your task. Any idea how you will do it?"

"Several," he said. He wouldn't risk his mission by uttering them aloud in the corridors, not when listening ears might overhear. Instead, he bid Jamie goodnight just outside his door, then slipped back into the shadows, ready to implement the next phase of his plan.

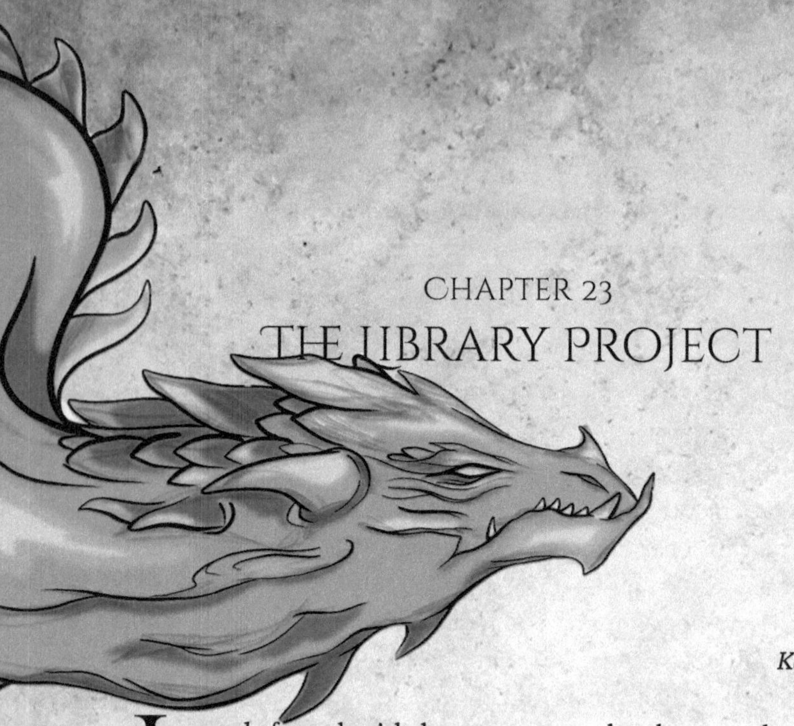

CHAPTER 23

THE LIBRARY PROJECT

Kastali Dun

Leah fussed with her gown, another borrowed piece from Saffra. They were close to the same size, and most of Saffra's gowns had ties that adjusted the waist and bust. She much preferred the simple homespun options, especially for the work she did in the royal library. But today was a special day, and she'd wanted to get dressed up.

"Here we are." Jovari pulled her to a stop, his hand gentle on her arm.

She looked around and gasped at the sight of the transformed building. It was nearly unrecognizable, hence why she'd almost walked past it. In its previous life, it had been a tavern with an inn on the upper floors. The owner had let it fall into disrepair, then listed the building for sale. That was years ago. It hadn't sold. Too many repairs were required to make it suitable.

The years hadn't been kind to it, but you wouldn't know that looking at it now. The outer walls were no longer leaning on their nearest neighbor. The paint was fresh. The roof, too. There were windows instead of boards.

"It's only been a week," she breathed, squeezing Jovari's arm,

200

lingering over the feel of him. He wasn't looking at the building, but her. Her cheeks heated under the intensity of his gaze. It was times like this that she questioned her decision to take things slow. Her lips still tingled with the memory of their last shared kiss.

Everything he'd done over the past couple of weeks had made this moment possible. He'd drafted a proposal, one she'd given plenty of input on. After she'd formally signed it, he'd gotten it in front of the king and lower council within the span of a few hours. Not only had it been approved, but the amount of funds Talon had set aside for this project was staggering.

She wished the king was here now, so that he could see how far they'd already come. More than that, she ached for her best friend. Would Claire be proud of her when she returned? Proud of the work she'd done to help the people of Kastali Dun?

After her proposal was accepted, she and Jovari had poured over city maps, looking for strategic locations that would allow less fortunate areas to access all the services the libraries had to offer. Far more than simply borrowing books, if she had anything to say about it. For now, baby steps.

Most children in poorer families did not attend school. Education was for scholars or families who could hire tutors. In this area of the city, parents needed their children home caring for siblings, or working in the family trade. While she wasn't yet ready to tackle the idea of public schooling—that was a monumental task in and of itself—she wanted a place for those who could read to access books, and for those who couldn't read, to enjoy other services the libraries had to offer. There would be programs like story time, for children who enjoyed storytelling, options to learn to read and write on rest days, even training sessions to gain marketable skills for those in between employment.

Her mind was filled with ideas she couldn't wait to implement.

The building before them was the first of three projects. "Shall we go in?" Jovari squeezed her hand. "I spoke to the contractor earlier this morning. Looks like everything is just about ready."

"Yes, please!" Her voice was barely a whisper.

They stepped up to the double doors. Jovari inserted a key,

leading them inside. The initial room was a simple atrium with a front desk for an assistant. She took in the finished wooden floors and freshly painted walls. Everything was bare, for now. A blank canvas she could decorate however she pleased.

When she walked through the archway leading into the main room, she gasped. "Oh!"

The ceiling had been knocked out, making it twice as high, giving the room an airy look. Shelves had been arranged in linear stacks. They were empty, for now. There were places for reading chairs. Large windows higher on the wall allowed for daylight.

"It's perfect!" Her voice came out breathy and excited.

"Come and see the gathering room, just through here." Jovari laced their fingers together and pulled her towards the other room on the ground floor. She relished in the feel of his hand in hers, loving the way it grounded her. His touch would never grow old.

The ceiling was lower here, giving it a more intimate feel. It had enough space for work tables. "Perfect for some of the workshops and lessons you talked about," he said, eyeing everything with an analytical air.

"Yes!" She pressed a hand over her chest, studying their creation come to life. She could already picture the ways the space might be used. They'd meticulously gone over the floor plan and sketches for each room. But seeing it in person was a huge difference.

They lingered in this room for several more minutes, exchanging ideas and adjustments before heading up the stairs to the second floor, and then the third. There were smaller rooms and another library, this one much smaller. She'd wanted a space for younger age groups, something more casual.

They spent another hour going back through each of the rooms and discussing plans. Jovari was careful and observant, drinking in every suggestion she made. She half wished he'd pull her into one of the darker rooms and kiss her, but he kept his hands to himself, giving this project the attention it deserved. When he finally took her back out onto the street, she blinked into the bright daylight. "These are yours now." He slipped the set of keys into her hands.

"Oh!" Her heart pounded. None of it had felt real until now. She slipped the keys into the little purse she carried. It clinked against the few coins inside. It was hard to believe this was really happening, and so soon from when she'd dreamt it up.

"We missed the midday meal, but what do you say we pop over to one of my favorite taverns for a bite to eat?"

"I'd love that." Truthfully, she simply loved being in his company.

"When do you need to get back to work?"

"Oh! Roland gave me the rest of the day off to work on this project."

"So, you're saying I get you all to myself?"

"Don't you have obligations from the king?"

"As it so happens, Verath cleared me for a day off as well."

She bit her lip, suppressing a smile. "Perfect. You can be my assistant, then."

"I'd love nothing more." He looped an arm around her waist, pulling her close and kissing the top of her head. "What sort of duties will I have?"

"Well, the library is going to need furniture and art, yes?"

"Then I guess we'd better come up with a plan."

OVER THE NEXT FEW DAYS, books began pouring in. She'd spent the week during renovations meeting with various merchants around the city, placing orders. She'd already curated a wide collection of options ranging from children's books, and fictional novels, to history and educational material.

"Wow! This is incredible!" Desaree, Jocelyn, and Saffra had joined her today. The king's shields were busy with court this morning, so a contingent of guards had escorted them through the city and remained stationed just outside.

The girls turned circles in the main room, their eyes darting everywhere, jaws slack.

"Pretty amazing, right?" She couldn't help her grin. The smile made her cheeks ache, but she didn't care. Seeing their awe made everything worth it. This was just a taste of how others would react, specifically, the people the library was intended for.

A hand slipped into hers. She turned to find Saffra wearing an expression of pride. "It's completely amazing. You and Jovari really did all this?"

"Well, we hired craftsmen to complete all the actual renovations. But we handled all the plans and everything."

"Well, now I know why you've been so busy! It shows."

"Wait until the common people see this," Des said, emerging from between a row of shelves.

"They're going to be so shocked." Jocelyn came to stand before her, her eyes glassy with emotion. "This is going to make a huge difference."

"You think?" Leah couldn't disguise the hope in her voice.

"I know." Jocelyn hesitated, then hugged her. "Thank you."

"Oh." Her chest burst with warmth and she blinked against the sudden blur in her eyes. They broke apart.

"So." Saffra eyed the crates stacked against the wall. "I'm guessing you need help with all of that?"

"Precisely. I've labeled the shelves. Our job is to put everything in its correct place. And... I heard rumors that there are ways to keep books from aging?"

"Magic," Saffra confirmed. "The royal library has it, to protect books from dust and light. But I'm not entirely certain how it came about."

Leah sighed. "Well, I guess it was worth a shot."

"Don't give up hope just yet." Saffra bumped her shoulder. "I think Isabella was responsible for the magic in the royal library."

"So you think Claire might be able to...?"

"Let's ask her when she returns." Saffra grinned. "I bet she would want to contribute in some way."

"You're right." She nodded. "She'll definitely want to help."

"Then let's do what we can in the meantime." Saffra squared her shoulders, walking over to the crates.

It was tedious work. They removed books and sorted them according to location and author. The hours sailed by.

Her back began to ache but she didn't mind. The work reminded her that she had a purpose. One she'd chosen for herself.

Despite her best friend's absence, she'd found herself smiling more and more. Everything was falling into place. Everything except...Jovari.

She'd chosen to take things slow with him. But he seemed to think slow meant at a snail's pace. They'd shared a few impassioned kisses here and there, but nothing more.

She pulled her lower lip between her teeth as she worked, thinking over their relationship. He'd surprised her, taking an active role in her library project. She'd expected him to offer advice here and there, but he'd handled the brunt of the work. And he'd done it all eagerly.

She wanted to find a way to thank him.

"What's going on in that beautiful mind of yours." The voice had her jumping. She almost dropped the stack of books in her hands. "Here, I'll take those. Just tell me where they go."

"Jovari!" She placed a hand over her heart.

"Didn't mean to sneak up on you."

A startled laugh burst from her chest. "Here, just put them on this shelf. They're already in order."

She caught the sound of distant murmurs. One voice sounded like Bedelth's. "We came to collect you. Well, Bedelth came to collect Desaree, Jocelyn, and Saffra. You and I are staying a little while longer."

"We are?"

"Yes."

The other three women rounded the corner, Bedelth lingering behind. His gaze darted to hers and he nodded in greeting before his focus returned to his mate. "Thank you for letting us be a part of this," Saffra said. The others echoed her sentiments.

"I should be thanking you! We got so much done."

"Can we come again tomorrow?" Saffra asked.

"If it's not too much to ask?"

"Count us in." Saffra grinned. "We've got to get this place finished before Claire's return."

"Thank you," she breathed. A warm palm slipped into hers and squeezed. Jovari's.

"Enjoy dinner, you two." Bedelth grinned before leading the others away.

"Dinner?" She turned to Jovari.

"Brought dinner," he explained, leading her through the aisles to an area near the entryway. He reached down and took a blanket off the top of a basket. He set it out on the floor like they were having a picnic, then pulled a few candles out, setting those up, too.

She watched his movements, fascinated. His hands were captivating. They were large and dexterous and she couldn't take her eyes off each movement. Everything he did was methodical. "You're staring," he murmured as he began pulling more items from the basket, setting everything up.

"Oh. Right. Well, you are my mate. I'm allowed to stare, right?" Saying those words had butterflies tumbling in her stomach. It made everything between them more real.

"I like when you watch me," he admitted. Taking a seat, he looked up at her. "Well?" He patted the spot beside him.

Eagerly, she sat down beside him. "You arranged all this?"

"I did."

Outside, the sounds of Kastali Dun were dying down for the night. Darkness had fallen, and people were settling in, eating dinner and spending time with their families. She jolted as Jovari set a small worn book in her lap. It had a maroon cover.

"What's this?"

"The library's first donation."

They'd talked about donations, and while she planned to send out a call for donated books among some of the wealthier citizens, she hadn't gotten a chance to yet. "You... You're donating a book?"

He hummed.

She read the title on the spine aloud, *"The Garden of the Drowned Sun."*

She paused. "Is this a common book?" Despite her time in the royal library, every book in this world was foreign to her. It would take years to learn more of them.

"Not very common, no. But it meant something to me, once. After Oralyn, that book was the only thing I could stand to read for a while. It's about a sun god who falls in love with a mortal and can only watch her age from the sky. He sends flowers in every season, but she forgets his name. In the end, he drowns himself just to be buried near her."

Leah blinked. "That's...incredibly sad."

Jovari smiled faintly. "It is. But it helped, somehow. Made me feel less alone. More understood."

"Isn't it incredible how books can do that for us?"

"It is."

They were silent for a few moments. "I picked it up again the other day. It's been over a century since I'd last read it. I'd almost forgotten the words."

"What did you think of it this time around?"

"I realized that the sun god never stopped giving warmth to the world. Even when his heart broke. It made me regret some of my behavior in the wake of Ora's betrayal. But everything ended up as it was meant to be. You, here with me."

"Jovari." Heart pounding, she leaned in and kissed him, letting the book tumble out of her lap. His lips were firm against hers, searching. Repositioning herself, she climbed onto his lap to straddle him, needing desperately to be closer, to be fused to him. He growled.

She thought of her frustration over the past few weeks.

Their kiss morphed into something untamed. She twisted her fingers into his auburn hair. Another growl rose in his chest until he spun them around. A breath whooshed out of her lungs as he repositioned them. She found him atop her, gazing down at her. The way he felt pressed against her was perfection. She angled her hips to better fit with his. A zing of pleasure shot straight to her core.

A little mew escaped her lips, quickly swallowed up by his mouth.

"Gods above." He wrenched himself away, scurrying off her. Like he needed to get himself under control. His pants were tented. He followed her gaze and grinned. "Yes, you see what you do to me, little minx."

"Why'd you stop?" she groaned.

"Because you wanted to take this slow and if I keep going, my claws are going to come out."

A shiver raced down her spine. "What happens when your claws come out?"

"Your gown gets shredded and I get to taste my prize."

"Oh." Fire flooded her already warm skin. "I... I wouldn't mind that, actually."

"No?" As he spoke, his pupils morphed. They turned to draconic slits before relaxing back into their natural appearance. It reminded her of what he was. A beast. She wanted more of that. She wanted to see what he was like when he lost control. But she also knew what the consequences would be if he did. She was close —so close to giving in to their mate bond. She wasn't all that interested in a ceremony. At least, not a large one.

She had no desire to put on a show for the world.

As tempted as she was to rip his clothes off, now wasn't the right time. She'd promised herself. She wanted some time to discover herself, to settle into a new life, before she bound herself to another. That didn't mean they couldn't have a little fun.

"Maybe dinner can wait?" She bit her lower lip. "I've always been partial to dessert before dinner, anyway."

A wicked grin spread across Jovari's face, making him look almost boyish. She loved it. Loved how handsome he was at that moment.

She leaned back on her elbows and bent her knees, letting her legs fall open. Her gown draped around her thighs, hiding everything from his sight, but that didn't stop his gaze from fixing on her center. "Truly?" A ripple of blue scales shot across his skin, there and gone again. Claire had mentioned something similar with Talon. It must have been a dragon thing. Something that happened when they were close to losing control.

She rocked her knees back and forth. An invitation. Her smile was coy.

"Very well. Remember, you asked."

A laugh burst from her chest. She was so ready for this, the ache was almost painful. His hand shot out, wrapping around her right ankle. He lifted it, removing her slipper. Then he did the same with her other foot. His palm was warm as it slid up her calf, dragging the skirt of her gown up around her hips. Then she was bare to him—because apparently no one wore underwear. She found she rather liked that about now.

Jovari crouched, lowering his head. The first brush of his lips on her leg made her gasp. He kissed a trail up to her knee. When he reached the apex of her thighs, his eyes turned to draconic slits again. This time, his pupils didn't change back. A low growl sounded. It made the hairs of her arms stand on end.

"You are utterly perfect. I don't—I don't even have the words." His voice was guttural and rough.

"Then don't bother with words," she whined. "Your mouth is good for other things besides talking."

"Little minx! I'll remember that next time you use that smart mouth on me."

She half giggled-half gasped. It helped to ease the tension building in her chest. Having his gaze on her like this, on her most private place, left her nearly trembling.

"If you change your mind—gods, I hope you don't—but if you do, then tell me to stop. Yes? That's all. You say stop? I stop."

"I don't want you to stop. Please," she all but begged, letting her legs fall open even wider.

His eyes held hers a moment longer, giving her another chance to back out. She didn't dare. With a final feral growl, he descended, putting his mouth exactly where she wanted it.

CHAPTER 24
COLLIER'S POISON

Kastali Dun

Dallin paused on his way down the dungeon stairs as Verath's voice filled his mind. *"I hear you've pulled a certain poisoner into your plans for Cobra."* He braced, half expecting Verath to scold him. *"Let me know if you need anything."*

"Thank—thank you. I will."

The shield's presence faded from his mind.

He blew out a breath. He still wasn't used to his shield brothers treating him like an equal. He'd given an oath. They'd welcomed him with open arms. But sometimes he felt like being the baby in the group meant they wouldn't take him seriously. That's why everything needed to go off without a hitch. This was his chance to prove himself.

Five days had passed since his initial meeting with Collier. Five days of planning. Of watching. Of learning Cobra's routine. He'd been lucky with the knife incident. Cobra hadn't discovered who the thrower was—thank the gods, since it had been Jovari—but the incident had cemented Dallin's place in his ranks. Cobra trusted him more than ever, or so he hoped.

Tonight would be the ultimate test.

He nodded at the additional presence of guards beside Collier's door and gave a perfunctory knock before opening it. The room was transformed since that first night. True to his word, Jamie had handled everything. A new cot and bedside table occupied one corner, and a workbench for cutting and brewing took up the majority of the extra space. It was a tight squeeze. A rug now lined the floor, illuminated by the increase in lamps that had been installed upon the walls.

Collier lounged in the only available chair, looking rather smug. His body didn't appear as frail as it had. Amazing what a few good meals could do for a man. A few good meals and a purpose.

"Finished it, have you?" he asked.

"All finished." Collier nodded towards the small glass vial sitting in a holder on the workbench. He moved towards it, lifting it into the light. The liquid inside was fully transparent, no evidence of Cobra's hair clippings. He'd covertly obtained them after the man had seen a barber just days ago.

"And it will do what I need? It will only affect Cobra?"

"It will work fast on your intended target. No antidote, you understand?"

He hesitated and then slipped it into his pocket. "I won't be needing one."

The faster the better.

"Very well. What comes next?"

"For you? Nothing. For me…" He lifted a shoulder then turned on his heel and left. If Collier wanted gossip, he was out of luck.

The guards closed the door behind him, locking Collier in.

Nothing dangerous remained in his cell. He and Jamie had been sure to only provide the exact ingredients necessary to brew this one potion. During that process, guards stood both inside and out to oversee and ensure Collier didn't brew something he could use for himself. They would remain just outside from now on, given all the added comforts the man now had. Who knew if he'd find some creative way to use the bed frame as an escape tool.

Opting for stealth, he took one of the secret passages that led him out into the city. A cacophony of sounds hit him as he entered the alley and stepped out onto the busy street. The remaining walk to The Tacky Stag took ten minutes. It was warm today, which made the stench in some of the lower districts more intense. His nose was more sensitive than a human's. He did his best to breathe through his mouth.

A block from his destination, a figure stepped out of the shadows.

"Remy, good to see you, my man."

"You too, Wasp." Remy cleared his throat, then nodded towards the alley. Dallin followed his gaze and caught sight of a figure filling the shadows. Bracing himself, he walked over.

"That will be all, Remy," Martel murmured, "you may go."

Remy slipped away.

Dallin crossed his arms and regarded Martel, casually standing with his back against the wall, one foot propped up. "Have you given any thought to our alliance? I assume you found my note useful?"

Dallin didn't respond right away. The street noise echoed behind them, distant but persistent. He kept his eyes glued to Martel, using his other senses to remain in touch with his surroundings. "You're assuming a lot."

Martel chuckled, the sound low and smooth. "I'm an optimist." He pushed off the wall, brushing dust from the shoulder of his coat. "But I'm also a realist. I know what Cobra is. What he *isn't*. He's not invincible. And he's not long for this world."

"That sounds a lot like treason in a regime like Cobra's." He kept his voice quiet but pointed.

"Only if it's said in the wrong company." Martel tilted his head. "But you're not the wrong company. You're the one who caught a knife midair to save his life. And yet..." His gaze flicked to Dallin's pocket. "You're also the one walking around with secrets."

His heart skipped but he kept his face calm. "If you had proof of anything, you'd be running to Cobra."

"I don't want to run to Cobra." Martel stepped closer. "I want a future where we're not groveling at the feet of a man who talks like a priest and slithers like his pet." Silence stretched between them. His next words were softer. "When it happens—whatever *it* is—I'll look the other way. I'll even help, spreading the word that you're innocent. Just a loyal guard who got unlucky. But when the dust settles, I want my share. I want the Syndicate."

His eyes narrowed. "That's a big ask."

"It's a fair one." Martel leaned in, his voice a whisper. "Better me than someone worse. You were at that meeting. You saw the inner circle he keeps. Better me than a power vacuum."

Dallin gave a slow nod, careful to keep his face blank. "I'll think about it."

He wasn't even sure he'd have a say in what came next. Talon had never shared his plans past the killing of Cobra. For all he knew, he'd have no involvement afterward.

Martel smiled, sharp and satisfied. "That's all I ask."

He took a step back, then another, until he was back out on the street.

He wished Talon were still in the city. Wished he could run this by the king. Verath would surely have answers. At the end of the day, his mission was clear. Cut the head off the snake. The only problem was, he was certain that the body would *not* follow.

LAUGHTER FLOATED through the closed door of the brothel room, a playful tone that sounded almost forced. Dallin ground his teeth. He respected brothel workers, he just hated that they were often exploited. Moon's Garden was a better sort than some of the establishments in the lower city. While Cobra didn't live extravagantly at The Tacky Stag, he didn't hesitate to spend money on other pursuits. Sex being one of them. He visited Nerina nearly every other night.

Dallin had been forced to stand watch outside the door each

time. Moments like these made him curse his drengr hearing. Fortunately, Martel's hints had served him better than he cared to admit.

He would have come to the same conclusions all on his own, it simply would have taken longer.

He pushed all thoughts of the crew leader out of his head. He didn't need that kind of distraction. Martel hadn't run to Cobra—that was the important thing. There had been a moment of anxiety in that alley earlier. A moment when he worried all his carefully laid plans might come crashing down around him. But Martel was too power hungry. He knew enough about Dallin, harbored enough suspicion about who he truly was, to risk his ire. Everything he did now was simply an attempt to grasp as much power as possible when the dust settled.

The question was, once Cobra was out of the picture, would Martel prove a more formidable opponent? There would be no repeat of this operation. He wouldn't have another chance to go undercover once this was done. Besides, it wasn't sustainable to think he could simply kill every leader who rose up to control the syndicate. At this point, the network was so vast, they'd need to kill every member inside if they wanted to eliminate it entirely.

Footsteps sounded on the stairs. On cue, Leora appeared with a tray in hand. An unopened bottle of wine and two pristine goblets rested on its surface. "I've the wine he ordered. Is now a bad time? Should I come back?"

He pretended to listen at the door. "Might be. Why don't you set that here and I'll wait for an interlude."

Leora hesitated. "Are you sure? It is my job, after all."

"Better not to disturb them at this moment. Why don't you leave your corkscrew on the tray and I'll take it to them at a better time. I can open the bottle well enough."

"Right. Thank you, Wasp. I just…"

"Here. I'll give you your tip now and let Cobra know I took care of it."

"You're sure?"

"Of course, sweetheart." He pulled a handful of coins from his pocket and passed it along.

Leora set the tray on a nearby hall table and bid him goodbye. He waited until her footsteps faded. With his enhanced drengr hearing, he listened for anything out of place. There were six doors in this hallway on the third floor of Moon Garden. Three of them were occupied, including Cobra's. None of them would be coming out anytime soon. Setting to work, he muttered an incant, effortlessly pulling the cork free of the bottle. He removed the vial and tipped it into the bottle, then replaced the cork. Everything looked as good as new.

Lifting the tray, he offered a tentative knock at the door. "Your wine's here, sir."

A hesitation, followed by a giggle and, "Door's unlocked. Bring it in."

He entered, setting the tray out on the table. The rooms in Moon's Garden were all decorated in shades of dusty blue and white, with hints of gold. Everything was gaudy and over the top. He caught a brief glimpse of Cobra stretched out on the bed, shirt missing, pants undone. Nerina straddled his hips, clearly in the middle of whatever it was they were doing. She was dressed in a long silk dressing gown, thank the gods. Still, he averted his gaze.

He made a show of lifting the corkscrew and setting about the process of opening the bottle.

"What happened to Leora?" Cobra gently removed Nerina and began doing up his pants, clearly eager for a drink.

"She stubbed her toe on the stairs on the way up." He didn't miss a beat as he twisted the corkscrew deeper into the soft cork. "Nearly dropped the tray limping around like she was. I offered to take it. She's seeing to her foot."

"You paid her, I hope?"

"Already taken care of."

"Good man. Good man." Cobra slapped him on the back and he flinched, nearly dropping the bottle. He made a show of struggling with the cork. "Here, I'll get it."

He handed it over. There was no reason to worry. Collier had plenty of motivation to do a thorough job. He'd lose every comfort he'd received if this poison didn't work as intended. Still, he hated that he had to rely on a criminal.

"There we go." Cobra made a show of sniffing the cork and humming with approval. "Can always tell a good wine by how the cork smells. Come, Nerina. What do you think?"

Nerina scurried over and inhaled, smiling. "Smells lovely."

Dallin gritted his teeth as Cobra poured one goblet, and then a second. "Sorry, my friend, but you're on the job."

"A job I take very seriously."

"Something I appreciate." Cobra handed the goblet to Nerina. Dallin's stomach twisted. If Collier messed even one thing up. If the hair didn't work...

"Tell me how you like it, dear." Cobra's eyes lingered on Nerina before darting to him. "Wasp! Back to your post."

"Yes, sir." He held his breath as he retreated, keeping his steps slower than necessary. With his back to the room, he was forced to listen to what transpired. This needed to go perfectly. If it didn't, Nerina would be the one to pay the price.

"Oh, it's...it's delicious. My favorite so far, I think?"

"Yes? Describe the flavors to me."

Nerina made a humming sound. Dallin's heart beat faster. "Cherries, I think? And oak. Oh, something...richer. A spice perhaps?"

"Very well, let's see." A long silence and then. "Yes, I see what you mean about the cherries and the oak." There came a slight choking sound.

Dallin stepped over the threshold and closed the door behind him, backing up to lean against the opposite wall. His blood roared in his ears, breaths coming faster.

"There's also...a hint of—" Cobra's words cut off in a sharp intake of breath. There came a muffled thud, the sound of a goblet striking the floor. Then the loud strike of a body crumpling to the ground.

A wave of relief crashed through him. Days of nervous anticipation had culminated into this moment. Now he had only to play the part of a shocked guard.

Nerina's scream lifted the hairs on his arms.

He waited a single beat, then burst through the door, letting it slam against the hinges as he drew a blade. Everything that happened next came in a blur. Wine had spilled all over the floor. Both cups had fallen and rolled away. Nerina was on her knees on the floor, shaking Cobra as her sobs filled the air. He lay prone, his eyes glassy and unseeing, his hand clutched to his chest. There came a hiss. He glanced over to see Sable slithering across the floor to reach her master.

Nerina's sobs grew more frantic when she caught sight of the snake.

Onlookers filled the doorway, gasping and muttering, most only half-dressed.

Dallin moved to pull Nerina away. "No!" She struggled against him. "He can't... He can't be dead!" She began beating at his chest.

"Stop! Nerina—stop. He's dead." He dragged her back, keeping a hold of her. "How did this happen?"

"I... I don't—?!" She pawed at her eyes.

"I've called the city guards," Madame Revelle announced. "They're on their way."

"I... He was fine and then... I don't know what happened. He clutched his heart and then..." Nerina tried to break free of him, to go back to Cobra, but he held on tight. "He can't be dead. He was just... We were just having some wine."

One of the men in the hallway stepped forward. "Can never trust these whores. I bet she poisoned him."

"Speak another word and I'll cut out your tongue," Dallin growled. He'd never been one for threats, but how dare this man? Nerina had nothing to do with any of this, and he hated the way the man made assumptions.

"Aren't you supposed to be his guard?" another man asked.

"What are you suggesting?" he demanded. "That I failed at my job?"

"He's lying dead, ain't he?"

"There was nothing I could have done," he snarled. "And I'll trust you to mind your own business."

Still, for show, he turned to Nerina. She saw the question in his eyes. "I drank the wine before he did, so it couldn't have been poisoned, right?"

"How much did you have?" he asked, an accusation ringing in his voice.

"Almost half a goblet!"

"Hmm... Perhaps not the wine then."

There came a pounding of boots on the stairs. Men in light armor pushed through, filling the doorway. Their eyes quickly swept over the room. The one in front stepped forward.

"Name and occupation," he demanded, looking directly at Dallin.

"Wasp. I'm his bodyguard."

"Him being...?"

"Cobra."

"And you?" The guard looked at Nerina.

"I was just... We both drank the wine. I swear it wasn't... I didn't..."

"She's right." Dallin squared his shoulders. "She couldn't have done anything. I was there when the bottle was opened. They both partook."

"Be that as it may." The guard stepped forward, hand on his weapon. "This looks a little suspicious from where I'm standing."

More of a crowd had gathered in the doorway.

"I'm afraid we must take you into custody," the first guard said. "Standard procedure and all."

Nerina crumbled to the floor, sobbing. "Come now, sweetheart. I'm sure they'll discover this is all just a misunderstanding." He hauled Nerina up and made a mental note to ensure she was properly compensated when this was over.

Another guard stepped forward, removing two sets of irons. "Afraid I'm going to have to..."

"Fine." Dallin held his wrists forward. Nerina did the same, silently sobbing the entire time.

The click of iron against his skin echoed louder than it should have.

"Contact the coroner," one of the other guards said. "The rest of you, back—this is a crime scene until further notice."

Sable hissed from the floor.

Cobra's body didn't move.

And just like that, it was done.

CHAPTER 25
TAYLYNN'S CEREMONY

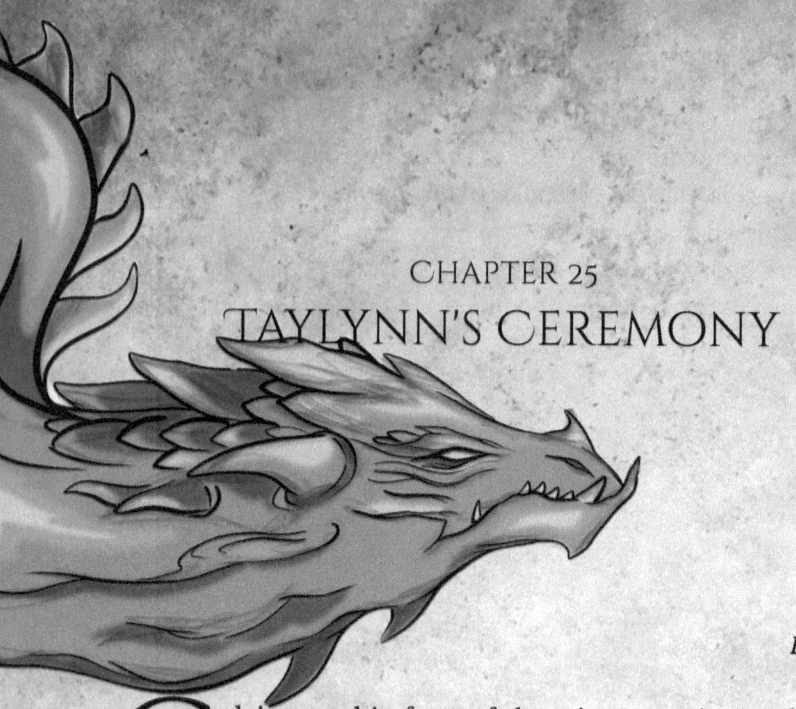

Esterpine

Claire stood in front of the mirror as Miera and Selphie readied her for the crowning ceremony. They dressed her in a gown that looked like starlight, with pools of shimmering silver that cascaded down her body. It was in the spriten style, though much more reserved than what most sprites wore. It only showed off her bare arms and the markings she had acquired. Her hair was pinned back, the tresses piled atop her head. Glittering jewel pins were pressed in to hold everything in place.

She sparkled like a star.

Taking in her appearance, she couldn't help but think of how very different this was to her own experience in taking over the spriten crown. For one, there would be no death to darken the moment. Her thoughts turned to Jade. The previous queen's selfishness had cost Taylynn and Feowen their mother. It had cost the forest a lot more than that, but she wouldn't allow those thoughts to linger. Wouldn't allow them to sour what ought to be a beautiful day for everyone.

"You look exquisite," Selphie said in *Ednuar*. Her handmaidens appeared happy to be back in Esterpine. They hadn't spoken a single word in the common tongue since returning. That made her stomach squirm uncomfortably.

"Shalaya." *Thank you.*

Her lip caught between her teeth. She glanced between them, hesitant. Had they missed their home so much that they'd want to remain here? What about Taylynn? When she became queen, would she want them for herself?

"What is it, my queen?" Miera pulled on her hand.

"Oh. I…" She shook her head. "It's nothing."

"Speak, please," Miera said.

She blew out a breath. "I am worried. Now that you are back, you will not want to return to the capital with me. But my time here is drawing to a close. I cannot keep you from your home. You stepped in as my handmaidens when I became the spriten queen. After today, I will no longer be your queen. Your duty to me will be fulfilled. You will have no reason to—"

"We will have every reason to!" Selphie drew herself up, face flushing with irritation. Her handmaidens were usually soft spoken. That Selphie had interrupted her took her aback. "Forgive me, Your Majesty. But you are still Dragonwall's queen. Our loyalty is to you, not the crown upon your head, spriten or otherwise."

"She speaks the truth," Miera confirmed, resolute. "We are with you. Forever. Until the end."

"You… You are?" Tears sprang to her eyes. Her throat tightened and she managed a swallow.

"We are." Selphie took a hold of her shoulders and pressed her back into position before the mirror. "No crying or it will smudge your eye lining. Hold still." She took a small handkerchief Miera produced and dotted at the corner of Claire's eyes. The motion made Claire want to burst into tears all over again. These women! They were making her feel too much.

Oh gods, was this what people talked about when they mentioned pregnancy hormones?

"I ought to warn you, you might have to be more patient with me than usual."

"Oh?" Selphie and Miera shared a glance.

"Wait." She stepped off the pedestal away from the mirror, putting distance between them. "No. Don't you *dare* tell me—"

"We know."

"You...? But how?!"

"Your Majesty. Forgive me but you have not bled at your bleeding time." Miera said this like it was so obvious.

"How—?! How do you—?!" She sputtered. "I could have bled on my trip from Shadowkeep to the forest."

Selphie lifted her brows. "Did you?"

"No, but that's beside the point!"

"She asked Feowen," Miera chirped.

"Miera!" Selphie's expression darkened as she turned to chide her.

"What?" Miera looked defensive. "There is no point in keeping secrets between us."

"She does not need to know we are prying into private matters."

"We were bound to discover it." Miera lifted her chin.

"Yes, but Feowen is her *cousin*. She does not need to know we were asking him about female matters."

"We?" Miera harrumphed. "*You* are the one who asked."

Claire pressed her cool hands to her warm face. "Stop it, the both of you! Oh, gods. What am I going to do with you? Nosey handmaidens. And now I am stuck with you for life!"

"Forgive us, Your Majesty." Miera pressed her lips between her teeth, trying not to laugh. "It is our duty to care for you."

"What is all this talk about taking proper care of my mate?" Talon strode into the room. She collected herself at the sight of him. Like her, he was clothed in sparkling silver. A tunic that shone like the stars, and black pants with polished boots. His sverak was strapped to his back.

Gods, he looked *incredible*. The feeling was mutual. He took her in, admiration and desire burning in his gaze. She hadn't noticed his approach, or that he was coming to collect her, too distracted by her handmaidens' antics.

"Ah. Interesting," he said, looking them over. "It seems our little secret is not a secret after all."

"No, it would seem not," she chuckled, too happy to feel annoyed. "I suppose with an inner circle like ours, everyone will find out before we tell them."

"Yes, but we will still give it a valiant effort."

"Indeed."

"Is she ready?" he asked her handmaidens in their native tongue.

"Almost." Selphie procured a carved box. "This is the ceremonial crown."

Miera lifted the lid and removed it from the box.

"I... How come I've never seen that before?" The piece was staggering. Vines of starlight silver studded with green gems. It seemed to radiate with light.

"Naeloria is purely ceremonial," Selphie said. "The king tree made it for the first spriten queen."

"For Ellia?"

"The very same." Miera stepped forward, holding the crown. Naeloria. It was a spriten name that meant hope reborn. How fitting that the king tree had crafted it for the first spirit singer, who later became Esterpine's queen.

She lowered for Miera to place it atop her head. "You did not have a conventional ceremony," Miera explained, "so it was never passed to you from Jade. I am glad that you might wear it at least once."

"That makes sense." She stood, feeling the weight of it. "It's... *Wow*." She lifted her hand, afraid it might slide off, but it remained fixed, almost as if it had molded to the shape of her head.

It was deceptively heavy.

Talon cleared his throat. "My father once said a crown should always be heavy—"

"—to remind you of the burden you must carry," she finished for him. Their gaze met and held. They were no strangers to burden. Not anymore.

"It suits you," he admitted. "But I am glad that you will not wear it for much longer."

"Me too." She found her shoulders relaxing.

"Ready?"

"*Neem.*"

"Good, then let us go down." He held out his hand.

She stepped up to him, lacing their fingers together. When they stepped out into the crystal corridor beyond, her entire queen's guard was waiting. She nodded to each of them, trying to ignore the uncomfortable squirming in her stomach.

"*Be calm, mate. Like your handmaidens, I am sure they will not abandon you.*"

"*It is within their right, should they wish. Their duty is to protect the spriten queen.*"

"*I'm sure Taylynn will offer them positions in her queen's guard.*"

"*I know.*" She let out a heavy sigh.

"*And, I'm sure they will refuse, insisting they continue with you.*"

"*But I'm not—*"

"*It's not about the spriten crown for them. Not anymore.*" Talon stopped her in the middle of the winding staircase that led down to the bottom level. He cupped her chin, turning her face to make sure she was looking at him. To everyone behind them, it was obvious they were holding a silent conversation. "*You have won their loyalty and trust. You have won their hearts. I am confident they will want to serve you until the end of your days. Just like your handmaidens.*"

Their gazes held. At last, she nodded. "*You... You're right.*"

They finished their descent to the palace's ground floor. When they stepped into the throne room, they found it packed with sprites. The room had been transformed into a living forest, with vines and blooms growing up out of the floor, creating a lattice high overhead. It was a world of living color.

She would never grow tired of the wonders of the spriten kingdom—*her* kingdom.

An aisle formed as they made their way, her people bowing to her as she passed. They murmured words of, "*Ayas Drollaya,*" and "*Nua bualta.*"

She reached the dais, the throne empty and waiting for its new monarch. Taylynn stood off to the side in a stunning green and gold gown, Koldis with her. She took note of their joined hands. Noticed the way Taylynn squeezed Koldis a little harder than necessary.

No one would ever guess that Taylynn might be nervous unless they looked closely.

"Nua bualta, Sarihon." *Well met, Princess.*

"Well, met," Taylynn returned in Ednuar.

"Please take your place before the throne," she said. Taylynn moved into position. Talon moved to stand beside Koldis, in the place she vacated. She turned to face the room, the hundreds of eager gazes that looked up at her. She did not need a herald to quiet everyone. They were already silent. Waiting.

Taking a deep breath, she said, "I came to this throne in grief. I wasn't born here. I wasn't raised in this forest or shaped by its magic. When I first laid eyes upon this place I was lost, heartbroken, and holding on to a promise I was not sure I could keep."

She paused, her gaze sweeping over the faces before her, many of whom had grown familiar. "But this forest...its people...you did not turn me away. You recognized my blood. You allowed me to try. You gave me the opportunity to learn, to fail, and to grow. You trusted me with something sacred, and I've carried it as best I could."

Her fingers tightened slightly around the edges of the crown as she lifted it from her head. It was a steady weight in her hands. "I was never meant to wear this forever. The forest has always known who its true queen is. And she has always walked among you."

She turned to Taylynn now, her voice softening.

"You were meant for this. Your wild heart. Your strength, your wisdom, your fierce love for this place. You are the true daughter of this forest." She lifted the *Naeloria*, holding it above Taylynn's head.

"Princess Taylynn, do you accept this crown and all that it asks of you?"

There was a long hesitation. Taylynn's gaze shot to Koldis. He gave her a firm nod of encouragement. "I accept."

Simple words for a promise that was anything but simple. With a relieved exhale, she set the crown upon Taylynn's brow. The response was instant. Magic rippled through the air. The vines trailing the walls shivered and curled as if wind had passed through them, though the air remained still. The crown flared with silvery light, then dimmed, settling as if it had always belonged there. Taylynn's markings, faint until now, lit like iridescent starlight scattered across her skin.

She was radiant.

Claire stepped aside.

Taylynn stood before her people, regal and glowing, her voice soft but sure. "I will serve you with all that I am. As I have served you before, now I will do so as your queen."

There was a beat of silence. Then, as one, the gathered sprites lifted their hands. A flower blossom appeared in each palm—some shaped like stars, others like bells, others like the wide, lush blooms of the forest.

The flowers lifted from their hands, floating into the air. They spun and danced, drifting gently down towards the crystal throne, affixing to it. Where they touched, they took root. Petals unfurled, transforming the seat into a thing of the forest, alive and ever-changing.

The forest had accepted her.

Claire blinked past the blur in her eyes, her chest tight and full. She wasn't sad—not truly. This was right. And beautiful.

It was perfect.

As a final act, she opened her palms, creating a series of jasmine blossoms, thinking only of Pelwynn and how they were his favorite, of how much he would have loved to witness this moment between his two favorite students. Her eyes met Taylynn's and held. The blossoms floated up into the air, swirling around the throne until they landed near the top, taking root with the other flowers.

"Shalaya," Taylynn murmured, as if reading her mind. She

wasn't just thanking her for the nod to Pelwynn, but for keeping the throne safe. For being patient and carrying the burden for as long as she had.

"It is done, Your Majesty," she said. "Now take up your seat as Esterpine's queen."

Blinking, Taylynn managed a nod. She turned and climbed the final steps of the dais, then turned and sat upon the throne. It was no longer crystalline but alive and thriving. As it should always be. A transformed throne for a new era.

The crowd in the throne room burst into merry cheers. Instruments appeared in several hands and music lifted around them. A hand found hers. Talon. He pulled her to his side, bending to kiss her brow. "You did well, *mih cralla*. That was beautiful."

"It was, wasn't it?" A tear fell down her cheek. She swiped it away.

Koldis was the first to position himself before the throne. He climbed the stairs, kneeling at Taylynn's feet. Their eyes met and held, and then he did the sweetest thing. He lowered his face into his mate's lap, resting his cheek against her thighs.

Taylynn let out a quiet gasp before a soft smile pulled at her lips. She ran her fingers through his hair. Koldis's eyes fluttered closed for a moment.

It was a new and strange world they were forging. But they were doing it together, and that was all that mattered.

CHAPTER 26

VERDENTINE

Esterpine

Koldis flexed his fingers, pushing away the nerves that tangled in the pit of his stomach. Now that she was Esterpine's queen, Taylynn's duties had increased tenfold. She had spent the entire day stuck in court, some of which was spent entertaining applications for her queen's guard. It was no surprise that Claire's queen's guard had requested to remain with Claire. It was unheard of for there to be two guard units, but given that these were unprecedented times, Taylynn had wholeheartedly agreed.

He was glad; they had all become his friends.

He kept a careful eye on the path before him, hoping the forest wouldn't toy with him. The last thing he needed was to get lost. This wasn't the first time he'd traveled this road, and it certainly wouldn't be the last. The forest didn't behave as it once had—purposefully misleading a drengr into endless wandering.

Night had long since fallen, and the beautiful night flowers were all open, casting an eerie beauty upon the world. His eyes remained in motion, searching out unseen danger. Did it usually take this long to reach her cottage?

228

Taylynn hadn't been at dinner. He'd allowed himself a few minutes of worry before letting it go. His mate could take care of herself. He wasn't her keeper. Their relationship would never be conventional.

The trees opened up around him and Taylynn's cottage came into view. He froze, letting out a breath and with it, the tension he'd been holding. Some of his nerves dissipated. Light glowed from the windows through the overgrowth that covered most of the dwelling. He'd worried he would find it cold and dark, that he'd be forced to hold fast to his anxiety a little longer.

Pulling his shoulders back, he set off down the overgrown garden path.

Magic hid Taylynn's cottage from the rest of the world, from those she didn't want finding it. She wasn't a fan of the crystal palace, and now that she was queen, she'd be expected to spend more time there. But after the past few days, he wasn't surprised that she'd finally managed to get away. This place was her refuge. When she wasn't out walking in the forest, she was here.

Taking a breath, he lifted a hand to knock. The door swung open before his fist landed. She was there, staring up at him. Of course she'd expected him.

Their gazes held, unspoken things passing between them. He saw her fatigue, even though she looked fresh as the morning. He knew the toll ruling was already taking on her.

Without a single word, he gently pressed a hand to her chest, forcing her back into the cottage. The door swung closed behind them. A blink later, his hands were tangled in her thick hair, tilting her head back for a kiss. She didn't resist him, going pliant in his arms. It was a small victory, each and every time she didn't fight him.

Her lips parted, letting his tongue explore against hers. A soft mewl sounded. He hungrily swallowed it up.

When they pulled apart, their breaths were labored.

"You weren't at dinner," he pointed out.

"I wasn't hungry."

"Did you eat?"

She lifted a shoulder. He sighed, dropping his bundle near the door. He stalked across the room to the trap door leading down to the food cellar and prep area. He spent a few minutes putting together a meal that would be light but filling, some olives, cheese, bread, infused oil for dipping, and boiled eggs. He loved that the magic of Taylynn's cottage kept everything fresh and ready for consumption.

When he reappeared, she was still standing in the middle of the room, but her eyes had fixed upon the bundle he'd dropped. A fresh wave of doubt made his steps falter. Did she know what it was? If she did, would she know why he was here tonight?

He set the tray on the table. "Come, mate. You need to eat. If you cannot properly take care of yourself, I'll be forced to remain here and do it for you. I refuse to leave if you give me reason to worry."

Her expression, once clouded, cleared as she looked up at him. "You are right. I was being..." She let out a sigh. "I will do better in the future."

"It is all right to slip occasionally. But please, try not to skip meals. Immortal though you may be, you still need to eat. Promise me that you will."

He hated the thought of being parted from her, but the day to depart was fast approaching. Claire and Talon were needed in the capital and he would go with them. That was part of why he'd come tonight. Their time together was fleeting.

Taylynn sat and began picking at the tray he'd assembled. He took the bench beside her, thighs caging her in as he focused his attention on every bite she took. If she suffered under his scrutiny, she did not let on. He merely observed, enjoying the sight of her methodical chewing and swallowing. Gods, he could watch her all day and never get bored. The way her dainty fingers picked at the spread before her. The way she took small bites, contemplating each item before placing it on her tongue.

They did not speak for a long time.

At last, she said, "I do not want a ceremony. I'm sick of ceremonies."

"I know." There was a reason the fates had paired them, after all.

"I know you know." She exhaled. "And I know why you've come, and what you've brought with you."

"Well," he growled, "way to take all the mystery out of it."

A laugh burst free of her chest. "If you like, I will act surprised. Will that help your male ego?"

It was his turn to chuckle. Taylynn was usually the serious one, while her brother, Feowen, was always joking. But occasionally she surprised him. He liked that he could bring her out of her shell.

"I would love your surprise," he rasped, reaching out to lift her hair from her neck. She had mostly finished eating and he wasn't sure he could wait another moment. Leaning in, he laid a string of soft kisses from the base of her ear down the column of her throat. She hummed.

"The king has amended the law, then?"

"Yes. There's no more hiding from what we are. Nor do I wish to."

"Nor do I."

He pulled back, surprised. He half expected her to have cold feet. For someone like her, mating could feel like another obligation. And yet, all he saw was her eagerness.

She studied his expression and laughed again. He shivered. The sound of her laughter was always a gift. "Gods, Koldis. I might be immortal but I am still of flesh and bone. I still have urges."

"This is about more than urges and you know it."

"You're right. That was flippant of me. Something my brother might say."

"And what's something *you* might say?"

"You are the male of my heart. I wish to bind us together, so that even when we are parted, I carry a piece of you with me. There will be times when I am within the forest and you are without, when I will not share your mind, nor you mine, but we will always be connected and I long for that. I never believed I would crave another the way I crave you. A *drengr*, no less. But it is our differences that speak so deeply to my soul. We fit together, you and I. The fates saw it when I didn't. I am glad of it. Aren't you?"

"More glad than I could ever put into words. Certainly not words as eloquent as yours. Thank the gods you are queen and I need not rule by your side, else I'd send half your kingdom running." He didn't wait for a response, scooping her up and walking over to the bundle he'd set by the door. She giggled in his arms, then settled down when he put her on her feet.

He bent, picking up the cloth bundle. "You know what this is?"

"I do, but I am no less eager to see it."

His heart began to pound like it might burst from his chest and race away. Swallowing, he held her gaze for another beat before removing the silky cloth, letting it cascade to the floor. Taylynn gasped, her eyes going wide. His stomach fluttered. Hers wasn't a feigned surprise. It was genuine.

"But how did you—?"

"I sucked up my pride and asked your brother to help me, that's how."

"But of course, he is good with starlight silver." She reached for the bow, no less eager knowing Feowen had helped to craft it. She took it from him to study it. It was nothing like most rider's bows, which were made entirely of wood. He had Claire to thank for the inspiration. She'd told him of the necklace she'd made for the dragonstones.

This, too, had been made from thin vines he'd woven together. Feowen had helped cast veins of starlight silver over it. The streaks of metal made the bow heavier than necessary, but still flexible enough that it would be nothing for a sprite.

Just to prove it, she lifted it, testing the weight and draw. It looked beautiful in her hands. He watched the soft flex of the bowstring in her fingers.

There was a matching set of arrows, each made from a thin vine, locked straight once cast with silver. The feathers were deep green to match his scales. The quiver was of spriten make, with markings etched into it.

He cleared his throat. "I do not know if you have ever attended a mating ceremony in person, but I assume you have not." She gave a small shake of her head, still focused on admiring her prize. "During the bonding ceremony, a drengr gives his mate a bow. I give you this now, so that you might protect me in your own way." He said the words, knowing it was the closest to a ceremony they would get.

He didn't mind. In fact, he preferred this. The two of them alone together, sharing these quiet moments.

She pulled her bottom lip between her teeth, letting her bow arm fall before spinning to face him. Her gaze lifted to the sverak secured across his back, to the empty pommel stone. He held his tongue, waiting.

A flush came over her cheeks. "Oh, all right," she said at last, more to herself than to him. Setting the bow gently on the table, she moved across the room to a set of shelves near her alcove. He gaped at her, not quite believing as she removed a small box from the back, hidden from sight. He licked his lips, not daring to breathe. When she opened the box, it was to reveal the most beautiful green stone. It glowed, almost like spriten markings did. "This is verdentine. Do you know of it?"

"No," he croaked. "I've... I've never heard of it."

"It's rare. As rare as the stone Claire used for Talon's pommel. It can only be found here in the forest, often at the base of ancient trees. I found this beneath one of the oldest, a tree I believe was one of the first after the spirit singers sang them into existence."

"That's... Oh, gods." He swayed on his feet.

"Are you going to be all right?"

"I'm not sure. I wasn't expecting—this." For her to not only get him a pommel stone, but something so rare that she had put great effort into. "When...?"

The flush on her cheeks darkened. "After our return from Ashvale."

"That long ago?!" he all but barked.

A soft smile parted her lips. He cleared the distance between them, leaning in to capture her smile for himself. His lips were hungry, but he couldn't let them get carried away just yet.

Pulling back, he said, "Will you place it for me?"

"I would be honored, as your mate and partner of your heart."

Reaching behind him, he removed his sverak and held it forward. The stone wasn't the perfect size for the empty pommel but as she sang her native words, the metal seemed to shape around the stone until it looked as if it had always been there. "I give you this pommel stone, mate of my heart, so that you might protect me in your own way."

He removed his scabbard and sheathed it, admiring the way it glowed. "You know, all of my brothers are going to be madly jealous when they see this, right?"

"I'm sure they will give you much grief," she cooed.

"They'll all want glowing stones after this."

"Well, yours will be the most unique. Just as you are the most unique creature in the world to me."

"Taylynn—" His voice was choked.

"I am here." She wrapped her fingers around his wrists.

"Tell me I can take you. Tell me I can make you mine completely."

"I would give you those words, but first I want you to understand what this might mean for our future." He frowned. "Claire reversed Isabella's curse, as you know. And spriten queens always bear at least one female child. Our daughter, for it is certain that we shall have one, will be a very different sort. Of both sprite and drengr blood. Presumably with the ability to shift. She will be something the world has never seen before."

He let her words sink in then said, "And we will love her all the more for it, will we not?"

She blew out a breath, as if she'd feared he might be too afraid to accept this last little detail. "We will."

Her words were the final barrier between them, now shattered.

They lunged at each other. He wasn't gentle as he disrobed her, ripping the flimsy fabric she called a gown until it fell in two halves down her body. "I'll get you another," he growled at her protest. "I'll get you a hundred more. A thousand more. I don't care."

Her fingers were already at work on the laces of his pants. He shed his tunic and shucked his boots until there was nothing between them but skin. Guiding her to the alcove that housed her bed, he stretched her out beneath him. Her beautiful hair fanned out upon the pillow. He hesitated, then chuckled, plucking a twig from her tresses. "My wild creature," he crooned. "As untamed as the fiercest storm, and as strong as one too."

Then his mouth was on hers, claiming her in the most primal way he knew how. She tasted like salt and starlight. When they joined, it was not frantic, but slow and sure—two warriors of a different kind shedding their shields. He held her like she was made of light, like he'd burn with her if that was what it meant to be hers. She moved with him, beneath him—fluid as a river, fierce as the wind, wild as the heart within her chest.

And when she tightened around him and called his name, not softly, but like a vow, he answered with her own, whispered like a prayer as he followed her into pure bliss. Their minds followed, fusing into one.

In those final moments, there was only the way they fit together, as if they'd always been meant to. Because they had. The fates had meant for it. And gods, he felt like the luckiest person in the world because of it.

CHAPTER 27
THE CROWN

Esterpine

Jeanine dodged a blow from Elyon, pivoting on her heel as she swept her blade around. Elyon anticipated the attack with plenty of time to spare. Growling, she struck out again and again, attempting to find a weakness in Elyon's defenses.

Sweat trickled down her back, only serving to irritate her. Their spriten blades sang as their fighting continued. She wasn't usually this emotional or heavy-handed. Feowen had taught her better. And yet, she couldn't help it. Not today.

The spriten female dodged another sloppy attempt, laughing with pure glee. "That's it. Let me have it all."

Her taunting, the fact that she could see Jeanine battling her own demons today, only made her jaw clench. She attempted another downward sweep, accidentally leaving her side open. Elyon sent a fist flying. The blow was so forceful she doubled over, dropping her sword and wheezing out a cough—

"Enough." A quiet voice rang out.

Elyon snapped to attention, taking a step back. "*Neem, mih sariho.*"

"What is going on?" Feowen asked, using the common tongue.

236

His silent footsteps stopped beside her doubled over form. She managed to stand, using her forearm to wipe sweat from her brow. It wasn't the first time Feowen had seen her sweat, not by a long shot. Still, it irritated her more than usual, a result of being around so much perfection.

"She wishes to be aggressive today. I am happy to trade blows, or...impart them, mostly." Elyon smirked. It made her want to dart forward and punch the look right off the female's face. Elyon only smiled wider. The female could probably scent the reason for her added emotions, which meant Feowen probably could, too.

Elyon was one of her favorite people in the world. But today, it felt as though everyone was her enemy. That would pass in a day or two.

"Elyon, you're dismissed. Training is over for the day—tell the others."

"*Neem*." She nodded and offered Jeanine a quick, friendly smirk before walking off.

"Come, sheathe your sword. Let's take a walk." Feowen's voice didn't carry its usual playful cadence. Great, was he going to scold her? She knew better than to fight with her emotions running wild.

Following her commander's orders, she sheathed her sword and followed him into the forest. He set out on a familiar path, one they had walked together many times before. He was silent for a time before he said, "You're not usually this worked up during your time of the month."

She snorted in dismissal.

Her menstrual cycle would begin either tomorrow or the day following. She was always extra irritable around that time. But he was right, nonetheless.

"Something happened to set you off, and I think I might be able to guess."

She scoffed but said nothing.

Feowen sighed, reaching for her hand and pulling her to a stop. "My sister and her mate sealed their bond yesterday. You cannot fool me. I know this has something to do with them. And I have a feeling I know why. But if you don't voice your concerns, then it will be impossible for us to move past them."

"There's no point in voicing what I've already voiced before."

"There is. If only so that I might reassure you. Again. I am happy to do so."

"You do not need to repeat yourself."

"Then let me do one better. Come." He tugged on her hand, lacing their fingers together.

They emerged into their clearing, the one with the boulder in the middle. How many times had she escaped here and sat on that boulder simply to get away from the city. From the presence of sprites occupying it? It was her favorite place to come and think. She hadn't been back since their return to the forest.

Only this time, resting atop the familiar boulder was a flower crown made of delicate white blossoms. She stared at it, not quite understanding why it was here. "Did you do that?"

"I did."

She arched her brow. "You made me a flower crown." It wasn't a question. "That's your idea of doing me one better?"

A short laugh burst from Feowen's chest, transforming his serious features, turning them into something more familiar. "My Jeanie." He blew out a breath, as if working up to something. "It is what the crown represents. I have done some thinking—mostly because a wise person in the form of my little cousin gave me good advice. So, I'm acting on it."

Her thoughts began to race.

"That crown is not simply a flower crown. It symbolizes something. When a sprite wishes to propose a life pairing with their partner, they present a crown of aevindra flowers. The aevindra is unique to our forest. It symbolizes beauty and eternity. Presenting the crown is a proposal of sorts, similar to how a husband might propose to a wife. But we do not have marriages in my culture. Only life ceremonies."

Her lips parted. She had heard whisperings about life ceremonies, but they were sacred and she knew next to nothing about them. She glanced back at the flower crown before finding Feowen's steady gaze. "You... You're asking me to...to marry you?"

"Of a sort."

She took a step back. Something akin to pain flashed over his features, there and gone. "Feowen... We... I... I could never live with myself if you regretted binding yourself to me. I know we have touched on this. I know you wish to spend our future together. But this? I cannot force you to watch me grow old and die. It would be unfair to bind you like that."

His expression softened. "That is my choice to make, not yours. I know what I am committing to. I have considered the consequences. I have no doubts, only hope."

She studied him, her chest aching. She wanted to have that same hope. But there was too much fear.

Learning of Koldis and Taylynn that morning had set her off. It had reminded her that yet another of her close friends had found their happily ever after. There was only one other person in their circle who suffered a similar fate. Desaree had accepted Verath knowing she would age and die. How did she live with the weight of it?

"You are not yet twenty-five, Jeanie." She softened at his use of her pet name. "You and I will have many decades together."

"Yes, but..." She chewed on her bottom lip, not daring to glance at the crown.

"If you like, I could age myself to match. We sprites can alter our appearance as we see fit. How would I look with gray hair, I wonder?" He appeared thoughtful.

She couldn't help the small laugh that lightened her emotions. "You really want to do this? To bind yourself to me?"

"I do. And I want you to bind yourself to me." Her throat felt thick, making it harder to swallow. "Forget about your doubts and worries for just a moment. Tell me what you want."

"I want you. I want us to be together." There was no question about it. Of course she wanted this. But the thought of seeing him fifty years from now, knowing he was whole while she wasted away...

Feowen casually clasped his hands behind his back and said, "Do you know that the aevindra flower only grows along the trunks of a specific kind of tree within this forest? Each of our ancient trees carries a spriten soul. You know of the tree shepherds? When a sprite dies, the shepherds take their soul away from the king tree and plant it within an ancient tree inside of our forest. It is why everything is so connected. When a life pair dies, their souls aren't always planted together. The shepherds don't know any better. And yet, because the forest is alive, because our trees move at the whim of the king tree, occasionally those souls find a way back to each other. Isn't that incredible? The aevindra flower only grows on pairs of trunks, on the trunks of two adjacent trees that are said to be life pairs to each other. Twin souls. They are very difficult to find. Some say that only those meant to find them, will. I was meant to find those flowers for you. I was meant to make you that crown. Just as I am meant to make you this proposal. Share your life with me, Jeanine. Your whole life. Bind yourself to me as I wish to bind myself to you."

A sob escaped her throat. It had been building since the moment he talked about life-bound souls. It was all too much.

"Come here." He crossed to her, pulling her into his arms. She let herself go. Let the frustration, the irritation, the fear, and the doubt leave her body in the form of tears. Gods, she hated this time of the month. Even if it wasn't entirely to blame for everything she was feeling.

He had done something truly incredible for her. He had gone in search of the aevindra flower and made her a crown. He was an ancient being. He had considered the consequences and still wanted her.

"I am not asking you for an answer today," he murmured against her hair. "In fact, I would prefer it if you think about it. Just as you do not wish for me to have regrets, I would not have you regret this decision years from now."

"Okay," she managed, hiccuping.

"The flowers will not age or die. Not unless you reject my offer."

"And... If I accept?" Her heart rate jumped at the thought.

"If you accept, it is customary to place the crown upon your head, so that I might see your answer. Promise me you will consider it?"

"I will. I promise."

"If you decide to do this with me, I would like to do it when we return to the capital. Just a small ceremony with our closest companions. While we cannot have a true life ceremony, I have a few ideas that would make it perfect for both of us. A little of the traditions from spriten culture mixed with those of yours. We could have the ceremony in the king's tower rooftop garden. I think it would make for the perfect spot, don't you?"

She nodded against his chest, already picturing the scene he wove with his words.

"Good." He hooked a finger under her chin, tipping her face up to his. The kiss was gentle. She let herself relax into him, allowing the feel of his mouth to comfort her. When he pulled back to kiss her forehead, she caught a flash of light. It was faint. Just a small green glow that spoke of sprite magic. Her gaze fixed on the crown. "Did you see that?"

"See what?"

"The crown. I thought..." But it looked the same as it had before. The beautiful white flowers on their delicate vines. "I thought it glowed with magic."

He made a humming sound. "I have never heard of that happening. But then, who knows? Perhaps that is the king tree, giving us its blessing."

Her breath caught. The idea of the king tree meddling in her life felt comical. But then...she was in love with a spriten prince.

"Come. We don't want to miss Claire's farewell feast." He released her, moving over to collect the crown, which he handed to her. She ran her fingers over the beautiful flowers, appreciating them all the more now that she understood what they symbolized and how rare they were.

They made their way back into Esterpine. She caught a few curious looks along the way. Those looks turned surprised when they caught sight of the crown dangling from her fingers. It seemed that every sprite knew what it meant as their eyes darted between her and Feowen.

"Is there going to be talk about how the spriten prince proposed and his intended didn't come back wearing his crown?"

Feowen's deep chuckle had heat blossoming low in her belly. "Oh, I'm sure there will be talk. But I am the trouble-maker prince. They will only say it serves me right."

She bit her lip to suppress a smile.

Taylynn appeared before them. Her expression faltered when it dropped to the crown. Jeanine braced herself. Surely the queen would disapprove. Instead, when Taylynn's gaze lifted, her face transformed into a brilliant smile, all warmth. She reached for Feowen and pulled him into a hug. "I am happy for you, brother."

Feowen barked a laugh. "Happy that she has not yet accepted me?"

"That you have found someone who means so much. And yes, that she has not yet accepted you." Taylynn pulled back, keeping a hold of her brother's shoulders. "It builds character. Your head is already big enough on a normal day."

This time Feowen did laugh. When Taylynn released him, it was to turn to Jeanine and pull her into a similar hug. She stiffened a fraction, then relaxed. "Trust your heart. It will lead you."

She pulled back to study the spriten queen. "Why do I feel like you already know what I'm going to decide?"

Taylynn only grinned before slipping away, leaving the two of them smiling in her wake. "Is it funny that I'm actually going to miss your sister?"

"Not funny at all. And, I'm sure she'll still find a way to meddle in our lives, even with her new role as queen."

"I can't decide if I should be excited or terrified."

"We should probably be both. Now, come." Taking her hand, he led her towards the feast. It was their final night in Esterpine. She wasn't sure when they would return to this place, but she hoped it wouldn't be too long. It had become a second home of sorts. It would always be the place where she'd found her purpose. Where she'd found Feowen.

CHAPTER 28
MERRIAN'S RETURN

Celenore

Merrian exhaled a relieved breath as Reyr descended towards the landscape below. Her thighs ached, her shoulders ached...everything ached. She envied the more powerful mages who healed faster. Her meager abilities with magic meant she was prone to longer bouts of discomfort and illness, even if it wouldn't kill her. She bit her lip. Perhaps she could ask Reyr for a massage.

Her cheeks flushed at the thought as the ground came up to meet them. So much had changed between them. Every time she thought back to those moments in the cave, her body rebelled with a fresh wave of desire that left her ravenous. They'd spent hours tangled up together, exploring each other's bodies with reverent touches. It had started with hungry kisses and ended with wandering fingers and mouths. He'd brought her to completion twice before he'd allowed her to do the same for him. And yet, they hadn't breached that final barrier between them. He hadn't given himself fully, and neither had she.

Reyr landed and she slid from his back, eager to be on her own two feet again. She removed her pack as she went, dropping it on the ground. He transformed moments later, his golden scales shimmering into skin, clothing materializing with the shift.

The wilderness stretched around them. Tonight was their last night alone. What would happen once they reached the capital? Would this thing between them keep evolving? Or would they go back to being friends?

For all she'd replayed every intimate moment between them in that cave, she'd also replayed Reyr's words. How he'd fought the thing between them. How he'd resisted it. Did that mean he didn't really want anything between them?

"You are doing a lot of thinking. What's going on in that mind of yours?" Reyr's voice broke through her contemplation.

"What?" She blinked. "Oh."

"You have that look. Like you are trying to untangle a knot that won't give." His eyes, amber and knowing, studied her face.

She cleared her throat. "Yeah. Just...lost in my thoughts."

"Care to share?" Reyr tucked his fingers beneath her chin, tilting her face up towards him as he studied her.

"It's nothing."

"Please tell me." She chewed on the inside of her cheek. "The truth. Not some deflection. We've been through too much together for that."

Gods, but he was right.

"I'm worried about where we go from here."

He made a humming sound, his thumb tracing along her jawline. "Well, I'd like to kiss you for a start."

Before she could correct him, he bent and pressed their lips together. Her traitorous heart beat out a series of heavy thumps. An arm snaked around her waist, pulling her flush to him. The feel of his hardening length against her abdomen was all she needed to know. He was just as affected as she was.

The warmth of his mouth, of his tongue as it slid along hers, had every coherent thought slipping from her mind. His arms tightened around her and he groaned. Their movements intensified. He pulled away to lay kisses along her jaw, stopping to nip her earlobe.

Heat exploded between the apex of her thighs, her knees nearly buckling. It didn't matter. Reyr held her against him, keeping their bodies flush.

It should have been impossible, the way he affected her. "Reyr." She placed her hands against his chest, giving a gentle push.

"Hmm?" He withdrew slowly, eyes still half-lidded.

"Shouldn't we get camp going before it's too dark to see?"

He blinked, his glassy eyes regaining a measure of clarity. "I can see just fine in the dark."

She frowned. "You can?"

"Mmm-hmm." He tried to pull her back to him.

"Reyr!"

"Yes?"

"You never told me you could see in the dark. I... I thought that was just a myth."

"Not a myth. Drengr can see perfectly well in the dark."

Her lips parted as mortification washed over her. She took a step back. All those times she had—oh, gods.

He made a grumbly sound, rubbing a hand over his face. "I swear on my honor as a shield, I respected your privacy."

"Yes, but—"

"Merrian." The way he said her name made her freeze. "Let's get camp going and then we can talk. Yes?"

"Right. Yes. I'm going to go and relieve myself while you do that —somewhere your keen eyes don't penetrate."

She would forever be mortified now. Why hadn't she considered the drengr's abilities all those months locked in a cell? Every time she'd used the chamber pot, she'd assumed that she'd had a measure of privacy. But he'd been able to see her doing her business all that time. Oh, gods.

She wanted to sink into a hole, let the earth swallow her up.

That was probably why she walked much farther away than necessary to take care of her needs. That and she needed some time to herself. Time to make sense of her jumbled thoughts.

When she returned, there was a warm fire going. Reyr had flattened the prairie grasses around it and spread a blanket across the ground. What remained of their rations was set out and waiting.

She could feel his eyes on her as she took a seat and dug in, her stomach growling in anticipation. This time tomorrow, she'd be treating herself to hot food. The thought of eating a feast in the keep's dining hall made the food in her mouth taste like sawdust in comparison.

Reyr took a seat, eyeing the rations before him with distaste. He hadn't gone hunting since the start of their journey, opting to eat the same food she did. Only, it looked like he was having similar thoughts. Good food was less than a day away.

After a moment, he lifted a strip of dried meat to his mouth and began to chew. They ate in silence for a while, their chewing drowned out by the crackle of the fire and chirping insects.

"You asked where we go from here," he said at last. She jolted. "The truth is, I don't know. I promised that I would accompany you on your tour of Dragonwall, helping those in need, and I will. Only, this trip has shown me that it is impossible to control myself in your presence. I've fought many battles, Merrian, but none as difficult as resisting what's between us."

"Why do you want to?" Hurt bloomed in her chest, snuffing out what little desire remained. "Am I... Do you not want me?"

"Oh, I want you." His voice darkened, a rumble in his chest that reminded her of his dragon form.

"Then, why?"

He turned to fully face her. "Merrian, I am a drengr. One whose mate has come and gone from this world. You might be mage-born, and that will give you a longer life than that of a human, but I cannot give you children, a family. I cannot marry you or become your husband—"

"I don't care about those things."

"I saw the way you looked at some of the children we encountered in Squall's End."

A strangled sound burst from her chest. "You... You *frustrating* male! You based your assumptions on how I interacted with children and assumed that I wanted my own, simply from that? You could have asked me. I would have told you that I don't want children or a conventional relationship."

Reyr blinked a few times. "You...don't?"

She made an annoyed sound and fell back on the blanket, looking up at the stars. Better than his infuriatingly handsome face. "You know my past, where I came from, why I do what I do. There isn't a whole lot of room for family in that, not unless I give up my dreams, and I know you wouldn't want that."

"I wouldn't. Not ever. And certainly not because of me."

"If there is to be a family, it would be one of my choosing. There are too many motherless children in this world. All they want is love. I could give that to them—if I chose to have children, that is."

Reyr grunted. She turned to look up at him. He appeared thoughtful, digesting all she had said. He leaned down, propping himself on an elbow to be closer to her. "I cannot promise that I'll be an easy male to get on with."

A burst of laughter fell from her lips. "You think I don't already know that? I have seen you at your absolute worst—or close to it."

The days following the loss of his mate would have been his worst. But losing the crown definitely came in second place.

"Then all my worries are unfounded."

"Exactly." She smiled.

He moved over to her, keeping their eyes locked. Her pulse began to race as he settled between the cradle of her thighs. She suppressed a groan at the feel of him. His gaze was dark, pupils blown wide. "So we're doing this? You and me? Us?"

"I want to." The words slipped out, barely a whisper, but in the quiet night they sounded like a shout. A proclamation for all the world to hear.

"As do I." He dipped his head to capture her lips.

The kiss was different from the ones they'd shared last night. There was no desperation, no frantic edge. It was a promise, slow and sure. She melted into it, into him, allowing herself to feel everything without reservation.

When he pulled back, his gaze was serious. "I want you, Merrian. All of you. But not here, not like this."

She blinked, coming back to herself. "What do you mean?"

"When I take you, I want it to be in a proper bed, not on the hard ground." His lips pulled up in a half-smile. "I want to be able to focus solely on you without having to listen for predators or worry about the weather."

"As if any predator would stand a chance against you!"

"Yes, well... Be that as it may, we have time." The words were a gentle murmur against her mouth. "All the time in the world."

She blew out a breath, relenting. "You're a terrible tease, you know that?"

"I've been called worse." His laughter was a rich, warm sound that seemed to fill the night air around them. She felt it radiate through her, burrowing deep in her bones.

They spent the rest of the evening talking, planning their return to the capital, speculating about what might have changed in their absence. When sleep finally claimed them, they were tangled together beneath a shared blanket, her head on his chest, his arm wrapped protectively around her.

THE TURRETS of the great keep in Kastali Dun glinted in the afternoon sunlight, a welcoming beacon on the horizon. Her heart lifted at the sight. After weeks away, the prospect of a hot bath and clean clothes was nearly overwhelming.

Reyr dipped low, turning on his wingtip. Below her, the city slanted with him. As they approached the keep, the guards on the battlements sent up shouts of recognition. There was no mistaking his golden scales.

She looked for the king's tower, expecting him to land in the same place they'd left. Instead, he circled around before bringing them down in the main courtyard near the royal gardens. Her cheeks flamed at the sight of the small crowd gathered. Gods, had he done this on purpose?

She quickly slid from his back, her legs only slightly wobbly from the long flight. He transformed behind her, his hand immediately finding the small of her back. The gesture was subtle but possessive, and she didn't miss the focused gazes from several onlookers.

Among them, she spotted Lady Owen, the widow of a prominent courtier, whose tight-lipped disapproval was evident even from a distance. The older woman's gaze flickered between Reyr's hand at Merrian's back, her eyebrows rising in silent judgment.

Was that what this was? Reyr's way of claiming her in front of an audience? A political maneuver? As a rule, only mates flew with their drengr. She wasn't his mate, and yet, he didn't care that the world saw what was considered by most to be inappropriate behavior.

"My lord!" A servant hurried forward. "Welcome back. We've been expecting you."

"Have you, now?" Reyr's voice held amusement. He shot her a glance and winked. Her lips parted.

"Lord Verath's requested your presence in the tower as soon as you arrive."

"Yes, I'm aware." Reyr nodded. "See that Lady Merrian's things are taken to her chambers."

"Of course, my lord." The servant rushed to grab the travel pack from her hands. He scurried off before she could protest. She let out a small scoff. She was perfectly capable of carrying her own belongings.

"Well." Reyr turned to her. "Duty calls, it seems."

"Go." She gave him a gentle push. "I'll find you later."

He held her gaze for a long moment, then he bent and pressed a swift kiss to her forehead, unconcerned about their onlookers. Heat bloomed in her stomach. "Tonight," he whispered before turning to follow the servant.

The word was a promise.

She stood still for a moment, watching him go. The kiss had been so casual, so natural—as if they'd been doing it for years. Her cheeks warmed at the thought.

She glanced at the small crowd, noticing whispers behind hands and widened eyes. "Well, don't you all have duties to attend to?" The words were spoken in the voice she'd mastered during her time as a healer, the one that made even the most stubborn patients comply.

Everyone rushed into action, scattering. She took a moment to look around, her gaze roaming over the entrance to the royal gardens. It was all so familiar, almost exactly like it had been that first day she'd arrived. When Taylynn had brought her here to stand in as Claire's body double. So much had changed since then. She wasn't the same woman anymore. She was stronger, more confident, more certain of her place in the world, more certain of the impact she wanted to have.

She noticed something new as she walked—a small statue of a bird near the garden entrance that hadn't been there before. A symbol of rebirth after Kane's occupation. The kingdom was healing, just as she was.

She made her way through the keep, nodding to familiar faces. When she reached her new apartment, the one she'd moved into after being released, she found everything just as she'd left it. Her pack rested on the foot of the bed. She went to it, reaching inside. Her fingers brushed against the letter. Caterina's letter.

She pulled it free, setting it on the table. The parchment was sealed with a simple blob of wax—no crest, nothing to identify its sender. Caution, perhaps, or shame.

After a quick bath and change of clothes, she set out in search of the recipient. The letter sat safely in the pocket of her gown, seemingly innocuous. There was no telling what weight it carried. Especially knowing what she knew about Caterina.

She found Desaree in the royal library, bent over a large tome with Saffra. They were so engrossed in their reading they didn't notice her at first.

"I hope I'm not interrupting anything important," she said softly.

Both women looked up, their faces lighting with surprise and joy.

"Merrian!" Desaree was on her feet in an instant, rushing forward to embrace her. The gesture made her warm all over. She'd never expected Claire's friends to welcome her with open arms, but they treated her like one of their own and she loved them for it. "When did you get back?"

"Just this afternoon." She returned the hug, surprised at how good it felt to be around them again. The air smelled of new parchment and fresh ink—the library seemed busier than she remembered, with several scribes copying texts at the far table.

"Your trip went well?" Saffra reached for her, squeezing her in a tight hug. "We've missed you."

"And I've missed you both." She meant it. Her time with Reyr had been impactful—life changing, even. But there was something irreplaceable about female friendship.

They settled at the table, and she gave them a brief account of her journey, carefully glossing over certain parts involving caves and Reyr. She wanted to keep those delicious bits to herself. But she did tell them that things had changed between them.

Desaree clapped her hands together, beaming. "Oh, gods. I'm so glad you two aren't at each others' throats anymore. I knew there was something there. All that palpable tension. All those simmering looks you used to throw at each other back in the beginning."

"You know what they say," Saffra teased. "There's a fine line between hate and love."

"I don't—that's not—we don't—" She couldn't quite bring herself to say she didn't love him. Because the truth was, she had fallen hard for the drengr she'd once despised.

Clearing her throat, she said, "What about you two? What have I missed?"

"Oh, the usual stuff," Desaree said with a wave of her hand. "Tons of court gossip. Leah's working on a library project you'll love. And Saffra here has been busy planning her bonding ceremony."

"Your bonding ceremony?!"

"We think it's time." Saffra's skin flushed.

"Congratulations!"

"Thank you." Her eyes glowed with happiness. "We're waiting on Claire and Talon's return before we announce a date. But hopefully they'll be back any day now."

"I can't wait," Desaree breathed. "We need her back. Then things can finally go back to normal. Or, a new normal, I suppose."

They fell quiet, contemplating. She reached into her pocket and pulled out the letter. "There's something else," she said.

She slid the letter across the table to Desaree, who looked down at it, frowning. "What's that?"

"Right before I left Captain Bennett's ship, a woman slipped this to me." Merrian hesitated. "She seemed pretty adamant that I give it to you."

Desaree's eyes darted between the two of them and the suspicious letter resting on the table. "Who?"

"A woman by the name of Caterina."

A small gasp was the only sign of Desaree's surprise.

"You found Caterina?" Saffra didn't bother to hide her shock. "But, she's a wanted criminal."

"Believe me, I know. Reyr made a fuss about it."

"Then why didn't he arrest her?" Saffra demanded.

"No jurisdiction out on the open ocean. Besides, what would he have done, carried her back in his claws?"

Saffra huffed. "It's no less than she deserves, after what she did to Desaree. To her mother."

"I completely agree," Merrian said.

"Right." Saffra made to stand. "Where is Reyr? I'm going to give him a piece of my mind—"

"Both of you, stop!" Desaree snapped. They both froze. She'd never seen Des lose her temper. "This is my fight. Saffra, sit down." Saffra complied, pressing her lips together. "I think I should see what's in this letter before we jump to any conclusions, don't you?"

"Yes, all right." Saffra leaned back in her chair, crossing her arms. "But if that snake of a woman says anything hurtful, I'm getting Bedelth and we're flying out to Captain Bennett's ship immediately. I won't have her hurting you any more than she already has."

Desaree nodded, still staring at the letter. Then she picked it up, staring at the seal. There was a slight tremble to her finger as she slid it beneath the flap of parchment. Merrian held her breath as Desaree broke it open and unfurled the parchment to discover the contents within.

CHAPTER 29
CAT'S LETTER

Kastali Dun

Desaree's hands trembled as she broke the seal and unfurled Caterina's letter. The paper was of an inexpensive quality that spoke to the conditions on Captain Bennett's ship. The calligraphic handwriting filling the page was a direct contrast, all elegant lines and beautiful flourishes.

Desaree,

I know you probably wish to burn this letter without reading it. I would not blame you. There was a time when I would have delighted in your pain. Today, that thought only brings shame.

For years, I have carried the weight of what I did to your mother. I was young and selfish. Even a little scared. It was too easy to fall for Kane's manipulations. Not that it's any excuse. My jealousy over the life you lived turned me into an ugly person. I took that out on you. Again, not an excuse.

I won't ask for your forgiveness. Some acts are beyond that grace. But I want you to know that working with Captain Bennett has shown me the person I should have been. Someone who makes a difference rather than someone who tears others down. I can only hope that with each little act, each little deed of merit, I can work towards righting all the wrongs I have done. No amount of good I do will ever fix what I have done. I understand that. But I am willing to spend the rest of my life atoning. We have saved a lot of lives, so many people snatched from the clutches of slavery. It made me realize that even though the scales will never balance, at least they will tip in the right direction.

You deserved better from me. Better than a childhood wounded by me and my father's cruelty. You deserved your mother, your title, and your dignity. All things I helped take from you. We could have been true sisters but I destroyed that. My father destroyed that. I admire your triumph over me, that you have stepped in to reclaim the title that should have been yours.

I deserve nothing less than the sentence King Talon was sure to pass. A lifetime spent in the dungeon beneath the keep. Instead, I am here. I hope you can see that my time and life were better spent serving Dragonwall. Perhaps that is a little selfish of me to say. I am, and will always be, imperfect in that regard.

Anyway, I will leave it at that. Assuming you have not burned this yet, I will just add that I do not expect a response to this letter. It would be impossible to find me out at sea. It's better that way. Better that you wash your hands of me once and for all.

I hope knowing I live with the consequences of my actions will be enough to bring you some peace. You were always the strong one. Far stronger than I gave you credit for.

If our paths should cross again, I hope that we might meet as indifferent acquaintances. But, if you wish to mete justice, I will accept whatever you deem appropriate. Until then, I wish you all the happiness I once so callously tried to deny you.

Sincerely,

Cat

A tear splattered the parchment. And then another. And another. Her breaths came faster with each word. A pressure built in her chest like a physical weight, making it difficult to draw air. When she finished, she was a mix of confusing emotions. Disbelief, anger, even relief.

"Caterina wrote this?" she demanded of Merrian, her voice barely above a whisper.

"Yes. She...she gave it to me herself."

Desaree blinked back the blur clouding her eyes. The words on the page swam before her, wavering like heat rising from summer-baked stones.

"What is it?" Saffra demanded. "Did she say something horrible? She did, didn't she! That *witch*! Let me see it."

Saffra reached for the letter but Desaree pulled it away and stood. "I think—I need a moment. I'm going for fresh air."

"Desaree!" Saffra and Merrian's cries followed her as she fled the library.

Her feet pounded the flagstones as she made her way through the keep's corridors. Minutes later, she found herself surrounded by the greenery of the royal gardens. She braced her hands on her knees, taking gasping breaths, all but choking. A cold sweat broke out across her forehead. Passersby regarded her but she ignored their questioning stares. The letter still trembled in her hands. She took off at a clipped pace, glancing back over the contents.

She'd never in her wildest dreams expected to receive any apology from Caterina, and certainly no admission of wrongdoing. Every word on the paper ripped something open inside her. And yet, those same words then knitted those open wounds back together.

There was no more wondering where Caterina had gotten off to. She hadn't run off to cause more trouble. She'd fallen into the hands of Captain Bennett, somehow turning her life around.

She pawed at her cheeks, wiping away the tears. A small laugh burst from her as she pictured Caterina on the deck of a ship, bedraggled as she secured ropes and used a mop and bucket. Her laughter intensified. Gods, it was so fitting.

In fact, it was rather perfect. She'd never have to face the woman again. Never have to worry about her storming back into her life, causing hurt.

Some of the anger she'd carried for years began to fade. The realization dawned on her that this tragedy no longer defined her existence. She didn't have to remain forever the girl whose mother was murdered, whose inheritance was stolen. She could simply be...herself.

"Desaree?"

She whirled. "Verath. Aren't—aren't you supposed to be debriefing with Reyr? What are you—?"

"Saffra said you were distressed."

She exhaled. Her friend meant well, but running off to Verath felt kind of like tattling. Then again, if anyone should be with her at this moment, it was the male who had helped her begin healing after all Caterina had done. He deserved to know what she was going through. They didn't hide things from each other.

Holding out the letter, she waited for Verath to take it.

The silence was stifling as he read its contents. She watched each expression flit across his face. Watched his frown deepen, the corners of his mouth turning down, his brow furrowing like storm clouds gathering. At last, he looked up. "You're sure this is from Caterina Rosen?"

"Merrian was positive."

Verath swore, pinching the bridge of his nose. "I can have guards stationed at the Port of Kastali. Have her arrested if she sets foot in the capital—"

"Verath, no."

"No?"

"No." She held out her hand, motioning for the letter.

He handed it back, his jaw tight. "You want to let her go?"

"I think so." She carefully folded the letter, slipping it into the pocket of her gown. It felt heavier than it should have.

"Help me understand why you wish to allow the woman who *murdered your mother*, who made your life a living hell, to sail off into the sunset."

She closed her eyes, letting the scent of roses wash over her. The garden was vibrant with late summer blooms—climbing roses in shades of pink and yellow wound their way up trellises, and lavender bushes attracted lazy bumblebees. When she opened her eyes again, Verath's steady gaze was locked with hers. She took a step forward, reaching for his wrist. "The heaviest chains are those we forge ourselves. I've been carrying the weight of what she did to me, to my mother. The hatred, the anger, the need for justice. It's been dragging like an anchor behind me. I'm tired of being a victim. I'm tired of giving her that power over me. This letter gives me something I never thought I'd have."

"And what's that?"

She squeezed his wrist. "The chance to set down that anchor. I'm ready to move on—fully and completely. Besides, sticking her in the dungeon accomplishes nothing. I'm all for a good redemption. And I rather like the idea of her being stuck on a ship."

Verath turned his gaze away from hers, looking off into the distance. His hand went to the sverak at his hip, unconsciously clenching the grip. "She could be lying. This could be another manipulation. Half those words didn't even sound like her."

"You could be right. But I like to think otherwise. Either way, I'm choosing to finally be free of her."

His eyes snapped back to hers. "Just like that?"

"Just like that. I'm not forgiving her. I'm simply...letting go. There's a difference."

"Very well. Then I support your decision." He reached out and pulled her against him, ignoring the passersby who gawked.

She pulled her bottom lip between her teeth. "You'll lay down the torches and pitchforks, then?"

"Only for you. Only because this is what you want." He leaned down, pressing his forehead against hers.

"Thank you. Thank you for being here with me. Thank you for pushing me that day, when you came to my room and insisted I take back my title."

"I only want the best for you, love. You know that."

Her throat felt tight. "I know," she croaked.

She swayed gently in his arms as he held her. They were silent for several minutes. Somewhere in the distance, a bell rang announcing the hour. "What time is Saffra's fitting?"

She jolted, going ramrod straight. "Oh, gods! I'm the *worst* friend. If I don't go now, I'll be late."

Verath chuckled. "Come, let me escort you."

"Okay, but first—" She went up on her toes, capturing his mouth in a grateful kiss.

He growled low in his chest. "Don't start something you cannot finish, little love."

She giggled, pulling away. "What if we finish it later? Tonight?"

"I'll hold you to that."

As they walked back toward the keep, she felt lighter than she had in years.

"SORRY I'M LATE!" she cried, breezing into Saffra's chambers. "Oh!"

The place was transformed. Bolts of fabric in varying shades of orange and sunset colors lined the walls. There were several books out on the table. Madame Rosanne hovered over Saffra's shoulder as she flipped through one of them. Jocelyn, Leah, and Merrian were at the table with her. Assistants stood around ready to jump into action at Rosanne's request.

"Desaree!" Saffra abandoned the book and surged to her feet, taking a step towards her before faltering. "Are you—?"

"I'm well. Really. More than well."

"The letter?" Merrian also stood.

"Everything's all right, I promise."

"Did Verath find you?" Saffra worried her lower lip.

"He did. I don't know whether to scold you or hug you."

Saffra barked out a laugh. "Hug me, please. I was worried."

Desaree moved to embrace her friend, careful of the pins that held swatches of fabric to Saffra's current outfit. "I'm sorry for running off like that. It was just...overwhelming."

"Do you want to talk about it?" Saffra asked quietly.

"Later, perhaps. Right now, I want to focus on you. This is your bonding ceremony preparation, and I don't want to take away from that." Desaree gestured to the fabrics. "Look at all of this!"

"It's a bit excessive, isn't it?" Saffra glanced around with a mix of excitement and anxiety. "Madame Rosanne has brought half her shop, I think."

"Nonsense!" the dressmaker exclaimed, fluttering her hands. "A drengr's bonding ceremony is a once-in-a-lifetime occasion. We must have options!"

"And what glorious options they are," Leah said, running her fingers over a bolt of burnished copper silk. "I've never seen so many beautiful fabrics."

"Come, Des." Jocelyn patted the chair beside her. "We're just getting to the good part. Madame has sketches!"

Desaree slipped into the open seat, leaning forward to see the book Saffra examined. It was filled with detailed drawings of gowns in various styles, each more exquisite than the last. Just like all of Rosanne's sketches, these came to life with a single touch, mesmerizing the room's occupants, especially Leah, who looked on with fierce longing.

"I was thinking of this one," Saffra said, pointing to a design with a fitted bodice and flowing skirt. "But with alterations, of course."

"Of course," Madame Rosanne agreed. "The bodice will feature scaled embroidery to honor Lord Bedelth's dragon form. And here," she tapped the sketch, "we'll add panels in burnished gold, orange, and pink, to complement his colors."

"It's perfect," Desaree breathed. "You'll look absolutely stunning."

"I still can't believe it's happening," Saffra admitted, a faint blush coloring her cheeks. "After everything..."

"You deserve this happiness," Jocelyn said firmly. "Both of you do."

"Indeed," Madame Rosanne clapped her hands. "Now, Lady Saffra, if you'll stand, we'll take measurements and begin draping some of these fabrics."

As Saffra stood and Madame's assistants swarmed around her with measuring tapes and pins, Desaree turned her attention to Leah. "Speaking of relationships, how are things progressing with Jovari? I noticed he barely takes his eyes off you these days."

Leah's cheeks turned a shade that nearly matched her lavender hair. "We're... taking things slowly."

"Which is very wise," Merrian said with an approving nod. "Given everything that's happened."

"But not *too* slowly, I hope," Jocelyn chimed in, not bothering to keep her voice down. "Anyone can see you two are perfect mates for each other."

"Oh, stop it," Leah protested, though she couldn't help smiling. "We're here for Saffra, remember?"

"Yes, please," Saffra sing-songed from her position surrounded by pins and fabric. "Let's focus on the ceremony that's actually happening."

"Fine, fine," Jocelyn conceded with a wink at Leah. "But we'll be discussing your blossoming romance later. Don't think you're escaping that easily."

Madame Rosanne draped a length of shimmering bronze fabric over Saffra's shoulder. "Oh, this is divine with your skin tone," she declared. "And imagine it catching the light during the dancing!"

Conversation flowed easily from there—discussing food, flowers, music, and all the details that would make Saffra's day perfect. Madame Rosanne and her assistants continued their work, draping fabrics, taking notes, and occasionally requesting Saffra to turn or lift her arms.

"Will your family be coming from Brushbridge?" Desaree asked, helping to hold a length of sheer, golden fabric that Madame was considering for an overlay.

"Yes, they're already preparing for the journey," Saffra said. "My parents and siblings are all thrilled."

"As they should be," Merrian said. "It's not every day that a loved one mates with a king's shield."

"And not just any shield," Jocelyn added with a wink. "The steadfast one."

Saffra rolled her eyes, but her smile was fond. "Don't let him hear you say that. His ego is big enough already."

"Speaking of egos," Leah said, "which of the other shields will be most emotional at the ceremony? My money's on Jovari."

"Oh, definitely Jovari," Desaree agreed with a laugh. "Though Koldis will pretend he has something in his eye."

"And Reyr will stand there looking stoic," Saffra added with a fond smile, "while trying not to let anyone see how affected he is."

The afternoon passed in a blur of fabric samples, design decisions, and laughter. By the time Madame Rosanne and her assistants packed up their supplies, the general design for Saffra's gown had been agreed upon—a magnificent creation of burnt orange silk with gold and pink accents, featuring subtle scale embroidery at the bodice and flame-like patterns cascading down the skirt.

"I'll have the initial framework ready for a fitting next week," she promised as she gathered her books. "Oh, and I'll bring some jewelry options as well. Orange fire opals, perhaps, or imperial topaz..."

After the dressmaker departed, the five women remained, lounging comfortably in Saffra's sitting room. A servant had brought tea and small cakes, which they nibbled as they talked.

"Thank you all for being here today," Saffra said, looking around at her friends. "I couldn't have done this alone."

"You never have to," Desaree said firmly, squeezing Saffra's hand. "That's what friends are for."

"Family," Jocelyn corrected with a smile. "We're family."

Desaree felt warmth bloom in her chest as she looked at these women—her chosen sisters. From Saffra who had been her first true friend in the keep, to newcomers like Leah who had found her place among them so easily. Even Merrian, once a stranger, now part of their circle.

"Family," Desaree agreed, raising her teacup in a toast. "To bonds stronger than blood."

"To bonds stronger than blood," the others echoed, clinking their cups together.

As afternoon stretched toward evening, Desaree found herself filled with gratitude. The letter from Caterina had closed one chapter of her life, but here—surrounded by love and laughter— many more chapters were just beginning.

CHAPTER 30
FRIGHT'S STONE

The Gable Forest

Claire breathed in the familiar, crisp mountain air as she and her entourage approached the entrance to the Forest Clan's cave. So much had changed since her last visit here. Kane's death. The loss of Cyrus. The weight of the sprite crown that no longer rested on her head—physically or metaphorically.

The morning sun cast long shadows across the mountain path, illuminating the vibrant greenery. Their departure from Esterpine several days prior had been met with mixed emotions—many sprites had lined the paths to bid farewell to their retired queen, tossing luminescent petals that clung to her cloak. Taylynn had stood at the forest's edge, regal in a formal gown, watching until they disappeared from sight. Claire had felt the forest's awareness shift then, its focus turning inward toward its new queen, leaving her free.

"Having second thoughts?" Talon squeezed her hand as they walked. His scars caught the mid-morning light, giving his face a rugged beauty that still made her heart flutter.

"Not at all." She smiled up at him. "Taylynn was always meant to be Esterpine's queen. I was just keeping her throne warm."

Her hand drifted briefly to her still-flat stomach, the gesture becoming habitual even though there was no outward sign of life growing within. Talon noticed immediately, his eyes softening.

"How are you feeling?" he asked, his concern evident.

"Fine. Excellent, actually," she replied, the private joy passing between them.

There were others traveling with them. Her queen's guard led by Feowen, along with her handmaidens Selphie and Miera, and Koldis. Everyone who had chosen to accompany them back to Kastali Dun. Though she'd abdicated, her guard still maintained their formation around her, protective as ever. Jeanine walked close to Feowen, their shoulders occasionally brushing. The crown of aevindra flowers he'd presented was carefully wrapped in silk and tucked into a pouch on her travel pack. She hadn't given him her answer yet, but they all knew what Jeanine would say.

The white dragonstone sat heavy in the pouch at her hip. She'd felt its pull growing stronger as they approached the caves, like it sensed its true owner was near.

As they entered the cave system, the temperature rose noticeably. The air grew sweet with the scent of warm sand and dragon musk.

The vast interior opened before them, revealing the multiple levels carved into the rock that overlooked the central hatching ground. The mothers and their hatchlings had settled into the ancient space as if they'd always belonged here, reclaiming the ancestral home.

They made their way down to the warm sands below where the final clutch of eggs still rested, their shells gleaming with jewel colors in the golden light filtering through strategic openings in the cave ceiling. A little over ten eggs remained.

A smile pulled at Claire's lips as she caught sight of the young dragonlings frolicking about. They'd grown. Fright was keeping them well fed, clearly.

"Claire!" a familiar voice called, and she turned to see Irelia approaching.

A copper-colored hatchling the size of a large dog trailed behind her, watching Claire with intelligent golden eyes.

"Grandmother," she said warmly, embracing the elderly woman. The sprite blood in Irelia's veins had extended her life far beyond normal human years, but age showed in the deep lines of her face and the careful way she moved.

Irelia pulled back, her old hands gripping Claire's arms as she examined her. "We did not expect your return so soon. Is everything well? Kane?"

"He's dead." The words were simple, but she felt the weight of them. "Truly and finally. Though the cost was high." She wouldn't speak of Cyrus's final sacrifice here, not when the wound was still so fresh. Sometimes in her dreams, she still heard his final goodbye, felt the emptiness where his presence had once resided within her.

"There was never any doubt in my mind that you would succeed." Irelia nodded, studying her face carefully. "Though I see you still carry a shadow."

Claire looked away, uncomfortable with how perceptive Irelia was. "Some wounds take time."

"And some never fully heal," Irelia said softly. "But we learn to carry them with grace."

The copper hatchling nudged Irelia's hand, making a soft trilling sound. "Yes, yes, I haven't forgotten you," Irelia said, stroking its head. "Claire, this is Ember. She just received her name three nights ago. She's quite proud of it and has taken to following me everywhere, like the spark that she is."

Claire bent down, offering her hand to the young dragon. Claire laughed and Ember scurried off to rejoin her siblings, joining in their game of rough housing.

"I've brought something that doesn't belong to me." She patted the pouch at her side, returning to the purpose of their visit. "Where is Fright?"

"In his cavern, resting. The little ones wore him out." Irelia pointed towards the upper levels, to a large opening that led to one of the dragons' sleeping chambers.

She thanked Irelia and gave the others a look that said they could make themselves at home while she tended to this business. Then she turned to her mate. "Talon, shall we?"

Together they ascended to the upper levels of the cave. They passed the room that had been theirs the last time they were here. Her cheeks flushed as she recalled some of the ways they'd spent their time together as he'd helped her master the last bits of mage magic that gave her trouble.

"Careful, mate," Talon's voice slid into her mind, tinged with amusement and heat. *"Guard your thoughts or we might need a repeat of our time here."*

She bit her lip to keep from smiling. A repeat wouldn't be a bad thing.

They found Fright dozing in his cavern room. He sensed their arrival, blinking before lifting his head to greet them. He turned as they approached, intelligent eyes fixing on Claire immediately.

"Little Queen," his voice resonated in her mind. *"You have returned."*

"I have," she said, stepping closer without hesitation. *"And I've brought something that belongs to you."*

The white dragonstone warmed against her hand as she withdrew it from its pouch.

"My stone." Fright lowered his massive head to better see what she held, putting him at eye level with her.

"Taylynn replaced it with another stone to prevent Kane from using all five original dragonstones against us," she explained, holding the stone out in her palm. *"It saved us all."*

The white stone radiated heat and magic, pulsing with power that seemed to recognize its master.

Fright blinked slowly. *"Clever sprite. I am in her debt."*

"As are we all," Talon added, standing just behind Claire's shoulder. *"Your stone prevented all of us from being turned back to our original stone forms."*

She could sense Talon's tension despite his calm tone. The

memory of how close they'd come to losing everything still haunted him. She leaned back slightly, her shoulder brushing his chest in reassurance. They had survived. They had won.

"*May I?*" She indicated the place where the stone had been removed.

Fright rose up on his forearms in invitation, looking every bit the proud dragon he was.

She stepped forward, humming a gentle tune, drawn to the area of Fright's chest where a cavity remained—the exact shape of the white dragonstone. With steady hands, she pressed the stone into place. The moment it connected with his body, light flared around the edges, forcing her to stagger back and shield her eyes. Talon's arm wrapped around her waist, steadying her.

When the light dissipated, the stone had melded perfectly with the dragon's body, as if it had never been removed. There was no seam, no indication it had ever been separate, carved from the marble he used to be.

"*It has returned to its proper place,*" Fright said, tapping a talon against his chest, "*as have I.*" His voice had changed, the grinding quality replaced by something clearer, more melodious.

"*What will you do now?*" Claire asked. "*Will you stay with the hatchlings?*"

"*For a time.*" Fright nodded his massive head. "*These young ones need to learn the old ways, the true ways, of dragon kind. Before they were corrupted by Rage's greed.*" He shifted his position, his white scales gleaming in the filtered light. "*We are ushering in a new era— one where dragons, humans, and drengr coexist as they were always meant to. These young ones must learn not only our past but how to build this shared future. It will not be easy after so many centuries of separation, but it is necessary.*"

"*And after your time with them ends?*" Talon asked.

"*After,*" Fright's eyes gleamed, "*I will return to the world. The time of dragons hiding in shadows and forgotten mountains is ending. We will fly under Dragonwall's skies again, not as conquerors, but as allies.*"

Claire nodded. "*I welcome that day.*"

"*Thank you for returning what was mine,*" Fright said, his gaze warm with gratitude. *"Taylynn's deception saved us all. A clever queen, that one."*

"We're fortunate to have her," she agreed.

"Should you need my aid," Fright continued, *"you need only call. I am bound to you, who freed me from my stone prison, gave me the revenge I sought. My loyalty is yours until the end of my days."*

"Thank you, Fright." She bowed her head slightly. *"But I've never sought anyone's servitude. Friendship and alliance are what I value."*

Fright's mouth opened in what she now recognized as a dragon's approximation of a smile. *"Then you shall have both from me, freely given."*

They spoke a while longer, Claire sharing details of her confrontation with Kane, omitting the most painful parts. Fright, in turn, updated them on the progress of the hatchlings, who were growing stronger by the day.

When they descended again to the main level, they found Irelia surrounded by the youngest dragons, who seemed to flock to her like children to a beloved grandmother. She spoke to them in low tones. They understood, bobbing their heads and chirping in response. Several of them had arranged themselves in a circle around her, their jewel-bright scales creating a living mosaic at her feet.

"Look at their organization," Koldis murmured from behind Claire. "They're already establishing a hierarchy."

She watched as a small silver hatchling deferred to a larger red one, ducking its head and offering a wing tip in what appeared to be a gesture of respect. The social complexity surprised her.

"They adore her," Feowen observed.

The dragons around Irelia gathered closer as the group approached. Ember pressed her head against Irelia's hand, trilling softly.

"I'm glad you found your place here," Claire said.

"For now." Irelia stroked Ember, who had wrapped herself around her arm like a living bracelet. "These little ones need someone who understands them. I believe I'm meant to guide them through their early years. The king tree's fruit can wait."

"I'm glad to hear it. I like the idea of having you around, having you a part of this world for a little longer."

Irelia nodded. "And what of you? Your kingdom awaits its queen."

She nodded. "We should be going if we want to make good time."

Ember suddenly detached herself from Irelia's arm, scurrying across the stone floor toward Claire. Before anyone could react, the copper hatchling climbed up Claire's skirts and pressed her warm snout gently against her stomach. After a moment, she chittered excitedly and returned to Irelia's side. Irelia's eyes widened slightly on Claire's abdomen, drawing her own conclusions from Ember's behavior, then she met Claire's gaze with a knowing smile.

"We haven't told anyone yet," Claire whispered so only Irelia could hear.

"Your secret is safe with me," Irelia promised.

They said their goodbyes, Claire embracing Irelia one last time. The older woman whispered in her ear, "I'm always here if you need me. Be sure to visit when you can."

Outside the cave, their party assembled for departure. The day had advanced, the sun beginning its western descent. She squinted against the light, looking toward the distant horizon where Kastali Dun lay waiting. The capital was several days' journey away, but she could almost feel it calling to her—another kind of homecoming.

The mountain air smelled of pine and coming snow, though the weather remained clear for now. Behind them, the Forest Clan's cave mouth yawned dark against the mountainside, ancient and enduring.

"The unicorns have agreed to carry those who cannot fly," Feowen announced, gesturing to where Tourmaline and seven other unicorns stood waiting. The magnificent creatures pawed the ground impatiently, their sleek coats shimmering with unnatural lustre in the afternoon sun. "They'll convey your handmaidens and queen's guard."

"We meet again, Queen." Tourmaline's deep voice resonated in her mind.

Claire suppressed a smile and said aloud, "We appreciate your generosity, Tourmaline."

"Will you not ride with us?" the black unicorn asked, sounding almost disappointed.

"I'm afraid we must travel separately this time," she replied with genuine regret. Though unicorn travel was faster, she and Talon needed time alone in the sky to prepare for their return.

Her queen's guard looked uncomfortable at the idea of separation, particularly Feowen, whose eyes kept returning to the sky as if assessing weather conditions. They had discussed this plan previously, but she recognized their protective instincts ran deep. The unicorns would arrive at the capital first, allowing her handmaidens to prepare for their monarchs' arrival.

"My lady," Selphie stepped forward, adjusting the traveling cloak around Claire's shoulders, "we'll have everything ready for your grand return."

"Take care on the journey," she said, embracing both her sprite handmaidens. Then she turned to Feowen and added, "Watch over them."

"With my life," he promised, bowing slightly. His eyes flicked to Jeanine, who stood nearby adjusting her sword belt. "All of them."

Jeanine looked up, catching his gaze, and a faint blush colored her cheeks.

Claire turned to Talon, who stood waiting in his full dragon form, his iridescent black scales gleaming in the sunlight. Koldis had also transformed, his emerald body crouched low. There was something different about him since his mating with Taylynn—a new calm in his movements, a contentment that hadn't been there before.

With practiced ease, she climbed onto Talon's back.

"Ready?" Talon's voice rumbled in her mind, warm with affection.

"Always," she replied through their bond, sending him her complete trust and love.

She turned back to the others one last time. "We'll see you in Kastali Dun."

"Safe journey, my queen," her guards called in unison, their fists pressed to their hearts in salute.

As Talon launched into the sky with powerful strokes of his wings, she felt the familiar rush of exhilaration. Her stomach dropped pleasantly as they climbed, the wind whipping her hair into a wild tangle. Koldis rose beside them, his emerald scales flashing in the sunlight as they gained altitude.

The forested mountains fell away beneath them, the trees spreading out in an endless carpet of green that eventually gave way to the patchwork of fields and towns that made up Dragonwall proper. For a moment, she looked back at the cave entrance growing smaller in the distance, where Irelia stood watching their departure, hand raised in farewell, dragon hatchlings gathered around her like a living skirt.

Then she turned her gaze forward, toward Kastali Dun, toward home.

Toward their future.

CHAPTER 31

THE BRACE

Kastali Dun

Saffra glanced towards the horizon, her eyes fixed north. The queen's garden offered unparalleled views of the city and landscape beyond. Somewhere out there, Talon and Claire were winging their way home. According to their latest update, they were just a day away. Her heart swelled. To say she had been worried was an understatement. Claire's disappearance had frightened every single one of them. Thankfully, she had her frustration with archery and all the details for her bonding ceremony to keep her busy.

She pulled her gaze away from the landscape and scowled at the target. Bedelth was supposed to meet her here at sunset. With preparations underway for the king's return, they hadn't gotten a chance to practice this morning. He'd been a bit cagey about it and rescheduled for this evening, opting to bring a picnic basket up with their dinner.

Removing an arrow, she went through the motions of nocking, aiming, drawing, and firing. Her elbow twinged and her bow arm jerked. The poor arrow didn't stand a chance. It went so far wide she might as well have just thrown it herself. Groaning, she

274

muttered an incant and brought it soaring back to her. It wouldn't do, allowing arrows to rain down upon the castle. One could find its way into a courtyard and hurt someone.

"I'm late. I'm sorry." Bedelth appeared.

She exhaled. It had been a little over a week since their conversation about her giving up. Since then, they'd gathered each morning for an hour to work. Sometimes Bedelth offered to brace her arm, knowing she would shoot better if he helped. She always refused. No progress had been made, and while she was determined to keep trying, she couldn't help that little nagging voice that said maybe she should accept defeat.

Bedelth set a picnic basket at their feet then stood, holding a long, cloth wrapped bundle. She eyed it warily. "That better be a loaf of bread."

"Hopefully something better." He hesitated, then unwrapped it. She blinked, uncertain of what she was seeing. "It's a brace. I worked with a few healers and Berbik to engineer it. After seeing how well you shot when I braced your arm." His expression was hopeful.

The contraption was made from a thin, dark metal, fitted with leather straps and golden clasps. There was an adjustable gear near the elbow. It was fine craftsmanship. That didn't stop the flash of betrayal and then anger taking hold.

She took a step back. "You don't think I can do this on my own?" Her voice came out louder than it should have.

"Of course I do. But you shouldn't have to."

"Why... Why would you do this? Undermine me like this?"

"That was not my intention." His voice remained calm. "You carry a heavy burden, my love. You always have. This is not a sign of weakness. It's a bridge."

"I... I can't."

"Please, just try. For me? If you hate it, we never have to use it again."

We.

Because they were in this together.

Soon they would be bonded, sharing minds and thoughts, their whole lives joined.

She swallowed, eyeing the contraption. Now she understood why he'd been so curious when bracing her arm with his hands. He'd been planning this. For her.

She felt equal parts anger and love.

"Is it...complicated?"

"No. I'll show you." He held it forward, motioning for her.

She took a tentative step towards him, then eventually lifted her arm. He fitted it over the sleeve of her gown. She hated long sleeves in the summer, but didn't want to scare off the palace staff with the state of her arm's disfigurement.

Bedelth set about fastening the leather straps. She felt the even pressure distribute along her arm, supporting muscles that had lost the ability to fight. His deft fingers were a wonder to watch. Her stiff body began to soften. He adjusted the gear at her elbow then placed the bow in her hand. She lifted her arm and he made a few more adjustments. The idea was genius, truly, the way it supported the position of her arm taking the strain off the elbow and muscles that were no longer there. But she hated what it represented. The finality of it, bridge or not.

"Give it a try." Bedelth stepped back.

Sighing, she nocked an arrow. She was half-tempted to miss on purpose, just to prove that the brace would be useless. But the hope in Bedelth's gaze, the open concentration as he watched, had her focusing her efforts on the tip of the arrow right before she released.

It cut through the air, landing with a thud two rings from the bullseye. The closest she'd gotten even with Bedelth's help. Her stomach sank. She should have felt pure elation. This was more progress than she'd made all week. Instead, she felt only dread.

Bedelth let out a whoop of joy, spinning towards her. He lifted her into his arms and spun her around, setting her down before capturing her mouth in a kiss. For a moment, she forgot to feel everything assaulting her and instead only felt the warm reassurance of his lips on hers. When he stepped away, grinning from ear to ear, it was hard to be angry or frustrated while taking in his boyish delight. He'd done something beautifully creative. Beautifully thoughtful.

She was furious and grateful all in one, and she hated that she felt both.

"Try again," Bedelth urged. Humoring him, she went through the motions, firing arrow after arrow. All of them struck the target, some closer to the bullseye than others. She didn't hit it a single time, but that wasn't the point. The point was that with this brace, there was a hope that she could improve.

Eventually, Bedelth stopped her. "Come, let's eat."

He helped her out of the brace and set it aside, pulling them over to a different part of the garden where they sat on one of the benches to eat. She was glad she couldn't see the brace or she'd have glared at it the entire meal.

They were silent as they ate. Eventually, Bedelth said, "Have I overstepped?"

"What? No. I mean..." She blew out a breath. "I'm struggling with what to think about it, if I'm honest."

"I always want your honesty."

"It feels like cheating. It feels like I'm giving up and accepting that I will never overcome my...disability. But to be able to hit the target again. That feeling of elation..."

"I think it's normal to feel all those things together. You are not broken. You are evolving. If this can help you along the way, then let it. If in time, you regain any strength in your arm, you can shed the brace and view it as the thing that held you over."

"The bridge." Like he'd said before.

"The bridge."

"It was incredibly thoughtful. Thank you." The words felt like ash on her tongue, even though he deserved them. She agreed with his thoughts on the matter, and yet she was still struggling. Was it wrong that she didn't feel open gratitude and nothing more? Should she have felt only relief at a problem solved? Was there something wrong with her because she didn't?

"You're welcome." Bedelth hesitated. "Would you like to practice a little more before we retire for the night? I bet you'll manage a bullseye before we go in."

A laugh burst from her chest, lifting the heaviness with it. He knew exactly how to goad her. Now she'd be determined to do exactly that.

They put away their things and he helped her again with the brace, this time showing her each of the straps and how to fasten them one-handed. "It's ice metal," he explained. "Berbik got a small supply of it on short notice and fashioned the supports with it."

She sucked in a breath, a new sense of appreciation dawning. "Truly?"

"Indeed. And look." He turned the brace over. She saw on the gear that there was a tiny emblem of a phoenix. "Remember how Claire got her phoenix feathers?"

"Because a phoenix rises from the ashes."

"And look at the strap here. And here. And here." She hadn't noticed that there were words stamped into the leather straps on the underside of each one. Her heart caught in her throat as tears sprang to her eyes. They were little quotes of encouragement. She read each of them aloud. "Strength in the draw. I rise, I aim, I endure. Bend, but do not break."

"This one is my favorite." He turned over the last strap and tears clogged her throat. "Not a crutch, a wing."

"Oh, Bedelth." Her eyes blurred and she threw her arms around him. A sob fell from her chest, and then another. He tightened his hold on her, absorbing every tremor as she let her tears fall. She hadn't even noticed these little details when he'd first shown her, immediately against anything that might help her. But the amount of thought and care and love he'd put into this gift, to help her regain something that meant so much to her.

Gods, she didn't deserve him. And yet, the fates had chosen this male to be hers. Her mate.

"I love you—so much," she managed as she pulled back.

"And I love you." He framed her tearstained face in his hands, leaning down to brush a kiss over her lips. It was gentle, soft. It spoke of promises and devotion. He was with her, through the good and the bad.

"Now, let's see if you can prove me right." Fitting the final fastening into place, he stepped away, then took a seat on a nearby bench to watch.

The sun had already set by now, but the little lanterns placed in the garden last year before Claire's bonding ceremony were still there. They filled the peaceful garden with a warm glow, complementing the scent of the spriten night flowers unfurling in the gathering darkness.

Letting out a breath, she calmed her racing heart and took up the proper stance, adjusting her feet a few times until she felt comfortable. Then she began working. Each arrow was a balm to her frayed emotions, just as it always had been. From those first days when she fought to discover her place in the keep, to the days when she found and then lost her first love. All the way until now. Each arrow seemed to knit a little more of her soul back together.

She had Bedelth to thank for that. Bedelth had given her a way. Even if it wasn't the way she'd initially envisioned.

The brace worked beautifully. While it didn't make her an expert with her opposite arm, it did allow her to hit the target and that was what mattered. When she'd fired the entire quiver, Bedelth rose and collected the arrows, returning them to her. There was no silent reproach in his gaze. No, I told you so. Just calm support. He said nothing as he returned to the bench and she began again.

Her draw arm was shaking by the time she called it quits. While she hadn't hit the bullseye as she'd hoped, she'd come damned close. Bedelth stepped over to massage her shoulders.

"What do you say to a hot bath and some massage oil," he murmured against her skin.

She shivered. "I think that's the second best suggestion I've heard all day."

"What was the first?" He bent to collect her quiver and took the bow from her hand, slinging it over his shoulder.

She set about the straps of her brace, intent on removing it herself. "You suggesting I should wear this brace."

"So you like it, then?"

She pulled her lower lip between her teeth. "I both love and hate it, Bedelth. I love it because it's beautiful and thoughtful. Because it's something that came from you. It's a sign of your devotion to me."

"And you hate it because it reminds you of your disfigurement." There was a flash of guilt in his eyes because he'd never forgive himself for what happened.

"No. I hate it because it reminds me that I can never be the girl I was before. And honestly, that's a good thing. But it is also a scary thing, filled with a world of the unknown. I'll always be different now."

"Different is good. Your differences will set you apart in the best way. But no matter how different or changed you are, one thing will always remain the same." They set off towards the tower's stairs.

"And what's that?"

"That we are mates. And that my love for you knows no bounds."

"Thank you—for all of this."

"You are most welcome."

As they descended the stairs, returning back into the main part of the tower, she knew one thing with certainty. She might not have hit the target's center tonight. But she was a fighter, and she would never stop trying, just as Bedelth would never stop loving her.

CHAPTER 32
INFINITELY BETTER

Kastali Dun

Dallin sat alone in a holding cell beneath the city guard's headquarters. They'd allowed him to wash up but had confiscated his knife and kept him in the same clothes he'd worn at Moon's Garden, now wrinkled from a night spent on the narrow cot. Unlike the dungeon beneath Kastali Dun, this cell was sparsely furnished but reasonably clean. The guards had been wary but not cruel, uncertain of his exact status in the complex web of Kastali Dun's underworld.

Through the small barred window near the ceiling, morning light filtered in. He watched the progress of sunlight across the floor, marking the passing hours. The cell smelled of damp stone and sweat, with an undertone of something bitter from previous occupants who hadn't been as fortunate as he would be.

His mind kept returning to Moon's Garden. The moments after the poison had done its job. Cobra's glassy eyes, his hand clutching his chest. The momentary, terrible silence before chaos erupted. Onlookers filling the doorway. Guards flooding the room, confusion on their faces as they tried to make sense of the scene. Nerina's panicked expression as they were separated, her dark eyes finding him in a silent plea that twisted something in his chest. In the aftermath, he couldn't help but think of Martel, who would surely be making his move now. The cunning bastard had positioned himself perfectly, and with Cobra gone, the Serpent Syndicate would be ripe for new leadership.

He ran his fingers through his hair, gritty despite his efforts to rinse it in the small basin they'd provided. The weight of the past weeks pressed on him—not from guilt or doubt about the mission—Cobra had more than earned his fate, and he had fulfilled his duty to the king without hesitation. Rather, it was the bone-deep weariness that had settled into his very marrow. Weeks of pretending to be someone else had taken their toll. Living in constant vigilance, never knowing if his cover would be blown between one heartbeat and the next. The mission was complete, but the cost to his spirit had been heavy in ways he hadn't anticipated when he'd first accepted the job. He was changed. But that's what it meant to grow. What it meant to be a shield for the king.

The echo of approaching footsteps drew his attention. Not the shuffle of guards making their rounds, but purposeful strides. Keys jingled, metal scraped against metal, and the door swung open to reveal Verath. The king's shield dismissed the accompanying guard with a curt nod before stepping inside and closing the door, his sverak at his hip.

For a long moment, neither spoke. Verath leaned against the wall, arms crossed over his chest, his expression unreadable. "You did it," he said finally. "Well done, the king will be pleased."

After wanting more than anything to please the king, to please his shield brothers and prove that he was capable, this victory felt hollow. He'd expected to feel a sense of accomplishment, and while he had accomplished the task, it hadn't left him feeling prideful. If anything, it left him feeling...emptier.

"Martel will try to take over," he pointed out.

Verath's expression shifted slightly. "Yes, but he's not Cobra. The Syndicate under him might be more... manageable now. We'll see how it plays out."

"I can help if—"

"No, I think not. It's no longer your concern. Or mine." Verath pushed away from the wall. "The city's guards will take care of it from here on out."

"Right." He glanced around. At any point over the past several hours he could have told the guards exactly who he was. He could have used magic to get himself out of here. That wasn't the point. The point was to maintain the ruse. Everyone in Cobra's circle needed to believe that their leader's death was unrelated to the monarchy.

As if reading his mind, Verath said, "We'll leave here quietly. Measures are already in place to cover your disappearance. None of the syndicate will be the wiser. Let's go." He held out a hand, helping Dallin to his feet.

"And the girl? Nerina?"

"She's being held separately. She's claiming she knew nothing of what happened."

"She didn't," he confirmed. "She's just one of the brothel workers. Actually...I was hoping she might be given a position at the keep. Under Tess, perhaps, in the kitchens."

Verath's eyebrow lifted. "Huh. Not a bad idea. It would keep her out of harm's way, in case any of the syndicate come sniffing."

"Exactly."

Verath nodded. "I'll see that she's exonerated and escorted to the keep. I'll make sure she knows that it is for her own safety."

"Good."

Verath moved toward the door. "Come. I'm sure you're eager for your bed, a bath, and perhaps some hot food."

"All of those, yes."

Verath chuckled, clapping him on the back as they left the cell. A few guards eyed them suspiciously, but as soon as Verath glared at them, they turned away.

With his mission complete, he could finally return to his life at the keep. He wondered if he might ever run into any of the crews he'd run with, and what would happen if they saw him and figured out who he was. Humans lived such short lives compared to the drengr. He might need to keep clear of the lower districts for a few decades.

That made him think of Jamie. His happy mood instantly dropped a measure.

They took a carriage back to the keep, mostly to stay off the streets. Golden morning light bathed the buildings. There'd be breakfast waiting. He could have a hot bath then stuff his belly full.

Guards nodded at their carriage as they passed through the portcullis. The familiar scents of the keep surrounded him as he emerged into the main courtyard. He breathed it in, exhaling with relief. Home. He was finally back. His shoulders relaxed slightly.

"Well, I'll leave you to settle back in," Verath said, giving him a nod. "We have court in an hour. I'll expect you to be present."

"I'll be there."

THE DAY FELT UNUSUALLY LONG, or perhaps that was merely because he had to wait so long to see the one person he ached for. After he'd cleaned up properly and changed into his own clothes, attended to his court duties and everything else, he made his way to Jamie's quarters. He paused outside the door, taking a breath before knocking firmly.

After a moment, Jamie called, "Come in."

He pushed the door open to find him sitting at his desk near the window, writing. Jamie didn't notice him at first, too focused on his work, quill moving across the page. He watched from the doorway, taking in the familiar sight: Jamie's furrowed brow, the way he tucked his hair behind his ear, the ink on his fingertips.

"Jamie."

Jamie's head snapped up, quill freezing. For a moment, he stared. Then he stood, nearly knocking over his chair. "Dallin? Oh, gods!" Jamie's eyes darted over him, as if cataloguing every part of him. His heart skipped under the perusal. "Did it work? Collier's poison?"

"It worked, thanks in part to you. I appreciate everything you did to help."

"It was..." Jamie rubbed the back of his neck. "You don't need to thank me."

He hesitated. The room felt too stifling. "Let's take a walk. I could use some fresh air."

Jamie straightened. "Sure. Let me just put these away." He quickly tucked the pages into his desk.

Dallin waited out in the hall, eager anticipation twisting him into knots. They walked in silence through the corridors. It wasn't until they reached the royal gardens, where afternoon sun lit the flowerbeds and cast shadows across the paths, that Jamie finally spoke.

"So... Want to talk about it?"

"Talk about it?"

"Your mission. I assume everything went okay, since Cobra is dead."

"Oh. Right. Yeah, it did. But, I'd rather talk about you. What were you writing just now?"

A gardener knelt nearby, carefully pruning dead blooms from a flowering shrub. The snip of his shears punctuated the quiet like heartbeats.

A flush crept up Jamie's neck. "Just a story."

"What's this one about?" he pressed.

Jamie bit his lip, and gods, he looked so cute when he did that. "A sea captain. He discovers a map to a hidden island where time flows differently. When he finds it, he has to decide whether to stay where a single day equals years in the outside world, or return to his life knowing he can never go back."

"That sounds strangely familiar."

Jamie's laugh was high pitched—nervous. "I might have used some inspiration from King Talon's trip to Claire's world. Is that too much?"

"No, I think it's brilliant." He reached out and squeezed Jamie's wrist in reassurance. The feel of his skin, soft and warm beneath his fingers, was a balm. Jamie's eyes darted down and Dallin quickly released his wrist. He cleared his throat and added, "What are stories but bits of information inspired by the things in our own world?"

"Exactly."

"Which does he choose?" Dallin asked, intrigued. "The sea captain? Does he stay or return to his life?"

"I haven't decided yet." Jamie glanced sideways at him, something vulnerable in his expression. "I'm still working out if what he'd be returning to is worth the sacrifice."

The weight of those words hung between them as they reached a stone bench nestled in a quiet alcove, shadowed by a weeping willow whose branches swayed gently in the breeze. By unspoken agreement, they sat, shoulders not quite touching but close enough that he could feel the warmth radiating from Jamie's body.

"I've been worried about you," Jamie admitted after a moment, staring at his hands. His voice was quietly fierce, laced with an intensity that was surprising. "Every day, wondering if your cover would be blown. I know you're *you*—" Jamie gestured, indicating what Dallin was. That there was no need to fear. "But still, it was irrational fear, I suppose."

"I like that you were worried." His heart began to pound.

"You... You do? You're not going to tell me I'm being ridiculous?"

"Nothing about you is ridiculous, Jamie."

Jamie's lips parted at the sound of his name. Their eyes were locked. Tension seemed to crackle between them.

A butterfly drifted through the branches, fluttering past them before disappearing. When had their faces gotten so close together? He wanted more than anything to kiss Jamie at this moment. It would be so easy to lean in and press their mouths together. But the fear that struck him, memories of what had happened the last time he'd tried that with another boy, burrowed beneath his desire, threatening to destroy it. He couldn't bear the possibility of what might happen afterward. Couldn't bear the thought of Jamie looking at him with a horrified expression.

But...what if he didn't? What if he kissed him back. Jamie wasn't Claude—

Jamie made the decision for them. He surged forward, pressing his lips against Dallin's. Dallin froze, eyes wide.

A beat later, Jamie panicked and pulled back. "I'm—sorry. I don't know what—"

He grabbed Jamie's face and smashed their mouths together, capturing his lips in a hungry kiss. Jamie let out a tiny huff, freezing for only a moment before relaxing into him. Sparks erupted everywhere they touched, as if fireworks were bursting above them, cascading down around them, landing upon their skin with sizzling precision. He deepened their kiss and Jamie groaned.

Their breaths came faster, hands roving, hearts beating in tandem.

Every fear he'd carried was swept away at the feel of Jamie's tongue against his. Every worry that his friend might reject him. Every doubt that the way he felt was wrong. Every moment of second guessing. All of it, gone in an instant.

Time seemed to stretch around them.

When at last he pulled back, eager to see the expression Jamie wore, it was to find his skin flushed, his lips swollen. Jamie studied him in much the same way. Their eyes remained locked, understanding passing between them.

"I've..." Jamie touched his fingers to his lips. "I've never really kissed anyone like that before."

"You haven't?"

"Not—not like that. There was this one girl. Well, it was a little awkward. I'll spare you the details."

"Then, you liked it?"

Jamie's throat bobbed. "Would it enlarge your ego to epic proportions if I said that I didn't just like it, but loved it?"

Warmth burst in his chest. "You mean that?"

"I do." Jamie's eyes darted between his.

"Well. Good. That's...good." They both scooted apart, sudden shyness building between them. He wasn't sure where they went from here, but he had a good feeling that the direction would be one they followed together, exploring this new thing between them.

"So..." He cleared his throat, eager to fill the charged silence. "Tell me more about your sea captain? What's his name?"

A rueful smile spread across Jamie's lips, like he knew what Dallin was doing and was both understanding and grateful at the same time. "Everett. Captain Everett Drake."

"That's a good name, that."

"You think?"

"I do."

"Will you tell me about him?"

As the sun descended, they remained on the bench, Jamie describing his sea captain's adventures with growing enthusiasm. He listened, asking occasional questions about the story. It wasn't the reunion he had imagined during those long nights in the Pauper's District. It was better. Infinitely better.

CHAPTER 33

CLAIRE'S RETURN

Kastali Dun

Claire's heart swelled as Kastali Dun came into view, the setting sun casting brilliant light across the city. From Talon's back, it was spread before them. Tears pricked her eyes, as was often the case when returning home. For the first time ever, there was no shadow of Kane looming over them.

Another thought, a more painful one, had a small sob catching in her throat. This was the first time returning to Kastali Dun without Cyrus. Even that initial, fateful arrival when his dead body had been present, he'd been in her mind. She hadn't fully realized it at the time.

"He is at peace," Talon reminded her.

"I know. But gods, I miss his unsolicited remarks."

"I know, mih cralla. *I miss him too."*

Taking a steadying breath, she took in the beautiful city before them. The jewel of the kingdom. Colorful banners fluttered from every battlement, vibrant blues and golds snapping in the evening breeze, welcoming their rulers home. Beneath them, people lined the streets, their faces turned skyward. Talon banked, his massive wings catching the wind.

They came into view and Talon roared, making their presence known. Beside them, Koldis echoed the announcement. A cry went up from far below, and then another, and another, until the swell of voices lifted into the sky. There was joy there. And victory. It looked as if every single one of the city's inhabitants were out of doors.

Dragonwall's rulers had returned.

"They are here for you," Talon said. *"To celebrate the return of their queen."*

Warmth blossomed in her chest. She loved her people. Loved them enough that despite her unbreakable promise to Cyrus, she would have gladly thrown herself through that portal to defeat Kane, simply to keep their kingdom safe.

"And I would have been even more furious," Talon pointed out. She could only laugh.

It would take time. Eventually her mate would move past the weight of her promise. What she had forced herself into. He never wanted to see her in danger.

The cheers continued, never ceasing. *"They'll be celebrating in the streets until dawn,"* Talon said. For show, he turned and completed a full circuit of the city before winging his way to the keep. She leaned forward, squinting at what appeared to be the entire court, servants and nobility alike, assembled in the main courtyard. She could make out her queen's guard and hand-maidens among them.

She laughed, the sound carried away by the wind. What a contrast to her last return, sneaking in to the city through the secret passages, uncertain of what awaited them. Now she flew above it, returning as a queen who had fulfilled her promise.

Talon descended, Koldis beside him. His massive wings sent gusts of wind across the courtyard as he landed. Koldis trans-formed, landing on two feet. The gathered crowd stepped back, giving them space. She slid from Talon's back before he trans-formed, her feet touching the stone of Kastali Dun for the first time in what felt like forever.

As one, everyone in the courtyard genuflected. She hesitated, looking out over the sea of bodies. She fought the urge to race over to her friends, to throw herself at them. Instead, she settled into the formal role she had agreed to. Dragonwall's queen.

Slipping her hand through Talon's arm, they walked forward together, the epitome of poise and grace.

Reyr was the only one to rise. "Welcome home," he said, striding forward with a broad smile that softened his usually serious features. His voice carried the warmth she had missed so much. "We've missed you."

His eyes settled on her and a small squeal burst from her lips. So much for dignity! She flung herself at him. He laughed, catching her up and twirling her around in a hug. "I missed you too," she breathed against his neck.

A throat cleared. Talon, of course. "I don't suppose it's my turn?"

She laughed, breaking out of Reyr's hold so that he could properly greet his best friend.

Meanwhile, she turned to the crowd. "Please, rise."

Everyone stood.

Her friends used that moment to break rank. Feowen came first, then Jeanine and the rest of her queen's guard. Desaree was openly weeping as they hugged, and even Saffra's eyes were misty. She and Leah broke into delighted squeals as they embraced, rocking back and forth. "We were so worried," her bestie whispered.

"I'm okay," she assured her. "We've got a ton of catching up to do."

"Tell me about it."

Claire hesitated, then leaned in. "So... You should have been the first to know. There are a few others who've figured it out already. I'm pregnant."

"What?" Leah whisper-shrieked.

"Shhh!"

Leah's face transformed into one of joy. "When?!"

"I figured it out in Esterpine. We're going to tell the others, but I wanted you to find out from me."

"I'm going to be an auntie?!" Leah's quiet voice was choked with tears.

"Yes."

"Oh, gods! I'm going to be an auntie!"

"I know!" They hugged again before she stepped away to observe the others, sharing in a happy reunion of their own.

Jovari clapped Talon on the back while Bedelth, Dallin, and Verath crowded around, all pretense of formal distance abandoned in this moment of homecoming. Their relief was palpable. These gruff warriors who had faced down many threats throughout their life looked like eager puppies, desperate for their king's attention.

The crowd remained watchful, taking in the greetings among their inner circle. This was a formality that always occurred when the king returned home. Now, she was included in that formality. She still wasn't used to it, not really, but this evening it felt right. They had earned this. She had earned this.

Talon's hand found hers. He lifted their joined hands in the air and shouted, "Our queen was victorious! Tonight, we shall feast!"

The assembled crowd erupted in cheers.

"Let's go inside," he whispered. "Home."

"Yes. Let's go."

They made their way through the castle.

The moment they entered the king's tower, she was hit by a wave of familiarity so powerful it nearly brought her to her knees. She hadn't realized how much she had missed this space until now. So many things had happened in this tower. So many moments of change.

Her gaze darted over to the chair—the place she'd sat when Talon first summoned her here, to answer for her behavior towards Caterina. The spot she had revealed her gift—Cyrus's presence—to everyone. Where she'd told them about her promise and their mate bond. This was the room they'd spent so many long nights, joined with their friends. Their family.

Her throat closed up.

Everything was just as she remembered, yet somehow more vivid—the rich tapestries, the warm glow of lanterns, the subtle scent of herbs that had always reminded her of Talon. A black streak shot across the floor and suddenly Batty was weaving between her ankles, his purrs nearly loud enough to echo off the stone walls.

"Oh my gods! Batty! Baby!" She dropped to the floor.

"Someone missed you," Talon smiled as she scooped up the cat, who head-butted her chin with surprising force.

"I missed him, too." She stroked Batty's sleek fur, her throat tight. "I can't believe I'm actually home."

Talon crouched behind her, his arms wrapping around them both. "We'll have time to explore everything later. Desaree has been overseeing the restoration since Kane's departure. But right now..."

"I know." She reluctantly set Batty down. The sun was quickly setting. "We've a feast to prepare for."

Talon pressed a kiss to her cheek. "And a very important announcement to plan."

She was vaguely aware of some of the others crowding in the doorway to watch them. Her queen's guard took up their positions along the nearby wall, while Talon's shields and their friends lingered.

"May we help you prepare, *Ayas Drollaya*?" Selphie appeared beside her, Miera hanging back.

"Yes, of course." She was eager for her handmaidens' attentive hands.

"We will *all* help," Desaree said, stepping forward.

"But first—" Talon stood, pulling her to her feet. "My mate and I will have a bath. I'll let you know when I'm through with her."

"Talon!" she hissed, seeing his meaning clearly in his mind.

The others didn't need to share his mind to know what he intended as he scooped her up, tossing her over his shoulder, a very undignified gesture that only their inner circle of friends was privy to. A few of them snickered before they scattered to attend to their own tasks.

~

STEAM ROSE around them as she sank into the bathwater. Talon hadn't waited for them to enter the bath before he'd taken her for himself, choosing to press her against the wall, using it as a brace as he reaffirmed his claim over her. One she relished in. Now they relished in the heat to soothe their quivering muscles.

His chest was warm against her back. After so many days of traveling, the simple luxury of hot water and scented oils felt decadent.

"How are we going to tell them?" she asked, trailing her fingers through the water. "About the baby."

He already knew what she meant. Yet, she still found herself falling into old habits. They had centuries together, yet she might never get used to some of the nuances that came with sharing his mind.

Talon's hand slid around to rest protectively over her still-flat abdomen. "Tonight, once we've gathered everyone together—after the feast. Perhaps at the end of our meeting."

"And our people?"

"We'll hold off a bit before making the public announcement. Unless you would rather we share it sooner than later?"

"Our people could use some joy. But…"

"You'd like to enjoy this news with our closest friends first."

"Exactly." She sighed, settling deeper against him. "I still can't believe we're actually having a baby."

"Some mated pairs wait centuries."

"Do you think it was because of what I did in the forest? Reversing Isabella's price?"

"You were pregnant before that, obviously. It happened either in Ashvale, or while we were in the cave, waiting to take back the kingdom."

"True. But you know how magic is. I can't help but feel like it's a reward—for what I did."

"That's a good way of thinking about it." His arms tightened around her. He pressed his face into the back of her neck and groaned. She could already feel him hardening beneath her. Insatiable male! "We should hurry," he groused. "Your ladies will want plenty of time to prepare you—something a few of them haven't had the luxury of doing in some time."

"Yes. You're right." Still, she wasn't ready to leave the comfort of the sunken tub.

"We'll have months, years, decades, centuries to enjoy this," he reminded her. "No more threat of Kane. We can finally...live."

Her breath caught at those words.

"Yes, we can, can't we?" She stood, water cascading off her body. Talon did the same. They climbed out of the bathing pool. She caught her mate's gaze tracking the droplets of water sliding down her skin as he began to towel her dry. He was already aroused, fighting the hunger that drove him.

"Later," she promised with a smile. "We have all night, remember?"

His only answer was a low growl.

There were several dresses on display in the room used to prepare her when she entered. Desaree and her handmaidens waited, looking eager.

"Where are the others?" she asked.

"They are getting ready before they join us," Des explained, already dressed in a blush pink gown. She looked stunning.

"Do you have a preference, *Ayas Drollaya*?" Miera asked.

"Hmm." She glanced between the options on display before settling on a royal blue number with silver trim.

"That is a perfect choice." Selphie clapped her hands together.

The thirty minutes was a blur of chatting and laughter. Desaree worked on her hair while Miera and Selphie fussed with her face and jewelry. Saffra and Jocelyn appeared, shortly followed by Leah. All of them were clothed in beautiful gowns.

"I didn't get a chance to compliment your hair!" she told her best friend. "I love the color."

"I'll take that compliment, thank you," Saffra teased. "Since it was me who fussed over batches of brew to get it right."

"You don't think it's too much?" Leah asked, hesitant.

"No! What does Jovari think?"

Leah's cheeks pinked. "He likes it," she admitted.

"I am not even a tiny bit surprised."

Before she knew it, the others had rushed down to the hall to get seats while Talon escorted her, bracketed by her queen's guards and his shields.

The great hall fell silent as they entered, hundreds of eyes following their progress toward the head table. She kept her chin high, though her heart hammered in her chest. The head table stretched across the dais, large enough to accommodate both her queen's guard and the king's shields. It was the piece they'd commissioned before the battle with Oshea. She'd almost forgotten about it. As they approached, she made a quick calculation and frowned.

"We'll need an even larger table soon," she thought as Talon pulled out her chair. A table that would not only accommodate the shields and guards, but some of their mates, too. For now, Desaree, Jocelyn, Leah, and Saffra were sitting at their favorite spot, over by one of the fireplaces.

Once they were seated, Talon remained standing, his hand lifted to signal for silence, though the hall was already quiet enough to hear a pin drop. She was surprised by his lack of discomfort. Usually he hated public displays, mostly because of his scars. But then she remembered the conversation they'd had in the little cottage, after her mind had been freed. When he'd chosen to keep his scars. Something about that had made him more comfortable in his own skin.

His voice was strong as it carried across the room. "Tonight, we celebrate not just our return, but the end of a shadow that has hung over Dragonwall for too long." He paused, his hand finding her shoulder. "Many of you have heard the rumors, and I can confirm that Kane is dead."

Excited murmurs grew into exclamations.

"Our queen faced him in combat and ended his threat permanently." Talon's voice grew tight with emotion. "The dragonstones have been recovered and placed somewhere they can never be found again. The wild dragons are subdued. It is time. We can finally heal. With that, I will officially announce the start of Dragonwall's Fourth Age."

Cries of shock and delight rang out. They had discussed this, once. The idea of reigning in a new age. One of prosperity and fresh beginnings.

He raised his goblet. "To Queen Claire, slayer of Kane, protector of Dragonwall."

The toast was taken up throughout the hall, hundreds of voices calling her name. She felt her cheeks flush as she nodded in acknowledgment, uncomfortable with the praise but understanding its necessity.

As Talon sat, servants began bringing out the first courses. The tension in the room dissolved into animated conversation, the news of Kane's demise speculated on from table to table.

"It's really over," she whispered, more to herself than to Talon.

His hand found hers under the table. "Yes. Now we begin the next chapter."

∼

Claire stepped into the main room of the king's tower, the familiar space alive with movement and conversation. The feast had lasted longer than she'd liked. She was grateful to finally be among just their closest friends.

She took in the room. Dallin stood by the hearth, a goblet of wine in his hand, laughing more freely than she'd ever seen. There was a lightness to him that hadn't been there before, a relaxed set to his shoulders.

Across the room, Jovari casually kept Leah within arm's reach, his hand finding the small of her back whenever she moved near him. The easy comfort between them spoke volumes. She caught Leah's eye and received a bright smile in return.

Her queen's guard was posted up along the wall, observing, like they often did. She didn't miss the way Feowen's gaze frequently darted towards Jeanine. Those two... She hoped Jeanine would accept Feowen's offer soon.

Talon disappeared, then reappeared with a goblet of water in hand, offering it to her. To everyone else, it probably looked like wine. She smiled up at him. "Shall we sit?" he murmured, guiding her over to his favorite armchair. They'd need to get more seating in here. The size of their inner circle had grown.

The others took seats, some on the floor, and a hush fell.

"We want to hear everything," Reyr insisted, his fingers naturally intertwined with Merrian's as they sat beside each other. She still couldn't quite believe that pairing, but she was happier for it. Reyr deserved joy.

"Start from the beginning," Verath added, pulling Desaree closer on his lap.

So she told them. She described the harrowing climb through Shadowkeep, the confrontation in the atrium, and the final battle atop the fortress. She didn't spare the details of how Kane had trapped innocent servants in a ring of fire, forcing her to make an impossible choice. Feowen helped, piping in with the little details she missed.

The room was tensely silent as she described Cyrus's final sacrifice—how he had given the last of his soul to immobilize Kane, allowing her to deliver the killing blow.

"He's truly gone then? Cyrus?" Verath asked softly.

She nodded, the familiar ache in her chest a little less painful than it had been. "Yes. But he found peace. I believe that with all my heart."

"To Cyrus," Dallin said, breaking the tense moment by raising his goblet. "The shield who sacrificed everything twice. I wouldn't be in your ranks if it weren't for him."

Hearty agreement rang out as everyone lifted goblets of wine. They drank solemnly, honoring the fallen shield whose actions had saved them all.

"What about you?" she asked, eager to shift the focus. "I want to hear everything I've missed."

The tension evaporated, and Bedelth leaned forward. "Well, for one thing, Saffra has finally agreed on a date for our bonding ceremony."

"What?" She gasped, delighted. "When?"

"Week after next," Saffra said, a full smile crossing her face. "We've already completed most of the preparations. We were just waiting for you to return. My family is already making the journey."

"Your family," Claire breathed. "I'll get to meet them finally!" That thought made her so warm and happy. "It's going to be the most perfect ceremony."

"That it will," Bedelth agreed, turning fondly to Saffra to plant a kiss on her forehead.

"Oh. My. God." Claire whispered to Talon at the sight of their affection, loud enough so the others heard. "I'm literally melting."

Talon's gruff chuckle reverberated through her. She shifted on his lap as Batty trotted over, leaning down to scoop him up.

"What about the library?" She turned to Leah and Jovari. She'd seen a little bit of that in Talon's mind but wanted more details.

Leah's face lit up. "The main building is complete! We're still organizing the books, but we plan to open soon. It's beautiful, Claire. Wait until you see what Jovari organized for the children's section."

"I just gave suggestions," Jovari demurred, though she didn't miss the pride in his voice. "Leah is the one with the vision."

She noticed the warm look they exchanged, and her heart swelled with happiness for her friend.

The conversation flowed naturally from there, updates on the kingdom's recovery, the rebuilding of villages damaged during Kane's reign, the gradual return of normalcy. She found herself relaxing completely for the first time in months, surrounded by those who had become family.

As the evening progressed, a natural lull fell in the conversation. She caught Talon's eye, and he gave her a subtle nod, his hand squeezing hers beneath the table.

"We actually have some news of our own," Claire said, her voice steady despite the flutter in her stomach. "Something we wanted to share with all of you first."

The room quieted, attention focusing on her.

"I'm pregnant."

For a heartbeat, there was complete silence. Then the room erupted.

"I knew it!" Saffra screeched, clapping her hands together. "I could sense something different about you!"

Desaree was instantly in tears, on her feet rushing over, throwing her arms around Claire. Leah smirked, clearly pleased that she had learned of it first. They were best friends, after all. It only took moments, but soon enough they were all on their feet. Even the sprites broke rank, coming forward to share in the excitement. Talon's shields passed him around, clapping him on the back as they congratulated him.

"We're going to have a little prince or princess," Jovari said wonderingly. "The first royalty born in Kastali Dun in centuries."

"When are you due?" Desaree asked, her eyes shining with excitement.

"Spring, I think?" She couldn't have been more than six to eight weeks along.

Verath went around refilling goblets for everyone except her. She continued to sip on her water. "To Claire and Talon," he said, raising his goblet high. "And to the future of Dragonwall!"

"To the future!" they echoed, goblets clinking.

As laughter and joy filled the room, her hand found Talon's, their fingers intertwining. The journey had been long and often painful, but looking around at the faces of those she loved, she knew every step had been worth it.

They were home. They were safe. And for the first time, their future stretched before them unobstructed by enemies and unbreakable promises. Just the simple, profound miracle of new life and the family they had built together.

EPILOGUE: ONE

Fort Squall

Tamara stood beside Byron, her hand in his, as they surveyed the completed reconstruction of Fort Squall. The sun was setting, casting golden light across the newly rebuilt eastern wall, washing the stone with an amber glow. Where once there had been rubble and destruction, now stood rebuilt stonework and gleaming wooden beams.

"It looks just like before," she murmured, though that wasn't entirely true. The new fort was stronger, with improvements they'd incorporated during the rebuilding. More efficient ventilation in the kitchens, wider pathways in the garden, sturdier foundations in the eastern apartments.

"Better than before," Byron corrected, squeezing her hand.

She nodded, allowing herself a moment of pride. When they'd first begun this project, the task had seemed monumental. The wild dragons had done so much damage, and more than once, she'd been overwhelmed with doubt. But they'd done it—she and Byron together—with the help of so many others.

"My parents would be proud," Byron said quietly.

She swallowed past the lump in her throat. "They would."

She straightened her shoulders and began walking the perimeter, methodically checking off items in her mental ledger—a skill Emmy had drilled into her during their brief time together. "Always have a system for keeping track of the fort's needs," Emmy had instructed. "It's easy to overlook something crucial if you're disorganized."

"The northern defense wall is complete," she noted, gesturing to where several drengr were removing the last of the scaffolding. "And the training grounds have been restored with the improvements we discussed."

"Fierran mentioned the new volunteer quarters can house twice as many now," Byron added, following her gaze. "We'll be able to give our supporting servants more space. Not to mention the new volunteers."

After the wild dragons had ravaged much of the north, people had lost their homes. While many had chosen to return home and rebuild, just as many had decided to stay. She didn't blame them. The exhaustion was overpowering, and many people didn't want to start from scratch.

"I'm so proud of what we've accomplished here, what you've accomplished, Tam."

Because they both knew he'd spent more time helping in Squall's end, leaving much of the fort to her. She ducked her head, fighting the blush that heated her cheeks. She was no longer that frightened girl who'd run away from Redport to escape an arranged marriage. She had found her place, her purpose—as a rider, as Byron's mate, as co-leader of Fort Squall.

"Lady Tamara!" A voice called from across the courtyard. A young messenger boy was running toward them, waving an envelope. A child from one of their pairs.

"Breathe, Elan," she instructed as the boy skidded to a halt before them. "What is it?"

"Message from Kastali Dun," he panted, holding out the envelope. "Marked with a royal seal."

She exchanged a glance with Byron before taking it. The seal was indeed the royal one—Talon and Claire's combined insignia.

With careful fingers, she broke the wax and removed two sheets of parchment, one thin, the other thick and opulent.

To Lord Byron and Lady Tamara of Fort Squall,

You are formally invited to visit our capital and attend the bonding ceremony of Lady Saffra Ndiaye and Lord Bedelth the Orange, to be held two weeks from the date of this letter, in the throne room of Kastali Dun. Please see the official invitation enclosed with this message.

Your presence would be most welcome.

With warmest regards,

King Talon and Queen Claire

P.S. We miss you!

"It's an invitation," she said, passing the letter to Byron before looking over the official invitation. "For Bedelth and Saffra's bonding ceremony."

It didn't matter that Byron had already seen what she read. Didn't matter that their bond connected their minds. Old habits were still habits.

"It's set for two weeks from the date of this letter," Byron said, "eight days from now. That's cutting it close."

She bit her lip. "I want to go. We missed Claire's bonding ceremony because we were dealing with all this." She waved a hand to encompass the fort. He knew exactly how much it had pained her. "Do you think they can manage without us?"

"Fierran is more than capable," he said. She hesitated, torn between duty and desire. Byron sensed all this and more, reading the turmoil of her mind. "We deserve this, Tamara. We've been working non-stop for months. When was the last time we took time for ourselves? When was the last time we saw our friends?"

The last time they'd been in Kastali Dun had been to swear fealty to Kane. The memory sent shivers down her spine—the fear, the wagon full of people bound for slavery, the cold terror at watching their comrades executed. It haunted her.

The decision crystallized within her. "We should go," she said firmly. "Not just to celebrate with Saffra and Bedelth, but to see the capital restored to what it should be."

Byron's eyes lit with approval. "Reyr will be there too. I'll speak with Fierran. We can leave tomorrow, if we hurry."

"That would be wonderful."

"We'll fly directly," Byron added. "Just the two of us."

The thought of days alone with Byron, flying over the kingdom, sparked a warmth in her chest. It had been so long since they'd had time just for themselves. "Yes," she agreed. "Just the two of us."

SHE SQUINTED against the late afternoon sun, one hand shielding her eyes as she gazed down at Kastali Dun in the distance. Byron soared steadily through the sky, his icy blue scales gleaming in the sunlight. After traveling for days, the capital finally lay before them, sprawled across the peninsula where the Dragonfire Sea met the bay.

The sight brought a lump to her throat. The last time she'd seen the city, fear had been a tangible presence in the streets. People had hidden in their homes, shutters locked, as wagons of prisoners were carted to the docks to be sold as slaves.

Now, even from a distance, she could see the difference. Colorful banners flapped in the sea breeze. People moved freely through the streets. Ships with trading flags, not slave ships, were docked at the harbor. It looked as it did before, when she'd come here for refuge after the fort had been destroyed, only...better. So much better.

"It's beautiful," Byron's voice filled her mind. Five days of flight had left them both weary, but she wouldn't trade a moment of it. Each night they'd made camp beneath the stars, talking for hours about everything and nothing. Days spent in the companionable silence, connected through their thoughts and feelings.

"So different from the last time," she replied, remembering the cold dread that had filled her.

"Much has changed."

She thought about all they'd done after that awful day—their secret alliance with Captain Bennett to rescue slaves bound for Oshea. Small acts of defiance that had felt so inadequate at the time, but combined with similar efforts across the kingdom, had helped keep hope alive until Claire and Talon returned.

"Do you think we'll learn what happened with Claire?" she asked. Information had been scarce at Fort Squall, despite their best efforts. After Reyr's visit, they'd heard rumors of Claire's victory over Kane, of her abdication of the spriten throne, but little else.

"I'm sure we will," Byron assured her, descending towards the keep's largest courtyard.

She tightened her grip on the harness. The space was already occupied by several people waiting to greet them. Byron's large wings stirred the air as he landed. She unbuckled herself, removing both their packs, and dismounted with the practiced ease that had once seemed so difficult. Her feet had barely touched the stone when she caught sight of Claire.

The queen was smiling, radiant in a gown of deep green, her hand resting protectively over her belly.

"Oh, gods!" She got Byron's attention as he completed his shift. "Look!"

"Is she...?"

"Pregnant. She must be." Her heart skipped. Pregnancy among mated pairs was rare and joyous. Before she could stop herself, she rushed forward.

"Claire!" She threw her arms around the queen, etiquette forgotten.

Claire laughed, returning the embrace. "Tamara! Gods! It's so good to see you both."

"You're pregnant!"

"How did you know?"

"You're glowing, and, well, you were holding your belly." She took hold of Claire's shoulders, looking her over.

"I guess I made that pretty obvious, didn't I?" Claire's whole face lit up with joy. "It's a habit now, and I'm not even showing yet."

"You're going to be the best mother," Tamara said, smiling warmly.

Talon stood beside his mate, a rare smile softening his scarred features as he gazed at his mate. "She will." He cleared his throat, turning to them. "I hope your journey went well. We worried you might not come."

Byron stood tall beside her. He clasped forearms with the king. "We wouldn't miss it. Five days of hard flying to get here, but worth every moment."

"I'm glad to hear that," Talon said.

"Come," Claire urged, linking arms with her. "You must be exhausted. We've prepared rooms for you, and there will be time to talk after you've rested."

As they followed Claire and Talon into the keep, she took in all the changes since her last visit. Gone were the black flags and Oshean livery. The corridors hummed with activity and life.

Claire led them to guest quarters in the Hall of Kings—the same chamber they had shared the last time they'd been here.

"Rest and refresh yourselves," Claire said. "Join us in Talon's tower in two hours, and we'll catch you up on everything."

After the monarchs departed, her eyes caught Byron's. Their thoughts jumped to the same thing, and she watched as the sly grin spread across his face. A steaming bath awaited in the bathing chamber, the sunken pool topped with floating herbs. They wasted no time in undressing and submerging. Byron pulled her against him, capturing her lips. "We've got plenty of time for what I intend."

A laugh burst from her chest. She knew exactly what he intended. "Well then," her voice was teasing. "What are you waiting for?"

His growl was absolutely draconic.

～

Two hours later, refreshed and dressed, they were ushered into Talon's tower. The room was warm and welcoming, with a crackling fire and comfortable seating. Claire and Talon were already there, along with many familiar faces: Saffra and Bedelth, their hands intertwined; Jovari with a violet-haired woman she didn't recognize; Koldis, looking extra broody; Dallin, the newest shield; and Reyr, sitting with Merrian.

"Uncle!" Byron moved over to embrace Reyr.

"Nephew." Reyr's smile was genuine as he rose to meet them. "Lady Tamara, you look well."

"As do you," she replied, meaning it. When she'd last seen Reyr, he'd worn lines of exhaustion etched into his features. Now he looked fresh and...happy.

"This is Leah," Claire said, introducing her to the one person she didn't know. "She came with me from my world."

"I love your hair!" She clapped a hand over her mouth after blurting the words.

"Oh!" Leah looked more than pleased. "Thank you."

They settled into comfortable chairs, and servants brought wine and refreshments.

"Tell us everything," Tamara urged, looking between Claire and Talon. "We've heard so little at the fort."

"That's my fault," Talon admitted. "I meant to send a long missive, but, admittedly, I was hoping you might come, so that we could tell you in person."

"No matter," Byron said.

Claire recounted the tale of Kane's defeat. As she described her pursuit through the portal and the final confrontation at Shadowkeep, Tamara found herself leaning forward, hanging on every word. When Claire spoke of Cyrus's final sacrifice to immobilize Kane, tears pricked her eyes.

"He's truly gone," Claire said softly. "But at peace, I think."

"And the dragonstones?" Byron asked.

"All accounted for," Talon replied. "The original five were given to the king tree for safekeeping, while the white stone was returned to Fright."

The conversation shifted to the aftermath—Taylynn's coronation as sprite queen, the defeat of the remaining Oshean forces, the kingdom's slow recovery. As they spoke, she couldn't help noticing the subtle changes in everyone. They all carried scars from Kane's brief reign, visible or not, but they had emerged stronger.

"That's not all," Claire added. "While I was in the forest, I took the liberty of...undoing some of the damage Isabella wrought on the race of drengr."

Tamara sucked in a breath. "Isabella's price?" She remembered her shock at learning from Emmy that drengr pairs could only have one child. "You... you broke the curse?"

Claire nodded, her hand resting on her belly. "I did."

"I remember when Emmy told me," she said, voice soft with memory. "We were having our first lesson in her chambers. She explained about the limitation, that each pair could only ever conceive once. I was so shocked. I couldn't believe it."

"But now?" Byron asked.

"Now you can have as many as you'd like to try for—I think. None of us really knows yet."

"We will discover more in time," Talon added.

She felt Byron's gaze on her, warm and questioning. Felt the gentle probe of his thoughts. They'd made love plenty, but knowing it could take decades, centuries, even, neither expected a child any time soon. Given Claire's news, that could all change. She'd once been terrified of the idea.

Now, she was more than eager. The mental growl that came from Byron had her squeezing her thighs together and shifting in her seat. She forced her mind to behave, forced Byron to stop sending her scandalous ideas.

The conversation drifted to Fort Squall's recovery, and she found herself speaking with unexpected confidence about their rebuilding efforts, the programs they'd established for those who'd lost homes, their plans for the future.

"You've done remarkable work," Claire said when she finished. "Fort Squall and Squall's End are fortunate to have you."

"We've had good examples to follow," Byron replied, his eyes shifting briefly to his uncle and then Talon.

The king inclined his head in acknowledgment. "Leadership is seldom easy, but it is always worthwhile."

"It helps," Claire added with a warm glance at Talon, "to have someone by your side who understands the weight of responsibility."

The words resonated with her. She'd never expected to lead anything, let alone a fort, when she'd fled her father's keep. But with Byron, the burden was shared, the path clearer.

As the evening drew to a close, Saffra approached her while the others were engaged in separate conversations.

"I'm so glad you could come," Saffra said, taking her hands. "It means a great deal to both of us that you'll be here for the ceremony."

"Thank you for including us. I missed Claire's and...it is one of my biggest regrets. Even though..."

"You had your own duties," Saffra said with understanding. "Would you like to help with some of the final preparations tomorrow? I could use another pair of hands."

"I'd be honored." Her chest exploded with warmth.

Saffra squeezed her hands. "You know, I never expected this life," she confided. "To be a prophetess, to find my mate in one of the king's shields. But now I can't imagine any other path."

Tamara nodded, understanding completely. "I feel the same. Running away from my father's house was terrifying, but if I hadn't..."

"Then we both found where we belong," Saffra said with a smile.

 ~

THE NEXT DAY dawned bright and clear. She slipped out of bed, careful not to wake Byron, and dressed quickly before making her way to Saffra's chambers. She found not just Saffra but a flurry of activity—Claire, Desaree, Jocelyn, and Leah busy with preparations for the ceremony, which would take place the following day.

"Tamara!" Saffra exclaimed, rising to greet her. "Thank you for coming. We're just sorting through favors to give each of the guests."

There were piles of little knickknacks like bags of toffee, small glass orbs that held a tiny orange flower inside, bottles of orange ink, and handcrafted wooden tokens that had Saffra and Bedelth's names engraved with the date of their ceremony. She joined them at the large table where they were assembling everything into decorative bags. "Each guest will get one upon entry, to keep as a memento. It was Claire's idea, actually. In her world, wedding guests often get things like this."

"I love it!" Tamara said. "What a wonderful idea."

She thought back to her ceremony. How simple it had been. They'd made the best of a horrible situation, and she wouldn't change a thing about it.

As they worked, conversation flowed easily between them. She found herself sharing stories of Fort Squall, of the challenges and triumphs they'd faced during reconstruction. In turn, she absorbed the details of life in Kastali Dun since Kane's defeat—the public library Leah had established, the reforms Talon was implementing in the kingdom's justice system, Claire's abdication of the sprite throne to Taylynn.

"So much has changed," she marveled, tightening the drawstring on one of the bags, tying it with a golden ribbon.

"For the better," Claire said. "Though there's still much to do."

"There always is," Desaree said pragmatically as she worked on her own bag. "That's the nature of growth."

As morning stretched into afternoon, she felt a contentment settle over her. She hadn't realized how much she'd missed female companionship. Fort Squall had female riders, of course, but few she'd connected with as deeply as she once had with Claire and her friends.

"Will you dance at the celebration?" Saffra asked, breaking her reverie.

"Oh, I haven't danced in ages," she admitted.

"Neither has Byron, I'd wager," Claire teased. "You should surprise him."

The suggestion sparked a memory—that day she'd fled her betrothed, racing across the dance floor to escape him, only to run smack into Byron. She'd fallen to the floor, embarrassed herself monumentally, and then fled. He'd found her, of course. She never would have imagined in that moment, when they sat under the willow tree, who he would become to her. What they would become together. That was before the weight of leadership had settled fully on their shoulders.

"Perhaps I will," she said, smiling at the thought.

"You absolutely will," came the growled thought from her mate.

"Quit eavesdropping," she scolded, but couldn't help her smile.

By late afternoon, they had created nearly two hundred bags. As servants began carrying them away, Saffra pulled her aside.

"Thank you for your help today," she said sincerely. "It meant more than you know to have you here."

"I was happy to do it," she replied. "It's been... nice. To be part of this."

She left Saffra's chambers, wandering the keep until she found herself in the queen's garden atop the king's tower, a space she was honored to have access to. The sun was setting, casting long shadows across the carefully tended greenery. To her surprise, Byron was there, deep in conversation with Dallin.

When Byron caught sight of her, his face lit with a smile that still made her heart skip. He excused himself from Dallin and crossed to her, taking her hands in his.

"I've been missing you," he said, drawing her close. "How was your day with Saffra and the others?"

"Wonderful," she replied honestly. "We were preparing favors for the ceremony."

He knew all this, of course. He'd seen her progress throughout the day. Just as she knew he'd met with Talon and the king's shields, and also spent time alone with his uncle. But, it helped retain normalcy to speak of it, as if they hadn't lived each other's days together.

Byron's contentment mirrored her own. They'd both needed this visit more than they'd realized—this reminder that they were part of something larger than Fort Squall, that they had friends and allies across the kingdom.

He guided her over to the garden's edge, overlooking the city. She said, "It's beautiful up here."

"It is," he agreed. Talon's inner circle had taken to using the space as their own personal refuge. She was honored that they considered her and Byron part of that.

She leaned against him, looking out over Kastali Dun, enjoying the glittering glow of the lights as the sun began to set. The evening meal would begin shortly. "What would you like to do for the rest of the night, after dinner?"

"Hmm. Now that we know Isabella's curse is broken, I think I'll work twice as hard at getting you with—"

"Byron!" She swatted his chest and he chuckled, the sound low and gravely.

"You cannot blame me."

"As if you haven't already been working at it with every spare moment we have," she teased.

He had.

She couldn't have asked for a more ardent lover. One who interpreted her every need. One who put her pleasure above his own.

Just the thought had heat pooling low.

"We can always skip the meal and order food to be delivered to our room," he murmured against her ear, reading her thoughts.

She giggled. "We really should go to dinner. But...I'm not opposed to enjoying your efforts afterward."

"Deal." He leaned in, kissing the top of her head.

The future stretched before them, bright with possibility. Fort Squall, restored and strengthened. A potential new generation of young drengr and riders to mentor. And someday—hopefully soon—children of their own.

She had fled Redport seeking freedom from constraints. What she'd found instead was a different kind of freedom—the freedom to choose her own path, to build something meaningful, to love and be loved in return.

Byron's arms tightened around her, and through their bond flowed his love, his pride, his absolute certainty that they were exactly where they were meant to be. She closed her eyes and let herself believe it too.

EPILOGUE: TWO

Kastali Dun

Saffra blinked awake, her mind immediately fuzzy with sleep. Around her, bodies shifted on the floor—a tangle of limbs and blankets and soft breathing. The vigil. Right. They'd stayed up through the night, taking turns dozing on sleeping mats and couches scattered throughout the queen's chambers on the lower level of the tower.

"Someone's awake." Claire's voice drifted from across the room. She stood by the terrace balcony wearing a white shift from the night before. Beside her, platters heaped with breakfast rested on the large table. They'd stayed up so late, she must not have heard the servants creep in to set everything up.

"Oh gods," she breathed, sitting up carefully. "I can't believe today is the day. This is actually happening."

"Believe it," Desaree said through a yawn, stretching from her place on the nearby couch. "You deserve every moment of this."

The others stirred. Leah mumbled something about needing tea, while Jeanine bounced upright with her usual morning energy. Miera and Selphie moved through the room, setting out cups and ensuring everyone had what they needed.

Tamara blinked and sat up, rubbing at her eyes before stretching and groaning. Her arrival three nights prior had been one of celebration. Rebuilding in Squall's End and Fort Squall had finally allowed the young fort leader some time away.

"Breakfast first," Jocelyn declared, clapping her hands together. "Then we make you beautiful."

"As if she isn't already," Saffra's mother said, appearing from the adjoining chamber. She was already dressed in her white ceremonial gown, every hair perfectly in place despite the early hour. She'd decided that all her favorite ladies would be dressed in white, so that her sunset colored gown stood out.

All of her favorite females were present, having kept vigil with her the night before, as was customary. Though they'd fallen asleep halfway through the night. She didn't blame anyone for that. After the past year they'd had, they were all bone tired. It would take months before they recovered.

The room exploded into chaos as people came and went, getting dressed for the ceremony, seeing to their needs, and gathering around the food—honey cakes and fresh berries with cream, warm bread with sweet butter. Tourines of scrambled eggs and potatoes, plates of ham. Tess had truly outdone herself.

Saffra's stomach fluttered, taking in the activity. Her nerves didn't save much room for an appetite, but she forced herself to nibble at a honey cake. Her sister Rana chattered about the decorations she'd glimpsed in the corridors a few minutes prior—orange lanterns and white ribbons everywhere.

"The guests are already pouring into the throne room," Leah said through a mouthful of eggs. "According to Selphie."

"Don't terrify her," Merrian scolded, though she was smiling.

"It's...overwhelming," Saffra admitted.

"Which is why you have us," Claire said firmly.

And it was true. As the morning progressed, Saffra found herself passed from gentle hand to gentle hand. Rana washed and braided her hair into an elaborate crown. Her mother applied cosmetics with a practiced touch—just enough to enhance, never to mask.

"Are you ready for the dress?" Madame Rosanne appeared at the door, her assistants behind her with the carefully wrapped gown.

Saffra's breath caught as they revealed it. The burnt orange silk glowed in the morning light, pink and gold accents catching and throwing back reflections like tiny flames. The scale embroidery at the bodice was even more intricate than she remembered. What started off as orange at the bodice faded into sunset colors near the hem.

"Oh my gods," she whispered.

"My thoughts exactly," Desaree said, looking a little awed.

They helped her into it—all those hands, all that care. No one commented on the appearance of her mangled arm. Nor did they treat her any differently because of it.

When Rosanne finally turned her toward the mirror, Saffra hardly recognized herself.

"Bedelth won't know what hit him," Jocelyn said with a soft grin.

"The jewelry," Miera murmured, producing a wooden case. Fire opals and imperial topaz, arranged in a delicate necklace and matching earrings that caught the light like captured flames.

Claire stepped forward with a gold circlet embedded with tiny orange gems. "Every bride needs a crown."

Saffra's throat tightened, making it hard to swallow. She already felt like a princess. But this?

A knock interrupted their admiration. Bedelth's mother peered in. That had been the biggest surprise of all. Bedelth's parents had gotten over their disapproval enough to attend the ceremony. She had her suspicions, mainly that they wanted to save face. People would talk, after all. Given that the king had changed the law, there was no reason for his parents to be against their bonding. If they weren't there, it wouldn't look good on them. But she wanted to think it was because some part of them wanted to support their son, despite their tendency for conditional love.

Regardless of how she disliked his parents, she could put that aside for this one day. She was determined to remain civil. Determined not to let anything ruin what was sure to be the most perfect day of her life.

"The guests have all arrived," Seishi reported. "And my son is wearing a hole in the floor."

Laughter rippled through the chamber.

"Then we shouldn't keep him waiting," Saffra decided, though her stomach did that fluttering thing again.

They formed up around her—her supporting ladies in their sea of white, making her sunset gown stand out like a beacon. Her heartbeat grew stronger as they moved through the keep, past corridors lined with staff and well-wishers.

The throne room had been transformed. Orange and white flowers covered every surface, silk draperies caught the light from hundreds of candles. She barely noticed any of it.

Bedelth stood at the base of Talon's dais.

He wore silk brocade that complemented her own gown. His hair was cut close to his scalp. When their eyes met, his expression shifted—from nervous anticipation to something that made her heart skip entirely.

Love. Wonder. Awe.

They were truly doing this. She couldn't think of another male she would rather tie herself to. While she hated the dark thoughts that rejoiced in Commander Daxton's circumstances, she also thanked the gods that everything had turned out as it had. That they were here. That they would get to be together, as they were meant to be.

None of that would have been possible had Kane won.

The ceremony blurred. Talon's words about eternal bonds and shared souls rang through the throne room—no doubt inspired by his own bond with Claire. Bedelth presented her with a bow of white wood inlaid with gold. Her own gift—a fire opal pommel stone—caught the light like a tiny sun.

When they spoke the bonding ceremony words, her skin erupted with chills. She could almost taste the magic swirling around them. Bedelth's gaze never left hers, not for a single moment.

Cheers and raucous chants erupted when the ceremony came to a close.

As they turned to face the crowd, she caught sight of her supporting ladies. They didn't bother hiding their tears. Claire and Leah were clinging to each other. The look of radiant joy and support on her queen's face made warmth explode in her chest.

Gods, she was so lucky.

The celebration passed in a blur of congratulations, music, and dancing that lasted all through the afternoon and well into the evening. Because they were the honored couple, Talon and Claire had shifted their position at the head table. She and her mate sat in the center, all eyes upon them. She felt like absolute royalty, minus all the extra duties, thank the gods. Bedelth held her steady whenever her arm spasmed during the dances. With his solid presence, she could do anything.

As the festivities roared on with no clear intention of ending, she grew overly aware of what came next. There were no nerves, only eager anticipation. She and Bedelth already knew each other intimately. All that was left was the final act, one she'd desperately craved for months.

They were moving through a dance as he caught her eye. Even though their minds were not yet melded, it was like he could read her thoughts. His expression morphed with desire. "I think I am done sharing you." The words were more of a growl than anything.

Her cheeks flushed, heat pooling low in her belly. "How difficult would it be to sneak away without notice?"

"Now *why* would we want to do that?" he challenged.

"Because—!" she spluttered, pulling them to a stop. "Everyone will know."

"Good." His expression was smug. Couples were forced to move aside and then stop as they noticed. "Everyone should know I plan to make you mine."

"I think they already know, you beast."

"What do you think?" He lifted his voice for the surrounding crowd to hear. Realizing what moment this was, the musicians stopped playing and a hush fell. "Is it time to make this beautiful woman mine?"

Bawdy shouts rang out into the hall.

Saffra pulled her lower lip between her teeth, unable to help her smile. She was going to make him pay for this later. Preferably by teasing him until he begged for reprieve. She'd already learned a few ways to do that successfully with her mouth.

Talon appeared beside them. He gripped Bedelth's shoulder, a silent look passing between them. Then the rest of Bedelth's shield brothers appeared, followed quickly by her supporting ladies.

"Have fun," Claire winked.

When she next blinked, Bedelth had swept her into his arms, carrying her out of the hall like a conquest. "Dragons," she muttered, feigning annoyance even if she felt anything but.

Her body throbbed with want. Her heart raced with anticipation. Her mind jumped through all the things that were sure to come.

They had the rest of the night to themselves.

Bedelth strode through the keep with silent purpose. She could feel the eager tension in his coiled muscles. When they reached his chambers—their chambers now—the door barely closed before he set her on her feet and was kissing her.

"Mine," he murmured against her lips.

"Yours," she agreed.

"There was a time I worried you would never be mine," he managed between kisses.

"I'm so glad you pushed me," she admitted. "Thank you for that. For not giving up on me."

"It might have taken a bit for me to realize it, but giving up wasn't an option. Giving you time was."

"I needed it."

"I know." He pressed their bodies together, pulling her hips against his. She felt his hardness and groaned.

"I wanted to take tonight slow," he whispered against her lips.

"We've had *ages* to take it slow."

"Needy little mate. Shall I mate you now, then, with no soft moments to get us there?"

"Now, Bedelth."

His chuckle was gravely as he snatched her waist and spun her away from him. He pressed her backside against him, leaning in to nip her ear. "As my mate wishes." Then he set about the buttons on her gown. He made quick work of the masterpiece, sliding it off her frame. The orange silk pooled at her feet. A brief bout of nerves overtook her as her mangled arm was revealed. Bedelth's hand ghosted down it before reaching around to span her belly. "There isn't a single part of you that isn't beautiful. Tonight, I am going to prove that to you."

"All right," she managed, pushing her nerves aside. This was Bedelth—her mate, her anchor, her choice. When his lips found her throat, she relaxed into him. He set kisses across her skin, mapping a path down her throat, to her shoulder.

"Your turn," he taunted, spinning her back around to face him.

She set about his clothes with feral delight, rushing through undoing the ties and buttons. When his rigid chest was revealed, she leaned in and licked a path up the hard lines of his muscles. Each one twitched in response and he groaned. "That is for toying with me earlier—in front of a crowd," she said.

"I had a feeling you would punish me for it."

"Oh, I haven't even gotten started, but we'll get to that later." She made quick work of the ties on his pants.

When they were both bare, she took a step back to admire him. He did the same. There was only adoration in his gaze as it roved over her like a heated touch.

"I love you," she whispered.

"And I love you," he replied, stepping forward and lifting her easily. "Let me show you just how much."

He wasted no time depositing her on the bed. What followed were hungry touches that turned urgent, desperate. Whispered words dissolved into breathless moans. He joined with her and her world felt complete for the first time. Everything about this was right. Inevitable.

"Gods, I will never get the feel of you out of my mind," he groaned.

It was mutual.

He moved inside her knowing exactly how to bring her to the brink. Exactly how to give her the pleasure she craved. Their names were whispered in tandem, eyes locked as they flowed through this profound ritual. When they crested the mountain's peak, their minds crashed together like waves meeting—merging, swirling until she couldn't tell where she ended and he began. Every sensation doubled, every emotion amplified.

She gasped out his name, riding each powerful pulse of pleasure, feeling him do the same. The sounds of their mingled breaths followed into the silence. If she listened hard enough, she could just make out the faint sounds of merriment still happening below. The party continued, unchanged.

But she and Bedelth? They were changed forever. Changed in the best of ways.

"That was..." She couldn't find words as they came down from the high.

"Perfect," he finished, pressing a kiss to her forehead. "You're perfect."

Her lip caught between her teeth and a low growl sounded in his chest. She saw herself through his eyes, felt the hunger in him rise, only moments after they'd finished. When he twitched inside her, she gasped.

"Now that you are in my mind," he said, "you know what you do to me, mate."

Then he was ravaging her again. Thank the gods they were bonded. His eager energy was boundless, his desire for her unrelenting. She matched him, savoring every moment, every measure of pleasure he wrung from her.

When their mating frenzy calmed, they lay tangled together, whispered musings over the ceremony breaking the silence. Her eyes grew heavy, and his did too.

Mates.

They were finally mated.

Complete.

"I'm still going to punish you for earlier," she reminded him, her words slurred with fatigue.

"Perhaps we ought to sleep first. There's always the morning."

"And every morning thereafter." A soft smile pulled at her lips. The idea of falling asleep in his arms and waking up beside him every morning for the remainder of their lives was pure bliss.

"That's a promise I'll hold you to," he murmured, pressing a kiss to her temple.

Today had been perfect. Getting to this point wasn't without its hardships, but it was worth it. Every moment. Just to be beside the one she loved more than life itself. Her last thought before drifting off was that she'd found exactly where she belonged—in the arms of her mate, surrounded by their connection, finally and irrevocably complete.

EPILOGUE: THREE

Kastali Dun

Leah frowned, propping her hands on her hips. "That banner is crooked," she announced, eyeing the colorful fabric hanging just opposite the main entrance. "Can someone—?"

"I've got it." Jovari appeared beneath it, adjusting the corners until it hung perfectly straight. She couldn't help her soft smile at his appearance. He'd been hovering for hours. Keeping out of the way unless she needed something, at which point he jumped in to help.

He stepped back, glancing her way. "Better?"

"Better."

The fabric proclaimed "First Public Library of Kastali Dun" in elegant script, the letters shimmering with subtle magic that made them catch the light. She took a deep breath, fighting the flutter of nerves in her stomach. Through the windows, she could already see the crowd gathering outside—far more people than she'd expected. Merchants closing their shops early, families with children in tow, even some of the nobility had come to witness the opening. A thing like this was unheard of, so naturally, no one

323

dared pass up the opportunity to insert themselves into history in the making.

She moved to complete the final preparations, checking that everything was exactly where it needed to be. "Leah, stop fretting." Saffra emerged from behind a bookshelf, her skin practically glowing in the morning light. Being newly mated had given her a radiance that was impossible to miss. "You're making me anxious with all those nerves rolling off you."

"I just want everything to be perfect." She twisted her fingers together, glancing around the main room one more time. The floors gleamed, the books were arranged by subject, the rule plaque near the entry sparkled, ensuring that everyone who entered would be aware of the stipulations for using the space.

"It's already perfect." Claire appeared beside her, reaching out to smooth Leah's hair. "Look at what you've created here. It's nothing short of spectacular. You should be proud of what you've pulled off. I know I am."

"I can't believe this is finally happening," she breathed, taking in the space with fresh eyes. Sunlight streamed through the tall windows, illuminating motes of dust that danced in the air. The scent of new wood and leather bindings filled the room. Colorful rugs marked cozy reading nooks. She'd already done her rounds upstairs, spending extra time in the children's section, which boasted tiny chairs painted in bright colors, tables for coloring and art projects, and fun murals painted along the walls.

"The crowd's getting restless." Jovari joined them. His hand found the small of her back, warm and reassuring. "Are you ready?"

"As ready as I'll ever be." She managed a smile. "Though I keep wondering—what if no one actually wants this? What if—?"

"Leah." Saffra interrupted, fixing her with a stern look. "Do you see those people outside? They've been waiting for over an hour. Some brought their lunches." She leaned in conspiratorially. "And trust me, if they're anything like new mates, they'll be devouring books the way Bedelth devours me." Saffra's brows waggled.

"Saffra!" Claire laughed, elbowing the seer with a knowing look.

"What? I'm just saying that when Leah and Jovari finally bond, she'll understand the appeal of losing yourself in something engaging."

Leah choked.

Jovari's hand flexed against her back. "Saffra, being mated has turned you wicked. I can promise you, I think my mate already understands just how engaging I can be."

"Oh, my gods," Leah muttered, heat creeping up her neck. "Can we please get back on track, to the matter at hand?"

"Ah, but notice how I distracted you from your nerves there for a moment?" Saffra grinned.

"Jovari's right!" Leah decided. "Being mated has truly turned you wicked."

"She's going to be a bad influence on us," Jocelyn said.

"Nonsense." Saffra lifted her chin.

Desaree rushed in, slightly breathless. "The king is coming! He's walking up the street as we speak."

"Oh, gods. The crowd is about to lose their minds," Saffra muttered.

"But I thought he had matters to attend to—" Leah managed before Verath appeared.

"He insisted." The shield leaned in and kissed the top of Desaree's head. "You truly believe he would miss something so significant? In his city?"

Jovari squeezed her wrist. "You deserve recognition for this, little minx."

The endearment sent warmth flooding through her. "I just wanted to help people."

"And that's exactly why this will succeed." Claire stepped forward, fussing with her gown. "Shall we?"

Leah nodded, though her hands trembled slightly. She suddenly found it difficult to speak, so she pressed her lips together. They moved toward the double doors. The murmur of the crowd grew louder as they approached.

"Remember," Saffra called out, "head high, shoulders back. You're about to show Kastali Dun what real magic looks like."

She faltered, then continued. Saffra had no idea how much those words meant to her. Most of her friends had magic. Some of them could utter a single magical word and make something happen. What she'd done here was magic of a different kind, but no less impactful. That thought lifted her confidence.

With Jovari's steady presence beside her, and her friends flanking her, she reached for the door handles. The moment she pushed them open, the waiting crowd erupted in cheers.

Her breath caught in her throat. There had to be hundreds of people packed into the street. Children perched on their parents' shoulders, elderly citizens leaned on walking sticks, and groups of young adults clustered together, all craning their necks to see. An aisle formed as a voice called, "Make way! Make way for the king!"

King Talon appeared and Claire immediately went to link their hands. Even without his crown, his presence commanded attention. The cheering died down as he raised a hand.

"Citizens of Kastali Dun," his voice carried easily. "Today marks a new chapter in our city's history. Lady Leah, dear friend of our queen's and a visionary in her own right, has gifted our community something invaluable—access to knowledge for all." He gestured toward the library, then to Leah. No one had ever addressed her as *Lady Leah* before. "Many of you know the hardships our kingdom has faced. But it is through innovation, compassion, and the dedication of individuals like Lady Leah that we rebuild stronger than before. This library represents not just books, but opportunity. Not just stories, but dreams."

The king's eyes met hers, and she saw warmth there. "Would you care to address your community?"

Her throat went dry. Public speaking had never been her strong suit, but looking out at all those expectant faces—children clutching their parents' hands, elderly faces creased with hope— she found her voice. "I..." She cleared her throat. "I come from a place where we had libraries everywhere. Where anyone, regardless of their station or wealth, could walk in and borrow a book. When I arrived here and learned that wasn't the case, I knew I had to do something."

She gestured to the building behind her. "Books aren't just entertainment. They're teachers, friends, and windows to worlds we might never see otherwise. Every child deserves the chance to learn, every adult the opportunity to grow, and every person the right to escape into a story when life becomes too heavy."

Jovari's hand squeezed hers in encouragement.

"This library is yours—all of yours. The only rule is respect. Respect for the books, for the space, and for each other. Take what you need, return what you borrow, and know that every time you open these doors, you're investing in your community's future."

The applause that followed was deafening. Children jumped up and down clapping their hands with excitement, not quite knowing or understanding the world that had just been opened to them, while adults nodded approvingly. More than a few people wiped at their eyes.

"I'd like to introduce our library staff," she continued, raising her voice. Three people stepped forward—a middle-aged woman, a young man with ink-stained fingers, and an elderly gentleman with kind eyes. "Head Librarian Marta, Assistant Librarian Edwin, and Master Geoffrey, who will oversee our children's programs."

Each staff member bowed slightly as she introduced them. Roland caught her eye from the crowd and nodded approvingly. Though he couldn't leave his post at the royal library, his presence here today meant the world to her.

"Now," she took a deep breath, "shall we cut the ribbon?"

The ribbon had been a joint idea between her and Claire. It wasn't something familiar to the people of Dragonwall. She liked that with the opening of a new library, was potentially a new tradition, too.

The ceremony proceeded smoothly after that. Merrian stepped forward and handed her a pair of ceremonial scissors, the handle adorned with small crystals that caught the light. As the blade met the ribbon, the crowd erupted again. The doors were officially open.

What happened next was controlled chaos. People surged forward, eager to explore. Parents guided children toward the upper floor, to the colorful room designated for young readers. Teenagers gravitated toward adventure novels. Elderly citizens settled into cushioned chairs with books of poetry. There were other things available for those who couldn't read. Craft tables and an entire room for creating artwork of every variety. The massive table of refreshments was especially popular. She would have to see about having some kind of snacks section that could be monitored in the future, knowing many people in less fortunate parts of the city often didn't get enough to eat. She never wanted people to go hungry while enjoying a good book.

"It's working," Jovari murmured beside her, his voice filled with pride. "Look at them."

She did look. A young girl clutched a book filled with pictures to her chest like it was treasure. Two boys argued amicably over a text about dragons. A woman who looked like she'd never owned a book in her life ran her fingers reverently over leather bindings.

"Thank you," Claire said, suddenly at her side with tears in her eyes. "For making this happen."

"We all made it happen." She hugged her best friend, happier than ever that Claire had insisted she come on the journey to Dragonwall. "I couldn't have done it without—"

"Without your brilliant mind and stubborn determination?" Saffra interrupted, joining them. "Please, we just helped with the manual labor."

"And the magical protections," Jovari added with a grin. "Don't forget those."

Claire had come to the rescue, using her spriten magic to cast spells over the space and all the books within. No book would suffer damage that often came with aging or poor treatment. Even while checked out, they would carry those protections. "It's some of my more genius work," Claire had admitted.

They spent the next hour mingling with patrons, answering questions, and watching the library come to life. Children squealed with delight around one of the craft tables, splattering paint everywhere. Adults discussed book recommendations with animated gestures. The staff moved efficiently through the space, helping people find what they needed.

"I hate to steal you away," Jovari said eventually, his breath warm against her ear, "but we should head out if we want to reach Irelia Island before dark. Are you ready to go?"

Her heart skipped. He'd surprised her last night with the invitation—a private getaway to celebrate her achievement. Just the two of them, no responsibilities, no crowds.

"Go," Claire urged, having overheard. "Your library is in good hands, I promise."

"You'll make sure Marta has everything she needs?"

"Of course." Claire squeezed her hand. "You've given our people something incredible. Let someone else manage the rest of the day."

She glanced around one more time. The library was thriving, her staff looked confident, and the patrons seemed perfectly content. "All right."

She said her goodbyes quickly, promising to return tomorrow to check on everything. As she and Jovari made their way through the streets toward the keep, she couldn't stop smiling.

"You did something amazing today," he said as they walked. "I'm so proud of you."

"We did something amazing. You helped with every step."

He squeezed her hand. "Only because you had the vision to see what was possible. I'm sorry if I ever doubted it."

"You have nothing to apologize for."

By the time they reached the king's tower garden, the sun was beginning its descent toward the horizon. Her traveling pack sat ready where she'd left it that morning. Jovari had already shifted into his dragon form, his sapphire scales gleaming in the afternoon light.

There was a large pack attached to his harness. She added hers, too.

She climbed onto his back with practiced ease, settling between his wing joints. The moment her skin was in contact with his scales, their minds merged. It was the first time she'd embraced him this way. She saw a glimpse of the ocean, the waves of his memory, before they sank into each other. She could feel his every emotion, his pride and adoration, the deep hunger for her that he often kept buried. He could feel everything from her, too.

Before they launched into the air, she glanced down towards the city, in the direction of her little library. Her eyes watered and she blinked away the tears threatening to fall. She had been so scared that she might not settle in. Here she was, thriving.

"Ready?" Jovari's voice rumbled through their shared minds. She jolted, unfamiliar with the caress of his words. A mental chuckle followed. *"You will have many human lifetimes with me, little minx. Many years to get used to it."*

She found that she was already looking forward to that, more than she had realized.

Jovari leapt from the ground, Kastali Dun shrinking below them. The wind whipped through her hair as they soared south-east, leaving the bustle of the city behind. Flying always filled her with a sense of freedom, but today was different for so many reasons. She was flying with Jovari as his mate, their minds melded. She was flying as a woman who had finally accomplished something she was truly proud of. A woman with a future and a purpose. Today felt like a celebration.

The sea sparkled in the sunlight. For a time, there was nothing but wide open water. Several hours passed in a rush, and then—

"See it yet?"

"Yes!"

The small island was covered with dense foliage. She could see from Jovari's mind what was in store for them. Irelia Island was a place that had once belonged to the ancient dragons of old, where they once lived and died, where they laid their eggs and started new families, just like the cave in the Gable Forest. Now it was a peaceful sanctuary that had become a favorite retreat for the inner circle.

As they descended, the unique feature of the island became visible through the canopy of trees: the hatching ground with colorful fragments of dragon eggshells scattered across the interior like confetti. Even from a distance, she could make out pieces in blues, greens, golds, and deep purples.

Jovari landed and she slid from his back, quickly untying both packs before he shifted to human form. The transformation always fascinated her—the ripple of magic, the fluid change from massive dragon to the man she was growing to love. "Should we explore the hatching grounds first?" he asked, though his eyes suggested he had other priorities.

"Maybe later," she decided. "I want to watch the sun set from the beach."

They made quick work of setting up camp. Jovari had brought a thick blanket, cushions, and a pack of food that smelled heavenly. As the sun painted the sky in shades of orange and pink, they settled onto the sand with goblets of fizzy wine and a selection of cheese, fruit, and fresh bread.

"To successful beginnings," Jovari raised his goblet.

"To unexpected adventures," she countered, clinking her goblet against his.

The wine was sweet and bubbles exploded on her tongue, warming her from the inside out. They ate in comfortable silence, watching the sun sink lower.

"Can I ask you something?" Jovari's voice was carefully casual as he refilled their goblets.

"Anything."

"Are you happy? I mean, truly happy, here in Dragonwall?"

She considered the question, gazing out at the water. "I think...yes. More than I realized I could be." She turned to face him. "Today proved it to me. Opening that library, seeing people's reactions—I've never felt so purposeful."

"You've found your place."

"I'm finding it," she corrected. "With help from amazing people. Especially you."

He set his goblet aside, reaching for her hand. Once again, she was struck by how handsome he was. There were moments when the sight of his face was a familiar comfort to her, and other moments when she saw him again as if for the first time, and the sight nearly knocked the breath from her lungs. She never dreamed she could be so lucky to find a person like him, both beautiful inside and out.

His thumb traced circles on her palm. "I love watching you discover yourself. Your passion, your determination—it's incredible."

The compliment made her stomach flutter. "You're pretty incredible yourself, you know."

"Am I?" His voice held a teasing note, but his eyes were serious. "Because there's something I've been wanting to discuss with you."

Her pulse quickened. "Oh?"

"The bonding ceremony," he said quietly. "I know you wanted to take things slow, to find yourself first. And I respect that completely. But I wondered... How are you feeling about it now?"

She took a sip of wine to buy time. Over the past few weeks, she'd felt herself settling deeper into her life here. The work at the library had given her renewed purpose. Her friendships had grown stronger. And her feelings for Jovari...

"I feel more grounded every day," she admitted. "Like I'm becoming who I was meant to be."

"And us?" His thumb continued its gentle caress. "How do you feel about us?"

"I think..." She bit her lip, gathering courage. "I think I might be ready to talk about timing."

His eyes brightened, but he didn't rush her. "No pressure. I want you to be completely sure."

"I am sure about you," she said firmly. "About us. Maybe we could...discuss a date? Something in the near future? A few months, perhaps?"

The joy that spread across his face made her chest tighten with emotion. "Really?"

"Really." She laughed at his boyish excitement. "I want to be your mate, Jovari. Officially. Completely."

He leaned forward, cupping her face with his free hand. His

expression turned serious. "You have no idea how happy this makes me."

Their kiss was soft at first, almost reverent. But as she leaned into him, it deepened. His hand tangled in her hair, her fingers gripped his shirt. The taste of wine lingered on his lips, sweet and intoxicating. It meant everything to her that he was patient. That he hadn't made a single demand of her—hadn't demanded they rush things or seal their bond. He was going at her pace.

When they broke apart, her heart was racing. "So...perhaps a winter bonding ceremony? The solstice, maybe?" She'd always loved the winter season, days where the world around her was blanketed in snow.

"That sounds perfect." His voice was rough with emotion. "Though I might not survive waiting that long if you keep kissing me like that."

She laughed, suddenly feeling bold. "Maybe I can take the edge off a little bit, since you didn't allow me to last time."

His pupils dilated, shifting briefly to draconic slits. "Leah..."

"I've been thinking," she continued, her cheeks burning but her voice steady. "About what Saffra said earlier. About losing yourself in something engaging."

"Have you now?" The words came out as a growl.

Instead of answering, she moved closer, until she was straddling his lap. The position brought them eye to eye, and she could see the desire there, carefully restrained.

"I want to make you happy," she whispered. "Let me?"

His control seemed to fracture. "Gods, little minx. Are you sure?"

For an answer, she kissed him again, pouring all her feelings into the gesture. His arms came around her, pulling her flush against his chest. She could feel his heart thundering against her, matching her own racing pulse.

Her hands trailed down his arms, marveling at the solid muscle beneath her palms. When she reached the ties on his pants, she hesitated for just a moment.

"We don't have to—" he started.

"I want to." She met his gaze. "Trust me?"

"Always."

With trembling fingers, she loosened the laces on his trousers. His breath hitched as her hand found him, warm and hard. Oh, the feel of him was perfection, smooth and unyielding. The intimacy of the moment struck her—they were alone on a beach, the sun setting behind them, no one around.

"Show me," she murmured. "Show me how you like it."

His hand covered hers, tightening, guiding her movements. "Like this. Just—yes, exactly like that."

A sound escaped him, somewhere between a groan and a prayer. The control he usually maintained so carefully was slipping, and she found she loved watching him unravel because of her touch. Nothing had ever made her feel more powerful.

She used his cues as her guide, moving her hand, gripping him how he liked. His breathing grew ragged, his hips bucking beneath her. The stars were coming out now, painting the sky with silver light.

"Leah," he rasped, his voice strained. "I'm close. If you want to stop—"

"I don't want to stop." She increased her pace, watching his eyes roll back.

"Gods above," he moaned, the sound strangled.

"Let go, Jovari. I've got you."

He shattered with a low growl that rumbled through his chest. Her name fell from his lips like a benediction as he found his release. The satisfaction that filled her was explosive—seeing him vulnerable and undone because of her actions. It was her new favorite drug. She would happily do this for him every night until their ceremony if necessary, just to watch him fall apart.

He wrapped his hand around the back of her neck and crushed their mouths together. His breaths fanned her skin as she breathed through their kiss. She swallowed each one greedily.

Eventually he shifted her off his lap and grabbed a cloth from their supplies, cleaning up before pressing a kiss to her forehead.

Sitting down beside her, he pulled her against his side, staring out over the rolling waves.

"That was..." he trailed off, seemingly at a loss for words.

"Good?" she prompted, suddenly nervous, like she was being graded on an exam.

"Incredible." He turned and tilted her chin up. "You're incredible."

She curled into his warmth, listening to his heartbeat slow. Above them, the stars grew brighter, and the gentle lapping of waves created a peaceful rhythm.

"Thank you," she said softly. "For today. For the library support, for this getaway, for...everything."

"Thank you for letting me be part of your dreams." He stroked her hair. "And for trusting me with more of yourself."

"Always." She guided him back upon the blanket until they were laying side by side, his arm propped under her head. They lay there in comfortable silence, the events of the day replaying in her mind. "I love you," she whispered, turning into his chest. The words had come unbidden, shocking her. But once they were out, she recognized how true they were.

There was a long hesitation. "Truly?" Jovari's voice held wonder.

"Yes."

His arms tightened around her, turning her and pulling her closer against him. "I love you too. More than I thought possible."

She turned her face up towards him and he kissed her forehead. When the breeze picked up, he muttered a word and a blanket near the edge of their makeshift bed appeared in hand. He spread it over them.

His fingers traced patterns on her skin, lulling her into sleepiness. She felt happier than she could remember. There was still a small ache in her chest where her family lived, the wish that they could be here to see the life she'd made. She knew her parents would be proud of her, and hoped that even though she'd come from a different world, that wherever they were, they could still look down on her and witness her successes. The waves continued their gentle song as she drifted off, safe and loved and exactly where she belonged.

EPILOGUE: FOUR

Verath shifted in his chair, trying to focus on the mundane dispute taking place in the throne room. Attending court was one of his least favorite obligations. Sitting still for hours on end, listening to grievances that often stemmed from selfishness. Sometimes it made him want to crawl out of his skin with irritation.

He wasn't alone in the feeling. His shield brothers suffered the same. Today they were all in attendance, as they had been since Talon's return with Claire. He couldn't remember a time when all six chairs bracketing the dais had been filled. Not since before Cyrus left the capital to hunt the stones.

A pang of sorrow tightened his chest at the thought of his shield brother—of his sacrifice. It was quickly replaced by relief, thinking Cyrus had found peace at last. They all missed him—dearly. Knowing a little part of him resided within Claire had brought comfort. But learning of his sacrifice, knowing he had finally moved on, that brought the closure they all needed.

"I didn't sign a twelve month licensing agreement," the disgruntled cloth merchant droned on, gesturing with increasing frustration. "Six months. Six! The next merchant gets to peddle his wares year-round, and I'm told I need to pack up in two weeks?"

These merchant licensing squabbles had become all too predictable. They'd gone through this same song and dance with the candlers just last week. And the spice vendors the week before that.

When Claire's voice broke in—soft but authoritative—to ask the merchant to clarify his initial agreement terms, Verath glanced over his shoulder. The sight of her on that throne never failed to catch him off guard. It wasn't just that she belonged here. Though gods knew she'd earned that seat a hundred times over. It was the image burned into his mind from a few weeks ago. The morning after her return feast, after Talon had announced her victory over Kane.

She'd chosen to wear silver that morning. Silver, of all colors. The same color as the gown she'd worn the first time she'd stood before Talon in this very room. Defiant and furious and absolutely magnificent.

But this time, when she'd settled into the throne beside Talon, it hadn't been defiance. It had been *rightness*. After Kane's darkness, after the uncertainty of her disappearance, seeing her there—their queen, where she belonged—had made something tight in his chest finally, blessedly loosen.

"...and I'll need written confirmation from the merchant's guild," Talon was saying, bringing Verath's attention back to the present.

"Of course, Your Majesty." The cloth merchant groused, clearly disappointed he hadn't gotten the answer he'd wanted.

As the man backed away with a deep bow, court proceedings began to wind down. He thanked the gods, every single one of them, that this was the last petitioner for the day. He was already preparing to stand, eager to stretch his legs, when Claire's voice slipped into his mind.

"Verath?"

He stilled. It was always a delight to hear her speak to him. There were times—more than he cared to admit—that he wished Desaree could do the same. But that was dangerous thinking, the kind of yearning that would only lead to disappointment, and there was nothing about Desaree that was disappointing.

"When court ends, can you gather Desaree and meet me in your chambers?" His muscles tensed. *"There's something I'd like to discuss with the both of you."*

"My chambers? Surely it would be easiest if we came to the tower?"

"This is something I would like to keep between the three of us—for now."

His mind erupted into speculation. *"Of course. But I must ask, is everything all right?"*

"Oh, yes. More than all right. I'll see you, then?"

"As soon as possible."

Rising from his chair, he didn't bother offering any explanation to his shield brothers as he strode from the throne room. Anyone who cared to look would assume he had some matter of urgency to attend to. And he did, didn't he? Anything his queen asked of him was certainly urgent.

He found Desaree in the queen's rooms of the tower, working with Selphie and Miera on a couple of gowns. There was a pile of trimmings around them as they laughed and chatted. He took a moment to silently observe, watching the happiness radiate from the woman he loved. Becoming a handmaiden had been one of her dreams as a young girl. She'd risen to so much more than that. A lady in waiting with a title.

He cleared his throat. All three females looked up. "Verath." Desaree stood, setting aside the hem she'd been dressing. "Is everything all right?"

"Fine. I hope. Might I borrow you for a little while?"

"Oh. Can it not...wait?"

"It cannot."

"Certainly, then." She looked to Claire's spriten handmaidens. "I'll be back in a bit."

"No rush," Selphie said.

"We'll be here," Miera added, disguising a smirk.

Gods, what did they think, that he was stealing her a way for a tryst?

She followed him out of the tower and down the hall.

"What is this about?" The words were whispered as they approached his door.

"No idea whatsoever. Claire wants to speak with us; that is all I know."

Desaree frowned. "She never mentioned anything about this to me. And I just saw her this morning."

He shrugged. "Shall we see what it is about?"

They hesitated outside his door. "Should I be worried?"

"If Claire wanted us worried, she'd have summoned us to the dungeons," he teased, trying to lighten her mood. She snorted, her expression relaxing. "Besides, when has our queen ever brought bad news to my chambers?"

"True enough."

Claire was already waiting when they arrived. He didn't mind that she'd let herself in. He had nothing to hide, and this wasn't exactly the first time she'd been in here. They'd shared a heartfelt meal once, when he'd told her about his past, about how he'd given up on taking a mate when he'd had the chance to.

Standing by his window with her hands clasped behind her back, Claire looked every bit the ruler. She turned as they entered, and something in her expression—purposeful but gentle—made his spine straighten automatically.

"Thank you both for coming," she said, moving towards them. The words were formal, which only made him more wary. "I have something for you."

Claire went to a small parcel on the table and removed the brown packaging. He frowned at the two round fruits. Purple, but like nothing he'd ever seen. With an otherworldly shimmer that whispered of magic.

He and Desaree both stared.

"What...?" Desaree took a step forward.

"They're from the king tree," Claire said simply. "A gift."

The blank stares continued.

Claire's lips twitched into a small smile. "They're for you. If you want them."

"But...what are they for?" Desaree's frown deepened.

Claire hesitated. "It struck me as most unfair that despite the depth of your love, you would face a mountain of suffering in your future. I petitioned the king tree to do something about it. It was, perhaps, selfish on my part. But I knew it would not hurt to ask. Much to my delight, the tree listened to my request. I believe the solution it offered will be most agreeable. You each eat one, and the magic of the king tree will tie you together, creating...a bond, of sorts. I believe it will be something akin to a mate bond."

"A mate bond?" Verath repeated the words aloud, not quite understanding or believing.

"How could something like this be possible?" Desaree mused.

Claire's laughter was musical. "You will find that when it comes to sprite magic, more specifically the king tree, impossibilities are not so uncommon."

Verath felt his heart stop, then pound more forcefully against his ribs.

"If this is some sort of trick..." The words came out rougher than he'd intended.

"No trick, I promise." Claire's features were soft and understanding. "Your life will be tied to Desaree's, just as mine is tied to Talon's. She'll age at the same rate as you. She'll..." She paused. "She'll die with you, rather than long before you. But even more importantly, I believe she will also be able to communicate with you, the way mates do. The only thing I am truly uncertain of is children."

"We would be fine without children," Desaree squeaked, looking dazed.

His world tilted.

In all the time since he'd acknowledged his feelings for Desaree, he'd accepted one brutal truth: he would lose her. Watch her grow old while he remained unchanged. Watch her weaken and fade and die while he continued for centuries alone. It was the price of loving a human when you were a drengr.

He'd accepted it. Made peace with it. Decided she was worth that inevitable heartbreak.

He'd never... *Gods*! He'd never even dared to dream.

"What about the others?" Desaree's voice was barely a whisper. "Reyr and Merrian? Feowen and Jeanine?"

A wry smile spread over Claire's face. "I plan to offer them the same, but I wanted to approach you first. I hope you'll keep this between us until I can speak with them? I'm hoping to offer Jeanine and Feowen theirs at their life ceremony—assuming Jeanine will decide to accept him, that is. Otherwise, I'll just pull them aside separately."

Desaree exhaled and her entire body seemed to relax.

He still didn't want to believe it. Didn't dare believe it.

Claire stepped forward and extended the fruit. "The choice is yours."

He stared at the impossible gift in her palm. His eyes were burning, which was ridiculous. He wasn't a godsdamned child, prone to fits of emotion. But the weight of all the accepted sorrow, all the future heartbreak that he'd braced himself for...

"Godsdamn it," he muttered, rubbing his eyes.

Desaree's hand found his arm. When he looked down at her, he saw his own emotions reflected on her face. Longing and shock and tentative, desperate hope warring for dominance.

"Why would the tree grant us something like this?" he challenged. Surely they weren't so special. Yes, Claire had asked for a favor. But, there had to be some catch. Plenty of drengr had fallen in love with humans over the ages. Drengr who were no better than him.

"Think of it as a gift, for services rendered to the kingdom."

"Verath," Desaree said, squeezing his arm again. He huffed. Did this little human truly think he would refuse? Even if there was a thimble of hope, he would take it. For her—always. She must have seen the answer in his eyes because when she next opened her mouth, her voice was soft. "Together?"

He nodded, not trusting his own.

They each took a fruit. The surface was smooth and cool. He sucked in a breath at the tiny zap he felt, like it was thrumming faintly with...something. Magic. Desaree met his gaze and held it. Together they each bit down.

The fruit was sweet. Almost honey-like, with an undercurrent of something wild and green and alive. They chewed in silence, Claire watching with an expectant expression that held not a trace of doubt.

"You'll have to finish it all."

"You're not trying to poison us and get rid of us, are you?" Desaree teased. "Because I'll have you know, finding a replacement for me won't be easy."

"Finding a replacement for you would be impossible," Claire laughed. "Which is why I never want to lose you."

Desaree's eyes glossed. They continued eating, until both fruits were polished off. He licked the juice off his fingers.

"At least if it doesn't work, it will have been the most delicious thing I've ever tasted," he huffed.

Seconds ticked by.

Nothing happened.

He felt a flicker of disappointment threatening to surface, followed immediately by a surge of skepticism. His eyes darted towards his queen. She merely stood patiently by, watching. There was nothing of the doubt he felt mirrored on her features. Her expectation was steadfast.

Still, he couldn't help but assume this was too good to be true—

Desaree gasped.

The sensation struck him straight in the chest. He gasped and doubled over, taking several deep breaths before he could stand again, and only so that he could ensure Desaree was all right. A presence bloomed to life in his mind, warm and bright and utterly, unmistakably *hers*. He froze, completely shocked. Completely devastated in the best way by what he felt. Desaree's joy crashed into him like a wave, her relief and disbelief and overwhelming gratitude flowing through their new connection until he couldn't tell where his emotions ended and hers began.

Was this what it felt like to be mated? This open connection. This feeling of...completeness?

Guttural sobs broke the silence. Desaree's sobs. She threw her hands to her face to hide behind them.

For a moment he remained motionless. The feeling of her crying—crying from inside him, inside his mind—was unlike anything he had ever felt. And though it was happy tears, the undercurrent of desperate relief felt grating on his mind. He didn't like experiencing the depth of her worry, of the burden she had carried, knowing what her death would do to him in the future. He never wanted her to feel those things—never again.

He exploded into action, pulling her against him, wrapping his arms protectively around her, caressing her mind with his, soothing her. The release of fear she'd carried since falling in love with him almost brought him to his knees. It gave way to wonder at this impossible new beginning, knowing they wouldn't be torn apart by time.

And gods help him, his own eyes were spilling over. Because he'd never felt so much at once. Her happiness was *his* happiness, doubly intense, feeding back on itself until emotion threatened to tear him apart.

"Verath?" Desaree's voice was trembling, wonder-struck.

"Yes." His mental voice was rough with emotion. The sound of his name spoken by her in his mind was something he would never forget. Not for as long as he lived. *"I'm here. Gods, I can feel you."*

Her laugh was watery and bright. *"I can feel you too. All of you."*

Through their connection, he felt her trying to process the magnitude of it. This gift they'd been given. This future they thought they'd never have, stretching out before them like an endless horizon.

Claire moved toward the door, giving them privacy. Right as she slipped past, he caught her arm.

"Thank you," he managed, his voice thick with emotion. "I don't... There aren't words..."

"There doesn't need to be." She squeezed his shoulder. "You both deserve this. The tree wanted you to have it. So did I."

He owed his queen so much, not just for what she'd done to protect his kingdom, but what she'd done for Desaree as a result of their friendship. Now for this? How could he ever repay her?

She slipped out quietly.

As she disappeared, he realized she wouldn't ever want him to repay her. That thought made his chest explode with love. *"She is truly something, isn't she?"* Desaree asked.

"We don't deserve her," he agreed.

"And yet, she is ours all the same."

"A gift."

"Just like the one she has given to us."

"Indeed."

Desaree pulled back and their eyes met, tears streaming down their cheeks. A watery laugh burst from her chest, echoed by his own, until they devolved into fits of hysterical laughter fueled by happiness that couldn't be described. "Let's go flying," they both blurted out at the same time, which only made them laugh harder.

Grabbing her hand, he raced from his chambers, pulling her down the hall towards the king's tower. They passed a few of their inner circle as they went, who eyed them with curiosity. He didn't bother stopping to explain. They exploded into the queen's garden and he wasted no time in transforming.

Desaree was quick to approach, placing a tentative hand upon his scales. Their minds were already connected, so there wasn't any grand mate moment the way there would have been. He didn't care.

She climbed up and settled into the dip between his shoulders and neck. *"Comfortable?"* he couldn't help but ask. It was a question he'd never been able to voice before, given their circumstances.

"Perfectly," she said, adjusting the harness straps.

"Good, then let us fly."

They might not have been mates in the traditional sense, but she was the mate of his heart, and they were paired in all the ways that mattered. As the world shrank away beneath them, he lifted his face towards the sky, relishing in the feel of Desaree's mind joined with his, and let forth a bellow of victory for all the world to hear. She was his, and he was hers, and they had an entire lifetime of lifetimes to belong to one another.

EPILOGUE: FIVE

Kastali Dun

Jeanine climbed the familiar spiral staircase leading to the upper levels of the king's tower, a bundle wrapped in delicate blue silk clutched to her chest. As a member of the queen's guard, she'd made this journey countless times, but today her heart pounded against her ribs with each step. She was doing this—she was *really* doing this.

She stopped outside Claire's study. Elyon and Gorded were on duty, bracketing the entry. Their eyes darted towards the bundle in her arms, then quickly away. Heat flushed her cheeks. "It's not what it looks like," she grumbled.

"I have no idea what you mean," Eylon said, keeping her gaze focused on the opposite wall. Gorded's mouth twitched but he said nothing.

She sighed. *Sprites.*

Because Claire was safe in the tower, it was never necessary to have all eight of her guards on duty at any given time. Granted that they were stationed outside, it was obvious that Claire would be within. Still, she said, "I assume our queen is in there?"

"Indeed. She only just returned from court," Eylon said.

347

"Good." She gave a gentle tap.

"Enter." Claire's voice was muffled.

She went inside. Claire looked up from her desk where she appeared to be reviewing documents. A smile bloomed across her face. "Jeanine." She set aside her work, leaning back with a small groan.

"I hope I'm not interrupting," she said.

"Not at all. Court ran long today with trade negotiations, and I'm grateful for the distraction. Come, sit. What brings you here?"

Jeanine took a seat, setting the bundle on the desk. "I've made my decision about Feowen."

Claire's eyes widened slightly, her gaze dropping to the bundle. "And?"

She carefully unwrapped the silk, revealing the delicate white aevindra flower crown. The flowers remained as pristine as the day Feowen had presented it to her, just like he said it would. "I'm going to accept." Her voice was stronger now that the words were spoken aloud.

Claire's face lit up. "Oh, gods, that's wonderful! I'm so happy for you both!" She stood and rounded the desk, leaning in to embrace her.

"I wanted to give the matter adequate consideration. I hope... I hope I didn't wait too long."

"You did what you felt was best. Feowen would never judge you for that."

She blew out a breath. "I know."

"The important thing is that you made a decision."

"Taylynn's words kept coming back to me," she admitted as they separated. Claire returned to her seat.

"Oh?"

"Trust your heart. It will lead you true." She ran her fingers lightly over one of the flowers, and to her amazement, it emitted a faint glow at her touch. "See that? It's been doing that whenever I touch it. I thought I was imagining it at first..."

"Sprite magic," Claire said with wonder. "The king tree's blessing, perhaps."

"I have fears still," Jeanine confessed. "About committing my life to him as a mortal. About forcing him to watch me age while he remains unchanged. But I love him. This commitment, this ceremony, it means a great deal to him. I need to trust that he knows himself best, and if this is what he wants, then I want to give him that. Even if..." She swallowed. "Even if things later down the road will be difficult for us."

"Love is always worth the risk," Claire said, something unspoken passing over her gaze. She opened her mouth to say more, then stopped. Jeanine waited. Claire cleared her throat and said, "So, are you going to tell him tonight?"

"Actually..." She hesitated. "I was hoping to surprise him. To make it special."

Claire's eyes lit up. "A surprise! But I do love surprises. What do you have in mind?"

"I'd like to wear the crown when he sees me. I want him to know my answer before I even say the words."

Claire nodded, tapping her finger against her chin. "The queen's tower garden would be perfect. It's private, beautiful at night..." Her expression brightened further. "You know, in my world, when someone proposes, sometimes they arrange for family and friends to be hidden nearby. After the proposal is accepted, everyone comes out to celebrate together."

"Really?" She was taken aback. She hadn't pictured telling Feowen the news within earshot of anyone else. And yet, the moment the words sank in, she realized how perfect the idea was. "That sounds wonderful, actually." Everyone in their inner circle had been to hell and back. That brought them together in a way that created unbreakable ties. They shared in each other's setbacks and triumphs. They shared in each other's sadness and happiness. Excluding them from such a big moment in her life when they had always included her didn't feel acceptable. "Could we do that? Have our friends there hiding?"

"Absolutely! We could surprise him completely. You'll need a special gown, of course. Let's have Miera and Selphie prepare you after dinner. We'll keep it secret, so you'll have to sneak into my chambers without Feowen knowing. I can arrange everything else —refreshments, drinks, getting everyone in place."

Relief washed through her. She was nervous enough simply giving the spriten prince her answer. The thought of putting the rest together made her want to renege. "You'd do that?"

"Need you ask? All you need to fuss about is yourself. I'll make sure everyone knows to act normally during the meal so Feowen doesn't suspect a thing."

"Thank you," she whispered. The enormity of her decision settled over her—a pleasant weight of certainty rather than the burden of doubt she'd carried for so long. "I can't believe this is happening."

"Believe it," Claire said with a warm smile. "You deserve this happiness, Jeanine. And every happiness that comes after."

THE QUEEN's garden glowed with the soft light of dozens of hidden lanterns. Claire had somehow managed to arrange everything without raising suspicion. Additional flower arrangements that hadn't been there earlier now adorned the stone benches and planters, adding to the already lush growth. A small table held an array of delicate pastries, fruits, and what appeared to be several bottles of wine.

She stood in the center of the garden wearing a golden gown, which had been perfectly tailored to fit her form. The aevindra crown rested upon her loose hair, the flowers occasionally emitting that mysterious glow when she touched them nervously to ensure they were still in place.

Around the garden, hidden behind strategic arrangements of foliage, waited all of their friends. She caught occasional glimpses of them: Desaree adjusting something on Verath's tunic, Saffra whispering to Bedelth, Jovari with his arm wrapped around Leah's waist. Even King Talon had joined them, looking somewhat amused at being part of the subterfuge.

The sky was decorated with glittering stars. The late summer night was warm, with a gentle breeze carrying the scent of jasmine from the climbing vines that Claire had coaxed to grow along the garden walls.

Her heart pounded when she heard footsteps approaching. She quickly moved behind a large floral arrangement, peering through the blooms as Claire led Feowen into the garden. "I don't understand why this couldn't wait until morning," Feowen was grumbling. "Is there truly an urgent matter concerning the queen's guard, or did you simply trick me to get me up here for...gods know what? Why are we really here?"

She almost snorted. Trust Feowen to see right through Claire's behavior. The spriten prince was too good.

"Trust me, it's important," Claire said, guiding him to the center of the garden. "Wait here a moment."

Jeanine watched as Claire disappeared behind a flowering shrub, joining Talon in hiding. Taking a deep breath, she stepped out from her hiding place.

Feowen turned at the sound of her movement, his expression shifting from mild confusion to shock as he took in the sight of her —the golden gown, and most significantly, the aevindra crown resting atop her head.

For a moment, he simply stared, speechless. Then his face transformed with such naked joy that she felt her heart swell almost painfully. She expected a smirk or playful smile to grace his lips, as was often his nature. Instead, his expression remained serious. "Jeanie," he breathed, using his special name for her. "You..."

"I accept," she said softly, her voice carrying in the quiet garden. "I want to be yours, Feowen. For the rest of my life."

He moved toward her with the fluid grace that always made her breath catch, stopping just before her. His eyes searched hers, as if seeking confirmation that this was real.

"You're certain?" he asked, his voice carrying both hope and disbelief.

"I am. Well, I'm uncertain of many things, but not of this. Not of us." She reached for his hand, lacing her fingers through his. "I love you. I want to bind myself to you, as you wish to bind yourself to me. We can have the life ceremony you wanted—the one you talked about hosting right here in this garden, surrounded by all our friends. We can start planning it as soon as you wish. I'm all in."

The smile that broke across his features was nearly blinding in its intensity. It was quickly followed by a whooping laugh of joy as he pulled her into his arms, lifting her and spinning her once around before setting her back on her feet. His lips found hers in a kiss that communicated everything words couldn't—relief, joy, promise.

When they separated, he cupped her face in his hands, his eyes shining with emotion. "I was prepared to wait months for your answer, if necessary. I would have waited years, even."

"Fortunately for us both, I didn't need that long," she teased, feeling lighter than she had in weeks.

Their moment was interrupted by a burst of applause as their friends emerged from their hiding places, causing the spriten prince to startle and then laugh in surprise. In the last couple of minutes, she'd completely forgotten they weren't alone. "What's all this?" he asked, looking around at the grinning faces of their friends.

"Claire said that in *her* world, family and friends sometimes hide nearby for proposals," she explained. "I wanted to surprise you. To show you that your life with me includes all of them, too."

His expression softened as he looked at their gathered friends. "A beautiful tradition. Thank you all for being here."

Claire stepped forward, beaming. "Congratulations! We have refreshments and wine. Let's celebrate!"

Everyone clapped and whooped again, making her blush as they converged around them with hugs and well-wishes.

"The crown looks perfect on you," Desaree told her, adjusting one of the flowers.

"I hope we get to help you plan the ceremony," Saffra said, clearly still riding the high of her own ceremony, which had happened less than two weeks ago.

"Of course we'll get to help," Jocelyn said, offering her a hug before letting Leah have a turn.

"It's going to be lovely," Leah said. "Whatever you need, we're here for you."

"Yes, anything at all, you need only ask." Merrian added, before leaning in for a hug.

Her heart was overflowing with love. "Does that mean you'll be able to attend? I know you and Reyr are planning a tour of the kingdom."

"Oh, we wouldn't miss it for the world. If we must postpone our adventure for a few weeks or even months, we will."

"You might have to postpone for a few months," Leah piped up.

"Oh?" Merrian turned to Claire's purple-haired friend, inquiring.

Leah flushed. "Well, I don't want to take away from Jeanine's night but, Jovari and I are talking about having our bonding ceremony on winter solstice. But shh! Keep it between us ladies for now."

"My lips are sealed," Merrian said. "And yes, we will be sure to attend. Perhaps waiting until spring to set off is the best decision, anyway."

"Good! We get to have you to ourselves longer," Saffra said, bumping her shoulder with Merrian's.

A throat cleared and the others around them fell silent. Jeanine sucked in a gasp. "Jahl?"

He stood by, waiting his turn. There was a female with him. She was petite and curvy, with dark brown hair and large eyes. In short, she was beautiful. "Hi," Jahl managed.

His eyes darted around, snagging on a few of the sprites and shields. She pressed her lips together to keep from laughing. Sometimes she forgot how intimidating most of the members of their inner circle were.

"I didn't ... How did you...?"

"I found him," Claire proudly said.

"But how did you know?"

Claire huffed. "Feowen and I had a lot of free time on our hands while we were traveling. I might have asked a few probing questions about you, including if you had any friends beyond—" She waved a hand to encompass their group.

"Oh. That... That was so thoughtful. Thank you."

Jahl stepped forward. "This is Kara. We've been courting for a little over a year now."

Her heart leapt. She recalled the last time they'd had a conversation, he'd mentioned that he was seeing someone. That he would introduce them.

"Hello, Kara. I'm Jahl's childhood friend. We used to hunt together, and get into all sorts of trouble."

"So I've heard." Kara's eyes sparkled. "Allow me to offer my congratulations on your engagement. We are both so happy for you."

"Thank you. And—thank you for coming. I know it was short notice."

"Wouldn't have missed it," Jahl said.

They shared a few more pleasantries, spending a few minutes catching up on each other's lives before she offered to introduce him around. He knew most of them, having met them at one point or another in Esterpine.

Goblets of wine were distributed. Talon raised his in a toast. "To Feowen and Jeanine, may your upcoming life ceremony bring you joy for all your days together."

"All our days," Feowen echoed, his gaze locked with Jeanine's as they drank.

The celebration continued late into the night. Lantern light cast a warm glow over their gathering, conversations flowing easily between pairs and groups. Jeanine noticed Talon pull Feowen aside at one point, the two males speaking with their heads close together. Feowen's laugh carried across the garden, and he glanced back at her with such warmth that she felt her cheeks flush.

Throughout the evening, Feowen never strayed far from her side. His fingers would brush against her arm, her back, her hand —each touch seemingly casual but sending sparks along her skin.

By the time things began winding down, she felt as though her entire body was attuned to his presence, burning with awareness.

During a moment when their friends were distracted by a story Jovari was telling, Feowen leaned close. "You are torturing me in that gown," he murmured. "All I can think about is removing it and tasting the delicacy beneath."

Heat rushed through her. He'd tasted her plenty and each time left her more desperate than the time before. "Perhaps we should make our escape soon," she murmured, all too eager.

His fingers traced a pattern on her lower back, the light touch making her shiver. "I was thinking the same. You've given me the greatest gift tonight—I'd like to properly thank you. In private. Obviously."

She turned her face toward his, close enough that their breaths mingled. "I certainly hope you won't be the only one doing the tasting."

The look he gave her was positively wicked. "I've been told I taste delicious."

She mock gasped. "Have you? By whom?"

"Oh, you know, the beautiful little human who just promised her life to me."

"Hmm...she sounds like she must have a very discerning palette."

"Only the most discerning," he confirmed. She bit her lip, desire coiling tight within her. They'd shared intimate moments before, but never with the knowledge that they had committed themselves to each other. Tonight would be different. Significant.

"Get me out of here," she begged.

Feowen's eyes darkened. "I'd love nothing more."

He straightened, clearing his throat to gain everyone's attention. "Friends, we are deeply grateful for your presence tonight. But if you'll forgive us, I believe we have...private matters to discuss."

The snickers and jests that followed them made her flush deepen, but she couldn't find it in herself to be truly embarrassed —not when anticipation thrummed so powerfully through her veins.

As they made their farewells, Claire embraced her one final time. "I'm so happy for you," she whispered.

"Thank you. For everything," she replied sincerely.

Hand in hand, they escaped the garden, Feowen leading her toward his chambers in the tower below. Each step increased the tension between them, Feowen's thumb drawing maddening circles on the sensitive skin of her wrist. The stairs seemed to take forever. The number of levels in the tower had never been so maddening.

"I'm going to worship every inch of you tonight," Feowen promised, obviously just as impatient as her, "starting with my mouth between your thighs."

She groaned. "I'm holding you to that promise."

The heat in his eyes when he glanced down at her was answer enough. "One of many I intend to keep, Jeanie. For all our days together."

They reached his chamber and he pulled her inside, spinning her around and pressing her front to the door. His teeth clamped down on her shoulder, a firm order to remain still as he began working at the buttons on her gown. When that seemed to take too long, he growled in frustration. A little hummed tune under his breath had the remainder of the buttons freed. The gown slipped down her overly sensitive skin.

She knew with absolute certainty that she'd made the right choice. Whatever the future held, whatever price they might eventually pay for their time together, this—this moment, this man, this love—was worth everything. He spent the remainder of the night confirming this, over and again.

EPILOGUE: SIX

Kastali Dun

Dallin shifted, stretching his legs out before him and getting comfortable again. Morning light cast soft rays across his private terrace, bathing the stone balustrade in warmth. A gentle breeze carried the scent of brine, mingling with the aroma of his steaming tea. He'd just ordered his third pot. The morning air held that perfect crispness—not too cool, not too warm—that made Kastali Dun's early autumn so pleasant.

The manuscript in his hands, bound with simple twine, pages slightly uneven at the edges, had captivated him all night. Jamie had finally finished it and allowed him—after much coaxing—to read the story of Captain Everett Drake.

'The captain stood at the edge of the waterfall, watching as the mist created rainbows in the morning light. Behind him, the island's peak rose like a sleeping giant, while before him lay the vast, unforgiving sea that had claimed his ship and crew. Ten hours had passed since the storm had driven him onto these shores.

He clutched the weathered journal he'd recovered from the wreckage. Within its pages, the expedition notes that had led him

357

here in the first place—tales of an island where time flowed differently. Where one day equaled years in the outside world.

"One day," he whispered to the roaring waters. "One day here, and every person I've ever loved will be gone."'

Dallin turned the page, pulse quickening as the captain discovered the ruins of a previous visitor's camp—a visitor who had chosen to eventually leave, only to find upon returning home that centuries had passed. His world had moved on without him.

He was impressed by the depth Jamie had created in such a simple premise. The captain's torment felt real, the choice impossible. Stay on the island forever but remain the same age, or return home to find everyone he loved long dead and forgotten.

'The goddess of the island approached him, her form shifting like the mist between the trees. "You must choose," she told him, her voice like water over stone. "Stay, and you will never age. Leave, and time will claim its due."

Everett thought of Sarah waiting for him back in Porthollow, her smile as bright as the fiercest star. By now, years would have passed for her.

"How long?" he asked. "How long can I stay before it's too late to return?"

The goddess's eyes were ancient, filled with the patience of mountains. "Time is not sand in an hourglass, Captain. It is water in a river. Some currents move swiftly, others barely at all. But they all reach the sea eventually."

She placed a smooth stone in his palm, warm as flesh despite the night chill. "As long as you hold this, you may return to those you left. One day only, to make your decision. After that, the river flows as it must."'

Dallin was leaning forward, gripping the edges of the manuscript tighter. Jamie had woven magic and mythology so seamlessly into what felt like a historical tale. The writing moved him, transported him. He'd known Jamie was observant and soft spoken, but he'd never realized how clever he was with words. The depth of his storytelling—it was something else entirely.

He turned to the final pages, where Captain Drake made his choice.

'The rowboat scraped against the sand as Drake secured it for the night. The goddess watched him from the tree line, impassive as the stone he clutched in his fist. One day—that's all he had. One day to decide whether to stay in this island prison or return to let time claim him as it claimed all men.

As he settled beneath the stars, he wondered which was truly the selfish choice: to stay young forever in paradise while the world moved on without him, or to return and ask Sarah to love the man he had become—a man changed by solitude and the weight of impossible knowledge.

The stone pulsed in his palm like a second heart as the decision crystallized in his mind.'

Dallin exhaled slowly as he finished the final page. The ending left him hanging, wondering what choice Drake would ultimately make. Would he remain on the island? Would Sarah still be waiting? Would she even recognize the man he'd become?

He placed the manuscript on the table, staring out over the ocean. He picked up the sounds of industry coming from behind him, from the city. Kastali Dun had woken up over the past few hours, merchants opening their shops, people going about their daily business. And here was Jamie's story, hidden away in private quarters where no one could experience it.

That seemed... wrong. Criminal, almost.

He sat up straighter, an idea forming. He knew exactly who could help Jamie share his stories with the world. But the question was, would Jamie be willing? He chewed on the inside of his cheek, torn. Part of him worried that if he pushed too hard, Jamie would retreat into himself. It had taken weeks just to get him to share some of his work.

Since their first kiss, they'd shared many more. They'd explored each other's bodies, taking things slow. This was entirely new for Jamie, and almost just as new for him. They had time, and he was determined to do this right. Not to rush or ruin the new thing developing between them.

Would pushing Jamie be overstepping?

He stood, strode towards the door, froze, turned around, then went back to his chair. He glanced down at the manuscript in his hands. A story like this deserved to be read. He could only try, and hope it went over well.

Glancing at the side table, he reached for his teapot and poured a fresh cup. He drained it, then stood, striding from his chambers.

~

Late morning sunlight shone on the cobblestone streets of Kastali Dun's upper merchant district. Colorful awnings created patches of shade over shop entrances, while brightly painted signs sitting outside shop fronts advertised the deal of the day. The scent of fresh bread wafted from a nearby bakery, mingling with the earthy perfume of flowers from a florist's cart.

He'd been careful these past weeks to avoid the lower levels of the city. While he could likely feign ignorance if any of his old crew spotted him, it was a situation he didn't want. Fortunately, he doubted he'd run into anyone this close to the keep.

"Are you going to tell me where we're going?" Jamie asked, his voice caught between exasperation and amusement. "We've been walking for nearly fifteen minutes."

Dallin smiled, giving Jamie's hand a gentle squeeze. "Patience. It's a surprise."

He'd taken Jamie's hand the moment they'd left the keep, a bold move that still sent a thrill through him. Years of hiding who he was, of careful secrecy, were behind him now. Being one of the king's shields had its privileges—chief among them the protection of the crown and his shield brothers, who had accepted him without question.

A noblewoman passing by with her maid cast a sidelong glance at them, her lips pursed in disapproval. Dallin met her gaze steadily, refusing to look away or release Jamie's hand. After a moment, she looked away and hurried past.

"People are staring," Jamie murmured, though he made no move to pull free.

"Let them." He spoke with a confidence he was still growing into. "I'm a king's shield. You're under my protection. They can stare all they want."

Jamie's smile was worth every questioning look. The warmth of his hand, the simple pleasure of walking together out in the open—these were things he'd once thought he'd never have. Now, he was finally finding the courage to be himself without apology.

They turned down a narrower street lined with specialized shops. The scents shifted subtly—ink, leather, and the distinct aroma of paper and binding glue.

"Seriously, *where* are we going?" Jamie tried again, peering curiously at the shops they passed. "I don't think I've ever been to this part of the district."

"Just a little further," Dallin promised, a flutter of excitement in his chest. "You'll see."

They passed a stationary shop with delicate quills displayed in the window, then a shop specializing in sealing wax and stamps bearing family crests. Finally, he slowed their pace as they approached their destination.

The shop's facade was elegant but understated—polished wooden trim framing large windows that displayed exquisitely bound volumes. Above the door hung a painted sign depicting an open book with gold-leaf pages. "Master Hartwin, Bookbinder to the Crown" was inscribed in flowing script beneath it.

He stopped, watching Jamie's face as realization dawned.

"A bookbinder?" Jamie looked from the shop to Dallin, confusion evident in his expression. "Why are we—?"

"I read your story," Dallin said quickly, the words tumbling out before he could think better of it. "Captain Drake's story. The one you let me borrow yesterday."

"Already?!" Jamie sputtered, his face flushing crimson. He pulled Dallin a few steps away from the shop's entrance. "You brought me here to—what? Have my stories bound?"

"Published," Dallin corrected gently. "Shared with others who would appreciate them."

"Dallin, I—" Jamie shook his head, lowering his voice. "My writing isn't... It's not ready for other people to read. It's just something I do for myself."

"It's extraordinary," Dallin insisted, keeping his voice low as a pair of well-dressed women passed by. "The way you wrote about Drake's dilemma, about time flowing differently on the island—I couldn't put it down. I was there with him, feeling what he felt."

Jamie looked away, his throat working. "You're just saying that because—"

"Because I care about you? Yes, I do. But that doesn't make me blind." He dared to reach out, touching Jamie's cheek lightly. "Your story moved me, Jamie. Truly moved me."

"I don't know..."

"Master Hartwin doesn't just bind books. He works with writers to prepare their manuscripts, helps arrange for copies to be made. He could advise you on the best way to share your stories." He gestured toward the shop door. "We don't have to commit to anything today. Just talk to him."

Jamie bit his lip, glancing at the shop. "I've never shown my writing to anyone but you."

"And now you have the chance to share it with others who might find the same joy that I did," he said softly.

Jamie was about to respond when the shop door opened. A young woman with striking lavender hair emerged, balancing a stack of ledgers in her arms. She nearly collided with them before stopping short.

"Oh! Dallin! Jamie!" Leah's surprise was evident as she adjusted her grip on the ledgers. "What are you two doing here?"

"Leah," Dallin nodded in greeting, his mind working quickly. "We were just... I was showing Jamie Master Hartwin's shop."

"Oh! Are you interested in bookbinding?"

"Something like that," Dallin replied. "What brings you here?"

"Library business," she said, shifting the ledgers to a more comfortable position. "I'm working with Master Hartwin to acquire some new volumes for our collection. He's been incredibly helpful with sourcing rare texts and recommending local writers."

"Local writers, you say?" It was as if the fates had aligned. "Are you looking to feature any Kastali Dun authors specifically?"

Leah's eyes lit up. "Absolutely! That's one of my priorities for the library—celebrating the stories and knowledge of those who reside more locally. It's been challenging to find local authors, though. Most published works come from all over the kingdom and overseas."

"That's interesting," he said carefully, aware of Jamie's rising tension beside him. "What if I told you I knew someone with remarkable talent? Someone creating stories that capture the essence of Dragonwall's spirit of adventure and discovery?"

He practically felt Jamie stiffen beside him.

"Really?" Leah looked between them, curiosity on her face. "Who is it? Would they be willing to have their work included in our collection?"

Jamie didn't move. Dallin squeezed his hand reassuringly. Jamie might get angry at him for this, or he might not. But it was an opportunity he couldn't pass up. He'd apologize later, if necessary. Besides, it wasn't like he was flashing Jamie's manuscript right in front of her face. He'd never betray Jamie's trust like that. The words were Jamie's to share, if and when he was ready.

"It's a possibility we're exploring," he said diplomatically. "My friend is considering whether to share their stories more widely."

Leah's gaze settled on Jamie's flushed face. "Jamie? Is it you?"

Jamie cleared his throat. "I...it's not... They're just stories."

"I'd love to read them," Leah said warmly. "Truly. I've been planning a special section for local authors. Prime shelf space, right near the entrance where everyone can see."

"It's really nothing special—" Jamie began.

"It's extraordinary," Dallin corrected firmly. "Trust me. His writing is captivating."

Leah beamed. "Well, whenever you're ready, bring them by the library. No pressure at all." She shifted the ledgers again and glanced at the sky. "I should get back. Jovari's expecting these records by midday. But think about it, Jamie. The library's doors are always open to you." With a friendly nod, she continued down the street, her lavender hair bright in the sunlight.

As she disappeared around a corner, Jamie exhaled heavily. "Gods, Dallin. I can't believe you just did that."

"I didn't say it was *you*," Dallin pointed out. "Not directly."

"She figured it out immediately!"

"Because she's perceptive. And because your face turned the color of a ripe tomato."

Jamie groaned, covering his face with his free hand. "I can't do this. I can't let people read my stories. What if they hate them? What if they laugh?"

"What if they love them?" Dallin countered gently. "What if your stories touch them the way they touched me?"

"You're different."

Dallin glanced around at the busy street just beyond their quiet one, at the people passing by, some still casting curious glances at their joined hands. "You know, when we left the keep today, I was terrified."

Jamie looked up, surprise evident in his expression. "You were?"

"Holding your hand in public? Absolutely terrifying. I was sure everyone would stare, would judge. And they did, most of them. But I decided the joy of being with you openly was worth whatever censure might come. Not that anyone would dare say anything to a king's shield—I hope."

Understanding dawned in Jamie's eyes.

"It's the same with your stories," he continued. "Yes, sharing them is frightening. Opening yourself up to judgment always is. But the potential joy—for you and for others—might be worth the risk."

"But what if—?"

"What if Captain Drake never leaves the island?" he interjected softly. "What if he's too afraid to risk the journey home, too afraid of what he might find? He'll never know if Sarah is still waiting. He'll never have the chance to see her again."

Jamie fell silent, his gaze drifting to the bookbinder's shop.

"This is entirely your decision," Dallin said, his voice gentle. "I'm not here to pressure you. If you want to turn around and walk back to the keep right now, we will. I just wanted you to know this option exists. That your stories deserve to be bound in books as beautiful as they are."

"I'm terrified," Jamie admitted quietly.

"I know," he squeezed Jamie's hand. "And that's perfectly reasonable. We can leave right now if you want. No judgment. I'll support whatever you decide."

Jamie took a deep breath, his eyes moving from the shop to Dallin and back again. "Would you... Would you stay with me? While I talk to him?"

Warmth bloomed in his chest. "Every step of the way."

Jamie nodded once, determination replacing the fear in his eyes. "All right. Let's do this."

Together, they approached the shop door. A small bell jingled overhead as Dallin held it open, their hands still firmly clasped together as they stepped across the threshold into a world of possibilities.

EPILOGUE: SEVEN

Dragonfire Sea

Bennett inhaled, savoring the salty air in his lungs. *Lady Faith* cut through the waves like a blade, her wooden hull creaking beneath his boots. He stood at the helm, one hand resting on the wheel, the sky a perfect blue above them. The distant coastline of Celenore was little more than a hazy smudge to starboard.

His thoughts drifted to the bag of gold dragons Reyr had delivered personally, along with a promissory note for a much larger sum waiting in a royal account at Kastali Dun's bank. King Talon's reward for services rendered to the kingdom—more wealth than he'd amassed in his entire life at sea. Enough to buy land and settle down if he wanted. But the sea was in his blood, and now that Kane's reign had ended, there were new horizons to explore with a ship that was truly his own. No more smuggling people to safety. No more battles with Oshean slavers. Just honest trade, exploration, and the endless freedom of open water. Like the good ol' days, but better.

He'd informed his crew of the reward. In the end, not a single one of them wanted to take the money and retire. Rather, they'd agreed to set up accounts with him, almost as if he were a bank. He'd divided the money between them, ensuring everyone got equal shares. When next they stopped in the capital, they could take out as much or as little as they pleased.

Movement on the deck below caught his eye. Cat wove among the crew with sure steps, tending to minor injuries from yesterday's storm. She knelt beside Emmon, examining a rope burn on his palm. Her hair was still shorn in a short style, which he'd come to love. His chest tightened at the sight of her. She might fight the admission until her dying day, but she belonged here—belonged with him—more than either of them had anticipated when she'd first sought passage with him. Now she was indispensable, not just to him but to every man aboard.

He'd asked her three times to move her things into his cabin. Three times she'd deflected with that maddening smirk of hers. He'd have to ask again. Perhaps the fourth time would be the charm.

A sharp cry split the air, followed by the telltale thump against the deck—sickening in nature. His head snapped up. Ferris had plummeted from the rigging, striking the deck, his body crumpled at an unnatural angle.

"Cat!" someone shouted.

Bennett was already moving towards the stairs, but his crew beat him to it. They crowded around the fallen man, then immediately made way as Cat rushed forward. She dropped to her knees beside Ferris, her hands hovering over his twisted form.

"Don't move him!" Her voice cut through the murmurs. "Jonah, bring my blue satchel. Tris, get clean linens. Emmon, fetch water."

The men scattered to obey without so much as a glance in his direction. He hung back, watching as she carefully examined Ferris, her fingers gently probing along his spine.

"His back is broken," she announced. "I need to stabilize him before we move him belowdeck."

Bennett stepped closer. "What can I do?"

She didn't look up. "Clear a path to my healing room and

prepare the table. We'll need to carry him carefully once I've stabilized his spine."

She worked with focused precision, laying out near invisible blue lines of magic along Ferris's body. Her words—incants—were too soft to understand. Not that he could. He'd learned that magic was spoken in the language of the asarlaí—an ancient language only the drengr understood. Sweat beaded on her brow as she worked, using her magic to create temporary bindings that would hold his spine in place. Only when she gave the nod did four men gently lift Ferris onto a makeshift stretcher.

He led the way, shouting orders to the rest of the crew to return to their duties. As they navigated the narrow passage to Cat's healing room, he found himself glancing back at her. She followed the stretcher, her eyes never leaving her patient, likely already strategizing what bottles and instruments she'd need.

"Set him down gently," she instructed as they entered the healing room.

The space had changed dramatically since they'd received the king's reward. They'd expanded it further, stocking more of the shelves with rarer ingredients that widened her abilities to treat even more maladies than before. There were now two tables, to treat more injured, if necessary. There was also a larger sleep area for her, both for personal use and as a convenience for when she needed to keep patients overnight. The work table held crystal bowls for mixing potions, scalpels that rarely needed sharpening, and a state of the art lamp that could focus light precisely where she needed it.

"Everyone out," she commanded once Ferris was settled. Her gaze finally lifted to meet his. "Including you, Captain. This will take time."

He wanted to protest, but instead nodded, backing out of the room. As the door closed, he caught one last glimpse of her leaning over Ferris, muttering soft words of reassurance. His chest swelled with a strange mixture of pride and something else—something that felt dangerously close to love. She didn't need him for this. But gods, he needed her.

Throughout the day, he checked on the healing room periodically. The door remained closed, soft light visible beneath it. Occasionally, he heard Ferris cry out as Cat worked to repair his shattered spine. Each time, he forced himself to walk away.

Night fell. The stars emerged, casting silver light across the deck. Most of the crew had retired, leaving only the night watch. Bennett stood at the railing, staring out at the endless black of the sea. In the stillness, he could practically hear Cat's voice in his mind, murmuring incantations and reassurances as she had when he'd left her.

She worked all through the night, fighting to save Ferris.

He wondered, not for the first time, how he'd gotten so damn lucky.

Dawn painted the horizon in stripes of pink and gold. He'd barely slept, his thoughts too full of Cat and Ferris and the strange web of loyalties that bound his crew together. He'd ordered the kitchen boy to prepare a tray with fresh bread, fruit, and hot tea, which he now balanced carefully as he approached Cat's healing room.

He knocked softly. "Cat?"

"Come in," came her weary reply.

He shouldered the door open to find her slumped in the chair beside her patient. Ferris lay unconscious on the table, his body covered with a clean sheet, his breathing deep and regular. Cat's face was drawn with exhaustion, dark circles under her eyes, but satisfaction gleamed in their depths.

"Brought you breakfast." He set the tray on her workbench.

"Thanks." She reached for the tea, wrapping her hands around the mug. The weak sunlight filtering through the porthole cast everything in a faint glow.

"How is he?" He nodded toward Ferris.

"He'll live. The break was severe, but I managed to mend the worst of it. I can mend bones, but the back itself? The spine? There's more to it than just bones, you know. I fear I might not have done the job well enough. My training—I never delved too deeply into the spine. Didn't have the time to before running away." She blew out a breath. "I cannot promise he will make a full recovery, but he will walk. We will have to monitor him over the coming days—weeks, even. If it's problematic, I would recommend we take him to a more experienced healer. In Kastali Dun, most likely. We can afford it now."

"We'll do whatever you advise." He moved to stand behind her, his hands settling on her shoulders, feeling the tension knotted there. He began to knead the muscles. Her groan of delight spurred him on. "You're amazing, you know that?"

"Just doing my job."

"Hardly." His thumbs moved up to work at the tight muscles of her neck. "A non magical healer would have said he'd never walk again, if he survived at all. Those with magic might have given it a decent effort, but never the same kind of effort that comes with being...close. That comes with caring for someone you claim as your own. This entire ship, the crew—it's yours."

"I don't know if I'd go that far."

"Things have changed since you came aboard. You've changed them."

She said nothing, just sipped her tea.

He cleared his throat, finding the bravery to forge ahead. "When we dock at Port Gallant, there's a decent shipwright there. I was thinking of using some of that reward money to commission a new bed for my cabin along with an additional set of shelves." He hesitated. "Room enough for two."

Cat stiffened almost imperceptibly. "Bennett—"

"Just think about it. Your things in my cabin. Waking up together every morning instead of sneaking between rooms."

She turned to look up at him, fatigue making her gaze more direct than usual. "I have thought about it."

"And?"

"And I'm not sure it's the right move." She set down her mug. "I work odd hours. I have patients come to me at all times. My space is separate from yours for a reason."

"Your healing room would still be yours," he clarified. "I'm talking about where you sleep. Where your personal things are kept."

She looked away. "I know what you're asking."

He fought down a surge of frustration. "Everyone already knows we're together, Cat. It's not exactly a secret when you spend half your nights in my cabin anyway."

"That's different," she snapped, her familiar claws showing.

He moved back, crossing his arms. "Different how?"

She opened her mouth to answer but was interrupted by a groan from Ferris. Immediately, she was on her feet, her professional mask sliding back into place as she checked her patient.

"We'll talk about this later," he said, disappointment sharp in his chest. "Get some rest when you can."

He left the healing room, closing the door quietly behind him. On deck, he barked orders with more force than necessary, driving his crew through their morning tasks while his mind churned. Why was she so resistant? What was he missing?

The question haunted him throughout the day.

Evening found him in his cabin, reviewing charts by lamplight. They were three days out from Port Gallant—a bustling trade hub where they'd offload spices from the Scattered Isles and take on textiles bound for Valoria. It was their first purely commercial voyage since Kane's defeat, and he was determined to make it successful. Not to mention, he'd promised ages ago that Cat would see the world upon the deck of his ship, and he intended to make that happen.

A soft knock interrupted his thoughts. He knew that knock.

"Come in."

The door opened to reveal the woman in question, freshly bathed, her hair still damp. She wore a simple linen sleep shirt and loose trousers—what she typically wore when she planned to spend the night in his cabin.

His pulse quickened despite his lingering frustration. She padded across the room and perched on the edge of his bed.

"How's Ferris?" he asked, setting aside his charts.

"Resting comfortably. Tris is sitting with him."

Bennett nodded, trying to read her expression in the dim light. She seemed distracted, plucking at a loose thread on his blanket.

"About this morning," she began.

He eagerly crossed to the bed, sitting beside her. "I'm listening."

She took a deep breath. "I need you to understand something. Before I came aboard this ship, I was Lady Caterina Rosen. My status, my worth—it all came from who I was connected to." Her voice hardened. "And before that, I was Kane's puppet. His tool. Not the way my father was, as you know. But he still used me."

He remained silent, sensing she had more to say.

"Here, I've built something different. I'm Cat, the healer. Not the captain's woman, not Lord Rosen's daughter. Just...me." She finally met his gaze. "When your men come to me with injuries, when they follow my orders during an emergency like yesterday's, they do it because they respect *me*. My skills. My knowledge."

Understanding began to dawn. "And you think moving in with me would change that?"

"I don't know." She twisted the fabric between her fingers. "Maybe it's foolish, but I worry they'll see me differently. That somehow having my possessions in your cabin means...means I'm just an extension of you."

Bennett felt a flash of hurt. "Do you think I see you that way?"

"No!" Her response was immediate. "Gods, no. It's not about you, Bennett. It's about them. About how they perceive me."

"So you're saying you don't want the crew to know we're together?" He couldn't keep the edge from his voice. "Because I hate to break it to you, but that ship sailed long ago."

"That's not what I'm saying." Frustration colored her tone. "Of course they know we're...something. But there's a difference between knowing we share a bed and seeing me as...as your possession."

"No one on this ship would ever think that," he insisted.

"You don't understand." She stood abruptly. "How could you? You've always been Captain Bennett. Your identity has never been in question."

Before he could respond, she was moving toward the door. "I should check on Ferris."

"Cat—"

But she was already gone, the door clicking shut behind her. He growled, staring at the empty space she'd left behind, torn between anger and confusion. He'd offered her everything—his bed, his cabin, his life—and somehow it wasn't enough. Or was it too much?

He cursed under his breath. Women were more confounding than the most treacherous seas he'd ever navigated.

~

"HEALER SAID I'll be back in the rigging by the month's end," Ferris announced proudly to the small group gathered around his hammock in the healing room. They'd installed it so he would be more comfortable while remaining under a watchful eye. "Said I'm healing faster than others with similar injuries."

Bennett paused outside the door, listening.

"Lucky you had Cat," someone—Jonah, by the sound of it—replied. "Regular healer would've left you crippled, or worse."

"She's a gift from the gods, that one," Ferris agreed. "Worth her weight in gold dragons."

"More than that," another voice chimed in. "Remember when half the crew came down with that fever in Galadhal? Any other ship would've lost men."

"Or when Emmon took those arrows. He should've died three times over."

Tris's voice joined the conversation. "Captain knows what he's got. Why do you think he's been after her to move into his cabin? Wants to make sure she stays put."

Bennett's breath caught. He leaned closer to the partially open door.

"She still refusing, then?" Jonah asked.

"Rumor is she wants her independence." Tris chuckled. Bennett suppressed a growl. How the hell did the crew know these details? Then again, he shouldn't be surprised. Doors on a ship were far too thin, and nothing ever stayed secret in close quarters.

"Can't blame the captain for trying, though. I would too, if I were him."

"Wouldn't matter if she did move in with him," Ferris said. "She's still the best damn healer in Dragonwall. I dare anyone to argue that."

"I certainly won't," Jonah agreed. "Though she's not just the healer anymore, is she? Half the time she's giving orders even when no one's bleeding."

"And the captain lets her," Tris added. There was no judgment in his voice.

Bennett stepped away from the door, a strange lightness filling his chest. A lightness that followed him through his tasks that morning. He found Tris later, pulling him aside as the first mate supervised the work on deck.

"Have a question for you," he said, keeping his voice casual. "About Cat."

Tris quirked an eyebrow. "Sir?"

"The men...how do they see her? Really."

Tris considered the question. "As the healer, first and foremost. Best we've ever had."

"And her relationship with me?"

Tris's expression grew thoughtful. "Permission to speak freely, Captain?"

"Always."

"The men know you're together. They respect it. But they also respect *her.*"

"Separately from me?"

"Aye." He paused. "It's actually something of a relief, if I'm honest. Having someone else they can turn to when needed."

Bennett frowned. "Relief?"

"A ship this size, crew this large...it's a lot for one man to shoulder alone, even with a first mate." Tris met his gaze directly. "Cat takes some of that weight. The men trust her. They know she has your ear, but they also know she has her own mind. As healer, she mostly outranks Jonah, don't she."

"She thinks if she moves into my cabin, they'll see her differently."

Understanding dawned on Tris's face. "Ah. That's what this is about." He scratched his beard. "Some might, at first. Change always causes talk. But she's earned her place here through more than just your favor. That won't vanish overnight because she changes where she lays her head."

Bennett clapped him on the shoulder. "Thanks, Tris."

A plan began to form in his mind.

He found Cat in her healing room that afternoon, cutting and mixing whatever latest concoction the crew needed. Ferris was awake, still resting while cheerfully recounting some tale about a tavern brawl in Bagradas that had Bennett shaking his head from the doorway.

"Captain!" Ferris greeted him with a grin.

"Ferris. Good to see you looking less corpse-like." He turned to Cat. "Mind if I borrow our healer for a moment?"

Cat glanced between them. "I was just finishing up."

"Don't hurry on my account," Bennett replied. "I'll wait outside."

He leaned against the wall of the narrow corridor, gathering his thoughts. When Cat emerged a few minutes later, he straightened.

"Your healing room looks better every time I see it," he began. "Those new shelves from Kisteg were worth every coin."

She tilted her head. "Did you really pull me away from my patient to discuss carpentry?"

"No." He took a deep breath. "I wanted to tell you I've been… difficult."

Her eyebrows shot up. "Oh?"

"I overheard the men talking about you this morning. About how they see you." He reached for her hand, relieved when she didn't pull away. "I didn't understand before. But I think I do now."

She waited, wary hope in her eyes.

"You aren't just the woman who shares my bed, Cat. You've

earned your place on this ship. The men respect you—not because of me, but because of who you are and what you do for them." He squeezed her fingers. "I was approaching this all wrong. Making it about us when it's about something more."

"It is about us," she said. "But it's also about me. About having something that's mine alone."

"I know." He cupped her cheek. "And I love that about you. I love that you've carved out your own place here. That you had the courage to build something new from nothing."

He wouldn't dare admit that he outright loved her. The last thing he wanted was to scare her off. He kept that little tidbit to himself.

She exhaled. "I was worried you'd never understand."

"I'm a slow learner when it comes to things like this—relationships," he admitted. "But I'll get there eventually."

"So where does that leave us?"

He smiled. "Wherever you want us to be. Your healing room is yours. Your position on this ship is yours. And yes, if you want your own cot to retreat to, that's yours too." He paused. "But I hope you know that my cabin is yours as well, whenever you want it."

Something shifted in her expression—a softening, a surrender. "Maybe I've been overthinking this."

"Maybe we both have."

"The crew already knows we're together," she acknowledged. "And they still come to me when they need healing. They still follow my orders in a crisis."

"That won't change," Bennett assured her. "Not because of where you sleep."

She studied him for a long moment. "I think... I think I'd like to wake up next to you every morning. Not just some mornings."

His heart leaped. "That can be arranged."

"But I need to keep my healing room. And I need certain times that are just mine."

"Of course. It was never my intention to take any of that away."

"And if I ever feel like the crew is treating me differently—"

"Then we'll find another solution," he promised. "This isn't about caging you, Cat. It never was. It's about building something together while still respecting what we each need."

She stepped closer, her body pressing against his. "Sometimes I wonder why you put up with me? I'm nothing but complications for you."

"Exactly the kind of complication I like." He kissed her forehead. "Besides, I need a good healer. Can't very well let you jump ship, can I?"

Her huff of laughter was soft against his chest. "Is that the only reason?"

"No." He wrapped his arms around her. "But the others would make me sound like a love-sick fool, and I have a fearsome reputation to maintain."

"Too late." She tilted her face up to his. "Your crew already knows their captain is completely besotted."

"Mutinous lot," he grumbled, but couldn't contain his smile as he lowered his lips to hers.

THE NEXT MORNING, he woke to find Cat already dressed, gathering items from around his cabin—her cabin now, too, since she'd agreed yesterday.

"What are you doing?" he asked, voice rough with sleep.

"Inventory. Making a list of what I need to bring from my quarters," she replied. "I thought I'd move my things today, while Ferris is stable."

He sat up, watching as she methodically sorted through her belongings. She had already claimed a drawer in his dresser and a hook on the wall.

"Need help?"

"Later, maybe. I want to check on Ferris first."

"There will be more room once I get the expansion done in Port Gallant."

"I know. But until then..."

He nodded, content to observe her. This was Cat—always the

healer first, organizing her world with the same precision she used to mend broken bodies. Yet there was something different in her movements now, a new ease as she navigated the space. As if she'd finally allowed herself to belong.

That evening, they worked together to move her possessions. It didn't take long; Cat had never been one for accumulating things. A few changes of clothes, several books, a polished stone from the beaches of one of the isles in the Scattered Islands, a silver hair comb that had been her mother's. The physical tokens of her life fit neatly among his own.

When the last item had been settled, she stood in the center of the cabin, turning slowly to take it all in.

"How does it feel?" he asked, leaning against the doorframe.

A small smile curved her lips. "Like something new. Another fresh start."

That night, as they lay in bed, the gentle rocking of the ship lulling them toward sleep, he traced the curve of her shoulder with his fingertips. The weight of her head on his chest was more precious than all the gold dragons in his strongbox.

Some treasures, he reflected, couldn't be measured in coin. Some were found in unexpected places—a noblewoman fleeing justice who became a healer, a woman seeking passage who became a partner, a relationship that began with secrets but grew into something true.

Cat's breathing deepened as sleep claimed her. He pulled her closer, feeling the steady beat of her heart against his own. Tomorrow they would see Port Gallant on the horizon. They would load new cargo, make much needed repairs and upgrades to the ship, then set a new course and face whatever adventures the sea had in store.

But tonight, in this cabin that was now truly theirs, Bennett had everything he needed.

EPILOGUE: EIGHT

Kastali Dun

Dallin's heartbeat kept rhythm with the faint tink of a hammer on metal drifting through the open window of Master Hartwin's shop. Midmorning sunlight streamed through the tall windows, catching dust motes that danced in the air above the craftsman's bench. The scent of leather, ink, and glue permeated the space, a smell he had come to associate with possibility.

"What do you think of this binding?" Master Hartwin held up a leather sample in a deep midnight blue. "It reminds me of the night sky in your story, the one Captain Drake sails beneath."

Jamie reached out, running his fingers over the textured surface. His touch was reverent, as if he couldn't quite believe this was happening. Over the past week and a half, the nervousness that had radiated from him like heat had transformed into something closer to cautious excitement.

"It's perfect," Jamie said, his voice soft. "I never imagined..."

"The illustrations are coming along quite well," Master Hartwin continued, pulling out several sketches. "Morrin has a wonderful eye for detail. See how he's captured the island's waterfall?"

That had been an extra surprise, having illustrations commissioned to bind into the book.

Dallin watched Jamie's face as he examined the sketches. The artist had indeed captured the scene beautifully—the imposing waterfall, the rainbow mist, and Captain Drake's solitary figure standing at its edge. The image perfectly matched the scene he'd read in Jamie's manuscript.

"They're incredible," Jamie murmured, touching the edge of one sketch with a fingertip.

Master Hartwin beamed. "I've also received word from Lady Leah, who has reserved three copies for their collection."

"Three?" Jamie's eyes widened.

"Indeed. Said something about featuring local authors prominently." The bookbinder winked. "She seems quite invested in your success, young man."

Jamie glanced at him, a mixture of disbelief and pride in his expression. Dallin squeezed his shoulder in response.

"And if this one does well," Master Hartwin continued, "perhaps we could discuss a series? Captain Drake's further adventures, perhaps? Or even one of your other works? You *do* have other works, don't you?"

"I... I do," Jamie admitted.

Dallin found himself only half-listening as Master Hartwin outlined the timeline for completion. His thoughts were elsewhere, circling an idea that had been growing in his mind for days. An impulse. A risk.

"Would you gentlemen care for some tea? I've just brewed a fresh pot."

Dallin blinked, forcing himself back to the present. "Thank you, but we should be going." He felt Jamie's curious glance but avoided meeting his gaze.

As they stepped out of the shop into the bustling street, the cool autumn air carried the scent of baking bread from a nearby bakery and cinnamon apples from a cart. Merchants called their wares, and a group of children darted past, laughing as they chased a rolling hoop.

"You're quiet today," Jamie observed as they turned down a less crowded side street. The cobblestones here were older, worn smooth by thousands of years of traffic. "Is everything all right?"

"Yes. Just thinking."

Jamie let the silence stretch between them for a moment before prompting, "About?"

Dallin slowed his pace, searching for the right words. How did one ask this? There was protocol, tradition. But none of that applied here, did it?

"Dallin?" Jamie stopped walking, concern creeping into his voice. "What is it?"

"Would you like to go flying with me?" The words tumbled out before he could second-guess himself further.

Jamie froze, his expression shifting from concern to something unreadable. He immediately began to backpedal. "I know it's not... I mean, I just thought you might enjoy seeing the city from above. It doesn't have to mean—"

"Have you taken anyone flying before?" Jamie interrupted, his voice carefully neutral.

Dallin swallowed. "No. Never."

As a general rule, only mates flew with their drengr. That had become less the norm since Claire had come into their world. But it was still frowned upon by the majority of the kingdom. Flying with a drengr was considered the most intimate experience outside of mating itself—something they hadn't yet done together during the intimate moments.

"I understand if you don't want to," he continued, forcing the words past the tightness in his throat. "It was just an idea."

"No, I want to. I *really* want to." His voice was steadier than Dallin had expected. "I've always wondered what it must be like, seeing everything from so high up."

Relief washed through him. "Really?"

"Really." Jamie's smile held something he hadn't seen before—

a quiet confidence, perhaps even anticipation. "Where were you thinking of taking me?"

"I thought we could head up to the queen's garden first. It's where most of us usually take off from."

Jamie nodded, and they turned their steps toward the keep, continuing through the streets in companionable silence. Anxious, nervous energy buzzed through him. He thought of a hundred ways the action of flying together could be interpreted, but just like when they held hands in public, he was finding that he didn't much care anymore.

The guards at the king's tower nodded in respect as they passed, one quirking an eyebrow at Jamie's presence but saying nothing. The privilege of being a king's shield meant few questioned his companions or movements. They climbed the winding stairs in silence, Dallin leading the way. When they reached the top, he gestured for Jamie to precede him.

Jamie's soft gasp as he emerged onto the rooftop was exactly what he'd hoped for. He scrambled up after him, watching as Jamie turned in a slow circle, taking in the panorama of Kastali Dun spread below them and the sea behind them.

"I had no idea this existed," Jamie said, moving to the edge where the stone balustrade protected against the sheer drop. "You can see forever."

Dallin joined him, leaning against the familiar stonework. "Not quite forever," he said. "But far enough."

From this height, the city was a sprawling tapestry of tiled rooftops, narrow streets, and open squares. The harbor glinted in the distance, ships looking like children's toys bobbing on the water. Beyond the city walls, farms and fields stretched toward the horizon, a patchwork of green and gold.

"It's beautiful," Jamie murmured.

"Wait until you see it from the sky." He stepped back from the edge, moving through to the center of the garden where there was ample space. "I'm going to shift. I... I don't have a harness, but that shouldn't matter. You can still fly without one. You'll have to climb up on my back, to the dip where my neck meets my shoulders. We can go from there."

"Okay." Jamie's voice was breathless.

He didn't allow himself to hesitate. He'd shifted hundreds of times before, though never with an audience who mattered quite this much. He closed his eyes briefly, then released the tension that always held his human form in place.

The transformation was swift, efficient. One moment he stood as a human male, the next his dragon form took shape, wings unfurling to catch the breeze. He lowered his head, watching Jamie through eyes that now perceived the world with new insight.

Jamie stood motionless, lips parted, eyes wide. The expression wasn't fear—he would have recognized that immediately—but something closer to awe. His stomach tumbled; he liked the way Jamie gazed at him. Jamie took a step forward, then another, until he stood within touching distance. He reached out a tentative hand, making contact with his scales.

The world disappeared.

Suddenly he was standing within an ancient library that stretched farther than the eye could see. Towering bookshelves rose toward a vaulted ceiling, the upper reaches disappearing into mist and shadows. Stained glass windows cast pools of violet and indigo light across worn stone floors. The air smelled of old parchment and ink, with a faint underlying scent of lavender.

He knew this place instantly, though he'd never seen it before. The books—hundreds upon hundreds of them—each contained a memory. *His* memories. As Jamie turned slowly, he noticed that while many shelves were filled, many more stood empty, waiting for memories yet to be formed.

"What is this place?" Jamie's voice echoed softly in the vast space. *"Did... Did you use magic to transport us somewhere?"*

"Gods above." Realization dawned—but it was impossible. Or, it should have been. *"You're in my mind."*

"Your mind?!" Jamie's eyes widened further. *"Is that why I can't see you?"*

"Yes." It was the only word he could manage. He was reeling,

like he'd been tossed in a gale and couldn't right himself. His heart pounded a rapid rhythm against his chest.

Jamie reached toward a nearby shelf, fingers hovering over the spines of several volumes before selecting one bound in deep blue leather. As he pulled it free, the book fell open in his hands.

Somehow, Dallin knew exactly which memory it contained before the images began to form between them. He was sixteen again, at Fort Edge, heart racing as he leaned toward another boy, Claude, in a shadowed corner. The anticipation, the fear, the hope —all of it crystallized in the moment before their lips would meet.

Except they never did. Claude's face had contorted in disgust. He shoved Dallin away, hard enough that he'd stumbled backward.

"What are you doing?" Claude had hissed. "Are you insane? If you ever try that again, I'll tell everyone what you are."

Dallin felt exposed, raw, as Jamie witnessed this most private moment of shame. Yet, alongside the exposure came something unexpected—relief. No more hiding, no more wondering if Jamie truly understood what this relationship meant to him.

"I'm sorry," Jamie whispered, closing the book gently. *That was private. I shouldn't have..."*

"You have nothing to apologize for. There should be no secrets between us."

Jamie didn't know what this meant yet, but Dallin did. That sudden reminder had him reeling back, breaking the connection between them. He shifted with lightning speed, until he was standing before Jamie on two feet.

"What was that?" Jamie gaped at him.

"We need to go. Come on." Without further explanation, he grabbed Jamie's hand and pulled him away.

"What's going on?" Jamie demanded as he led him down the stairs, hoping Talon would still be in the tower. "Dallin!"

"We're mates." He didn't stop. Didn't award this moment the reverence it deserved. Mainly, because it felt too good to be true. Too impossible to be real.

"What?! But... That... How?!" Jamie began sputtering, his

protests turning weak as Dallin dragged him along. "Where are we going?"

"To see the king."

"The king?"

They burst through the door of the king's council chamber. Talon froze mid-word, his head snapping in their direction. "Dallin."

"Your majesty. I—we—I must speak with you. Immediately."

He could have wept with relief at the immediacy at which Talon quickly dismissed his lower council, snapping at all of them to *get out*. He was already on his feet and across the room, taking Dallin's shoulders in his hands. Searching him for some unseen threat. "What's happened?"

"I... I have to tell you something. Something...happened."

He hadn't let go of Jamie's hand. "But I need to speak with you and the queen."

Understanding dawned in Talon's eyes. "I see." His eyes went unfocused for a moment. "She's on her way."

The silence that followed was taut with anticipation. Dallin found he couldn't bring himself to let go of Jamie's hand, drawing strength from the contact. Jamie stood beside him, quiet but present, his thumb occasionally brushing over Dallin's knuckles in silent support.

The door opened moments later, and Queen Claire entered. To her credit, she didn't show a thimble of surprise, probably because she already knew she was walking into something tense, from whatever she'd seen in Talon's mind.

"What's happened?" She moved to stand beside Talon, a united front.

Dallin drew himself up. "Jamie and I are mates," he said simply.

Talon's eyes widened with confusion. "What?"

"You are?!" Claire's face transformed with immediate joy. "But...that's wonderful!"

Dallin frowned and he took a step back, dragging Jamie with him. "You... Wait, you believe me?"

"Why wouldn't I?" She stepped forward, embracing first Dallin, then Jamie. "It's not exactly something to lie about. Dallin! I'm so happy for you both!"

Talon remained where he stood, shock gradually giving way to a genuine smile. "How is this possible?" he asked, looking at his mate. "There has never been any record of male pairings."

"That we know of," Claire said smugly. She appeared to be fighting a satisfied smirk. "When I reversed Isabella's curse on the drengr, I restored balance to the world. I believe this is yet another result of that balance. Who can say what new changes the future will hold once the dust settles? I think they will all be changes for the better."

Talon appeared thoughtful.

"Then... Is this acceptable?" Dallin winced at the vulnerability in his own question. "I know there's no precedent for this. No one has ever..."

Talon silenced him with a raised hand. His expression softened, the scars on his face shifting with his smile. "It doesn't matter who you bond with or love. You have your king and queen's full support. Always."

"Absolutely," Claire added, beaming at them. "And I wouldn't be surprised if you're just the first of many."

Relief washed through him, so powerful it nearly brought him to his knees. He'd expected acceptance—Talon had always been fair—but the enthusiasm in both their faces was more than he'd dared hope for.

"Thank you," Jamie said quietly, speaking for the first time since entering the chamber. "For your understanding."

"Understanding has nothing to do with it," Talon replied. "This is cause for celebration. The mate bond is sacred, regardless of who shares it." He turned back to Dallin. "Does this change anything for you as my shield?"

Dallin straightened. "No, Your Majesty. My oath remains."

"Good." Talon nodded. "Then I believe you have a flight to complete, don't you? That was the original plan, I assume? How this revelation all came about?"

Dallin cleared his throat. He felt heat rise to his face. "Yes, Your Majesty."

"Then don't let us keep you." His smile held genuine warmth. He stepped forward and slapped Dallin on the back in true brotherly fashion, then moved over and grasped Jamie's forearm, as if welcoming him to the family. "Go. Enjoy your first flight together. We can discuss the implications for the kingdom another time."

"Thank...thank you. We will." He tugged on Jamie's hand to lead him out of the room.

"Dallin? Jamie." Claire called after them.

They paused, looking back.

"I'm truly happy for you both," she said, her eyes shining. "For what it's worth, I think you make a perfect match."

THE QUEEN's garden was exactly as it had been minutes ago, and yet, everything had changed. He stood in the center, facing Jamie, their hands still linked.

"We don't have to do this now," he said. "If you'd rather wait..."

Jamie shook his head. "I've wanted to fly ever since you mentioned it. The fact that we're mates only makes me want it more."

He nodded, releasing Jamie's hand and stepping back. The transformation came even more smoothly this time, his dragon form eagerly taking shape in a matter of seconds. Jamie approached with newfound confidence. As he climbed onto his back, settling between the ridges just behind his neck, the connection between them was renewed. He felt a surge of protectiveness—one Jamie immediately sensed through their bond. This was his mate—his *mate*—trusting him completely.

"Are you comfortable?"

"I think it will take some getting used to." He could sense Jamie's nerves.

"I'll have a harness commissioned as soon as we return, one that fits your measurements."

"That would be...perfect." Pleasure over the idea radiated out of Jamie.

Gods, what would have happened if they had flown sooner? If they had flown together before Claire had reversed Isabella's curse? If he'd had the courage to take this intimate step when Isabella's meddling would have prevented them from knowing what they truly were to each other? The thought was devastating.

"Everything happened when it needed to," Jamie reassured him. *"As it needed to."*

"You are right. There is no use in lingering over the what ifs."

"Then shall we fly?"

"At once." He gathered himself and launched into the sky. They soared upward, wings catching the updraft from the keep's walls, spiraling higher until Kastali Dun spread beneath them like a detailed map.

Jamie's gasp of delight was snatched away by the wind, but Dallin felt his excitement through their shared minds. As they leveled out, he felt Jamie relax slightly, adjusting to the rhythm of his wingbeats.

"It's beautiful," Jamie's declaration left his heart bursting with warmth. To be able to share this with him...

They banked toward the west, the city falling away behind them as they skimmed over the sea, blue waves turned dragon fire gold in the afternoon light. It wasn't called the Dragonfire Sea for nothing.

"I love you too, by the way." Jamie's declaration had his stomach swooping.

"You're snooping through my thoughts."

"Isn't that what mates are supposed to do?" Jamie laughed.

"Yes." He hesitated. Even though he could feel Jamie's love, could see that it had been building for weeks, he still said, *"Say it again."*

"I love you."

"And I love you back."

Everything about this moment felt right. Complete. The loss and loneliness that had chased him south, pushing him to become a king's shield, then following him even after that, the certainty that he would never know the mate bond for himself, had vanished completely. He hadn't dared to let himself hope. And yet, here they were.

Now there was only acceptance, belonging, and the promise of a future with someone who saw him completely. As they soared over the sea, waves shimmering like scattered sapphires beneath them, their minds intertwined with the ease of two puzzle pieces settling into place. What they shared wasn't just unprecedented—it was inevitable. The world had simply been waiting for them to find each other, to prove that love, in its truest form, had always been more powerful than ancient curses or outdated traditions.

EPILOGUE: NINE

Kastali Dun

Claire fidgeted with the sleeve of her silver gown as Miera made a final adjustment to the back. In the mirrors surrounding them, she could see the subtle glow of excitement on her face. After weeks of planning, Jeanine and Feowen's life ceremony would finally take place tonight.

"Hold still, *Ayas Drollaya*," Miera gently scolded, nimble fingers working at the intricate fastenings. "Almost finished."

Her luminescent markings cast a faint glow over the fabric. She found herself wondering if her own child would someday have markings like hers. The pregnancy was just beginning to show—a small, firm curve beneath her gown that most wouldn't notice unless they were looking for it.

"There." Miera stepped back, admiring her handiwork. "Perfect."

She turned to the open doors that led to the adjacent chamber, where the other women were helping Jeanine prepare. Through the doorway, she caught glimpses of golden fabric and heard soft laughter.

"I should check on our bride," she said, smoothing her hands over her dress one final time.

"Not a bride," Selphie corrected with a smile. "Life-bound. Different."

"Of course." She returned the smile and moved toward the connected room.

Jeanine stood in the center, a vision in shimmering gold. The dress had been Selphie and Miera's design—elegant, flowing, with subtle details that honored both human and spriten traditions. Desaree fussed with the hem while Saffra carefully wove tiny blossoms into Jeanine's hair.

"You look stunning," Claire said, pausing in the doorway.

Jeanine's eyes found hers in the mirror. "I'm terrified."

"Completely normal," Leah assured her, adjusting a sleeve. "I was a mess before my senior prom, and that was just a dance. This is a life-changing ceremony."

Never mind that the others in the room hadn't a clue what a senior prom was. Something she and Leah got to share. Little bits of knowledge that tied them to their roots.

"You don't look terrified," Claire observed. "You look radiant."

"That's Desaree's doing." Jeanine nodded toward the dark-haired woman. "She's been surprisingly calm throughout this entire process."

Claire's gaze shifted to Desaree, who worked with a quiet confidence that hadn't been present months ago. The lingering effects of the special fruit she and Verath had shared were subtle but unmistakable—a new awareness in her eyes, a vibrant glow to her skin, a fluid grace to her movements.

"Some of us are simply better under pressure," Desaree said with a secretive smile that Claire understood all too well.

Her thoughts drifted to the small wooden box hidden in her chambers containing the four remaining purple fruits from the king tree. She'd been waiting for the perfect moment to offer them to the others. Tonight, when their circle was complete and joyful, the time would finally be right. A life-bond gift to Feowen and Jeanine, and an added bonus for Merrian and Reyr.

"Claire?" Saffra's voice pulled her from her thoughts. "You've got that look."

"What look?"

"The, *I-know-something-you-don't* look," Saffra teased, securing another blossom in Jeanine's hair. "The same one you had before you announced your pregnancy."

Claire laughed, deflecting. "I'm just happy. It's a beautiful day for a life ceremony."

"You're glowing," Merrian remarked from where she sat carefully arranging Jeanine's golden slippers.

"Pregnancy will do that, I think," she quipped, earning chuckles from the women. She loved that she could be entirely herself around them, that they never made her feel like she was an outsider. Not just because of where she'd come from but because she was their queen.

"Speaking of glowing..." Leah's gaze shifted pointedly to Desaree, whose cheeks flushed slightly.

Claire silently thanked her friend for the timely distraction. Desaree and Verath had kept their enhanced bond secret at her request, though she suspected Saffra might have guessed something had changed between them.

"Is it time yet?" Jeanine asked, clearly eager to get a move on things. The nerves in her voice were impossible to miss.

"Soon." Claire moved to stand behind her, placing gentle hands on her shoulders. "The queen's garden is ready. Taylynn arrived an hour ago to prepare the ceremonial space."

"Is Feowen—?"

"He's with Talon and the others," Claire assured her. "Probably being subjected to whatever passes for male bonding among drengr and sprites."

This earned a laugh from Jeanine, some of the tension visibly leaving her shoulders.

"I never thought I'd have this," she confessed softly, her voice dropping so only Claire could hear. "This kind of...love."

Claire squeezed her shoulders. "Life has a way of surprising us."

A gentle knock announced one of her spriten guards. "Queen Taylynn says all is prepared, *Ayas Drollaya*. The guests are assembled."

"*Shalaya*, Elyon." Claire turned back to the women. "It's time."

~

THE QUEEN's tower garden had been transformed, much like how it had been for her pre-bonding ceremony party all that time ago. Glittering, colorful lanterns hung from trellises, casting rainbow prisms across the stone paths. Flowering vines climbed around them, their blooms glowing softly in the twilight. In the center of the garden stood two slender saplings in ornate pots, their leaves rustling gently in the evening breeze.

Claire entered on Talon's arm, feeling the familiar warmth of his presence both physically and through their bond. He looked magnificent in formal black and silver that matched her gown. Crowns of gold gleamed upon their brows.

"Does this bring back memories?" he murmured as they walked to their designated place near the saplings.

"The best kind," she replied softly. It was impossible *not* to think of their own bonding ceremony. The same had happened during Saffra's ceremony. Seeing others so deeply in love, committing their lives to one another, had a way of reminding her of what she shared with her mate, of those joyous moments when everything had changed for the better.

The gathering was small but significant—their inner circle complete. Saffra and Bedelth stood close together, his arm wrapped possessively around his mate's waist. Jovari and Leah were nearby, their fingers intertwined in a way that hinted at their own eagerness to celebrate such a ceremony in the near future. Dallin and Jamie stood across the way, their sides pressed together. Mikkin, Berbik, and Unka had also been invited to join them, crowding in behind them. She gave them soft smiles of welcome. Even Jeanine's childhood friend Jahl and his partner had come.

Her gaze found Reyr and Merrian, their heads bent together,

whispering. She couldn't wait to share her surprise with them later. Reyr said something that made Merrian giggle, her expression content in a way Claire had never seen before. The relief she'd felt upon discovering their...*relationship* was monumental. Seeing one of her favorite people in the whole world happy? It was the best gift.

Along one side of the garden, several members of her queen's guard had assembled with instruments—Gorded with a carved flute, Jassin with a string instrument resembling a lyre, and two others with small drums. They began a gentle melody as Taylynn took her position between the saplings.

The sprite queen was resplendent in emerald green, her markings glowing bright against her skin. Koldis stood a respectful distance behind her, his eyes never leaving his mate. The pride on his face as he watched Taylynn officiate was unmistakable.

At the garden's entrance, Feowen appeared. He wore formal sprite attire in forest green, his midnight blue hair bound in intricate braids threaded with small white blossoms. He moved to stand before Taylynn, his expression a mixture of nervousness and joy. The two of them shared a soft smile, the kind exchanged between siblings.

The music shifted, growing more elaborate, and all eyes turned to the entrance.

Jeanine appeared, radiant in gold. In her arms, she carried a small woven basket filled with what Claire knew were her most precious possessions—tokens of her journey that had led her to this moment. She moved with grace that belied her warrior background, her eyes fixed on Feowen.

The look that passed between them as she approached made Claire's heart tighten. She felt Talon's fingers squeeze hers gently, his thoughts tangling with hers in silent understanding.

When Jeanine reached the center of the garden, she and Feowen stood facing each other before Taylynn. The music faded to a soft background melody. She placed her basket beside the one he'd brought up for himself.

"We gather beneath the stars," Taylynn began, her voice

carrying easily through the garden, "to witness the binding of two souls who have chosen to walk life's path as one."

She gestured to the saplings. "In true spriten tradition, life ceremonies begin with the joining of two living things, symbolizing the joining of two lives."

Normally this was done with both partners, but since Jeanine didn't have magic, Feowen stepped forward, placing his hands over the soil of both saplings. He closed his eyes, and began to hum. The saplings trembled, then slowly began to grow and bend toward each other. As the gathered friends watched in wonder, the trunks twisted together, becoming a single intertwined tree, their leaves mingling.

"As these trees grow as one," Taylynn continued, "so too shall your lives grow together."

Jeanine and Feowen each placed a hand on the newly joined tree, their fingers touching.

"Now," Taylynn said, "for the sharing of treasures."

Jeanine opened her basket, removing each item with care. A sword—the one she'd carried when she'd led refugees to safety. A wooden carving of a bird that had once belonged to her mother. A pressed flower from the day she'd first joined Claire's queen's guard.

Feowen's items followed—a small crystal from the heart of Esterpine, a medallion he'd received from a mentor when he was younger, and a silver clasp that had held his cloak the first time he'd met Jeanine.

"These tokens of your separate journeys," Taylynn explained, "now become the first treasures of your shared path."

The items were placed carefully in a new basket, woven with both blue and gold threads.

"Now, standing before those gathered as witnesses, speak the promises you choose to make to one another."

Feowen took Jeanine's hands in his. "Jeanine, from the moment I first saw you—fierce, determined, protecting those who needed strength—I knew you were unlike any other. I promise to honor your strength and courage for all our days. I promise to stand beside you, not before or behind you, but as your equal. I promise that each day we share will be treasured, each moment held sacred. My immortal heart is yours, for however long we walk this world together."

Tears glistened in Jeanine's eyes, but her voice remained steady. "Feowen, when I fled my village, I was running from death and destruction. In finding you, I found hope and a future I never imagined possible. I promise to meet each day with the same bravery that brought me to you. I promise to remind you of joy and wonder in the world around us. I promise that whatever time we have—be it days, years, or decades—will be filled with love, laughter, and adventure. My mortal heart is yours, completely and without reservation."

Claire felt her own eyes growing damp. She sensed Talon's emotions through their bond—a mixture of happiness for their friends and deep contentment with their own connection.

"Water from the king tree's spring," Taylynn said, producing a small crystal vial, "to nourish your joined roots."

She poured the water over the entwined saplings, the liquid shimmering with an inner light. Where it touched the tree, the bark glowed briefly.

"By the ancient traditions of the sprites," Taylynn proclaimed, "and with the blessing of the forest, I declare you life-bound. May your days together be full of light and love."

Feowen pulled Jeanine into his arms, and their kiss was met with applause from their gathered friends. The soft notes of music began again, a lively, joyful melody that filled the garden.

"Now, shall we celebrate?!" Taylynn announced, her formal demeanor melting into a wide smile.

The evening flowed like the sweet wine being passed among the guests. After Jeanine and Feowen's first dance, others joined in. Claire's spriten guards played with extraordinary skill, their music carrying an almost magical quality that made it impossible to stay still. She was glad that they had volunteered.

She watched from a stone bench, one hand resting lightly on her abdomen. The scene before her filled her with a satisfaction she couldn't quite name. Saffra and Bedelth danced together. Leah had convinced Jovari to attempt some famous social media dance move from her world that had everyone laughing. Even Dallin and Jamie had joined in, moving somewhat hesitantly but with evident joy.

Talon returned from speaking with Reyr, offering her a goblet of water. She accepted it gratefully, shifting to make room for him beside her.

"Happy?" he asked, his scarred face softened by the gentle lighting.

"Incredibly."

His arm slipped around her waist, his hand coming to rest over hers on her stomach. "Thinking about our little one?"

"Among other things." She leaned against him, drawing strength from his solid presence. "I think it's time."

He didn't need to ask what she meant. He knew. He *always* knew.

"Are you certain?"

She nodded. "It feels right. Tonight, when everyone is already celebrating love and connection."

Talon pressed a kiss to her temple. "Then do it, *mih cralla.*"

She stood, moving to where a small wooden box had been discreetly placed earlier. She caught Desaree's eye across the garden and gave a slight nod. Understanding dawned on the woman's face, and she whispered something to Verath.

"May I have everyone's attention?" Claire called, her voice carrying over the music, which gradually faded to silence.

Their gathered friends turned toward her, conversations halting.

"Today we've celebrated the binding of Jeanine and Feowen's lives," she began, "and there is no greater joy than seeing two people find each other across all odds."

She opened the box, revealing four purple fruits nestled inside.

"Some months ago, during my time in the Gable Forest, the king tree granted me six fruits of extraordinary power. Each one capable of binding two lives together in a unique way."

Murmurs rippled through the group.

"Some of you may have noticed," Claire continued, her gaze moving to Desaree and Verath, "that Desaree and Verath have seemed...different lately."

Desaree stepped forward, Verath's hand clasped firmly in hers. "Claire gave us two of these fruits weeks ago," she explained. "Since then, we've carried a bond almost identical to that of a mate bond."

"We can communicate telepathically," Verath added, "and Desaree will age at the same rate I do."

Gasps and shocked exclamations followed this revelation.

"Tonight," Claire said, "I wish to offer the same gift to two more couples who face similar challenges."

She turned first to Jeanine and Feowen. "For you, these fruits will bind Jeanine's human lifespan to Feowen's immortal one. While it won't grant sprite magic, it will allow you thousands of years together rather than mere decades. Which, I suppose, means you will outlive the rest of us."

Jeanine's hand flew to her mouth, her eyes widening and filling with tears. A sob burst from her. She almost crumpled, were it not for Feowen catching her, steadying her.

Claire turned to Reyr and Merrian. "And for you, a bond like that of drengr and rider—thoughts shared, lives connected."

Reyr's expression was complex—hope warring with lingering grief and guilt.

"This is a choice," Claire emphasized. "There is no obligation to accept. But it is offered freely, with love, in hopes that it might bring balance to those whose hearts have already chosen."

For a moment, silence hung in the garden. Then Taylynn stepped forward, tears glistening in her eyes. "Claire..." Her voice wavered. "This is beyond generous. You're giving my brother the greatest gift possible."

"Your brother gave me his loyalty and protection," Claire replied. "This seems a fair exchange."

Feowen looked to Jeanine, his question unspoken but clear in his eyes.

"Yes," Jeanine whispered, then louder: "Yes!" She moved toward Claire, pulling Feowen with her.

Claire offered them two of the fruits. "Eat them together. The magic works when you both partake."

Reyr and Merrian approached more slowly. "You're certain about this?" Reyr asked Merrian quietly.

"I'm sure," she answered, holding his gaze steadily. "As long as you are."

"I am."

Claire placed the final two fruits in their hands. "The effect is different for each pair," she explained. "For Jeanine and Feowen, it binds human life to sprite immortality. For you two, it will create something akin to a true mate bond, though born of choice rather than fate."

The couples stood facing each other, fruits in hand.

"Together," Feowen said to Jeanine, raising the purple fruit to his lips.

They bit into the fruits simultaneously, chewing and swallowing. Each pair polished the fruits off a few minutes later. Feowen's markings began to glow brighter and brighter, until the luminance spread to Jeanine. She gasped, her hand flying to her chest. "I can feel... something. Warmth." The glow faded, until all that was left was a luminescent marking on the back of Jeanine's hand. She lifted it, gawking.

Feowen's expression was one of wonder. He took her hand, lifting the marking to his lips, pressing a kiss there.

Reyr and Merrian gazed at each other in wonder. The effect of their bond was different. No light or visible sign marked the merging of their minds. Just a gasp from Merrian before their faces broke into brilliant smiles.

"Gods," Merrian breathed. "Is this what it's like? For drengr and rider pairs?"

Reyr nodded slowly, seemingly at a loss for words. When he finally spoke, his voice was thick with emotion. "I never thought I would feel this again."

Claire stepped back, allowing the couples their moment. She

felt Talon's presence behind her, his arms encircling her as they watched the magic take hold.

"You've done a remarkable thing," he said, for her alone. *"It was incredibly selfless to think of your friends during your time with the king tree."*

"I just wanted everyone to share the same happiness and future you and I share."

Taylynn sidled close, her expression grateful beyond words. She drew Claire aside, clasping her hands. "What you've done for my brother... There are no words sufficient to thank you."

"No thanks needed," she assured her. "Your brother deserves happiness, just as you found yours with Koldis."

"Still," Taylynn insisted, squeezing her hands, "you will always have my gratitude." Her eyes sparkled with unshed tears.

Their spriten musicians for the night, sensing the moment had passed, began playing again—a softer, sweeter melody that invited couples to dance. Jeanine and Feowen moved together as though in a dream.

She returned to Talon's side, leaning against him as they watched their friends adjust to their new connections.

"Happy?" he asked again, his lips brushing her temple.

"Perfectly," she replied, feeling the gentle flutter of their child within her. "Everything is exactly as it should be."

Around them, the garden glowed with lantern light and the hum of magical bonds both old and new, a testament to love that defied all boundaries—of time, of species, of fate itself.

EPILOGUE: TEN

Kastali Dun

Dallin stared at his reflection in the polished silver mirror, barely recognizing himself. An attendant had just finished fastening the final clasp on his formal attire—deep violet fabric that matched his scales, with silver accents in the form of embroidery and buckles. The ensemble had been crafted specifically for today.

His bonding day.

A day he never dared imagine would come.

"Would you stop fidgeting?" Jovari said, appearing at his shoulder in the mirror. "You're like a fledgling about to take his first flight."

"Can you blame him?" Reyr's voice carried a hint of amusement. "It's not every day history is made."

The word *history* sent a tremor through his stomach. Oh, gods. He was really doing this—in front of the kingdom, no less. He suddenly regretted the king's suggestion to make this public, even though he knew why Talon had requested it. Why he had agreed to it. He was about to become the first documented male drengr to bond with another male in the recorded history of Dragonwall. He'd spent his youth preparing for a solitary life, believing fate wouldn't be so cruel as to bind a female to someone who could never love her that way.

And then Jamie had touched his scales, and everything had changed.

"Your father wants to speak with you," Verath said, entering the chamber with fresh water. "Shall I send him in?"

A fresh wave of nerves crashed over him. His father had arrived three days prior with Evelyn, his mother. Their journey from Fort Edge had been surprisingly swift—Lord Averaen clearly hadn't wanted to miss his son's ceremony.

"Right. Yes." He tugged at his collar one last time. "Send him in."

King Talon's shields retreated to the adjoining chamber, Talon giving his shoulder a reassuring squeeze as he passed. Moments later, Lord Averaen entered, wearing formal attire in a lighter lavender that complemented the dark of his bonding clothes. Averaen was the oldest drengr in history to have found a mate and fathered a child.

"My son," he said, his voice unusually thick.

"Father. Is everything all right?" He found himself scanning his father's face for signs of hesitation.

Lord Averaen smiled, the expression transforming his stern features. "More than all right. I am prouder than I have words to express." A lump formed in his throat as Averaen crossed the room and placed both hands on his shoulders. He'd never expected this—his mother and father's open support. It was partly why he'd run, so he wouldn't have to explain himself. It was cowardly, he saw that now. But also understandable. "Like me, you found your mate against impossible odds. Must run in the family."

He huffed a laugh, appreciating his father's attempt to lighten the mood.

"But I'm especially proud of you because you've shown courage by embracing this bond when many would have hidden from it."

He reached into a pouch at his belt. "Your mother and I wanted something that would honor the significance of today."

He withdrew a small object wrapped in silk. When he placed it in Dallin's palm, the weight was substantial. Dallin carefully unwrapped it to reveal a silver chain bearing a pendant of polished violet crystal. The stone caught the light from impossible angles, refracting it into rainbow patterns.

"This belonged to my grandfather," Lord Averaen explained. Dallin's great grandfather had also been violet in color. "It's verdite from the heart of the Northern Barrier Mountains. It changes its appearance depending on who holds it." He smiled. "Look closely."

Dallin raised the pendant, staring into its violet depths. As he watched, the light within seemed to glitter, like twin flames dancing around each other. It was beautiful.

"Thank you," he whispered, fastening the chain around his neck.

A knock at the door interrupted them. "It's time," Talon called.

When they emerged into the corridor, the shields had assembled in formation. Further down the hall, Dallin saw Evelyn waiting beside a familiar figure that made his heart skip.

Jamie.

He wore formal attire in the same deep violet as Dallin's, though styled differently to complement his build. Someone had swept his hair back from his forehead, revealing more of his face. As their eyes met, Jamie's expression transformed, nervousness giving way to a smile that lit him from within.

"You look..." Jamie's words trailed off as Dallin approached.

"So do you," Dallin replied, feeling the inadequacy of speech. "Ready?"

Jamie nodded, his throat bobbing as he swallowed. "I think so."

Evelyn pressed a kiss to Dallin's cheek, then Jamie's. "We'll see you inside," she whispered, taking Lord Averaen's arm.

As his parents departed with the procession, Dallin turned to find himself alone with Jamie in the corridor. They took off at a steady pace, making their way through the keep to the throne room far below.

"I had a dream last night," Jamie said suddenly. "About the first time I touched your scales. How we found ourselves in that library."

"Dreaming about me, are you?"

Jamie let out a nervous laugh. "I guess."

Dallin's stomach fluttered. He loved the idea of Jamie having dreams about him. "And what did this dream have to offer?"

"It showed me that we're doing the right thing, sharing our day with the world."

"I think we are, too. I just wish I wasn't so godsdamned nervous."

They stopped outside the double doors leading into the throne room. Guards nodded, obvious respect in their expressions. From inside, trumpets sounded. Traditionally, Jamie would have been escorted in by his friends and family to where Dallin waited beside the king. But when they'd begun planning the ceremony, Jamie had hesitated. While his family was here, thanks to the unicorns Claire convinced to ferry them here, he'd wanted something different, something that departed from traditional male-female pairings.

"We found each other as equals," Jamie had said. "Shouldn't we enter that way?"

So they had planned this instead—to walk in together, side by side, breaking one more tradition in a bonding ceremony already unlike any before it.

The massive doors swung open, revealing the transformed throne room. The space was adorned with bookshelves and hanging banners in deep violet. Hundreds of candles cast golden light over the assembled guests. He wouldn't have minded flowers, like what Claire and Saffra had done. But this felt so much more... them. More masculine and tasteful. A better representation of who they were. Especially who Jamie was.

At the base of the dais stood Talon and Claire, waiting for them. Verath stood on the steps, prepared to officiate—a conscious decision. Verath had been his mentor, the one to champion him becoming a shield. Their other closest friends and loved ones stood waiting. Behind them was a sea of faces—every member of the court, representatives from each dragondom, crowded in the massive space to witness history.

"Together?" Jamie whispered.

Dallin squeezed his hand in response. "Always."

They stepped forward as one, and a murmur swept through the onlookers. Dallin spotted a few raised eyebrows and speculative whispers—but he saw far more smiles of approval. Most surprising were the looks of open wonder on the faces of several younger boys who stood among the crowd.

As they walked the length of the aisle, he felt a curious lightness spreading through him. Every step forward felt right, inevitable—as though his entire life had been leading to this moment. He caught sight of his mother, weeping openly, and his father, whose pride could not have been more evident.

When they reached the base of the dais, Claire stepped forward and placed a hand on each of their shoulders. "Are you ready?"

Gods, he loved his queen. He loved that she had been the first one he unburdened himself to. The first one to openly support him for who he was.

They nodded in unison and she moved to join Talon at the dais's edge. The hall fell silent as Verath raised his hands to address the gathering.

"People of Dragonwall." His voice carried to every corner of the room, "We are here to celebrate a historical moment. Since the time of Queen Isabella, the drengr and their riders have formed bonds that transcend ordinary connection. But now, we witness a bond unlike any recorded in our history, yet still familiar in its essence."

Verath descended the steps to stand before them. "As is tradition, you will now exchange the gifts that symbolize your commitment to protect one another."

Jovari stepped forward, bearing a long bundle wrapped in violet silk. Dallin accepted it, his fingers trembling slightly as he unwrapped the bow. He'd commissioned it weeks ago. The weapon was crafted from flexible yew, its limbs carved with intricate patterns reminiscent of dragon scales. The grip was wrapped in leather, dyed to match the color of his scales.

He presented it to Jamie, who accepted it with reverent hands.

"I present you with this bow, so that you may protect me in your own way," Dallin said, his voice steadier than he'd expected. "May you always fly with me, and may we face every battle side by side."

Jamie's eyes glistened as he ran his fingers over the bow. "I accept this gift and pledge to use it well. I thank you for this token of your love."

Mikkin stepped forward next, presenting Jamie with a small wooden box. Jamie handed the bow to Jovari, then opened the box to reveal a pommel stone of polished verdite, with subtle golden flecks trapped within its deep violet depths.

"I present to you this stone," Jamie said, his voice clear and unwavering, "so that your sverak may be complete, so that you may protect me in your own way."

Dallin's throat tightened as he accepted the stone. "I accept this gift and thank you for this token of your love." he responded.

He unsheathed his sverak and handed both it and the stone to Verath, who placed the gem in the previously empty socket at the pommel's end. "*Asamat*," Verath murmured as he fused the stone in place. When he returned the sverak, the weight felt different—balanced in a way it had never been before.

"Now," Verath said, smiling at them both, "join hands and recite the drengr-rider words that will seal your bond."

He sheathed his sverak and took Jamie's hands once more. Together, they began to speak the ancient words. To his surprise, other voices joined theirs—first Claire and Talon, then his parents, then the shields, and finally the entire assembly.

As the final words faded away, he felt a subtle shift in the air. A promise had been spoken. A bond had been acknowledged.

"And so it is said, so it shall be," Verath proclaimed, and the crowd erupted in response.

Before he could think of what came next, Jamie stepped

forward and kissed him. The touch of his lips was brief, proper for public view, but filled with promise. When they parted, Jamie was smiling so brightly that he felt momentarily dazzled.

"Now," he said, "shall we celebrate?"

The dining hall had been transformed, tables laden with delicacies from every corner of Dragonwall. As guests of honor, Dallin and Jamie sat at the head table framed in the middle, flanked by the king and queen and the rest of their closest friends and family, receiving a seemingly endless stream of well-wishers.

"That went better than I expected," Jamie murmured after accepting congratulations from another nobleman.

Dallin squeezed his hand beneath the table. "Did you think someone would object?"

"I wasn't sure how people would react to us."

"Look," Dallin nodded toward a young drengr standing with several others near the musicians. The youth's gaze kept returning to them with an expression he recognized all too well—hope mingled with disbelief.

"I think we've given some people something they never thought possible," he said softly.

Leah approached their table with a beaming smile. "I couldn't wait another moment to congratulate you both," she said. "And I have wonderful news, Jamie. Your book has been checked out fourteen times already! We might have to order additional copies if the demand continues."

Jamie flushed with pleasure. "Really?"

"Really. And I've had three different people ask if you're writing anything else."

"Uh..." Jamie collected himself. "I've been working on some new stories," he admitted, his flush deepening. "Nothing ready to show yet."

"Well, when they are, you'll have an eager audience waiting." Leah leaned over the table and squeezed his shoulder. "But for now, I think your presence is requested elsewhere." She nodded toward the dance floor, where the musicians were beginning a more traditional melody—one often danced to by bonded pairs.

Dallin stood and offered his hand to Jamie. "Shall we?"

Jamie hesitated. "I should warn you, I'm not much of a dancer."

"Neither am I," Dallin confessed. "We'll manage it together."

As they stepped onto the open floor, the other dancers moved back, creating a circle of space. Dallin placed one hand at Jamie's waist, the other clasping Jamie's hand. They began to move slowly, following the gentle rhythm of the music.

"Everyone's watching," Jamie whispered, his steps slightly unsteady.

"Only you matter," Dallin replied, drawing him closer.

As they turned in a slow circle, he caught glimpses of familiar faces —his parents watching with pride, Claire and Talon with knowing smiles, the shields with varying degrees of amusement. Yet most of the faces surrounding them were simply happy, caught up in the cele-bration of a bond that, only months ago, no one had believed possible.

"I never thought I'd have this," Jamie admitted quietly. "Someone who sees me and appreciates that. I certainly never thought it would be…"

"A male?"

"Exactly." Jamie gave a high pitched laugh. "I just thought I wasn't cut out for…a partner, you know? Now I know it was because I was waiting for the right one."

"If you hadn't touched my scales that day..."

"But I did." Jamie's smile was radiant. "And here we are."

"Here we are," Dallin echoed, feeling as though his heart might burst from his chest.

HOURS LATER, they made their way through torch-lit corridors to Dallin's chambers. Unlike most mated pairs, they'd opted to slip away unnoticed, allowing the party to continue in full swing. Only Talon had spotted their retreat, giving them a nod of farewell, his eyes glimmering with his unspoken blessing.

Dallin pushed through the door to his chambers, then faltered.

The room beyond had been transformed. Fresh linens adorned the bed, while dozens of candles cast a warm glow. Someone had scattered deep violet flower petals across the floor. Most notably, a writing desk now occupied the space near the window, complete with fresh parchment, ink, and quills.

"It looks like our friends have been meddling," he muttered, feeling warm and appreciated.

"They did this for us?" Jamie wandered over to the desk, running his fingers over its polished surface. "This is beautiful."

There was a slip of parchment declaring the desk a bonding gift to Jamie, from the king and queen.

Dallin took his hand, pulling him back to the middle of the room. His pulse kicked up a notch, knowing what the rest of the night held in store for them. But first—

He cleared his throat. "I need to be certain you understand what comes next for us. What it means."

Jamie's eyebrows drew together. "We've discussed this. I know about the bonding—"

"Once our minds connect permanently, there's no going back. No changing your mind. Our thoughts, our feelings...they'll be intertwined for as long as we both live."

"Dallin." Jamie reached up to cradle his face between his palms. "I've thought about all of this. I've had weeks to consider what it means to be bonded to a king's shield. I know the risks. I know the responsibilities." His thumb traced the line of Dallin's jaw, then brushed his bottom lip. Sparks followed in its wake. "And I've never been more sure of anything in my life."

The simple conviction in his voice loosened something tight in Dallin's chest. He bent his head, capturing Jamie's lips with his own. The kiss was different from their others—deeper, more purposeful, laden with the knowledge of what was to come.

Jamie's hands began to wander first, setting the precedent. They removed their elaborate attire piece by piece, reveling in every measure of exposed skin with reverent hands and lips, every touch an affirmation of the bond they were about to seal. He memorized the curve of Jamie's shoulder, the sharp line of his hip, the soft sound he made when kissed just below his ear.

Their touches grew more urgent. He felt like a ship caught in a perfect storm, waves of sensation crashing over him as Jamie's hands mapped territories they had yet to fully explore. They moved together like dancers following an unheard melody, each responding to the other's needs without words.

In all their previous intimate moments, they had held something back—a final barrier neither had dared to cross because it had never felt quite...right. But now? Tonight? Tonight, there would be no holding back. Tonight, they would give themselves to each other completely.

"I love you," Jamie whispered against Dallin's lips as they moved together. "Part of me wonders if I've always loved you, even before I knew who you were. Like I was waiting for you."

Dallin groaned. He answered Jamie's heartfelt words with his body, as they climbed higher together and their breaths mingled. The world narrowed to the space between their bodies, to the heat where they joined, to the rhythm they created with each movement. Like waves breaking against the shore, like flames consuming kindling, like birds soaring through endless skies, they carried each other toward the inevitable peak.

The moment came when he felt as though he might shatter. And then he did. Every muscle tensed, every nerve singing as pleasure crashed through him. Jamie followed an instant later, crying out his name like a prayer.

And then—

An entirely new sensation bloomed in his mind. It was sudden and profound. A shift as an invisible wall between them dissolved. Where once had been only his own thoughts, now there was more —Jamie's consciousness flowing into his. No longer two separate minds but one shared space, impossible to determine where his thoughts ended and Jamie's began.

Disorienting. Overwhelming. *Perfect.*

"Oh, gods," Jamie cried, his breaths rough. "You—we—it worked?"

"Of course it worked," he laughed, overcome by infinite joy.

But part of him, a small, scared part, had worried that this was all a horrible trick the fates wanted to play. That once they got to this moment, nothing would happen. That they'd discover they couldn't be mates, after all.

But they were connected—mated!

He felt what Jamie felt. Wonderment, joy, and a bone-deep certainty that this was right. Jamie's memories lay open to him as his own were to Jamie, a lifetime of experiences suddenly accessible. He no longer had to transform to create a connection. Emotions flowed between them unfiltered—Jamie's love for him, his relief at finding acceptance, his lingering surprise that someone like Dallin could want him.

"Dallin?" Jamie's voice had never sounded sweeter.

"I'm here." The response came without effort, natural as breathing. The concept of "here" had changed—they existed within each other now. *"We're here. Together."*

For a long moment, they simply existed in the bond, marveling at its completeness. There were no boundaries to push against, no barriers between them. When Dallin focused on a memory of their first meeting, Jamie saw it too—not as Dallin described it, but exactly as Dallin had experienced it, with all the accompanying emotions.

Eventually, their physical bodies reasserted themselves. Jamie became aware of Dallin's weight against him, of their shared heartbeats gradually slowing, of the softness of the sheets beneath them. Yet even as they shifted to lie side by side, their minds remained as one, neither able to retreat from the newfound unity even if they'd wanted to.

"I had no idea," Jamie murmured aloud, though Dallin experienced the formation of the thought before the words were spoken, feeling Jamie's wonder as his own. "It's like I've been living in black and white, and now there are all these... colors."

Dallin pressed his lips to Jamie's forehead, his contentment flowing freely between them. "And now we live in color."

They lay together in comfortable silence, catching their breaths. It didn't feel real. Any of it.

But it was, and just like Jamie had said, everything looked so much more vibrant than it had hours before. A laugh burst from his lips, and then he simply couldn't stop. Jamie started laughing too. They were both utterly, and incandescently happy.

It was exactly as it should have been. Perfect in every way.

EPILOGUE: ELEVEN

Kastali Dun

Leah held her breath. The massive throne room doors swung open. Holy. Shit.

Her mouth dropped. The sight before her was beyond anything she'd imagined when she'd drawn up the plans and explained her vision. Rows of evergreen trees were scattered throughout the giant space, adorned with silver orbs and sapphire ribbons that caught the light from a thousand floating lanterns that someone had magicked into position. Ice crystals sparkled on the needles—Claire's handiwork, obviously, making them glitter like diamonds.

It was the epitome of Christmas. In another world. *Christmas.*

And beyond the transformed space, through the stained glass windows surrounding the space, delicate white flakes drifted from the sky—actual freaking snow. In Kastali Dun. Where it almost never snowed.

Several court members had already gathered at the windows, pointing and exclaiming like children. She couldn't blame them.

"Is that why everyone's running late?" Saffra asked, adjusting Leah's sapphire blue gown with a quick tug.

"It's snowing," she whispered. "On winter solstice. On my wedding—*bonding* day."

"A blessing from the gods themselves," Desaree said, smoothing a nonexistent wrinkle from her gown. Floor-length sapphire blue silk lined with tiny silver stars made her appear draped in the night sky. "Though if anyone deserves such a gift, it's you."

She touched the silver chain at her throat, the small sapphire pendant Jovari had given her last month. Her fingers were steady now, though they'd been trembling as Miera and Selphie had helped her dress. Now, seeing the space transformed exactly as she'd envisioned, the nervousness faded into certainty.

The crowd parted, clearing an aisle.

And then she saw him.

Jovari. Standing tall at the base of the dais where King Talon waited. His sapphire-colored formal tunic and black trousers made him look like some fantasy prince from a Disney movie. He'd grown his auburn hair longer, the sides pulled back, showing off his sharp jawline that could cut glass. His eyes locked with hers, darkening instantly.

How had she gotten so lucky?

Claire appeared beside her, a dainty gold crown atop her head. Her pregnancy was obvious now—that baby bump impossible to miss beneath her formal gown.

"Ready to rope yourself to your dragon-man for eternity?" Claire asked, squeezing her hand.

"Born ready."

"Then let's not keep your mate waiting."

With her ladies behind her, Leah began the walk down the aisle. The music shifted to a melody she'd chosen—reminiscent of traditional wedding marches from Earth, but played on instruments that gave it an otherworldly quality.

The Christmas trees. Gods, they were perfect. Better than she'd imagined when she'd first brought it up to Claire. They were magnificent—taller and fuller than the scraggly ones she'd put up with her parents each year. A piece of home in her new world.

Jovari's eyes never left hers. That intensity made her cheeks flush. Each step brought her closer until finally, she stood before him.

He reached for her hand, and when their fingers laced, a jolt of awareness shot up her arm. Despite her initial hesitance about the mate bond, about tying herself to another, she was finally ready. This was meant to be.

"My star in the night sky," Jovari murmured, so only she could hear.

King Talon's deep voice filled the throne room.

"People of Dragonwall, we have come together on this winter solstice—the longest night of the year—to witness the bonding of two souls who found each other across worlds. Jovari the Blue, shield to the crown and defender of our kingdom, and Lady Leah, keeper of knowledge and bringer of light to our people."

Lady Leah. She still wasn't used to that title.

"In the tradition of our kingdom, since the days of King Eymar and Queen Isabella, we honor the sacred bond between drengr and rider, a connection that transcends the physical to unite two minds as one." Talon glanced at Claire, his expression softening for a moment before he continued. "Jovari will now present his mate with her bow, that she may fly with him and protect him in her own way."

Jovari turned to Reyr, who stepped forward with a long object wrapped in blue silk. After a nod, Jovari turned back to Leah.

"I helped craft this for you with my own hands," he said, unwrapping the silk to reveal a bow unlike any Leah had seen in Dragonwall.

She gawked. The wood was black as night, inlaid with actual sapphires along its length. Silver filigree wrapped around the grip, forming patterns that resembled stars.

"So that when we fly together, you may stand equal to me in battle and in peace."

"It's beautiful," she whispered, running her fingers along the bow arms. She'd been practicing archery for months, and even though she was total crap at it, she'd get better.

"Not as beautiful as you," he replied with that smirk that still made her knees weak.

"Flirt," she mouthed, making his smirk widen.

She handed the bow to Claire, who stood as her attendant, before turning back to the king.

"Lady Leah will now present her mate with a pommel stone, so that his sverak may be complete, so that he may protect her in his own way," Talon intoned.

Desaree stepped forward, offering Leah a small wooden box. Inside, on a cushion of blue velvet, lay a sapphire the size of a plum. She'd spent weeks searching for the perfect stone, finally finding it in the royal treasury where Claire had insisted she look.

"This stone," Leah said, her voice steadier than expected, "bears the color of your scales and the strength of my commitment. May it serve you well in battle and in peace."

Jovari's eyes darkened with delight. "I will carry it with honor," he said, his voice husky.

He handed both stone and sverak to the king, who performed the attachment ritual. When Talon returned the weapon, Jovari secured it at his side with practiced ease.

Leah took a deep breath and nodded to Claire, who stepped forward with another, smaller box. Time for her surprise.

"In my world," she began, addressing both Jovari and the crowd, "we have a tradition of exchanging rings during wedding ceremonies." She opened the box to reveal two bands of silver, one inlaid with tiny sapphires, the other with a single larger sapphire. "A ring is a circle without beginning or end, symbolizing eternal love and commitment. Would you honor me by wearing this symbol of my world, as I have embraced yours?"

The court erupted in whispers. Jovari's eyes softened with understanding.

"I would wear anything that binds me to you," he said, his voice sending shivers down her spine.

With trembling fingers, Leah slid the larger band onto his left ring finger. He then took the smaller ring and repeated the motion. The metal was cool against her skin but quickly warmed.

King Talon looked briefly surprised, and even a little impressed. His eyes darted to Claire's bare hand, like he was suddenly realizing he wanted *her* in a ring too. He recovered quickly. "And now, the traditional words that have bound drengr and rider since our kingdom's founding."

Together, they recited the ancient poem, their voices joining.

As the final words echoed, Jovari pulled her against him and claimed her mouth in a kiss that left her breathless and dizzy. The crowd erupted in cheers, breaking the solemn atmosphere. When they separated, she couldn't stop smiling.

"And so it is said, so it shall be," the crowd chanted.

"I present to you Jovari the Blue and his mate, Lady Leah!" Talon announced, his voice filled with genuine warmth.

What followed was a blur of faces and congratulations. Nobles and commoners alike offering blessings. She registered almost none of it, too focused on the feel of Jovari's hand at her waist, anchoring her to this moment, to him.

They had a position of honor at the head table, where they feasted. Then, it was time for dancing. Jovari led her to the middle for their first dance as a mated pair. As he pulled her close, his hand hot against the small of her back, she finally relaxed.

"Has this been as terrifying for you as it has been for me?" she murmured against his chest.

He chuckled, the sound vibrating through her. "You? Terrified? The woman who faced every moment of her father's treatment with a brave face? The woman who left her world behind for a new one? Who taught us king's shields how to play *poker* with cards she had commissioned? That woman?"

She snorted. "Yes, that woman. I kept thinking I'd trip on my dress or say the wrong words or drop your beautiful pommel stone."

"I'd have caught you. And the stone." His hand tightened at her waist. "Thank you for the ring, by the way. That was unexpected."

"You like it, then? It's not too much? I've never seen any of you shields wearing rings but—"

"I love it," he said firmly. "I want everyone to see that I belong to you as much as you belong to me."

Her heart did that stupid flutter thing again. She was about to respond when a chorus of young voices interrupted them.

"Lady Leah!"

A group of children approached, clutching handmade books and drawings. She recognized them immediately—regulars from one of her libraries. She'd made sure that the guest list to her ceremony included many of the faces she loved seeing. Over the past few months, what had begun as a single converted building had expanded to three locations.

"We made these for you, my lady!" A girl with bright red curls thrust a bound collection of papers forward. "Stories we wrote about our favorite adventures!"

Another child offered a drawing of Leah surrounded by books, her violet hair rendered in vibrant hues. "This is when you helped me find the dragon book!"

Jovari chuckled. "It appears you've cultivated quite the fan club, little minx."

Leah knelt despite her formal gown, accepting each gift. "These are wonderful. Thank you all. I'll add them to the special collection."

The children beamed, clearly thrilled.

"Lady Leah hopes to bring libraries to other cities someday," Jovari told them, his hand resting possessively on her shoulder. "Perhaps some of you will grow up to be librarians yourselves."

The idea seemed to excite them tremendously, and they scampered off, chattering about books and adventures.

She moved to hand the gifts off to an attendant who had been summoned.

"I have something for you too," Claire said, approaching with a leather-bound volume. "Though I fear it can't compete with crayon artwork."

Leah accepted the book curiously. Inside, she found pages filled with handwritten notes, sketches, and small keepsakes—brief messages from each member of their inner circle, recounting memories and moments they'd shared with her. Claire had documented her journey from newcomer to beloved friend, from nervous Earth girl to confident Dragonwall woman.

"So you'll always remember how far you've come," Claire explained, "and how many people love you here."

"You're going to make me cry, and Desaree will murder me if I ruin my makeup," she warned, hugging her friend carefully, mindful of her belly. "Thank you. For everything. For dragging me here, for believing in me—"

"For introducing you to tall, dark, and scaly over there?" Claire teased.

"That too," Leah laughed, wiping at her eyes.

The celebration continued around them. Dallin and Jamie approached, their own bonding still fresh.

"From one unconventional pair to another," Dallin said with a grin, "may your bond bring you as much joy as ours has brought us."

Jamie smiled shyly. "And thank you for believing in my stories. The new collection couldn't have happened without you."

"Our readers would riot if we didn't stock Captain Drake adventures," she said honestly. Jamie's tales had become the most requested books in all three libraries.

As the night progressed, she noticed Taylynn and Koldis slipping away from the celebration, exchanging secretive smiles. There was something different about Taylynn tonight—a subtle glow that made Leah wonder if Claire wasn't the only one carrying.

Hours passed in a whirlwind of music and dancing. The snow continued to fall outside, casting an enchanted glow over everything. It was perfect—more perfect than she could have imagined when she'd first decided on a winter solstice ceremony.

Eventually, Jovari pulled her aside. "It's traditional," he said, voice husky and low, "for the newly bonded pair to retire before the celebration ends."

Her pulse jumped into overdrive. "Is it?"

"Indeed." His fingers traced a path down her arm that left

goosebumps in their wake. "And I find myself eager to honor that particular tradition."

Heat bloomed in her cheeks and spread downward. Despite their previous intimacy—they had, after all, been sharing a bed for months—tonight was different. Tonight, she'd invite him into her body completely. They would be truly, completely bonded in every way.

"Well, we certainly wouldn't want to break tradition," she managed, her voice suddenly breathless.

They made their goodbyes quickly, enduring knowing looks and ribald teasing. Claire hugged her tightly, whispering, "Have fun."

The journey from the throne room to Jovari's chambers seemed to take forever, yet ended too soon. By the time they reached the door, the anticipation was almost painful. While she'd originally had Claire's old chambers, she'd been slowly moving her things to Jovari's. They'd agreed that they would settle in his, rather than hers. She liked all of his personal touches, things he'd acquired over decades, and she'd started to make her own mark too. Mostly in the form of stacks of books and increased number of bookshelves.

Inside, the room had been transformed. Fresh flowers scented the air, and dozens of candles cast a warm glow over everything. The bed was turned down, scattered with blue rose petals.

"Nervous?" he asked, closing the door behind them.

"A little," she admitted. "Even though we've done...stuff before."

He cupped her face in his hands, his callused palms rough against her skin. "After tonight, there's no going back. We'll be joined in a way that can never be undone."

"Good," she whispered. "Because I don't want to go back. I want this. I want you."

His pupils dilated at her words, briefly shifting to draconic slits. "Then let me help you out of this beautiful gown before I tear it off you."

"Yes, please," she breathed.

His fingers found the clasps at her back, deftly undoing them one by one. The fabric loosened, then fell away, pooling at her feet in a swirl of midnight blue and silver. She stepped out of it, now wearing only a thin silk shift that left little to the imagination.

"Gods, you're beautiful," he breathed, eyes roving hungrily over her body.

She reached for the ties of his formal tunic, working them open with less grace but equal enthusiasm. Soon, they stood before each other nearly bare, the candlelight playing across their skin.

When he lifted her into his arms and carried her to the bed, she went willingly, heart thundering against her ribs. His kiss was tender at first, but quickly turned hungry, months of restraint finally abandoned. Their hands explored with new urgency, each touch igniting a trail of fire along Leah's skin.

"I've wanted you since I first saw you," he murmured against her throat. "Pink-haired and defiant, challenging everything you encountered—including me. Maybe that's why I told you to stay home that night. I knew, even then, you were going to change my life. It terrified me."

She arched into his touch as his hand cupped her breast. "How about now, do I still terrify you?"

"In the best godsdamed way." His teeth grazed her collarbone, making her gasp.

Words became increasingly difficult as his hands and mouth staked their claim, drawing sounds from her she'd never made with anyone else. They had already learned each other's bodies, but the intensity was different—heightened by the knowledge of what was to come. Not just with sex, but the joining of their minds.

There had been tastes of it before, during their flights together. Extended periods of time where she got to share his mind and he got to share hers. But those had been fleeting. This, what was to come, it would be permanent. Forever.

He wasted no time in exploring between her thighs, first with his fingers and then his mouth, until she was bucking desperately. Begging for more. "I like that word on your lips," he teased, coming up for air. "Please. I wouldn't mind hearing it more often."

She growled at him and he took that as his cue to give in.

Their bodies joined in a familiar dance. As he sank into her, she came alive. The rising pleasure he'd stoked turned to an inferno. She cried out and he stilled, waiting for her to adjust before he began moving. His eyes remained locked with hers, reading everything through her expression. Through the sounds she made. His breaths came faster, his expression turning frantic. Gods, she loved what she did to him. She was his undoing.

She ran her hands up and down his back until she found his backside and squeezed.

She felt the moment his control snapped, when he took both of her hands and pinned them to the bed, growling. "Enough of that or this will be over before it starts."

Her laugh came out breathless and he kissed her. Their mouths dueled at the same frantic rate as their bodies as he picked up speed. And then she was racing towards the edge of a precipice, throwing herself over it. Pleasure exploded from her core as she cried out. As Jovari followed her over, falling with her.

Her emotions swelled. At first, she thought it was the aftermath. The overwhelming feel of having him inside her. But the feeling blossomed. She gasped. "I can feel you," she breathed aloud.

"Well that's good, little minx," he drawled, rocking his hips to prove a point. "I would have wondered how you had managed to come if you hadn't."

"Jovari!" She pinched his nipple and he growled. His thoughts wrapped around hers, mingling.

"*That* was not very nice," he chided. "Shall I teach you a lesson in being nice?" He took her arms again, pinning her wrists to the bed. Then he began to move anew.

"Again?" She gaped at him, her lips parted. She saw his every intention, plain as day.

"I have an insatiable appetite for one specific female," he explained. But he needn't have. She could feel the swell of his desire in their shared connection. Feel how badly he wanted her, even after just having had her.

"I think I find that I, too, have quite the appetite." With that, she squirmed free. He let her, when he saw what she had in mind. She pushed him to the bed and straddled his waist.

What passed were several hours where they slaked their hunger and thirst in each other's bodies. She had never felt such perfect unity. She finally understood what it meant to be someone's mate. Not just a partner or lover, but a genuine extension of oneself—separate, yet forever connected.

When they eventually lay together, limbs tangled, breaths slowing, she nuzzled against him, wanting to get closer, impossibly closer.

"Is it always going to be like this?"

He hummed. "Yes. Probably more so with time. That's what it means to be mated."

She turned the ring on his finger, the silver catching the candlelight. "A connection that never ends."

Outside, the rare snow continued to fall, blanketing Kastali Dun in white on the longest night of the year. But wrapped in Jovari's arms with their minds and hearts completely entwined, Leah had never felt more warm, more sure, or more home.

EPILOGUE: TWELVE

Talon continued to pace. The storm outside mirrored the one within him. Thunder cracked, rattling the windows of their bedchamber as he prowled from one end to the other, hands clasped tightly behind his back. Every single one of Claire's cries sent a physical pain straight through his chest. Their bond meant that her suffering was his own.

"You're wearing a path in the floor," Essie said firmly. The human midwife had delivered hundreds of babies in her decades of service to Kastali Dun. Her gray hair was pulled into a severe bun, and her weathered face showed little patience for his pacing. "*And* you're making everyone nervous."

He shot her a dark look but stilled his movements. The best midwives in Dragonwall stood assembled around his mate—Essie with her practical knowledge, Hedra who specialized in drengr births, and Lunara, a spriten midwife he'd specifically requested from Esterpine. He'd spent months researching, questioning, investigating to ensure the very best care for Claire and their child. And yet, for all his preparation, he felt utterly helpless.

Claire's face contorted with pain from another contraction.

Her golden hair lay damp against her forehead, her skin flushed. Her grip on the bedsheets tightened until her knuckles turned white. The pain flowed through their bond, and he clenched his jaw against the echo of it, sending her one reassuring thought after the next. Telling her how perfect she was. How much he loved her. Even if she snipped at him each time.

Another contraction passed, as did her ire, and she gave him a weary smile. "It's all right," she breathed.

He was at her side instantly, taking her hand. "No, it's not. I should be able to help somehow."

"You are helping. You're here."

Lunara approached with a small cup of something steaming. "Drink, *Ayas Drollaya*. It will provide strength."

Claire obediently sipped the herbal mixture. Taylynn hovered nearby, her expression unusually concerned. She'd arrived just after Claire's labor had begun, because somehow she always knew when she would be needed. They'd learned of Taylynn's pregnancy a few months prior, shortly after Leah and Jovari's bonding ceremony. It had been a joyous discovery. No doubt the spriten queen was cataloging this moment, taking notes for when her own child arrived.

He pressed his lips to Claire's temple, breathing in her scent. It had changed during her pregnancy—richer, warmer, with something uniquely their child mixed in.

"You are the strongest person I've ever known," he whispered against her skin.

She let out a pained laugh. "Even if I can barely breathe."

"Even if." He placed his hand on her rounded belly.

Another contraction seized her. She cried out, clutching his hand so fiercely that if he had been human, she would have broken bones. He felt her pain spike through their bond, and a growl built in his chest—instinctive, protective, useless.

"I'm here. Take my strength." He pushed against her mind, knowing it was pointless. He could not shoulder this pain for her. He hated that.

"How long?" he demanded of Essie when Claire collapsed back against the pillows, panting.

The midwife glanced up from where she was examining Claire. "Babies come when they're ready, Your Majesty."

His lip curled at the non-answer. "That's not what I asked."

"Talon," Claire murmured. "Don't frighten the midwives away. We need them."

Hedra, the stoic older woman who'd helped deliver drengr children before, merely raised an eyebrow at his display of temper. "Progress can take time for a first birth, Your Majesty. But I suspect before the sun sets."

It felt like an age away.

Another hour passed in this rhythm—Claire weathering contractions while he stood helplessly beside her, the midwives checking and preparing, Taylynn offering quiet support. Eventually, Claire asked about the others.

"They're all still waiting," he told her. "Desaree is wearing a path in the floor out there. Leah's been reading the same page of her book for an hour. Jovari had Tess prepare food for everyone."

Claire smiled weakly. "And Saffra?"

"Resting. Bedelth is hovering even worse than I am, if you can believe it."

Her lips quirked. "With good reason."

Because Saffra had discovered her own pregnancy just weeks ago.

Between contractions, he murmured, "We received word yesterday. Another pair are expecting their second child."

Claire's eyes widened, then filled with tears. "I get emotional every time," she whispered. "Isabella's curse is truly broken."

This was their third missive. They'd requested that drengr-rider pairs inform them if they encountered second pregnancies. It was a way to track how successful she'd been reversing the curse. Three so far. It was incredible. Three in less than a year. There were so few pairs, especially at Fort Kastali and Fort Squall after Kane and Oshea. Especially compared to the numbers Dragonwall had seen back in the early days.

Talon brushed damp hair back from her forehead. "I know this is difficult, but I'm grateful that it won't be our only time experiencing this miracle."

He couldn't imagine what it was like for pairs, knowing that witnessing the birth of their child was a once in a lifetime occurrence. That they had to cherish every moment, knowing it would never happen again.

"If you think I'm doing this again anytime soon—" She broke off as another contraction hit.

He could only murmur soothing words against her skin.

The hours blurred. Twice, he stepped out briefly to update their friends. The first time, he found them in various states of anxiety. Dallin and Jamie stood by the window, hands clasped. Verath paced while Desaree watched him worriedly. Bedelth sat with his arm around Saffra, whose hand rested on her still-flat stomach. Their eyes met in silent understanding—expectant fathers, though Bedelth was somewhere around eight months behind him in the journey.

The second time he emerged, Koldis immediately pressed a cup of liquor into his hand. "You look terrible," he said bluntly.

He drained the cup in one swallow, feeling it burn down his throat. "She's in pain," he growled. "And I can't stop it."

Reyr, ever practical, said, "Is there anything we can do?"

He shook his head. "Just wait."

When he returned to the bedchamber, things had progressed. Lunara and Taylynn stood on either side of the bed, sprinkling sacred water from the king tree while singing in Ednuar. The melody and its words washed over him, easing some of the tension in his shoulders.

"What is this?" he asked quietly.

"A water blessing," Taylynn replied without breaking rhythm. "To ease her pain and grant the forest's protection to the child."

The next hour passed in a blur of activity. Claire's contractions came faster, stronger. The midwives moved with practiced efficiency. Hedra directed Claire when to push. Essie prepared swaddling clothes. Lunara murmured sprite words of encouragement.

"Would you like to step out, Your Majesty?" Essie suggested at one point.

The look he gave her would have withered a lesser woman. "I will not leave her side."

Claire's grip on his hand tightened painfully. "Don't you dare leave me."

"Never," he promised.

Then suddenly, everything changed. Claire gave one final, powerful push, and the air filled with a new sound—their child's first angry cry.

"A girl!" Hedra announced, lifting the squirming, wet infant.

His heart stopped, then raced. Time seemed to slow as Essie cleaned the baby and placed her in Claire's waiting arms for skin-to-skin contact.

His mate's exhausted face transformed. Despite hours upon hours of labor, she glowed with triumph and love as she looked down at their baby daughter. "Ellia," she whispered. "Ellia Hope."

He could only stare, struck silent by the tiny being they'd created. Dark hair—his—already dusted her perfect little head. He wanted to touch her, but feared that he would hurt her. That his strength would be to much for the tiny infant resting on his mate's chest.

The midwives efficiently tended to Claire while he stood transfixed. Eventually, they finished their work and quietly withdrew, Taylynn and Lunara remaining just outside the door.

"Would you like to hold her?" Claire asked softly.

His throat tightened. "I might break her."

She smiled. "You won't."

Carefully, more carefully than he'd ever done anything in his long life, he took the child from her. "Ellia Hope," he breathed. She felt impossibly light in his arms, impossibly fragile. And yet, she was of his blood, of Claire's blood—sprite and drengr all in one. She would be stronger than anyone he knew.

"She's perfect," he managed, his voice constricted. His eyes watered. He didn't cry, but gods, he was about to.

"She is. And she's ours."

The silence of their regard—his and his daughter's—was powerful. Claire reached up to touch his face, wiping one of the tears from his cheeks.

They remained like that, the three of them alone in their small circle of wonder, until a knock at the door broke the spell.

"They've been waiting for hours," Claire said. "They deserve to meet her."

He reluctantly placed Ellia back in her arms, watching transfixed as she wrapped the baby in a soft blanket, then he went to the door. Their friends looked up expectantly, faces anxious.

"We're ready for you," he said, unable to keep the pride from his voice. "Come meet our daughter."

They filed in quietly, gathering around the bed where Claire sat propped against pillows, holding Ellia. Desaree immediately burst into tears. Leah beamed. The shields tried—and failed—to maintain stoic expressions.

"Her name is Ellia Hope," Claire told them.

"Ellia. After the first spriten queen," Taylynn said approvingly. Koldis stood behind her, peering over her shoulder, his arms wrapped around her waist, a hand resting protectively on her belly.

"And the hope she brings to Dragonwall," Talon added.

Jovari elbowed Dallin and Verath. "Pay up. I told you it would be a girl."

"I hate when you're right," Dallin grumbled, reaching for his coin purse.

Claire's smug smile answered all of them. She'd been insisting for months that they were having a daughter. That was the way of spriten queens, even if she'd given the title to Taylynn.

"When she's a bit older, I'll teach her to use a bow," Saffra said, leaning closer to see the baby's face.

"And I'll teach her to spar," Bedelth added.

"You'll do no such thing until she's at least ten," Claire retorted with mock indignation.

Everyone laughed, and the tension that had filled the tower all day finally dissipated. Their friends took turns offering congratulations and making increasingly outlandish promises about what they would teach Ellia as she grew.

Claire's spriten guards each placed a blossom within Ellia's cradle, for when it was time to put her to bed. A spriten tradition. A flower that would remain in bloom throughout the child's infancy. They offered their own spriten blessings.

Gods, he'd never been so happy, except, perhaps, on his bonding day.

He watched Claire's face as she glowed despite her exhaustion. His chest felt too small to contain the emotions surging through him—pride, love, fierce protectiveness, and something else. Something like awe at the miracle they'd created.

He noticed Taylynn standing slightly apart from the others, her eyes fixed on Ellia with an unusual intensity. When she felt his gaze, she looked up. "The forest has known of her coming since before she was born." Taylynn murmured. "When her magic manifests, the forest will call her home."

Before he could ask what the princess meant, Ellia began to fuss. Taking it as their cue, their friends started to withdraw, each offering final congratulations.

The midwives slipped back in to help guide Claire on proper feeding techniques, and ensure she had everything she needed going forward. He could only watch in reverence.

When they were alone again, Claire sighed deeply. "Would you take her? I can barely keep my eyes open."

He carefully lifted Ellia from Claire's arms, cradling her against his chest. "Sleep, *kiya cralla*. You've earned it."

Little heart. Because while Claire was his heart, she was his little heart, and she would always be.

Claire smiled drowsily, already drifting off. "Stay with us?"

"Always."

He settled onto the bed beside the woman he loved, watching over his mate and child as they slipped into sleep. Ellia's tiny hand had worked free of her swaddling and now curled reflexively around his finger. Her grip was surprisingly strong.

Outside, the storm had passed. Moonlight streamed through

the windows, bathing the room in silver. In this perfect stillness, he made a silent vow to his daughter: to protect her, to teach her, to love her more fiercely than he'd ever loved anything except her mother.

There would be challenges ahead, as there always was with royal children. But she would never face those challenges alone. She had them. She had their friends, who were more family than anything. She had all of Dragonwall.

Ellia Hope. Their daughter. Their future.

He gazed down at her sleeping face on his chest and whispered, "May your wings grow strong, your fire burn bright, and your heart remain true."

In her sleep, Ellia's fingers tightened around his, as if she heard and understood every word.

EPILOGUE: THIRTEEN

Reyr caught the scent of the northern wilderness—pine trees, wild herbs, and the distinct sharpness of mountain air. Below, rolling hills unfolded, streams cutting silver paths through valleys of grassy hills. Northedge's watchtowers appeared on the horizon, stark against the morning sky.

Merrian shifted against his back. Her thighs tightened around his scales before relaxing. Six months riding dragonback had changed her. No more wobbling, no more death grips on the harness.

"Almost there."

"Thank the gods. My legs are killing me."

He huffed, smoke puffing from his nostrils. *"My spine is perfectly formed."*

"Says the dragon, not the rider."

Reyr banked right, adjusting his approach. Things between them were so different now. The fruit from the king tree had changed everything—giving them a bond like mates, letting thoughts slip between them as easily as breathing. More importantly, it bound their lifespans together. She might have been a mage, but mages didn't usually live as long as the drengr. And while he had several hundred years behind him, he still had many more to go. It was an unexpected gift he would cherish.

Below, guards scattered as Reyr circled Fort Edge's courtyard. He felt Merrian tense through their bond.

"*Worried?*"

"*It's been decades since I last saw this place.*"

He understood. Tomorrow they'd visit her village. The place she'd lost her entire family to plague. The place that had played a role in shaping her.

"*You don't have to do this. We can skip the village and focus solely on Northedge and its people.*"

Her hands tightened on the harness. "*No. I need to.*"

Reyr landed with a thud that sent guards scrambling. Lord Averaen and Evelyn waited as Merrian slid from his back. Reyr transformed immediately, scales shimmering into skin, clothing materializing with the shift.

"Reyr." Averaen stepped forward, clasping his arm. Though his hair had gone completely silver, his grip remained firm as iron-wood. "Good to see you."

"And you, my lord." The respect came naturally after so many years.

"Liar," Averaen laughed. "But I appreciate it."

They'd seen each other less than a year ago, when Averaen and Evelyn had traveled south for Dallin's bonding ceremony.

Evelyn moved forward to embrace Merrian. "My dear, you look exhausted."

"Completely exhausted."

"Then let's get you settled. Come."

He felt relief wash through Merrian as the fort leaders led them through the fort.

Evelyn stopped before a large door, pushing it open to reveal spacious quarters with a wide bed and a steaming bath already drawn. Her smile held no surprise or judgment—clearly, everyone understood their relationship by now. The king tree's fruit wasn't common knowledge, but among the inner circle, their bond was accepted as fact.

"Thank you," Reyr said, noting the thoughtful touches like fresh flowers by the window, and extra blankets. He deposited their travel supplies that Merrian had removed from his harness before he'd transformed.

"We'll leave you to settle in," Evelyn said before disappearing.

After she left, Merrian raised an eyebrow. "Not even pretending to give us separate rooms anymore, are they?"

"Six months traveling together. I'd say the secret's out."

She shook her head, lips quirking. Then she reached for him, pulling him fully into their room. "Bath first," she said, voice low, "then dinner."

Reyr closed the door behind them. The steaming tub waited in the corner, water still fresh and hot. Merrian stood before him, fingers already working at the ties of her traveling clothes.

"Help me?" she asked, turning to present the remaining laces.

Heat spread through him as his fingers worked the knots, brushing against her skin with each movement. It took mere seconds before he was hard and ready for her. Six months together, and still this—the simple act of untying laces—quickened his pulse. When the dress loosened, she turned back to face him, letting it pool at her feet.

"Your turn," she murmured.

After his clothes were removed, they tumbled into the bath together, a tangle of limbs and hungry kisses. She straddled him, and managed to splash out more water than they saved. But it was worth it, every moment, to feel her stretched around him.

Afterward, they rushed to finish washing. He had to heat the water twice more with magic to ensure they didn't shiver throughout.

Eventually, they were cleaned and dressed and presentable.

~

"Have you any word from Dallin?" Reyr asked, breaking apart a freshly baked roll. Given that they hadn't spent too long in any one location, it was nearly impossible to receive letters.

Evelyn beamed. "He writes every few weeks. He and Jamie have settled nicely together."

"The king appointed him to help train some of the new guards in the barracks," Averaen added, pride evident.

"A good fit," Reyr nodded. "His fighting technique is excellent —trained by Verath, you know."

"I never imagined—" Averaen paused, voice catching. "I wish he would have told us of his preferences before leaving. I hate that he thought we wouldn't support him. But...I'm glad he told us eventually."

"He was scared—and young."

"Indeed." Averaen nodded. "It all worked out. If he hadn't gone to the capital, he wouldn't have found Jamie."

"Claire's reversal of Isabella's curse changed everything," Merrian said softly.

"To Queen Claire," Averaen raised his glass.

They drank in unison, northern wine warming Reyr's throat.

"And Ellia Hope?" Evelyn asked. "Seven months now, isn't she?"

"And surely stealing hearts everywhere," Merrian smiled, though it was sad. That was one thing they had sacrificed to come on this trip. But it was better to do it now, during Ellia's first year, then when she grew older and had the ability to remember them, and notice their absence.

"She's probably driving Batty mad," Reyr added. "That cat's never shared Claire's attention before."

"What of Saffra's baby?" Averaen asked.

"A couple more months," Merrian answered. "I'm sure Bedelth's beside himself with worry. He was when we left, and she was only at the start of her pregnancy."

Few knew of Taylynn's pregnancy. She had remained in the forest after Claire's delivery. If all went well, she should have given birth a few months prior. They wouldn't know for certain how everything had gone until returning home.

Conversation flowed easily as they shared stories of their journey—cities they'd helped after Kane's occupation, villages with new healing centers, reformed shelters, and corrupt officials exposed. Six months had yielded impressive results, though they'd covered barely half the kingdom.

"You've accomplished so much," Averaen commented, setting down his goblet. "When the king wrote and mentioned your planned tour, I doubted two people could manage it."

"Being a king's shield helps," Reyr admitted. "But Merrian deserves all the credit. She sees what's truly needed—not the facade officials present. It's her thorough planning that gets it done."

Color touched Merrian's cheeks. "I just point out problems. Reyr convinces stubborn lords to part with coin. Talon helps to match it with the capital's coffers."

"A formidable partnership," Evelyn said, her smile knowing.

Reyr felt Merrian's exhaustion leaking through their bond. Six straight days flying had drained her, and tomorrow would tax her emotionally. Their dinner was drawing to a close, the food long gone.

"I think it's time for us to turn in for the night," he said, rising. "Tomorrow will come too early."

Averaen nodded. "Of course. Rest well."

Once they were tucked away inside their sleeping chamber, he turned to her.

"Are you sure about tomorrow?" he asked, watching her finger trace patterns on the glass as she gazed out the window, looking over the courtyard below.

"No," she admitted. "But it's time to stop running."

He came up to stand behind her, giving her space. "Whatever you feel tomorrow, it's valid."

She turned, reaching for him. He pulled her close, her head resting against his chest. They stood silent, her heartbeat steadying against his.

"Are we making a difference?" she asked, voice muffled by his tunic. "All these cities, all these reforms...will they last?"

"Yes." He drew back to meet her gaze. "Every shelter reformed, every healing center—they continue after we leave. You've trained people who will carry on. It endures, Merrian."

She rose on tiptoes, pressing a gentle kiss to his lips. "Thank you for agreeing to come here."

"It matters to you," he said simply. "That's enough."

They undressed and he led her to bed, holding her close, listening to her gentle breaths after she drifted off to sleep.

The next morning brought clear skies—perfect flying weather. They broke their fast with Averaen and Evelyn before preparing to leave for Merrian's village.

"You're sure you don't want horses?" Averaen asked. "It's not far."

"Better to get there quickly," Merrian replied, fastening her cloak. "Dawdling will only make me more anxious."

Reyr transformed in the courtyard, his golden scales catching the morning light. Merrian mounted with practiced ease. Within moments, they were airborne, Fort Edge shrinking behind them.

"*Head east-southeast,*" she directed. "*There's a river. The village sits on the northern bank.*"

Reyr banked, adjusting course. The wilderness gave way to farmland, neat squares of plowed fields interspersed with autumn-colored woods.

"*How long?*" he asked. "*Since you've been back?*"

Her pause stretched. "*Sixty-seven years.*"

Nearly half a century. For a drengr, sixty-seven years wasn't so long. For a human, it represented most of a lifetime.

Reyr remembered their dungeon conversation, when she'd first spoken about her past. How plague swept through their small village, claiming her family one by one. How she'd been away, training as a healer, and hadn't heard a word of their passing until well after they'd been gone. How they'd been too poor to afford mage healing.

Reyr adjusted his flight path, descending gradually. Ahead, a collection of buildings came into view—Merrian's village, undoubtedly changed since she'd left.

"*It's smaller than I remember,*" she thought, surprise evident.

As they circled, Reyr counted maybe thirty structures gathered around a central square, with scattered farmhouses in surrounding fields. A wooden bridge spanned the river, connecting to a road toward Northedge.

He landed in a meadow outside the village, not wanting to cause panic. Merrian dismounted, her anxiety spiking through their bond.

"*I'm here,*" he assured her as he transformed. "*Every step.*"

She nodded, squaring her shoulders. "Let's go."

They walked in silence toward the settlement. Curious faces peered from windows as they passed. They weren't so far from the city, but to have a drengr in their midst was likely unsettling.

Merrian moved with purpose despite her uncertainty. The village had changed, but she found her bearings at the square. A stone well stood at its center, surrounded by a small market. A modest inn occupied one corner, sign creaking in the breeze.

"This is all different," she murmured. "The well was near the southern edge when I lived here."

An elderly man sitting outside the inn squinted at them. "Haven't seen a drengr here in decades," he commented, gap-toothed smile spreading. "They usually fly right over and ignore the likes of us."

Reyr grunted.

"What brings you here?"

"My companion," Reyr gestured to Merrian. "She once lived here."

The old man studied her with new interest. "Been a while, has it?"

"A very long while," Merrian replied. "I doubt anyone would remember me."

"You'd be surprised what these old eyes recall," the man cackled. "What family name did you carry?"

Merrian hesitated. "Voss. My father was Erian Voss."

Recognition lit the weathered face. "Voss? All taken by the fever back when I was just a lad."

Merrian stiffened. "You remember them?"

"Aye, though I was young then. Ten or twelve, maybe." He scratched his chin. "Your folk lived in the cottage near the east bend, didn't they? With the herb garden out front?"

"Yes." Merrian's voice had gone quiet. "That's right."

"Still standing, though only just," the old man said. "Nobody's lived there since. Folk say it's haunted." He shrugged. "Nonsense, if you ask me."

Reyr placed a hand at the small of Merrian's back, feeling tension run through her.

"Could you point us in that direction?" he asked.

"Just follow the river east," the old man gestured. "Past the mill. Only cottage with blue shutters still hanging."

Merrian nodded tightly before continuing, her pace quickening as they left the square. He knew that she already remembered the way. The old man's directions were merely a formality. He kept stride beside her, saying nothing but maintaining his presence through their bond.

They reached the eastern edge quickly. A small cottage stood back from the riverbank, partially hidden by overgrown bushes. Though clearly abandoned, it remained intact—stone walls weathered but standing, thatched roof patched in places, and faded blue shutters still clinging to windows.

Merrian stopped at the edge of what had once been a garden, now nothing but tangled weeds and herbs gone wild. Her breath came in short, shallow gasps.

"I can't—" she started, voice breaking.

"You can," Reyr said quietly. "But you don't have to go inside."

She shook her head. "No. I need to see it."

The door hung ajar, hinges rusted. Merrian pushed it open, the creak setting Reyr's teeth on edge. Inside, dust motes danced in the dim light filtering through dirty windows. A table and chairs remained, a broken bed frame in one corner, remnants of what might have been a cupboard.

Merrian stood in the center, turning slowly. Her face showed nothing, but through their bond Reyr felt a whirlwind—grief so keen it made his chest tight, regret like a physical weight, and something unexpected. Relief.

"It's smaller than I remembered," she said finally, voice steadier than expected. "So much smaller."

"You were practically a child when you left."

"Yes." She moved to the far wall, where crude markings remained visible—children's heights at different ages. "Look. Espen was just starting to catch up to me." Her fingers traced a mark labeled with a childish "E."

Reyr stayed silent, giving her space.

"I've spent years blaming myself." Her voice dropped to a whisper. "When my magic showed, we thought I would be my family's salvation. I left to train as a mage. No word was ever sent, that they were sick. I often wondered if...if I had been here, if my magic could have done...something. I don't know."

"You were a child," Reyr reminded her. "Untrained. Do you truly believe that, knowing what you know about healing?"

"I... I don't know. I guess I always expected more from myself." The words cut with decades-old pain.

"Merrian. It wasn't your failure," he continued, wiping a tear with his thumb. "It was a tragedy. One of many in this cruel world."

"I know," she whispered. "Logically, I know. But standing here..." She gestured around the empty cottage. "It all comes rushing back."

Reyr drew her into his arms, holding her as silent sobs shook her frame. Through their bond, he sent waves of comfort, understanding, love. Yes, love—he'd finally admitted it to himself. Somewhere between resentment and respect, between shared captivity and shared purpose, he'd fallen completely in love with this remarkable woman.

They stood like that for long minutes, her breaths gradually slowing.

"I think," she said finally, voice muffled against his chest, "I've carried this too long. This guilt. This idea that I should have saved them."

"Yes," he agreed simply.

She pulled back, looking up with reddened eyes. "Does it ever stop hurting? Losing everyone?"

The raw honesty pierced him. He thought of his mate, lost centuries ago, and the hollow ache that had lived in his chest for so long he'd almost forgotten what it felt like to be whole. He thought of his parents. Of his twin, Davi, and Davi's mate, Emmy.

"No," he said truthfully. "But it changes. Becomes something you carry rather than something that carries you."

She nodded, understanding. "Thank you for coming. I couldn't have done this alone."

"You won't have to do anything alone again," he promised. "Not while I breathe."

They lingered a moment before Merrian moved toward the door. "I'm ready to leave now."

As they exited, Reyr spotted an elderly woman watching from the path, silver hair caught in a loose braid.

"Pardon," she called. "Terril at the inn said the Voss girl returned."

Merrian tensed. "Yes, I—I grew up here."

The woman's face broke into a gentle smile. "I thought so. You have your mother's eyes."

"You knew my mother?" Merrian's voice caught.

"Oh yes. Liena Voss." The woman nodded. "She was a good midwife. She delivered my oldest baby. Saved him when the cord wrapped around his neck." She paused. "I'm Petra. I was a decade older than you, I think. Five years married when the fever came."

"Petra?" Recognition dawned. "Petra Holman? You lived across the square?"

"Petra Wycrest now, but yes." Her smile widened. "Never thought I'd see any Voss family again. After you left, we assumed..."

"I finished my training in Northedge and then left for the capital. I've been there since, helping others. Others who need it."

Petra nodded. "Liena would be proud."

Merrian's breath hitched, but she managed a tremulous smile. "Thank you for saying that."

"Would you take tea with me?" Petra gestured toward a cottage just visible in the distance. "I've stories about your mother you might like to hear."

Reyr felt Merrian hesitate through their bond. "*Whatever you want,*" he thought. "*We have time.*"

Merrian looked up at him, then back to Petra. "I'd like that. Just for a little while."

As they followed Petra to her home, Reyr sensed a shift in Merrian's emotions. Grief's sharp edges softening, making space for something new. Not healing, exactly. Some wounds never completely healed. But perhaps acceptance. The beginning of peace. It was so much more than he could have hoped for. It was everything.

EPILOGUE: FOURTEEN

Kastali Dun

Ellia withheld a groan of delight. The scent of caramel and cinnamon wafted through the air, making her mouth water. Tess had outdone herself with the desserts for tonight's feast—honey cakes with crystallized sugar, apple tarts still bubbling from the oven, and her personal favorite, caramel-dipped sweet rolls drizzled with cinnamon and nuts.

"El, you're drooling," Cyrus whispered, nudging her with his elbow. His silver eyes—identical to their father's—glinted with mischief despite his otherwise serious demeanor. With his dark hair and strong jawline, at twelve he was already catching the eyes of girls his age.

"Am not," she hissed back, quickly wiping her mouth just in case. "And keep your voice down or they'll hear us."

They were crouched behind one of the massive storage barrels in the shadowy corner of the cookery. The perfect vantage point to observe the bustling kitchen staff as they prepared for tonight's feast. To celebrate her mother's third pregnancy. Third! She was going to have another sibling, on top of her twin brothers. She wasn't sure how to feel about that.

"I still think this is a terrible idea," Micah said from her other side, pushing his golden hair out of his eyes. Unlike his twin, Micah had inherited their mother's coloring—fair hair and vibrant green eyes that always seemed to be dancing with some private amusement.

Ellia unconsciously traced the luminescent marking that curved across her right wrist—the only visible testament to her spriten blood. It had appeared last year when she'd begun her transition into womanhood, after she'd accidentally gotten irritated and grew an entire rosebush in the corridor outside her room. To block her mother from entering. The mark had appeared immediately afterward, accompanied by a minor stinging sensation to announce its presence. Needless to say, her mother had quickly dispensed of the bush, oversized thorns and all, and instead of being angry, had rejoiced.

"Don't be such a whispertoes," Ellia hissed, using her favorite made-up insult for her more cautious brother. "Besides, if we get caught, Father will just make us train with Aunt Saffra for a month."

"Says the only one of us who can actually keep up with her at archery," Cyrus muttered.

"It's not my fault I've got superior skills."

"More like superior cheating," Micah scoffed. "You've got sprite magic."

"I don't use magic when we're training," she insisted, though truthfully, she wasn't entirely sure. Sometimes things just...happened when she got excited. Or irritated. Or...anything, really. Objects would move, plants would suddenly bloom, water would ripple without being touched. It was one of the reasons her parents kept insisting she needed proper training. Ugh. She knew exactly what that meant. *No thank you.*

"Focus," Cyrus whispered. "Tess just went into the other room. This is our chance."

Ellia nodded, calculating the distance between their hiding spot and the cooling rack where the sweet rolls sat, practically begging to be stolen. If only her magic would actually do what she wanted it to, which would be, make a few of those caramel dipped rolls disappear, and reappear in her waiting hands. Alas...

"On my signal," she whispered. "One...two—"

"And just what do you three think you're doing?!" The voice, aged but commanding, made all three royal children freeze in place. Tess towered over them in her billowing kirtle, wooden spoon in hand, her gray hair tucked neatly beneath her cap. Deep lines fanned from the corners of her eyes as she fixed them with her most fearsome glare.

"Princess Ellia Hope. Are you leading your brothers into mischief again?" Ellia's mouth popped open to protest, but she wasn't given time. "Prince Cyrus, Prince Micah. Sneaking about my cookery with your sister? You should both know better!"

Ellia straightened to her full height, recovering and flashing her most innocent smile. "Aunt Tess! We were just...admiring your culinary artistry." She lifted her chin, trying her very best to appear princess-like. "The desserts look absolutely divine today."

Tess raised a single gray eyebrow. "Is that so? And I suppose you were admiring them with your fingers, not just your eyes?"

"We wouldn't dream of touching anything," Micah said, his voice dripping with false sincerity.

"Absolutely not," Cyrus added, attempting to look dignified despite the flour that had somehow found its way onto his sleeve.

Tess wagged her wooden spoon, advancing on them slowly. "Out! All three of you troublemakers, out of my cookery this instant before I inform the king and queen that their children are nothing but common sweet-thieves!"

They began backing away, but Ellia's hip caught on the edge of a low table laden with prepped ingredients. She stumbled, grabbing Micah's arm to steady herself. What happened next seemed to unfold in slow motion. A peculiar fission of warmth spread from her chest to her fingertips—a sensation she'd felt before, but never learned to control. A faint green glow emanated from her just as a surge of invisible energy pulsed outward.

Every bowl, platter, and utensil within ten feet suddenly launched into the air. Flour exploded in white clouds. Eggs cracked against the ceiling. A bowl of berry compote upended over a chef's head. Knives clattered to the stone floor, narrowly missing the feet of scurrying kitchen staff.

"Gods above!" Tess shrieked, ducking as a tray of pastries flew over her head.

"Oh, gods! Oh, gods! Oh, gods! I—I didn't mean to!" Ellia cried, frantically trying to rein in her magic. She concentrated, straining to pull the energy back into herself, but that only seemed to make things worse. A pot of honey lifted off its warming stand and turned upside down, creating a golden waterfall that splashed across the central preparation table. She began to tremble, big fat tears pooling in her eyes.

"Run!" Cyrus shouted, grabbing both his siblings by their sleeves and dragging them toward the door. She could only numbly let him pull her away, gawking at the absolute mess she'd made.

They burst into the corridor, pursued by Tess's outraged voice: "Your parents will be hearing about this immediately! I've had enough!"

Micah was already laughing as they ran, but Ellia felt sick to her stomach. This was the third incident this month, and by far the most destructive. Her parents were not going to let this slide. Her father, she might be able to convince him, rally him to her side. He'd always had the softest spot for her. But her mother? No. She was done for—absolutely done for.

"Stop laughing!" she snapped at Micah. "It's not funny. Do you have any idea how much trouble we're going to be in?"

"We?" Cyrus said, his expression sobering. "El, that was all you, big sis."

"I didn't do it on purpose!"

"Sounds like your problem, though. Isn't it? We were just... tagging along." Micah's laughter faded.

"Yeah!" Cyrus chimed in. "Besides, you never do it on purpose, but it keeps happening anyway."

Ellia's retort died on her lips as a pair of guards approached from the end of the corridor, doing their rounds.

"Quick, this way," Cyrus said, pulling them down a side corridor. They took a round-about way through the castle. There was no telling how quickly Tess worked. Best to avoid any guards.

It worked out well until ten minutes later, Uncle Verath stepped into their path, his expression grim. "Little terrors. I certainly hope you don't think you can outrun me."

Cyrus's chest puffed up. Verath had always spoiled him rotten and he knew it. "We were just—"

"Having a walk," Micah cut in. "Enjoying the scenery."

"Right. Is that why your parents just issued a castle-wide search and sent all of us to find you?"

"But we're not missing," Cyrus demanded.

Verath sighed. "Enough games. I am here to tell you that—" Verath hesitated, clearing his throat as if to add to the seriousness of the moment. "Your presence is required by the king and queen in their tower. *Immediately*."

The way he emphasized the last word told Ellia everything she needed to know. They were going to be in big, big, *big-big-big* trouble.

"Here we go again," she muttered, unconsciously stroking the spriten mark on her wrist as all three siblings followed Verath toward what would surely be a stern royal reckoning.

Both their parents were waiting. What was worse, they should have been in court. Golden crowns rested atop their brows, making them look more formidable than ever. It was said that drengr and their mates aged ten times more slowly than humans once they reached maturity, and she believed it. Her parents had always looked like adults to her, but as she'd approached womanhood, they'd started looking less...old. More...normal aged? If that made sense. And right now, both of them were glaring.

She swallowed down a gulp, stopping in the middle of the main chamber. Her brothers cowered behind her.

"Come and sit," King Talon said, his voice calm and even. The three of them did as ordered. She sat in the middle, her brothers bracketing her like protectors, even though she was two years older.

"Explain yourselves—no, better yet, just you, Ellia Hope." Her mother stepped forward. She wore a gown of gold and purple. The queen made her frustration clear as she squeezed the bridge of her nose. "I would like to know why we were forced to cancel the remainder of court in the middle of a tense shipping negotiation."

Ellia opened her mouth. Closed it. Then sank lower into the sofa. "It was an accident, I swear. We just...wanted some sweets."

Micah snorted, the dumb traitor.

Because they all knew that as royal children, whatever they asked for would probably be granted, even though her parents tried to ensure everyone in the castle did the opposite. They didn't want their children raised spoiled rotten. Still, most of the staff secretly catered to the royal siblings.

Ellia loved her parents. She really did. She hated disappointing them. Like now. But sometimes the pressure of being a princess overwhelmed her, no matter how badly she wanted to make everyone proud. She'd been born to rule, the first child from an ancient lineage. She wanted to fill her role properly, but sometimes, something inside her rose up and tempted her to rebel.

"Ellia..." King Talon sighed. "I have oft turned a blind eye to your behavior, but this? Destroying the cookery? It is unacceptable." His deep voice resonated through the main tower room. To everyone else, her father was frightening, but not to her. Never to her. His scars were just an ordinary part of his appearance.

She did her best to look appropriately contrite.

"Do you have any idea how disruptive your actions were?" the king continued. "The feast tonight is a way for the kingdom to celebrate your mother—to celebrate our family. Tess and her staff have been preparing for days." He threw a fond look at his mate, who looked both exasperated and concerned. The luminescent markings that covered her body seemed to shimmer with suppressed emotion.

"What were you three thinking?" her mother asked, her green eyes—so like Ellia's own—focused primarily on her daughter.

"It was my idea," Ellia finally admitted, followed by a loud sigh.

There was no point in denying it. "I convinced Cyrus and Micah to come with me. To prove that I could do it—steal the rolls, I mean."

"We didn't cause the magical explosion," Micah added helpfully.

Ellia shot her brother a glare. "Thank you for that clarification, *Micah*."

"Did you use magic deliberately?" Claire asked, her expression clouding with concern.

"No! It just...happened." Her voice dropped. "Again."

Her parents exchanged a meaningful look—one of those silent communications that mates shared through their bond. Ellia had always fought between disgust and envy over that connection, wondering what it would be like to have someone understand your thoughts so completely, but immediately hated the idea that she would have to share herself so openly. *Ugh.*

She might have been fourteen. She might have had "*the talk*," as her mother put it, but she had no interest in...that. Yet. Very well, perhaps she'd imagined it a couple of times. Particularly the mechanics of it. With Rylan, the cute boy in her mage class who was two years older than her. But mostly, she'd just thought about kissing him. And only because she'd seen him kissing Briar after their lessons one day, and it had done really uncomfortable things to her chest.

King Talon sighed deeply. "Ellia, these incidents are becoming more frequent. Just last week, you accidentally made the flowers in the royal garden bloom all at once."

"The gardeners weren't complaining," she muttered.

"And the week before that," Claire added, "you somehow turned the water in the eastern courtyard fountain into ice in the middle of summer because Cyrus splashed you."

"He deserved it," she groused, but there was little heat in her words. She knew where this was heading.

"Ellia," her father said, his voice softening slightly, "we've discussed this before. Your heritage is unique. You have two types of magic in your blood."

"And that magic is growing stronger as your emotions deepen," her mother continued. "Without proper training, these incidents could become more dangerous."

Ellia's stomach clenched. Here it came.

"Your Aunt Taylynn has agreed to begin your formal training in the Gable Forest," Claire said gently. "It's time for you to go to her."

"The forest is calling you home," Talon murmured, a thoughtful look on his face.

"You want to send me away." The words came out sharper than Ellia intended. It hid the fear taking root in her belly.

"Not permanently," her father said. "Just until you learn to control your abilities."

"But you're not sending *them* away, are you?" She pointed at her brothers. "They get to stay here, in Kastali Dun, with their friends and family and everyone they care about."

"That's different," Claire began.

"How is it different?" Ellia's voice rose. "Because they're boys? Because they're not freaks with unpredictable magic?"

"Ellia!" Talon's voice took on the edge that usually silenced even the most argumentative council members. "You know that's not true. Your brothers don't have sprite magic—yet. And until they do, they will remain here."

"Though I'd love some," Micah murmured under his breath, earning an elbow in the ribs from her.

"Why can't you just teach me, Mother?" Her voice softened slightly. "You're the most powerful sprite alive, besides, I guess, Aunt Taylynn."

Claire's expression was gentle. "Sweetheart, it's not just about learning techniques. Sprite magic is connected to the forest itself. It comes from the heart of the forest—from the king tree. To truly master it, you need to be immersed in that world, to feel the energy that flows through the trees and the earth." Her mother's expression morphed, a flash of raw sadness there and gone.

"But you learned to control your magic here, at Kastali Dun," Ellia argued.

"No, I didn't," Claire said quietly. "I had to go to the forest, too.

I spent months training with Pelwynn and even Lord Marquin—Elyon's father."

"Auntie Elyon's father trained you?"

"Yes. Sort of." Claire sighed. "There are some things that simply can't be taught outside the forest."

Ellia's anger faltered momentarily. She could see the understanding in her mother's eyes, the recognition of how painful this separation would be.

"I know it's difficult," Claire said, coming to crouch before her, reaching for her daughter's hand. "I know how much you love your home and your friends. But this is necessary, Ellia. And it's also a rite of passage—connecting with the sprite side of your heritage."

For a moment, Ellia allowed herself to be comforted, squeezing her mother's hand. Then a thought occurred to her, and she pulled away.

"But that was different for you," she said, a hint of her previous defiance returning. "You were an outsider here. You arrived in Dragonwall as an adult. You didn't have to leave behind everything you'd ever known."

Claire's expression tightened almost imperceptibly, and she realized the error of her words, even if she refused to backtrack. Because she'd never met her grandparents. Her mother had painfully left them behind.

Squaring her shoulders, she tried to recover. "Everyone I care about is here. All my friends, my training partners, my tutors. Saffra just started me with the longbow. I'm supposed to begin formal court duties next month! If I'm to be a good ruler someday, my training at court is compulsory. How many years are you planning to exile me to the forest?"

"This isn't exile, Ellia," Talon said firmly. "It's training—of another kind."

"Right. Training that conveniently gets the uncontrollable princess out of the way before she embarrasses you in front of the kingdom." The words tumbled out before she could stop them, sharp with indignation.

Claire's eyes widened in hurt. "Ellia, that's not—"

"Maybe if I was born normal, like Cyrus and Micah, you wouldn't be so eager to ship me off to the forest," Ellia continued, unable to stop now that she'd begun. "Isn't it just *sooo* inconvenient that your daughter is a walking magical disaster? Better hide me away with the sprites for a few years until I'm presentable!"

"That is *enough*!" Talon's voice cut through the room like a blade, his royal authority fully present. She flinched. "You will not speak to your mother that way. This discussion is over. You will depart for the Gable Forest in one week's time, and that is final."

Panic surged through her at her father's tone and the finality of his decree. A week? So soon? The reality of what was happening crashed over her—she would be sent away from her home, separated from everything familiar, pulled from her training. Fear and anger collided inside her chest, a volatile cocktail of emotion that seemed to ignite something deep in her core.

"You can't do this!" she cried, her voice cracking with emotion. "You can't just—"

The words died in her throat as a strange heat bloomed within her, different from anything she'd ever felt before. It wasn't the familiar warmth of her sprite magic but something deeper, more primal. The sensation spread rapidly through her body like dragonfire.

"Ellia?" Claire's voice sounded distant, concerned.

Ellia looked down at her arms in confusion and then horror. Iridescent pricks of color were flickering across her skin, white and black, appearing and vanishing like ripples on water.

...Scales?

"What's... What's happening to me?" she gasped, panic clogging her throat.

The scales were spreading, growing larger and more solid with each passing second. Pain lanced through her shoulderblades and she cried out.

Talon was across the room in a flash, recognition and alarm filling his silver eyes.

"Gods above," he breathed. Then, without hesitation, he swept her into his arms.

"Talon?" Claire's voice was sharp with concern.

"She's shifting," he cried, already moving toward the tower stairs, his daughter cradled against his chest.

Ellia barely registered her brothers' shocked cries or her mother's quick intake of breath. The burning sensation had intensified, becoming almost unbearable as more scales erupted across her skin.

"Hold steady, Ellia. Just for a few more minutes."

"Daddy," she whimpered, suddenly feeling like a small child again. "It hurts."

"I know, little heart," he said, his voice steady despite the urgency in his movements. "Be strong for a few more moments, all right?"

The world blurred. She was vaguely aware of the sound of a door slamming, a narrow stairway, heavy steps. Her body felt strange, as though it were trying to reshape itself from within. Bones ached. Muscles stretched. Her spine seemed to be attempting to elongate beyond the confines of her skin.

And then brightness replaced darkness and she could breathe fresh air. Talon set her down in the center of the garden and stepped back.

"There. Let the transformation come."

The pain crescendoed and she screamed—a sound that began human but ended in a distinctly inhuman roar. Her body convulsed, then expanded as her form grew rapidly. The world tilted dizzily as her perspective changed. Colors shifted, becoming sharper, more vibrant. Scents intensified until she could smell the individual flowers in the garden, the stone of the tower, the distinctive scent of her father nearby.

And then, just as suddenly, the pain vanished.

Ellia blinked, disoriented. She felt...different. Larger. Much larger. And stronger. Her body responded strangely when she tried to move, new muscles and limbs answering her commands imperfectly.

"There now. How do you feel?"

She yelped, or tried to. It came out as a pitiful sound.

"Daddy?"

"I'm here."

Later, she would realize that they were speaking telepathically. That she now had this ability, because she was a drengr. But for now, she was too preoccupied. She looked down at what should have been her hands and saw taloned forelegs covered in white pearlescent scales that shimmered with hints of pink and lavender in the sunlight. When she glanced behind her, she snarled at the sight of black luminescent scales on her lower half. She was, *somehow*, two colors. One blending to the other.

"I'm a freak!" she cried, wanting to wail.

"You are beautiful, that is what you are." Her mother's voice. Because her mother could hear and speak to all dragons. *"Absolutely magnificent."*

"Have you ever seen anything like it?" Talon asked aloud, taking in the way her head and shoulders were pearlescent, fading morphing to black like her father's coloring. Drengr almost never took on the coloring of a parent. They certainly never took two colors so drastically. So opposing.

"The first of her kind, in so many ways." Her mother sounded... proud.

She perked up. *"So I'm...not a freak?"*

"Not even a little," Claire said.

She spun around to try and get a better look at herself, trampling a section of her mother's favorite night flowers. *"Oops. Sorry,"* she managed pitifully.

"Easy," Talon's voice came from somewhere below her as he lifted his arms to calm her. *"Don't panic. Everything's all right."*

Every movement felt awkward. Unnatural. A strange sound escaped her throat—a confused warble that was nothing like human speech.

Her brothers chose that moment to emerge into the garden.

Micah bounded forward, circling Ellia with undisguised excitement.

"This is amazing!" he crowed. "My sister's a dragon! Can I ride you? Can you breathe fire? Do you eat grazers now?"

"Micah," Cyrus chided, though he looked equally fascinated. "Give her some space."

As the initial shock wore off, a thought occurred to Ellia. *"You don't seem that surprised,"* she said to her father, a note of accusation creeping into her mental voice. Females weren't supposed to become dragons...were they? She'd never heard of it in all the history she'd studied. And she'd checked. It was how she'd learned about Princess Lena and what she'd been forced to do—the Tournament for the Crown—all those thousands of years ago. *"Did you know this would happen?"*

Talon's expression grew slightly guilty.

"We...hoped it would," Claire admitted. *"When I reversed Isabella's curse, I knew it would affect future generations of drengr, including the potential for female drengr."*

"And you never told me?" The hurt in her voice was unmistakable.

Talon sighed. *"We didn't want to burden you with expectations that might never be fulfilled."*

"I knew in my heart that I had succeeded, but there was no proof," Claire explained. *"Moreover, you were conceived shortly before the curse was reversed. My guess is, you hadn't had enough time to develop in my womb for Isabella's curse to take effect. Or, perhaps some other magical reason is to blame. We can never know for sure. Ultimately, we had no proof that you would be the first. We've been waiting."* Her mother sighed. *"We wanted you to have a normal childhood without feeling like you were waiting for something that might never come."*

"Did you know about my sprite magic too?" Ellia asked, still processing this revelation.

"Now that we were more certain of," Talon admitted. *"Given your mother's heritage. Spriten queens have daughters first."*

"What else haven't you told me?"

"Nothing important," Talon assured her. *"Just the normal things parents keep from their children until they're ready."*

Claire reached out to stroke Ellia's scaled snout. *"We're sorry we didn't tell you this was a possibility. We wanted to protect you from disappointment if it never happened."*

Ellia considered this, then sighed. She considered the implications. Took things from an unbiased perspective, as she was always being trained to do. At last, she said, *"I understand. It's just... a lot to take in."*

Experimentally, she flexed muscles she'd never flexed before, feeling the massive wings spread from her back. They caught the wind, nearly lifting her off her feet. A very un-draconic squeak left her huge lungs.

"What do I do now? Am I going to fly?!"

"First, you need to learn control," Talon said, his voice calm and instructive. He spoke aloud for the benefit of her little brothers. "The most important skill is learning how to shift back when you need to."

"How do I do that?"

"Focus on your human form. Visualize yourself as you normally are," he instructed. "It's about intent and mental clarity. Picture your hands, your feet, your normal height and perspective."

Ellia tried to concentrate, but her new senses were overwhelming—scents she'd never detected before, sounds that seemed impossibly clear, the feeling of scales where skin should be.

"Don't get distracted by the new sensations," he advised, noticing her wandering attention. "Control comes first, exploration later."

Claire approached, gently touching Ellia's scaled snout. "Take a deep breath, sweetheart. There's no rush."

Ellia nuzzled against her mother's hand, struggling to process the magnitude of what was happening. She was a dragon. She could shift, just like her father and her uncles. It was unprecedented—revolutionary.

And terrifying.

The realization of how much she didn't know—how unprepared she was for this new reality—crashed over her. She had no idea how to control this form, how to shift back, how to manage this new aspect of herself.

She already couldn't control her sprite magic. Now this? It's like the fates were trying to curse her. It wasn't just raining, it was a full on deluge.

As if responding to her surge of anxiety, her body suddenly began to heat again. The world shifted, perspective changing rapidly as her form contracted. Pain lanced through her once more, though less severely than before, and then she was kneeling on the garden floor in her clothing, fully human again.

"Does it always hurt like that?" she croaked.

"No, the pain only occurs the first few times. It will fade. In fact, you probably won't even feel it next time," her father said, coming to crouch beside her. He reached out and tucked a strand of her dark hair—hair just like his—behind her ear. "How do you feel?"

"Okay, I think."

"Good." He took her arm and helped her to stand.

"Now, more than ever, it is important for you to understand yourself, all of yourself," her mother said, reminding her of why this had all happened in the first place. "Starting with your spriten magic."

Ellia looked down at her hands, then touched her wrist where her spriten mark still glowed faintly. She thought about the rush of power she'd felt, the terrifying but exhilarating sensation of becoming something more than human.

"You're right." She hated that. But she had learned years ago that a good ruler was willing to admit when others were right. She glanced around at the trampled flowers and the small bit of destruction she'd wrought. Thank the gods her father had been quick on his toes. She would have demolished the tower. That was what lack of control caused. "I'll have to go train with the sprites."

"Yes." Her father placed a hand on her shoulder. "But just think, now you can fly yourself there. After you learn, that is."

Her chest exploded with excitement. "You're right! Could you... teach me? Before I go?"

"I'll be damned if I allow anyone else to teach my daughter to fly." There was so much fierce pride in his silver eyes that it made her chest ache with love.

"Thank you, Daddy," she whispered, using an endearment

she'd mostly grown out of now, often calling him father instead. She threw her arms around his waist. She was tall for a girl, but even still, her head only came to his chest.

"We will begin tomorrow. Learning to control the shift comes first, then basic wing control, flight positioning..." He trailed off, leaning down to see the excitement in her expression.

"How long will the training take?" she asked, a calculating look in her eye.

"That depends on how quickly you learn," Talon said. "But I promise not to delay unnecessarily. Just until you're truly ready."

"So much for dragging this out," she admitted. Both Talon and Claire huffed at that.

"No dragging it out," Claire said, her voice firm.

"And you'll really let me fly there myself? No escorts?"

"Oh, there will be escorts," Talon countered. "But how about I let you choose them?"

"Really?"

"You are fourteen, Ellia. Much as I hate to admit it—you are growing up."

"Talon," Claire admonished, like he'd spoken a bad word.

"She is. We will let her choose. In exchange for learning to fly as quickly as possible, not drawing it out, and agreeing to go without further complaint, to Esterpine, so that she may learn her magic and return to us stronger and more adept to fulfill her role some day."

A commotion came from the stairwell and then a group of people emerged—some of her favorite people in the whole world. Talon's shields. Claire's guards. Some of the other women she considered family, like Desaree, Jocelyn, Leah, Merrian, and Saffra. Women who had helped raise her.

Talon cleared his throat, noticing that everyone had assembled. Later, she would realize that he'd summoned them. But for now, she just watched warily as Talon put on his *king face*.

"Ellia Hope," he said with quiet pride, "daughter of Dragonwall, first female drengr born in our history. Your journey is just beginning."

Several gasps sounded from the gathered group.

"It's true, then?" Reyr sounded absolutely dazed. She couldn't help the smirk threatening to break free. She loved when the others were surprised. Usually it was because she was getting into trouble —that dark streak breaking free of her propriety—and couldn't believe the lengths she was willing to go to do it. But this time... This was a *much* better way to shock them.

"She transformed before our very eyes," Talon confirmed.

"What color?" Koldis demanded.

"Colors," Claire corrected.

"Colors?" several of them echoed, blinking.

Then, every pair of eyes fixed on her, waiting. Planting her feet, as if about to do battle, she proudly lifted her chin and said, "Black and white. In equal measure."

Her onlookers gaped, stunned. When she glanced up at her father, he winked. Her mother only beamed, radiating with happiness.

Black and white. Light and dark. Just like what she felt inside. A little of both. Two sides. Sides that would hopefully coexist some day, just as they did for her mother.

Whatever challenges lay ahead in mastering both her flight and her magic, whatever secrets her unprecedented abilities might hold, she would face them with the same courage her parents had shown in their own battles.

In that moment, Ellia Hope, princess of Dragonwall and first female dragon shifter to be born in history, embraced her name's promise and looked toward the future—not with fear, but with possibility. And a whole lot of stubborn determination.

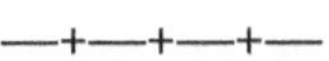

THANK you so much for reading! Please consider leaving a review for the books in this series.

Can't get enough of Dragonwall? Check out Captain Bennett's short novella "Through the Mists" for free by subscribing to my mailing list and receive access to my Reader Vault of bonus material:

https://www.authormelissamitchell.com/newslettersignup

You can also find more Dragonwall stories in my spin off series: Royals of Dragonwall, starting with *For the Crown*, which follows Princess Lena (Claire wears her ring in the final books). The third book in this series will follow Claire and Talon's daughter, Ellia. So be sure to keep an eye out.

https://a.co/d/0bIirGn8

Now, turn the page for the final artwork of the newest female dragon shifter.

ABOUT THE AUTHOR

Melissa Mitchell is a fantasy romance author and creator of the seven-book *Dragonwall* series. Her love of fantasy began with *The Dragonriders of Pern*, and she now writes stories full of dragons, magic, hidden royalty, and slow-burn romance. She holds a PhD in physics and lives in Atlanta, Georgia with her husband, a husky, and four very spoiled bunnies. When she's not writing, she enjoys baking cookies, bullet journaling, and figure skating—usually while plotting her next book.

Visit her online at: authormelissamitchell.com

Also by Melissa Mitchell

The Arcane Artifacts

Bound by the Blood Ruby

The Dragonwall Series

Talon the Black

Reyr the Gold

Verath the Red

Koldis the Green

Bedelth the Orange

Jovari the Blue

Dallin the Violet

The Lady Witch Series

Wielder's Prize

Wielder's Bond

Wielder's Might

Witch's Ruin

Witch's Heart

Witch's Crown

Royals of Dragonwall Series

For the Crown

Stand Alone Titles

Blood and Ballet